TEHRAN NOIR

TEHRAN NOIR

EDITED AND TRANSLATED BY
SALAR ABDOH

Published by Akashic Books
©2014 Akashic Books

Series concept by Tim McLoughlin and Johnny Temple
Tehran map by Aaron Petrovich

ISBN-13: 978-1-61775-300-8
Library of Congress Control Number: 2014938701

All rights reserved
First printing

Akashic Books
Twitter: @AkashicBooks
Facebook: AkashicBooks
info@akashicbooks.com
www.akashicbooks.com

ALSO IN THE AKASHIC NOIR SERIES

PHOENIX NOIR, edited by PATRICK MILLIKIN
PITTSBURGH NOIR, edited by KATHLEEN GEORGE
PORTLAND NOIR, edited by KEVIN SAMPSELL
PRISON NOIR, edited by JOYCE CAROL OATES
QUEENS NOIR, edited by ROBERT KNIGHTLY
RICHMOND NOIR, edited by ANDREW BLOSSOM, BRIAN CASTLEBERRY & TOM DE HAVEN
ROME NOIR (ITALY), edited by CHIARA STANGALINO & MAXIM JAKUBOWSKI
SAN DIEGO NOIR, edited by MARYELIZABETH HART
SAN FRANCISCO NOIR, edited by PETER MARAVELIS
SAN FRANCISCO NOIR 2: THE CLASSICS, edited by PETER MARAVELIS
SEATTLE NOIR, edited by CURT COLBERT
SINGAPORE NOIR, edited by CHERYL LU-LIEN TAN
STATEN ISLAND NOIR, edited by PATRICIA SMITH
ST. PETERSBURG NOIR (RUSSIA), edited by NATALIA SMIRNOVA & JULIA GOUMEN
TEL AVIV NOIR (ISRAEL), edited by ETGAR KERET & ASSAF GAVRON
TORONTO NOIR (CANADA), edited by JANINE ARMIN & NATHANIEL G. MOORE
TRINIDAD NOIR (TRINIDAD & TOBAGO), edited by LISA ALLEN-AGOSTINI & JEANNE MASON
TWIN CITIES NOIR, edited by JULIE SCHAPER & STEVEN HORWITZ
USA NOIR, edited by JOHNNY TEMPLE
VENICE NOIR (ITALY), edited by MAXIM JAKUBOWSKI
WALL STREET NOIR, edited by PETER SPIEGELMAN

FORTHCOMING

ADDIS ABABA NOIR (ETHIOPIA), edited by MAAZA MENGISTE
BAGHDAD NOIR (IRAQ), edited by SAMUEL SHIMON
BEIRUT NOIR (LEBANON), edited by IMAN HUMAYDAN
BELFAST NOIR (NORTHERN IRELAND), edited by ADRIAN McKINTY & STUART NEVILLE
BOGOTÁ NOIR (COLOMBIA), edited by ANDREA MONTEJO
CHICAGO NOIR 2: THE CLASSICS, edited by JOE MENO
HELSINKI NOIR (FINLAND), edited by JAMES THOMPSON
JERUSALEM NOIR, edited by DROR MISHANI
LAGOS NOIR (NIGERIA), edited by CHRIS ABANI
MARSEILLE NOIR (FRANCE), edited by CÉDRIC FABRE
MEMPHIS NOIR, edited by LAUREEN P. CANTWELL & LEONARD GILL
MISSISSIPPI NOIR, edited by TOM FRANKLIN
NEW ORLEANS NOIR 2: THE CLASSICS, edited by JULIE SMITH
PROVIDENCE NOIR, edited by ANN HOOD
RIO NOIR (BRAZIL), edited by TONY BELLOTTO
SAN JUAN NOIR (PUERTO RICO), edited by MAYRA SANTOS-FEBRES
SEOUL NOIR (SOUTH KOREA), edited by BS PUBLISHING CO.
ST. LOUIS NOIR, edited by SCOTT PHILLIPS
STOCKHOLM NOIR (SWEDEN), edited by NATHAN LARSON & CARL-MICHAEL EDENBORG
TRINIDAD NOIR 2: THE CLASSICS, edited by EARL LOVELACE & ROBERT ANTONI
ZAGREB NOIR (CROATIA), edited by IVAN SRŠEN

ELBURZ MOUNTAINS

EVIN PRISON

QEYTARIEH

DIBAJI

VANAK

NARMAK

SHAHRAK-E-GHARB

TEHRAN

GRAND BAZAAR

REY

BEHESHT E ZAHRA CEMETERY

TEHRANGELES

VARJIN PROTECTED AREA

LATYAN DAM

KARIM-KHAN, KUCHE ABAN

KARIM-KHAN, VILLA

AZADI TOWER

UNIVERSITY OF TEHRAN

TEHRAN

GRAND BAZAAR

MOWLAVI

SHAPUR

GOMROK

SHUSH

SALEHABAD

To the memory of Ali Abdoh, old Tehran's boss of bosses, and to his grandson, Ashil.

In addition to the remarkable efforts and patience of the writers themselves, there are several friends who should be especially acknowledged in this anthology: Hooshyar Ansaarifar, Mitra Elyati, Maryam Haidari, Somayeh Nasiriha, and Hassan Shahsavari. A warm thanks to each and every one of you for your invaluable suggestions and encouragement. This book could not have come together as it did without you.

TABLE OF CONTENTS

INTRODUCTION
THE SEISMIC CITY

Back in the day, so my mother tells me, on the rare occasions when my father took her along to one of the cabarets of old Tehran, the tough guys—the *lutis*—the bosses, the knife brawlers, and the traditional wrestlers, would lay out their suits and jackets on the floor of the place for my mother to walk on. It was a gesture of supreme respect for one of their own. And it says a lot about a Tehran that simply doesn't exist anymore—a Tehran of chivalry and loyalty, a place where allegiances meant something, where friendships harked back to a classical world of warriors from the great Persian epic, the *Shahnameh* (*The Book of Kings*), and to the medieval Islamic notion of the *ayyar* brotherhood in Iran and Mesopotamia where the bandit and the common folks' champion were one and the same, and where every man followed a code of honor set in stone.

Or else, all of this may simply be wishful nostalgia for something that didn't exist even back then. *Back then* means a time before the Islamic Revolution of 1979. That watershed event that sits in the mind of every Iranian as a chasm, a sort of *year one* after which everything strange became law. The brutal eight years of war with Iraq—the longest conventional war of the twentieth century—the persistent pressures from America in its own everlasting twilight war with Iran, the official corruption of the new ruling class, and the snowballing inflation turned just about everyone into a "night worker." Living an honest life was no longer an option. Prostitution, theft, an explosion in the drug trade and addiction, the selling off of raw materials and historic national treasures—plus endemic, in-your-face bribery—became a way of life. Meanwhile Tehran grew and grew, until it was one of the megacities of the world, now pushing at fifteen million stray souls—a leviathan that can barely stand itself, a purgatory of unmoving traffic, relentless pollution, and noise and anger and inequity, surrounded by some of the most beautiful mountain scenery in the world.

Tehran, then, is a juxtaposition of ugliness and beauty that breaks the heart. A place where not one but two inept dynasties came to miserable ends, and where, arguably, the third most important revolution in history (after the French and the Russian) was started. It is also the city where Churchill, Stalin, and Roosevelt met to divvy up the world while the flames of WWII were still burning. And it was where one of the CIA's first manufactured coups (with the prodding and support of the British—who else?) against a democratically elected government was put into motion, thus ushering in years of a dictatorship which in turn was swept aside by the first real fury of fundamentalist Islam, a harbinger of the world we now live in and call *post–9/11*.

In other words, there is something of both the absolutely spectacular and positively disgraceful about Tehran. But most writers around the world are inclined to think that their own sprawling metropolis is the capital of every imaginable vice and crime, of impossible love and tenderness and cruelty and malice in measures that seldom exist anywhere else. For me, Tehran's case is no different—except that there really is a difference here. The city may be a hothouse of decadence, a den of inequity, all that. But it still exists under the watchful eye of a very unique entity, the Islamic Republic. The city enforces its own morality police, and there are regular public hangings of drug dealers and thieves. Because of this, there is a raging sense of a split personality about the place—the imposed propriety of the mosque rubbing against the hidden (and more often not so hidden) rhythms of the real city. At the start of each day, and particularly in late evenings, Tehran remains a schizophrenic beast always at odds with itself, always trying to figure what will be the next design for it that won't fit, or fit horribly.

None of this is of course helped by the fact that Iran happens to be one of the biggest drug conduits on the planet. The vast Afghan opium crop, transformed into heroin, needs its transit routes for the European markets, while Iran itself remains a major supplier of methamphetamines. The country and its slatternly capital sit at the crossroads of the world—to the north is the specter of Russia, ever daunting, to the west there is Turkey and the gates of Europe, to the south is the Persian Gulf, the Arab lands, and the immensity that is Africa, and to the southeast and east is India and the rest of the great Asian continent. Each of these have had their say in Iran at some point. Each has left its indelible mark. And you only have to traverse the country to experience the dozen languages and as many shades of color and appearance—all of them inevitably converging on Tehran, impregnating it and aborting it, lending it life and destroying it, and, sometimes, praying for its redemption.

You would think that such fertile terrain would be the stuff of powerful fiction from the past. Not so. And the reason why so little of it all has been tapped thus far is something worth noting here: censorship. That ogre which hounded Iranian writers before the revolution and even more so afterward. Before 1979, there were two types of censorship, and at opposite ends of the political spectrum. One was the predictable and narcissist censorship of the king's court, and the other the knee-jerk braying of the leftist/Communist intellectuals who believed that any written work that was not in the service of the "masses" was bourgeois and of no consequence and therefore in the royal court's favor. This boded particularly unwell for serious genre fiction of any sort—which is why, for example, a minor gem like Qasem Hasheminejad's *An Elephant in the Dark* went utterly ignored.

Nevertheless, with the advent of the Islamic Republic, what had mostly been a thorn in the side of writers and their creative lives ballooned into absurd and unfathomable proportions. Consider this typical example of the censor's verdict regarding a sentence in a simple children's manuscript: There is a conversation between an apple and a pear. The apple tells the pear, "Come and take a bite of my red cheeks and see how delicious I am." The Ministry of Culture and Guidance's ruling on the sentence: "Too sexy. Too provocative. Must be removed." From this small example you can imagine what Iranian writers have had to contend with for the past thirty-some years. Imagine having to write in an alternate universe where there is to be no mention of sex, little genuine interiority of character, no delving into social issues, no politics, and nothing that could convey a society at some internal conflict with itself. In such a universe, if a writer does not kill himself first, or instead simply gives up and becomes a cab driver (I've known cases of both), he might resort to one of three modes of writing that have, unfortunately, a fighting chance to pass the censor's obtuse gaze: 1) fluffy and vague symbology meant to say one thing and mean another; 2) derivative and tired magical realism that has every other character and their mother growing wings and flying to who knows where; 3) thin, bloodless texts of angst and self-absorption with little context or reference to the troubled world outside.

In such an atmosphere, to even begin to attempt the noir mode—which at its best is in complete, albeit harsh, engagement with the world—is an act of courage, a political act. Which is why the writers drawn for this collection happen to be those who have tasted the city and know its wounds. They depict a Tehran at its most raw and least forgiving—Sima Saeedi and Majed Neisi in their inimitable portrayals of life after a war or revolution; Mahsa Mohebali and Danial Haghighi unmasking underground life in the Islamic Republic; Farhaad Heidari Gooran, Yourik Karim-Masihi, and Lily Farhadpour showing the tough, multicultural reality of a pullulating city bursting with prejudice; Azardokht Bahrami and Javad Afhami revealing the lugubrious weight of religion; Mahak Taheri and Aida Moradi Ahani exhibiting the systematic and inescapable corruption in the chambers of power; and Vali Khalili and Hossein Abkenar displaying the grit and harshness that is the quintessence of the capital. (Since I translated all but two of the stories from Farsi into English, I've included a glossary of Persian terms at the back of the book.)

In each story you can find more than one and often all of the themes I just mentioned. But Tehran's narrative would not be quite complete if we did not cross oceans in at least one tale to land smack in the middle of Southern California. In Los Angeles, to be exact. In the Los Angeles Valley, to be even more exact. After the revolution, the exodus of many Iranians took them all over the globe. But nowhere did they flock to with more verve and the sense of finding a home away from home than a city that is often dubbed *Tehrangeles*. LA, then, is where Gina B. Nahai's story takes us—this other unwieldy Goliath of occasional instant riches but mostly shattered dreams, the noir city par excellence, where the two Tehrans finally converge. And it's only right that they should, as both cities, Tehran and Los Angeles, sit on top of major tectonic fault lines. The clock is ticking for them. But who cares about dire predictions of earthquakes and eventual annihilation when there is real estate money to be made today? Who gives a damn about the day after tomorrow?

So take what you can get when you can get it. It is this sense of impermanence about a place, expected one day to be swallowed up whole and disappear, that drives the inhabitants of Tehran, *my* Tehran, to—as we say in Persian—*press hard on the gas pedal*. There is always an element of the end of the world about this city. A feeling of being once removed from the edge of the precipice. Elsewhere I have called it the "Seismic City"—the seismic sanctuary. All of this will end one day. Yes. And maybe sooner than later. And when it does, by God, we will miss it.

Salar Abdoh
Tehran, Iran
July 2014

PART I

THE CRIME PAGES

THE FAT, FAT STORY OF THE FAT CITY

BY DANIAL HAGHIGHI

Mowlavi

I'd made up my mind to go to work for Naser the Tiger. I hadn't had a real job in three months and was getting tired of watching everyone get ahead except me. Besides, Eid was coming, the New Year. The math of it is simple: A fella needs some new clothes. He needs to be able to buy things and give gifts to people and look important. I mean, all we had in this world was the butcher shop on Mowlavi Street. A rundown little shithole I didn't care to work in or inherit from my father. We'd bring anything you can think of to this place: chickens, rats, sick pigeons—we'd grind them all up together and sell it to places like Akbar Amu's sandwich shop.

Yeah, I was sick of it all. This jungle of a neighborhood. Look in every corner and someone's keeping a squirrel or a bunch of snakes or miserable dogs. I'm serious. They trade animals here and I was sick of animals. Just the other week someone showed up with some crazy creature that looked like a crocodile. They called it a dragon. They said it was poisonous, so they kept it on a leash and fed it morphine to make it stay calm. Then some old fart with money came and bought the thing.

You can imagine then how the stink of these beasts was driving me nuts. And in the end what should happen? I lost my own poor brother, Abbas, over this shit. Abbas got fucked. He died right here in this stinkhouse over nothing at all.

Still, in the beginning the money I made with Naser the Tiger was turning out to be all right. But less than two weeks into the New Year and my new job, everything went bad. It was actually the thirteenth day of the holidays, Sizdah Be Dar, the day you're supposed to throw away all your bad luck and begin fresh. I was Naser the Tiger's wheel man. I did the driving while Naser did the actual dealing. His main merchandise—cocaine—meant he had less competition to worry about in Tehran. Now imagine this guy—he is over six-six. He has a hammer face, a shaved head, and tattoos running up and down his arms. From the Janat-Abad end of the city to Nezam-Abad, he's fucked every woman who crossed his path. Another thing: it was two years since he ran away from the army. He'd beaten the crap out of his sergeant and had simply taken off. And nowadays he was in love with some married woman who sent him pictures of her tits over the phone. That's Naser the Tiger for you in a nutshell. The big gangster. And how old do you think this guy was? All of twenty. A junior giant who had been my brother Abbas's friend since back in middle school. And I, eight years older than them, was working as Tiger's chauffeur, his boy.

Tehran was almost empty that day. Everybody had driven outside the city to celebrate and throw away their bad luck on the thirteenth day of the New Year. None of the usual traffic. I was on the clock with Naser. He paid ten an hour, plus extra for gas and booze and women. In other words, he was treating me more than right. Now we were waiting to get word about a new shipment when Fat Rambod called and asked if he could come along. Bad idea. I should have known better than to allow that lazy fuck in our mix. You see, if I've learned one thing living in this fat town, it's that you can't ever be a nice guy. You can't let other people get too close. You have to be dirty and not let on.

Take this same Naser the Tiger as an example. There's not a part of his body that doesn't have a knife mark on it. Do you think nice guys have that many knife marks on them? Of course not. You have to be a son of a bitch like Naser to get ahead in this

world, hence the knife marks. And now he was sitting there telling us about a tattoo on his left arm. A house. "Yeah," he sighed
like he was nostalgic for something, "I want to sell this stuff for a
while and then buy me a nice house up there in Damavand and get
a rose garden going. Know why? Because my baby, Mrs. Fataneh,
told me roses mean love."

Now this Fataneh was the same married woman who sent him
her titty pictures. So Fat Rambod said, "Right, Mrs. Fataneh sure
has a delicate soul if she likes those roses."

Naser nodded appreciatively. "Yeah, that fucking beautiful
bitch, that's why I love her. She has a delicate soul."

I sat there saying nothing. Truth be told, I wanted to beat the
living shit out of Rambod. Until two years ago he was living out
in the boonies around Azadi. Then his grandma died, left him a
nice piece of cash, and the fat bastard moved uptown next to the
pretty people.

The text message we'd been waiting for finally came: *Good
news. The New Year's shipment is in.*

Naser the Tiger immediately called the number back and got
an okay on the quantity we wanted, so we drove out to the Na-
vab District. The place was an old family home with its basement
turned into some kind of teahouse. Smoke everywhere. People sat
behind their *qalyans* smoking and watching TV. There was a soccer game on, and guys were betting hard on some European-league
match while phones rang off the hook.

We walked to the back of the teahouse to meet up with some
blond faggot kid who'd also been a classmate of my brother and
Naser the Tiger in middle school.

Naser said, "I've come to get the receipt for the New Year's
shipment."

The kid wrote up a receipt while Naser laid ten New Year's
gold coins on the table.

The kid took the coins and started up the stairs, then gestured
for us to follow him. Upstairs, an old man sat by himself waiting.

He examined the gold and glanced up at us. "All good. Have a nice year, boys."

Now we drove to Bani Hashem. This time the place sold bathroom knickknacks. Another kid sat behind the desk here. Why not admit it? I wanted to rip the heart out of every one of these queers. I felt like I was miles behind in the game of life, while these little bitches with their slicked-back hair and attitudes were having all the fun and getting all the profits.

Naser said, "Brother, here's my receipt. Give me the New Year's shipment. I need to get a move on, the holidays are almost over."

The kid met Naser's eyes. "We're all in the same boat, brother. If you can't sell, you won't come to us next time." Then he turned to me. "Isn't that right?"

I mumbled something that was supposed to mean yes. What I really wanted to do was cut the boy's nose off.

Naser said, "But how am I to get gold coins for you every time? In the rest of the world they deal in cash, you know?"

The guy shrugged. "The rest of the world you're talking about is America. America has dollars. When you're in Iran it's gold you need to use. Cash means nothing here."

This kid couldn't have been more than sixteen. But he understood things. Some people, even by sixteen they're wise. They know how to get ahead. While other people can live fifty years and still get nowhere. I was disgusted with myself. I felt like I didn't even know half the things this girly boy did. I was thinking of the words he'd used—*America, dollars* . . . all of them words that smelled of life and success. Words that I knew nothing about.

They measured out the stuff for us in a little bag and even put a pink ribbon around it. You could have lifted the thing with a couple of fingers. Then I was driving us back to Mowlavi. My mood had changed for the better now. It was as if we carried the world in that pink-ribboned bag of possibilities. Suddenly I felt myself closer than ever to dollars, to gold, and to pretty girls who put red nail polish on their lovely feet.

I drove us fast. But then less than a minute away from the butcher shop, I had a snake—I kid you not—slithering and showing its fangs on the front windshield of our car. I hit the brakes and we all watched the monster in awe. It was Indian Ebrahim's snake. As long as I'd known the guy, that was what he did, dealt in snakes. He came lumbering up to the car, stoned as a doorknob. Yet he was expertly able to grab the creature by its head.

"Fellas, my apologies. This is one wild fucker. I'm taking him to Javad the Cadaver to give him some morphine, slow him down a bit."

And then he was gone and we were parking the car by the shop. It was the four of us: me, Naser the Tiger, Fat Rambod, and my brother Abbas.

Abbas grabbed a tablecloth and laid it out on the floor in the back of the shop. We sat around that cloth and started cutting up the New Year's powder and preparing it for business.

We were measuring out the coke on a scale and wrapping it. Meanwhile, Naser had texted a select list of his customers who quickly began to reply with their wishes.

When we were done, Naser took out a bill from his pocket and rolled it for the leftovers. It was time to have a little fun and try the stuff for ourselves.

And that's when it started. That lazy fat fuck Rambod! At first he said how great he was feeling. How he wanted to dance. And then, after the second or third sniff, suddenly his face went white. Cold sweat appeared on his forehead and he began shouting that he was dying.

Naser laughed, "You're not dying. You look fine." Naser had actually sniffed three times more than the rest of us.

Rambod started screaming, and I mean at the top of his voice. "My balls are on fire!" He ran around the place yelling and tearing his clothes off until I finally managed to wrestle him to the ground. Abbas threw me a small pillow which I stuffed in his mouth. "Shut the fuck up!" We were lucky so many people had left town that day, including my father who had gone out to Karaj to kiss his older, richer brother's ass as usual so he could borrow money from that asshole.

Anyhow, it was as if Rambod, in his nakedness, had grown supernatural powers. He threw me off and began his screeching again. We were all scared. I know I was. We didn't know what to do with this fool.

Abbas and I watched in horror as Rambod now took a sandal and threw it in Naser's face and began cursing him. We were dumbfounded. This guy was cursing one of the most frightening tough guys in the city and tossing things at him. We saw blood written all over Naser's face. Meanwhile, Rambod ran into the bathroom and turned the water on, all the while screaming and swearing at Naser.

Naser slowly got up and went to where my father kept his butcher knives. He came back out with the biggest cleaver in the shop. The thing had an ominous-looking blot of dried brown blood on it.

I ran up to Naser. "Tiger, what are you up to?"

"I'm going to cut him up."

"Let him go, brother. He snorted too much. He's not himself."

The powder that had gone up Rambod's nose had gone up mine too. My head was already starting to spin. I was talking to Naser and in the back of my mind I was still thinking about why I was so behind in life.

Rambod screamed, "Bring me some ice! My balls are on fire!"

"I'll strangle him," Naser growled.

I turned to Abbas. "Lend a hand here, won't you?"

Abbas shrugged. "When Naser the Tiger makes a decision, who are we to get in his way?"

I held my ground: "Naser *jaan*, they call this idiot Fatso Rambod. He's a mama's boy. You shouldn't let yourself get worked up over his going nuts."

"Abbas, I'm burning up! Help me!" Rambod screamed.

Abbas muttered, "Don't worry, son. Naser the Tiger is going to put you out of your misery in a second."

Naser pushed me out of the way and took two giant steps toward the bathroom. I grabbed his hand but he pulled it back.

Rambod stood in the door of the bathroom now, the long hose from the bidet in his hand. "Naser, what are you going to do to me?"

"I'm going to rip your heart out. There's not a man born yet who dares mess with Naser the Tiger. Now you're cussing at me?" He took another step and raised the cleaver.

Rambod lifted the hose and shot water into Naser's face. "Fuck off! If you were a real dealer, this wouldn't be happening. My eyes are popping out of their sockets. This stuff isn't coke. I don't know what it is. But they fooled you." He moaned, "Everything's turning purple. I swear. Somebody give me some ice!" He began jumping up and down.

Naser turned to my brother. "This isn't cocaine?"

"He's full of it, *aqa* Naser. It's the real thing," Abbas said, swallowing hard.

Rambod started to bawl. "Everything is purple. What the hell is this stuff?"

"Shut up!" Naser raised the cleaver again, and again Rambod doused him with water.

"Naser, fuck your mother! Naser the Tiger is Naser the Donkey. This isn't coke. I'm telling you, it isn't!"

"One more scream and I'll strangle you with my bare hands."

Rambod's eyes closed. The hose fell from his hand. He began shaking and fell to the floor. I ran up to him, scooped water from the sink, and splashed his face. Naser had turned beet-red; he stood there with the cleaver half raised and a soaked face, not knowing what to do.

I called to Abbas who brought over a glass of sugar water. We opened Fat Rambod's mouth and poured some liquid in there. Rambod choked and began uttering nonsense—something about the alphabet and how we should all learn our first-grade lessons.

We gave him more sugar water.

He called to me and grabbed my wrist. "Mahmud, I'm a heavy sort of guy, right? I'm better than all of you, right?"

"Yes, you are, my friend. You're the best." I held his head up and dried his face.

"You learned everything from me, right? I'm the one who made a man out of you. Isn't that the truth?"

"That's the truth, as long as you get better."

Now he turned to Naser. "You're a real pimp, aren't you?"

Naser looked like he could kill all of us just then. But he kept his cool. "Yes, I am. I'm a real pimp."

He turned back to me. "Anything you guys do, I can do better. You're all jealous of me—"

Abbas cut in, "Rambod *joon*, are you really sick or are you just using this opportunity to give us a piece of your mind?"

Rambod seemed to drift off again. I was afraid we were going to end up with a dead body on our hands and didn't know what to do. Then there was some noise from the outside. It sounded like Indian Ebrahim was wrestling with a snake.

I shook Rambod. "You're right about that; we're all jealous of you. You're number one. You're the heaviest of the heavies in town. Stay with us." I saw some color returning to his face.

He opened his eyes a bit. "Naser, do you promise to drop Mahmud and have me drive you around instead? Do you promise to forgive me for cursing at you?"

I wanted to smash his head in. I said, "Look, Rambod *joon*, it's true you're not feeling well. But don't exploit the situation." He began screaming worse than before, but I didn't want to take any chance with this son of a bitch dying on us. "Anything you want, Rambod *joon*. You're right, I'll get out of the way and you can work with Naser." I turned to Naser. "Isn't that right?"

Naser grimaced. "Sure. We'll work together. You know what?

You can take over my position too. You be the boss and I'll drive for you. How's that? Just don't die right now. All right?"

This quieted him down. He glanced Naser's way and said, "There's a lot we'll have to do. We have to make tons of money. Come Ashura, we have to feed the whole city. During Nim e Shaban, all of Tehran has to eat sweets and sherbet from the hands of Rambod and Naser. We have to make so much money that we keep a separate house just for ourselves. Agreed?"

"Agreed."

Rambod leaned half of his face into my thigh, smiling. "We'll get us a nice-size place behind Niavaran Park. You know, in that area where the Americans built years ago. Any girl who steps into our place will instantly fall in love with us."

Naser said, "That's right, Rambod *joon*. Whatever you say. As long as it's a duplex. One for you and one for me and Mrs. Fataneh."

I already felt left out of this conversation. It dawned on me I'd never even been to Niavaran Park.

Rambod went on, "We'll go skiing in Dizin. We'll use our cell phones to take lots of pictures. We'll put them on Internet. Each one of our pictures will get a thousand hits."

I was out of the loop and my eyes were filling with tears.

Abbas, my poor brother, asked where Dizin was.

I called out, "Fellas, how about Abbas and me?"

"No worries," Naser winked. "You guys are with us. We just want our business to grow. We want to have top customers."

Rambod: "We'll turn all the areas around Tajrish into cocaine land. All of Darrous and Fereshteh. Anywhere there's rich people, we'll feed them coke."

Abbas: "Don't forget there's also Shahrak-e-Qarb."

Me: "And Saadat-Abad. There's plenty of rich folks over there waiting for our coke."

Abbas: "That's right. Around Kaj Circle up there. They'll be salivating over our goods."

Rambod: "And then we'll conquer other cities too. Esfahan, Shiraz, Dubai, Istanbul."

Naser: "And we'll go on a pilgrimage to Mashhad to visit Imam Reza. Don't forget that."

Rambod: "No doubt. We have to go on a pilgrimage." He reached for the sugar water and drank. "We'll marry. We'll have kids."

Abbas: "I want two daughters."

Naser smacked him in the back of the head. "What good is a daughter to you, stupid? Have sons so your flag will always be up and straight."

Rambod: "Daughters are as good as sons. As long as they're healthy. *Enshallah.*"

We all repeated, "*Enshallah.*"

Now Rambod sat up. There was light in his eyes. He said to me, "Mahmud, remember that song you sang the other night? Will you sing it again?"

Naser said, "I even got my harmonica in my bag. I'll play along with you." He went and got the little instrument and started playing some bullshit and I began singing.

Rambod sprawled out comfortably and shut his eyes. He was peaceful.

The rest of us went back to where we'd cut up the coke. Naser said, "How about we snort just a little bit more?"

Abbas said, "Most definitely."

Naser made a few more lines and we sniffed. We lit our cigarettes and each man was in his own world. I was back to thinking about my life. It seemed like I wasn't going to see the color of peace and tranquility for a long, long time. I thought to myself, *To hell with it, Mahmud! Stick to the high you got right now; forget about tomorrow!*

Naser was quiet. My brother was playing an old song on his phone. And I . . . suddenly I was burning up. My jaws locked and my balls were on fire. As if a thousand worms were creeping inside me. I saw everything go purple. This thing we had snorted, it wasn't coke.

"I'm burning!"

That was my brother Abbas shouting. Next was Naser. All three of us were jumping up and down like men forced to run on hot coal. We were ripping our pants off and reaching for our scorched testicles.

At that moment Rambod finally got up. He looked like a whale coming to life and he had purpose in his eyes. He went into the freezer and came back with slabs of frozen meat and told us all to stick our nuts in it.

We did.

I almost passed out, but the iced meat soothed my eggs. Naser was in far worse shape, though. He had taken way more than us. And by the time the frozen meat arrived he wasn't together enough to properly cool his balls. Something happened to him that night. And I'll tell you what that something is: Naser the Tiger became Naser the No Nuts that evening. Man can barely get it up anymore. I'm sure of it. But no one dares talk about that. And if it hadn't been for Rambod's quick thinking, I would have lost my balls too.

But all this, as I said, is only between us. I mean me, Rambod, and Naser. And why not Abbas? Because my poor dear brother died that night. That's why.

I'd rather think it was Indian Ebrahim's snake that killed Abbas than the shit we snorted. Because it's more profitable to think like that. What happened was that while we were jumping around trying to save our manhoods, that evil snake took off again and somehow ended up with us and the frozen meat.

You can imagine the rest.

But Abbas's death wasn't all meaningless. His death was blamed on the snake, and Indian Ebrahim had to shell out a sizeable *diyye*, blood money, to my father. Now like I said, I don't know if it was the fake coke that killed my brother or the snake or a heart attack from seeing a snake at the critical moment when his eggs were on fire. Indian Ebrahim says that the snake was not poisonous and he's probably right. But in this neighborhood, a death that has a snake in the equation carries a price. If Indian Ebrahim didn't give the blood money he wouldn't be able to do business here anymore. One call to the cops and they'd confiscate his damn snakes and throw him in jail.

But all that aside (including the fact that my father got to spruce up his butcher shop a bit because of the blood money, and that I may stay here and inherit the dump after all), there's one thing that still burns me: I should have let Naser the Tiger cut up Fat Rambod that night. Because after that, they threw me out of the game and the two of them started working together. Turns out Fat Rambod has a sharp nose for fake powder. If it's not real, he'll know it before anybody else. We got an example of this that very night.

And that works for Naser. Fat Rambod drives Naser around now and examines the goods. Also, Naser raised such hell over the fake stuff from that night and rearranged so many faces that the two of them have already turned into legends, and cocaine is their domain.

As for me, every time I think of Rambod I get heartsick. But there's a catch: if I had let Naser cut up Rambod, I guess I wouldn't have my balls either. Let's not forget it was Rambod who saved us with the frozen meat. I love my balls. I'd like to keep them. I wouldn't trade them for all the money and cocaine in the world. Even if they told me I could become the biggest gangster in the city in return for my balls, I'd say no.

To hell with that.

For the time being I'm not even working the butcher shop. I'm playing hard-to-get with my old man and I hate the meat business. I want things on my own terms. And my own terms means keeping my honor and my testicles.

That's right.

Because, well, just imagine you are the fattest gangster in all of Tehran but you can't even fuck Mrs. Fataneh with the fat tits. Imagine your balls had melted away. Who's going to do Mrs. Fataneh now? Who's going to stick it between her ample breasts? This is why wise men have always said: *Don't count your eggs before they're hatched.* And, if possible, always keep a little frozen meat around.

FEAR IS THE BEST KEEPER OF SECRETS

BY VALI KHALILI

Rey

I t all began on a really slow day. One of those days when there's just no news. The hour hand on the office clock was pushing three p.m. and I still didn't have a report to turn in for the newspaper. Nothing. No murder. No calamity. No burning building. Some days are just like that and they make a crime reporter's job that much more difficult. Desperate, I'd even called my contact at the Criminal Investigation Department only to be met with the silence of a sleepy Thursday afternoon. So I started hitting the other papers to see what I could find. Which was when I came across it, a little ad about a young man who had gone missing.

His name: Asghar Ahmadvand Shahvardi. Age, twenty-eight. The photo showed a round face with a fat nose and olive skin. He wore a striped shirt and wasn't smiling. The ad said he'd left his house exactly three months and ten days earlier. He'd supposedly been on his way to work on a Wednesday morning but hadn't been seen since. At the bottom of the ad there was a contact number to call if anyone had news about him.

There was little time to waste. Deadline was around the corner and I needed to get five hundred words in for the day. I figured I'd make a call to the number in the ad, get some inside scoop about the young man from his family, and write my five hundred words. It wouldn't be the first time I was doing something like this, and sometimes it even paid off in interesting ways. One time I wrote about an autistic sixteen-year-old boy who apparently just got up and started walking alongside the railways tracks. Ten days later they found him 350 kilometers away still walking the tracks. Another time I wrote about a lost teenage girl who was finally located, the victim of a serial killer who'd murdered six other women.

So I made the call. The old man on the other end of the line had the familiar accent of a Lur, not unlike my own grandfather. I told him I was a reporter and was calling him about the ad.

The poor old guy started to weep and it took some time before he could offer any words. "I live way out in Malayer nowadays. I came to Tehran several times. Talked to the police. Nothing. They tell me every day dozens go missing in that evil city and at least four are murdered. They say if they find out anything they'll call me. When? I know they won't call. I was ready to find a good wife for the kid. Now I don't even know if he's alive." Then he started to beg me to do something for him and began weeping again.

Guilt had gotten the best of me. I'd done a hack's job of calling for a heartbreak story and now the ache in the old guy's voice wouldn't let go. His son, Asghar, was the same age as me. And I could just imagine what my mother—what with her bad back and bad heart—would do if I suddenly went missing for three months. I was hooked on that call. Sometimes this happens. It happens even to a crime reporter who thinks he's seen it all; the proverbial ants in my pants were on the move and I wouldn't stop until I had something.

The next day I had to go to the criminal court to follow up on some reports. Before that I called Asghar's father again and hit him for some information—Asghar's job, where he lived, his friends, anything to set me in the right direction. Turned out he'd been living in Tehran for about eight years and apparently worked night-shift security at a pharmaceutical company's offices in midtown. He had a best friend, Mohammad, whom he shared a room with around Sepah Circle.

I got Mohammad's telephone number from Asghar's father and set up a meeting with him for later that day. Mohammad turned out to be a small, dark-skinned guy who seemed a bit thrown off at first when I got there and couldn't quite imagine what a reporter wanted with him. But I broke the ice between us with the only thing in that room that still bore a trace of Asghar, a photograph. It was a picture of Mohammad and Asghar by a waterfall.

"It's from four, five years ago," he volunteered. "We went on a trip to Luristan and Khuzestan. There were six, seven of us altogether. It was a nice trip. I won't forget it."

Mohammad seemed depressed, like he really missed his friend. They'd gone to college together, and while Mohammad had quickly found a job with an oil company, Asghar was still looking for more permanent work when he went missing.

"I'd been sent by my office on a job down south. I called Asghar a couple of times when I was away and he didn't answer. I thought nothing of it. He keeps . . . *kept* things to himself, you know. Never talked much about his troubles. But then when I came back to Tehran and he still didn't come home, I started to get worried. I called his father."

I asked him if Asghar had left anything behind. Mohammad hesitated for a moment before he pulled a small bag from underneath a bed. In it were a few shirts, a bottle of cologne, an electric shaver, a pack of condoms, and a paystub with the name of the company he'd worked for: *Pars Pharmaceuticals*.

"Did the police ever ask to look at these things?"

"The police?" He gave a bitter laugh. "They never even stepped into this place. They couldn't care less about a missing person unless he lives in a mansion."

Another three days went by. In the midst of dealing with my girlfriend who was threatening to leave me if I didn't spend more time with her, and reckoning with my mother's doctors—not to mention putting in time at the news desk every day and chasing ambulances and police chatter—I found time to call the numbers on Asghar's paystub. But there was never any answer. Finally I called information, got an address for the place, and was getting ready to go there when an earthquake hit the Eastern Azerbaijan Province. The paper wanted me there right away. So Asghar had to wait yet again. Then, by the time I returned to Tehran, my mother's back had taken a turn for the worse. I spent more days trying to get her into a proper hospital and calming my sister, who was worried sick about her and our father who was already half bedridden. Meanwhile, my girlfriend had stopped returning my calls and my boss wanted to know why my reports never left a ray of hope for readers—didn't I know people can't live without hope?

Maybe he was right. Asghar's father certainly needed to hope. Two weeks had gone by now since I got the address for Asghar's workplace. I called his father and let him know I had the address and meant to visit it. He sighed and said he'd pray that I'd marry well.

So on a late September day I finally got around to paying a visit there. The address was off Kheradmand Street, but when I reached it, there was no trace of the building. They'd demolished it and were preparing the groundwork for a new structure. I asked around, yet no one there had any idea where Pars Pharmaceuticals had moved to, nor did they recognize the photo of Asghar that I showed them. Only the corner-store guy recognized him. As he was bagging groceries he grumbled, "Are you serious, man? In this jungle of a city we don't even remember what we had for dinner last night. And you're asking us where this nobody named Asghar might have disappeared to? You reporters sure have time on your hands. Time and plum, useless jobs."

I was tired and feeling hopeless myself. Around the corner from where Asghar had been working was a park. I walked there and sat on one of the benches watching kids play badminton. My mind drifted and I recalled how only a few months ago I'd had to cover the public execution of a twenty-one-year-old street thug named Ali Big right here. Three days before the execution I'd interviewed Ali Big at the lockup in the Shapur District. I'd been to that place countless times, interviewing every kind of criminal you

can name—murderers, kidnappers, muggers, burglars, drug dealers, guys who shoplifted, and guys who trafficked in humans. The
list was endless. Now then, sometimes my job is nothing more than
getting a nugget of a sound bite out of a man who's about to walk
the plank. I think that day I got that nugget out of Ali Big. He'd
sat across from me, a truly big guy, his hands shaking with tension
so that the sound of the metal handcuffs rattling on the table was
unnerving both me and the officer standing watching over us.

"Why do you rob people?" I'd asked. He gave me the look
of death and said nothing. I persisted, like I always did at these
interviews: "Didn't you think you might get caught and executed
one day?"

"Where I come from, Mr. Newspaperman, we have a saying
that goes like this: *If you sell your ass enough times, you gotta pay up
with the hemorrhoids eventually.*" Of course, the newspaper wouldn't
let me publish that sentence, but it was a beauty and maybe I could
rephrase it and get it past the censors. Ali went on, "All the fellas
like me who do this stuff for a living, they already know they'll get
caught one day. But they got no choice. We all grow up with just
one option: crime. I got unlucky this time. That's all. In this city
of fourteen million motherfuckers, there's a thousand muggings
every day. I got unlucky there happened to be cameras to catch
me in action. Fuck their cameras. You know for how much they're
hanging me for? For less money than you and your bright friends
spend on coffee in one of your fancy restaurants."

Three days later I was at his hanging—a couple of dozen yards
from where I was sitting now in the park. They'd hung him for
taking something like five dollars. They were making a public example of him.

I hadn't been able to step inside a café to get a cup of coffee
ever since.

Back at the newspaper I didn't have the heart to call Asghar's
father and tell him they'd demolished the building his son used
to work at. Yet his story wouldn't let me go. Sometimes a reporter

just sniffs something unique. I don't know how that really happens. Something just pulls at you. I kept asking myself, *Why him?* Granted, I only had general information on the guy. But what I had didn't point to him just going missing like that. He had a job, albeit a lowly one for someone with a college education; he also wasn't an addict, had a family that cared about him, and wasn't in love. I wrote all these things down in my notepad, trying to make sense of what I had before me. That afternoon, besides having to cover a robbery at a gold dealer's near Resalat Circle, I did some detective work and figured out the new location of Pars Pharmaceuticals.

They'd moved to a corner of Mottahari and Mirza-e-Shirazi, not too far from where they'd been before. I showed up around noon the next day. The security guard drew a blank when I showed him Asghar's picture.

"You haven't worked here long, have you?"

"Three months."

"Who was here before you?"

"No idea. You need to talk to the office manager for that. His name's Mr. Suleimani."

Suleimani's first response was a short laugh. "Well, we're looking for him too. The guy melted away. If you find him, tell him to come get his last paycheck. It's still with me."

I replied, "Like the ad says, he's been missing over three months now. Did he have a friend in this place? Someone who knew him a little bit better?"

I didn't expect Suleimani to be so forthcoming, but he seemed genuinely intrigued all of a sudden, if not concerned, and told me to look up a fellow named Mohsen who worked the third-floor security desk.

I found Mohsen sitting behind a row of television monitors playing with his cell phone. When I asked him about Asghar, he didn't bother answering. I repeated my question. Now he put his phone down and looked up at me for the first time. "You are?"

I showed him my journalist's ID and told him I was searching for Asghar on behalf of his family.

The initial suspicion left him. "I never had an address on Asghar. After he disappeared like that, I called him a bunch of times. But there was no answer. I thought maybe it was because of the thing that happened between him and the general manager that he didn't want to come back to us." Mohsen glanced away. "I mean, so he had an issue with the manager; it wasn't right he just vanished like that. I thought we were friends."

Something had happened between him and the manager? This was my first clue and I felt myself getting excited. "What happened exactly?"

He lowered his voice. "Asghar got in hot water with the general manager over a surveillance video of the company he sold to a reporter. The general manager wanted to fire him, but several people intervened."

"He sold a video to a reporter?" I felt the stirrings of a narrative and could barely contain myself. "What was in the surveillance video that was so important?"

Mohsen's reply floored me. Suddenly I was sure I was in the middle of something far bigger than a simple case of a missing person, and in a minute I'd realize that as a reporter I'd in fact been a part of this story from the beginning.

The security guard got up and took a careful look around to make sure no one was nearby. Then from a flask he started to pour tea for us and began: "It was last winter. I don't know if you recall that mugging off Kheradmand Street. Two huge guys on a motorbike stopped a man at knifepoint right in front of our building. Our cameras recorded the whole thing. I was on night duty back then, same as Asghar, so we weren't there when it happened. Usually after the place closed down we'd sit and watch the surveillance videos just to pass the time. There's a college girls' dorm annex across the street. We'd sit there and get our kicks watching those girls' comings and goings. So one night we're watching the video and there it is, the whole thing. The bike stopping, the guys pulling out a huge dagger and taking the guy's briefcase, and the people in the neighborhood who were there pissing themselves from fear and doing nothing about it. All of it was recorded. Need I say more? Unless you were asleep half of last winter, you must have seen the video on nightly news, right?"

I was too agitated to do or say anything except nod my head.

"The victim, he ended up going to the police station to put in a report. But the cops did nothing. It was just a simple mugging and what those thugs got away with was barely a day laborer's wages. I can tell you for sure the police sent no one to the neighborhood to investigate, or they would have come to our building. So what could Asghar and I do? If we told our bosses about the video, they'd ask what the hell we were doing at night watching old videos when we should be manning the building. So we stayed quiet. I mean, until two weeks later when one night I'm watching the eight thirty news on TV and I see our video being shown to the whole country. Asghar was on duty on the second floor. I called him upstairs right away. I was scared out of my wits. He made a face and asked me to promise I wouldn't tell anyone. He'd sold the video to a journalist. That's all I know. Next day there were pictures of the video in a bunch of the newspapers. It was like the thing had taken on a life of its own. It was crazy."

He was right. That video of the mugging had gone viral last winter. People were saying that the government had lost control. There was robbery and murder in broad daylight, *and* it was recorded, yet the police still did nothing. It had become a national issue all of sudden. The tech people at Criminal Investigation managed to zoom in on the license plate of the bike and quickly figured out who the perpetrators were. One of them was Ali. The very same Ali Big I'd interviewed for the paper three days before his execution. I recalled asking him then if he was angry that his partner in crime hadn't been caught, but he had. Ali Big had glared at me with an expression of utter loathing. "It's only you uptown bastards who'd sell your own mother for a song."

Mohsen checked his watch. Now he wanted to get all of his story out before anyone showed up. I could tell the whole thing had been weighing on his mind and Asghar's disappearance had gotten him thinking. "A few days after they showed the video on TV, Asghar and I were called into the manager's office. He introduced a guy in civilian clothes as a detective from the CID. Boy, was the manager angry! And he had every right. He told us he knew that besides us no one else really had access to the videos, and from the angle of the shot it was obvious it was a video from our building. I remember looking at Asghar and seeing him turn white as chalk. He confessed he'd sold the video to some reporter. Someone like you, I guess."

After a long pause where we both stared into space for a while, deep in our own thoughts, I asked him, "Do you know what the upshot of all this was?"

"That detective never came around again. I read in the paper they caught one of the robbers. Ali Big. Later they hung him right down the street, at Honarmandan Park. That was, I guess, about nine months ago? Our manager was still mad though. Several times I heard him tell people he knew of cases where relatives or friends of the guy they executed came back for revenge. Maybe he had a point. I mean, they're not going to take their revenge on the police, are they? The manager was scared they'd come after our company because it was our video that got them caught."

Or they could simply come after Asghar. That's if they found out it was him who sold the video to the newspeople.

The first thing I did back at my desk was go online and watch the whole video again, which was barely even a minute long. In the bottom right side of the screen I could plainly see the logo of the TV channel, Iran Afternoon. So the reporter was from that news station. I called my contact there and got the name and number of the city desk correspondent who had bought the video from Asghar.

Now I sat down and tried putting it all together. When Ali Big was caught he'd admitted that he and his partner first planned the mugging spree at a teahouse near the Imam Hossein Circle. But that was all he'd given the police about his partner, a guy people knew as Abi the Lisp. Back then I had tried to follow up on the man. But his vanishing act was complete. Then, after they hung Ali Big, no one really bothered about Abi the Lisp anymore and soon he was forgotten. I thought of calling the CID and seeing if the file on him was still open. But that would be grasping at straws. Those detectives had a thousand other things to worry about; besides, they'd already executed one of the two culprits, and as far as they were concerned they'd probably closed the case to their own satisfaction, if not the public's.

I finally called the reporter at Iran Afternoon. He was cautious at first. We both realized we were basically talking to competition here. But after a few minutes of chatting around the subject he opened up to a fellow journalist. What he gave me wasn't much. Just that the TV station had given him the green light to buy the video off Asghar. But afterward he'd had no contact with him. I could tell he had no idea Asghar had gone missing. And, of course, I didn't tell him anything about it.

My last option was to go to the teahouse Ali Big and Abi the Lisp had hung out at. This may sound easy enough, but it wasn't. What if I went there and started asking around and Abi the Lisp happened to be back in town and was sitting in that very teahouse just then? I was playing with fire. And I made the mistake of calling my girlfriend to ask her what I should do. She was still not talking to me. But she picked up this time, and as soon as she heard what I was up to she hung up again, though not before telling me not to call back until I was sure I wanted a life beyond being a newspaper reporter.

For three days I didn't do anything but weigh my options. I could call Asghar's father and tell him all that I'd found out so far and let him and the cops take it from there. But then . . . I thought about my life and where it was heading. Half my friends had left the country to work for organizations that beamed news into Iran; they had good lives and good salaries—at least I imagined they did—in places like London and Prague. They got to travel, see the world, and they didn't have to deal with this maddening everyday censorship. I'd stuck it out here because I knew if I went away I might have that good life, but I wouldn't be much of a journalist anymore. I'd have all the gadgets and all the audience who hungrily watched Persian-language satellite news coming from abroad. But I'd only be deluding myself. I wouldn't be a reporter anymore; I'd just be someone else's mouthpiece. I needed to be in the belly of the beast, so to speak. I needed to be in Tehran—to smell it, taste it, feel it, know its aches and pains and the sadness of its people. My friends had left and pretty much turned into collectors of paychecks. I didn't want that. I needed to walk through the Grand *Bazaar* of the city and sit in the teahouses where criminals sat and smell the stink of desperation and poverty. London wasn't for me.

And if I could somehow get to the bottom of Asghar's story and end up writing a feature article—one of those once-in-a-lifetime stories that makes a reporter's career—then maybe I could reach my dream of becoming a war correspondent. It wasn't impossible. And God knows, there were plenty of wars in the neighborhood for me to cover. I wouldn't have to go far.

I set out for that teahouse, alone. On the way there, I called my boss and told him what I was up to and where I was going. "If you don't hear from me in another three hours, call the police." He didn't have full faith in me and insisted he accompany me; I insisted he didn't. Truth was, there was only one person in all of Tehran I would have wanted to tag along. And that was Hassan. Better known as Hassan Underpants. I just didn't know if Hassan was in or out of jail nowadays. Hassan was nineteen, and his specialty was stealing cars and car stereos.

As for his name, they called him Underpants because one time his father had gotten into a fight in their neighborhood and had his pants pulled down by the other guy. I'd met the kid a couple of years back at the criminal court. They'd brought him in straight from juvenile detention to face the judge, and I happened to be there to cover another story. Somehow I managed to speak to him and we hit it off. He was smart, quick on his feet, and incorrigible. I got to liking him and ended up convincing the judge, whom I knew, to go easy on the boy. So Hassan felt he owed me. But more than that, he was simply an honorable thief. If he was your friend, he wouldn't steer you wrong. We hooked up every once in a while and he always had some technical details to fill me in on for my crime stories.

Now I decided I needed him. I called, giving him the rundown without saying anything obvious about a possible murder.

A half hour later he zipped up alongside me on his motorcycle not far from the Imam Hossein Circle. "Get on, brother. I wish I could be a reporter like you."

He had the body of a small wrestler and looked a good bit older than his nineteen years. I asked him if he had gotten in any trouble lately.

"Always. But as you can see, I'm on the outside, not the inside. So I must be doing something right. Now listen, the teahouse we're going to is called Shokufeh. I know all about the place and I'm glad you called me to come with you. We'll go in there, sit in a corner, order some tea and a *qalyan*. Leave the rest to me."

I had to shout into his ear as he zigzagged on his bike in the crazy early-evening traffic. "Let me guess: you're going to ask for Abi the Lisp and pretend you have car stereos to sell."

"Who says pretend?" he shouted back.

"I don't know about this. I mean, why would we be directly asking for him? There's a lot of other people you could sell your stereos to."

Hassan parked us next to a row of other bikes in front of the teahouse. "I did my homework, boss. Abi the Lisp does fence stereos, besides other things. We're in luck."

We ordered our tea and the *qalyan* from the tea man who gave us a once-over, smiled, and said they didn't serve smoke to uptown pussies around here.

Hassan shot back, "Do you see any uptown pussies right now?"

"Hmm, I don't think so," the guy said, and ambled off.

I'd been to my share of rough teahouses. But this place was in a class of its own. The air was thick with smoke and it seemed like every other customer was recently out of jail or was heading back there. Every kind of tattoo you could think of was inked into those forearms and the walls of the place were crammed with pictures of wrestlers and famous tough guys of old.

We sat for another twenty minutes, smoking and drinking. When our tea man brought another round for us, Hassan made his move. "We're looking for Abi the Lisp. They said this is his hangout."

"They misinformed you, son."

"Maybe they didn't misinform me. Maybe someone can let him know we got a few things we want to get rid of."

As Hassan was talking, I slipped several notes into the man's hand. He counted the money. "You guys sit tight. I'll be back."

We ordered omelets and more tea. If something was going to happen it would be now. Soon the tea man came back giving us a look that meant he wasn't convinced. "Never seen you two around here. How can I trust you? How do I know you're not chasing after *agha* Abi?"

Hassan didn't waste a moment. He took out his cell phone and showed several pictures of car stereos he had for sale. "Look, boss, they know us all over the Yaftabad District. We're here to make a living."

After seeing the pictures the man seemed more convinced, but not completely. "I'll be back," he said again, and disappeared behind a giant old fridge where we couldn't see him. I expected him to return with more questions, or maybe the entire teahouse now figured we were cops and they were planning to do us in.

In the middle of these thoughts Hassan gave me a nudge while taking a drag off the *qalyan*. "Get yourself together. Here he comes again."

The tea man stood examining us once more. He had the shrunken cheeks of a true opium addict and he didn't seem any more forthcoming. "I made a few calls. No one knows where he is. Some say he's been over in Pakistan for a while. Others say his new hangout is the Chaman teahouse over in the Mowlavi District. One thing's for sure though: he's not in the business of buying and selling stolen goods anymore. He's gone straight."

I was watching Hassan as he replied coolly, "Too bad. But since we're here, can you hook us up with anyone else who might be in the business?"

Now the tea man smiled and immediately dialed a number on his own phone and handed it to Hassan. "Don't forget my commission then!"

I nodded to the guy, telling him I'd guarantee his cut myself. Meanwhile, Hassan spoke quietly into the phone and I knew he was speaking to Abi the Lisp himself. After a couple of minutes he took down a number and whispered that he'd be in touch. He winked at the tea man and gave his phone back to him. "Peace!"

Five minutes later we were out on the street and Hassan Underpants could barely contain his excitement. "Did you see how I handled all that? Am I your Hassan or am I not? Did you see how I showed him pictures of the car stereos and asked him to find us anyone to take them off our hands?"

I nodded. But I was far from excited. Actually, I was getting pretty paranoid and kept glancing behind my back thinking we were being watched. Hassan must have noticed the panic in my face because he pulled me close. "Relax. What do you want to do now? Do you want us to go over to that other teahouse he mentioned in case we can find your man tonight?"

"I don't know what I want to do, Hassan *jaan*. Let me think about it a couple of days. I owe you big. And I'd like to pay you for your trouble."

"Come on, brother. What do you think I am? I mean, you can pay me for other stuff. But not tonight. Tonight I found a customer for all those stereos I've been sitting on." He started his motorbike. "Can I take you somewhere?"

I told him no and he took off like the wind, satisfied with a good night's work. He had no idea what I'd really gotten us into and at this point I could hardly tell him. I quickly grabbed a cab and headed home, all the while thinking about the description of Abi the Lisp that the tea man had given us when I'd asked him: almost six foot six of muscle, with that unmistakable lisp and a tattoo on his eyelid.

"On his eyelid?" I'd repeated to the tea man.

"That's right. You can't miss him. And when you do see him, tell him Sleepy Ghasem sends his greetings."

Now my days turned into one long bout of watching that mugging video over and over again. I was frustrated and angry at myself for my indecision. There was a scenario here and it made sense: Abi the Lisp seemed to have hightailed it quickly south of the border to Pakistan as soon as the video of the mugging came out in the news. By the time he returned, his partner, Ali Big, had been hung months earlier and no one could care less about what happened the previous winter. No one but maybe Abi the Lisp himself, who now sought revenge for the hanging of his friend. What I couldn't figure out was how he would have found out it was Asghar who sold the video to the newspeople. But that was neither here nor there at this point. What was certain was the following: Asghar had disappeared and Abi the Lisp was back in town and he'd changed his hangout so that people wouldn't be able to find him so easily.

I was stuck. On one hand I kept telling myself I was a newspaper reporter, not a detective. On the other hand, I knew if I let this story go I'd never forgive myself. I'd think about it for the rest of my days as the one scoop that might have catapulted me to a new place in my career. It got bad enough that I stopped answering most phone calls and could barely turn in any reports. The more I thought about it, the more I realized there were three choices in front of me: 1) call Hassan Underpants and tell him to set up that meeting with Abi the Lisp; 2) pretend none of this ever happened, call my girlfriend, tell her she was right, and take her away on a long holiday somewhere; 3) call the police and Asghar's father and tell them everything I'd learned so far and let them deal with it.

There was one other factor: I couldn't even be sure Abi the Lisp was the one who had murdered Asghar. In fact, I couldn't even be sure that Asghar was dead, though my reporter's intuition told me that he probably was.

Meanwhile, Hassan Underpants wouldn't stop calling. I answered his calls because I didn't want him thinking I'd changed my mind. And to give him credit, he was smart enough never to ask me too pointedly why I was so interested in Abi the Lisp. I knew that he knew Abi the Lisp had been implicated in the infamous mugging. But that was as far as we went. Hassan thought I was nosing for some story while he was simply hoping to sell his goods.

So I decided to consult a mentor, Mr. Boluri, an old hand who had done some of the best newspaper reporting since before the Islamic Revolution over three decades earlier. I met him in a sandwich shop on Komeyl Street one day and told him everything—I hadn't even told the whole story to my boss at the paper. As soon as I was finished he grabbed my wrist from across the table, stared at me intensely, and spoke: "You've already done 80 percent of the legwork. If you let this one go, I suggest you look for another occupation altogether. You won't be suited for this anymore."

Boluri's reply was like a shot of adrenaline through my body. I called Hassan and told him to meet me near the Chaman teahouse that night between eight and nine when it was sure to be at its most crowded.

We met at Mowlavi Circle. Chaman teahouse was at the end of a series of meandering alleys behind the Grand *Bazaar*. Junkies filled the dark, ancient passageways. Once we entered the teahouse we'd have to come back the same way. It was a cul-de-sac here; if I'd been worried before, now I was pretty much beside myself. Hassan parked his Honda alongside the usual motorbikes and nodded towards the teahouse.

I took a peek through the window inside the smoky place and remarked, "It's the kind of place a man could get raped."

As always, Hassan knew when I was feeling the heat. He smiled and made light of it. "If we do get raped, just relax your asshole and try to enjoy it at least. That's what I always do."

He grinned and we both burst out laughing. Though on my end it was mostly nervous laughter.

I asked, "Did you set up the meeting with Abi the Lisp?"

Hassan shook his head. "I almost did. Then I thought twice about it. Whatever it is you got us into, brother—and let me tell you, I'm willing to go with you all the way—I didn't want to take the chance and give the man a heads-up. This is his new hangout. So if he's here tonight, he's here. If he's not, then we'll come back another night, and another night till we catch him. What's important is nobody should be expecting us when we don't really know what we're walking into. This way, it's us who have the element of surprise, not Abi the Lisp."

"Hassan, did I ever tell you you're the smartest nineteen-year-old I ever met?"

"Tell that to the judge next time I'm in trouble." He smiled. "Come on, it's time."

The pungent smell of *qalyan* smoke hit us as soon as we entered. Behind the owner's desk there was a red sign that said, *Chaman teahouse, under Haj Morteza's management.* There was no space for us to sit. Men sat shoulder to shoulder drinking tea, smoking, playing backgammon, and wheeling and dealing in low whispers.

I turned to the busy tea man. "You have somewhere we can sit?"

"Apologies," the thick voice said. "Give me a few minutes."

Hassan came closer to the tea man and opened up the sack he

was carrying. "Brother, I'm looking for Abi the Lisp." He gestured to the goods inside the sack. "I got a few things I need to get off my hands."

The tea man took a curious look at the car stereos and then pointed to Haj Morteza, the owner. "You'll have to speak to the boss."

To get to Haj Morteza we had to pass men who could have come right out of murder lineups and horror films. I felt weak-kneed and a bit desperate. If Hassan hadn't been there, I would have tiptoed out and never looked back.

Haj Morteza was your classic tough guy, the kind with the fedora and a large prayer bead constantly churning in his right hand.

Hassan spoke in a respectful tone: "I have a few things to sell and they told me I could find Abi the Lisp here."

Without getting up from behind his desk, Haj Morteza pointed to Hassan's bag. "Let's see what you got, son." Hassan showed him. "No good. We don't allow for small transactions in our place."

"Haj Morteza, these are just samples," Hassan said quickly. "There's a lot more where this came from. And if the deal happens, your commission is a given."

Haj Morteza glanced up and met my eyes, probably wondering what part of the equation I was. "The teahouse takes its 5 percent. It's the rule here."

"Upon my eyes, boss," Hassan said in a tone of utter respect.

It was a good time to ask again, so I did: "Is Abi the Lisp even here, by any chance?"

Haj Morteza laughed. "Of course he's here." He pointed to a giant of a man sitting and talking with two others. "But I warn you guys, he doesn't like being called Abi the Lisp anymore. I suggest you just call him by his first name. I'll take you to him myself when he's not so busy. Just wait awhile."

Five minutes later, when Abi the Lisp's visitors were gone, Haj Morteza led us to his table.

Abi the Lisp wasn't big; he was huge. I'm a guy who's bigger than average, and yet my wrists must have been half the size of his.

"They're businessmen," the teahouse owner offered. "They're all yours."

Hassan opened his bag. "We spoke before on the phone. Business is not so good in Yaftabad. Lot of roundups. We thought we'd come straight your way, *agha* Abi."

The big guy took a glance at the goods and said, "Gentlemen, why are you still standing up? Let's sit." He definitely had a lisp, but who'd be man enough in that teahouse to admit they heard it?

We watched the owner walk off and tell one of the workers to bring three cups to our table. Then it was the usual rounds of underworld etiquette, offers of cigarettes and one man lighting up for the other—all the little things that made this world real and instantly flammable.

While Hassan and Abi talked, I stayed focused on the big man's face. There was a moment when he was drinking his tea that he closed both eyes. I saw them: one eyelid was tattooed *Good* and the other *Night.*

Good night?

Was that the last thing he'd said to Asghar before killing him?

But had he even killed Asghar?

The two men settled quickly on a price that included the teahouse's commission. Hassan then turned my way as if to get my okay too, and I nodded my head like the silent partner I'd become in all of this. The meeting was set for tomorrow night at ten, and in a minute I found myself finally shaking hands with the man who had come to occupy more and more of my thoughts.

Afterward, Hassan offered to give me a ride home. We barely spoke the entire way. It was some kind of an unspeakable victory for both of us. For Hassan, he suddenly had an in with a whole new crowd in a district he hadn't been operating in, and he had the shadow of Abi the Lisp to protect him. It meant he would be going on to bigger and better things, and those bigger and better things would probably get him in jail faster than if he just stuck to car stereos. And who had brought him to this? Me. As for myself, I had my own "in." But I still didn't know where I stood and what I should do about it. It's like when you chase a story and see and hear so much that you need to pull back at some stage, breathe deep, and get your head in order before you can write a word.

At home I put myself to sleep watching a Spanish-league soccer game. In the morning when I woke up I no longer had any doubt that Abi the Lisp was Asghar's murderer. How did I know? My heart told me. I think it was the moment we'd gone to pay for our tea at Haj Morteza's desk and Abi the Lisp called out to the teahouse owner that he'd cover our bill. It had been a gesture of friendship, of more profitable transactions to come between us, of showing good faith. But somehow the gesture had also crystallized something in my mind. Abi the Lisp was a man who called shots, who killed, who escaped to another country and came back and carried on as before. It wasn't that no one could touch him. Police, after all, had caught and killed Ali Big, his partner. Which made me wonder why these two guys who had a hand in everything would want to do a simple mugging for so little money. And then I thought about it like this: they did it because the victim was there and they happened to be passing that way. They'd sat in a teahouse and decided today they were going on a fast mugging spree. Why? Because they could. Some men climbed mountains, other men went on a mugging rampage for a day. Because it was there. Because victims were plenty. And it was this bad luck of getting caught on camera that had stuck to Abi the Lisp's craw. He'd felt foolish amongst his own kind. So when he came back from Pakistan or wherever he had been, he'd done the first thing he thought would set him standing tall again. He'd found out who the video source was—Asghar—and he'd buried him.

I hadn't a shadow of a doubt about this anymore.

I called Hassan and asked him if he still intended to see Abi the Lisp tonight.

"Are you out of your mind, brother? Of course I'm going to see him. This is what you call opportunity. And you? You coming?"

I didn't know, so I didn't answer.

"I tell you what," he said. "Think about it. I don't mind going alone. Or I might take one of the neighborhood boys with me."

I tiptoed out of the house without anyone noticing. I'd been made to feel guilty from every corner lately. There was my girl-friend who'd already sent me her ultimatum. There was my sick mother in the other room whom I hadn't been taking enough care of lately. There was my aging father who could do little for any of us and who kept saying that he only wanted to see me married and settled before he was dead. There was the newspaper and the hardly scintillating articles I'd been putting out recently.

Asghar's case was beginning to feel like a bad marriage—I couldn't live with it, and I couldn't let it go so easily. What would happen if I showed up with Hassan at the teahouse tonight? I couldn't go on shadowing Abi the Lisp forever. And even if I did, what made me think he'd turn around one day and show me where he'd buried Asghar's body? Worst part of all this was, what if Abi the Lisp somehow got suspicious of me? Then I'd be putting Hassan's life in danger too.

I was in the middle of these thoughts as I walked aimlessly on the streets when my cell phone rang. Asghar's father. I was debating with myself if I should even answer it when the phone went quiet. Now I noticed there had been six missed calls. All of them from Asghar's dad. I'd been so preoccupied that I hadn't realized he'd been calling.

I dialed his number.

He was crying. "They've found Asghar's body. The police called me. They said they found him in the Rey District." His voice broke up and he fell into a fit of uncontrolled sobbing. In between, he managed to tell me that Asghar had been strangled with a rope and then stabbed countless times with a knife. They'd only managed to identify him by his ID.

I felt gut-punched and disoriented. All I could do was tell him to wait for me. Then I hung up and quickly hailed a motorcycle cab to the medical examiner's office on Behesht Street where the poor man had been called to claim what remained of the body.

Cold wind hit my face on the back of the motorbike. Again I had a dozen thoughts racing in my brain. Yesterday I had shaken hands with the probable killer of Asghar, and today I was about to go meet Asghar's father. What could I possibly tell the old man? If I said anything at all—which I didn't intend to—would he not ask me what had kept me from telling him and the police this news until now? Would they understand a reporter's need to pursue a story to its last detail and get it right?

Asghar was dead. That was now the indisputable fact. What would telling anyone about Abi the Lisp accomplish at this point? Would it bring Asghar back? No. What it would accomplish was, arguably, another round of revenge. This time on me. And maybe not just me, but also Hassan, who was well known now by the thugs who frequented the Chaman teahouse. I thought about my mother and sister and father again, and even my fast-disappearing girlfriend. I pictured my own funeral—if there was even to be a funeral and I didn't just end up buried somewhere down there in the Rey District.

And then I tapped the biker-cabbie on his shoulder.

"We're not there yet, boss."

"I know. I'll get off here."

"The fare remains the same."

I gave him twice that and started walking in the opposite direction. The phone rang again. It was Asghar's dad.

I didn't answer it. I had other work waiting for me at the crime pages of the newspaper.

A WOMAN'S GEOGRAPHY IS SACRED

BY LILY FARHADPOUR

University of Tehran

T he shock of the blast is so loud that I find myself thrown to the foot of the bed. My first thought: tomorrow is the anniversary of the American invasion of Iraq; maybe someone is playing a terrible joke on us. Ali is sitting bolt-upright in the middle of the bed, staring down at me and looking like he's just been walloped over the head.

I can barely bring words out: "What happened? Are they here? Have the Americans finally come for us?"

We stare at each other for a second longer and then both run to the window. All the car alarms in the neighborhood are barking together, a deafening ruckus. The building across the street does not have a single window that isn't smashed to pieces. Still, the sky looks impossibly lovely on this early morning in mid-March. It hints of freshness and spring, of the Persian New Year and hopefulness. But then my eyes naturally follow the length of our blood-spattered window where a human finger presses against the glass like an exclamation point. As Ali opens the window to reach for it, I hear the sound of a woman screaming above the din of the car alarms. Ali has the bloody finger in his hand now and examines it curiously while I gag all the way to the bathroom.

By the time I come back he's already dressed and heading outside. I have no idea what he's done with the finger.

I call out to him, "Wait for me!"

"Bring your voice recorder," he yells back, and hurries out.

He's already grabbed his camera, naturally. Because this is how it is: to be a reporter means to have no life at all. Worse still is when your husband is the senior reporter for the crime pages while you work the city desk. It's then that your life turns into one never-ending bout of chasing accidents and robberies and murders and having to meet deadlines.

But there's another point of view to all this, one that Emily, my close friend, confidante, and supervisor at the city desk, reminded me of the other day: "Stop complaining! You and Ali have a good thing going. Have you already forgotten the crappy no-life you had with your last husband?"

Maybe Emily is right. Though maybe not 100 percent right. Truth is, I still don't know if I was the one who ran away from my ex's horrible moods, or if it was he who left me because of the way I make my living. I mean, what kind of a life is this? We spent most of yesterday in front of Evin Prison. A woman had murdered her husband and was set to be executed. Ali was there too; he was there because we still don't know if reporting on executions should go to the city desk or the crime pages. Emily had already written an article about the efforts to try to commute the woman's death sentence. So in the end we decided Ali would write about her execution while we'd cover the public effort to keep her from being hung.

This is our life.

As for Shahla, the condemned woman, she was hung anyway. No stay of execution.

Which means both Ali and I got our reports in for the day. We earned our keep.

Back on our street, broken glass carpets the block. The ambulance was unbelievably fast getting here, and they've already managed to cover what appears to be half of a body in a white sheet. A white sheet soaked in blood. The air is heavy with the scent of smoke and burn. The police have the area perfectly cordoned off. This is what you get for living so close to Tehran University:

efficiency from the authorities. They are so afraid of student demonstrations in this area of the city that they'll be at your doorstep in a flash if anything happens, let alone a blast of this size.

The police won't let Ali take pictures. As soon as he sees me, he comes over, grabs the voice recorder out of my hand, and pushes for an interview with the cop who appears to be in charge. I try listening, but Orzala's screams are deafening. Orzala is the wife of the Afghan super from the building across from us. And then there's Aqdas *khanum*, who is trying her hardest to find out what Ali and the policeman are talking about. Aqdas *khanum* is the neighborhood busybody. You can always find her behind her kitchen window surveying the street. I'm still in a daze and wondering at the doggedness of this woman who looks as animated as I've ever seen her. Then I turn around and see Abbas *agha*, our street sweeper, casually brushing bits of burnt flesh onto his dustpan and dumping the contents under the white sheet. This does it. I start to gag again. I hear someone calling out Ali's name and telling him I'm about to pass out.

When I open my eyes in Ali's arms, he says quietly, "Nasir is dead. He was carrying a bunch of fireworks for Chaharshanbe Suri when the whole thing blew up in his face."

The ambulance finally leaves. The car alarms have quieted down. But the blood on the asphalt is still there. And Orzala, Nasir's young wife, stands in the middle of the street and weeps uncontrollably. Next to her, her frightened daughter Khorshid pulls on her mother's *chador* and screams.

Poor Nasir! Only yesterday I bought fireworks from him to take to my nephews and nieces at my mom's house. The Afghan had been the super of the ten-story building across the street for only a few months. Once in a while I'd pay him to clean the stairways in our little building too. He was small and quick and spoke with a delicious Kabul accent that stayed in your ear long after he'd stopped talking.

I still cannot wrap my mind around the fact that Nasir is dead.

I'd been in the middle of writing a feature article on Iranian women who marry Afghan men when Nasir and Orzala moved into that building. In a way, they were perfect subjects for my piece, because although Orzala was born in Herat in Afghanistan, her family had escaped the civil war there and she pretty much grew up in Tehran. She doesn't have an Afghani accent at all and Nasir happened to be her cousin. It was an arranged marriage which allowed Nasir to move to Tehran from Kabul, then with Orzala's father's help he got the job in the building. It was really a dream job for Nasir. And the only person in the neighborhood who gave them trouble was the racist Aqdas *khanum,* who is convinced all Afghans are thieves and cutthroats. One time a few months back, I saw her slapping Nasir and Orzala's little girl. I went up to her and told her if she ever put a hand on that child again she'd have to deal with me. Ever since then, she hasn't said one word to me. But today she's on a roll. I can even hear her telling the policeman how nothing good ever comes of Afghans.

Ali sits me down on the curb. "If you're feeling better, I'll go back and talk to that cop for a bit longer."

I nod, then get up and head over to Khorshid, Orzala's daughter. Several of the other women from the neighborhood join me. Slowly the little girl's crying stops. We take turns caressing her until her grandmother, Orzala's mother, shows up. Ali comes over. He has that look that seems to say he's already completed a full day's work. I have a thousand questions to ask him, but he pulls on my hand. "Let's go. We need to be at the paper."

The whole way to work I'm in a daze. Nasir blown up, just like that! Gone. What can you possibly say about something like that? As soon as we get to the paper, Emily rushes over and hands me Shahla's file so I can write more about her execution yesterday. She seems so distraught over yet another hanging that I can't even bring myself to tell her about what happened this morning on our own street.

"You didn't sleep last night, did you?" I ask her.

"It's about losing, you know? It's about the taste of this kind of defeat. I mean, the poor girl was hopeful we could somehow save her. I talked to her husband's brother and got him to finally relent. But that mother-in-law, that witch, when it was time for the hanging, she asked to pull the seat from under Shahla's feet herself. Of course they let her. It was her right. Her fucking right by law. She was hell-bent on an eye for an eye, and she got exactly what she wanted."

"We could write about that. What do you think? We could write how she insisted on *qesas* to the very end."

"And have the authorities come hassle us? Like I said, *qesas* is law. She had the right to pull that chair. They don't give a damn why Shahla killed her husband, or if it was an accident; they just care that she killed him."

"The poor girl didn't want to live in a village."

"Exactly. So she kills the husband. It was wanting to be back in Tehran that made her do it."

I shake my head. "Wanting to stay in this monster of a city is that important for women, isn't it?"

"You and I take this place for granted. But a girl like that—she gets to be herself here. She can go to school, work, make money, go to the park, to the movies. She can stop wearing a stupid *chador*. So what's she supposed to do? Remain in the village with that mother-in-law while her husband stays in the city and pretends to work? No. She had a right to want to be in Tehran. And I guess she was willing to do a lot for it, including murder."

"I can't write about all this, can I?"

"Of course not. They'll send their thugs in and close down the paper. Even this useless anti–capital punishment campaign we have going is getting us in trouble. You wouldn't believe the kinds of calls and e-mails I get sometimes."

We both grow quiet for a minute and I have a feeling we're thinking about the same thing: a woman kills so she can stay in the city, so she can be free. Call it murder for freedom, if you will. Murder for a place of your own. I could have a field day with an article like that, if my hands were free to write it.

Finally I walk over to my own desk, put the headphones over my ears, and begin listening to Shahla's voice from the interview telling Emily why she killed her husband:

It's true. I'd promised I'd either kill myself or I'd kill him. But I just wanted to scare him. Because he wouldn't listen to me. I was born and raised in Tehran. How could I go live in a village? And next to that awful woman, his mother. My husband was a laborer, construction worker. Said he couldn't afford the rents here. So he took me and my daughter back to his village and left us there. He pretended he was sleeping at the building sites in Tehran. But he was lying. He had met some woman who had money and an old, dying husband. Mohsen drove her around. You know the rest. I'm certain it's that woman who's making sure I'll hang. She's the one spending the money on this.

Nowhere in Shahla's file is there a mention of this other woman. I listen on:

After a while he would barely ever come visit us. The last time he came, we had a big fight. I told him I wanted to see where he was working. He said I couldn't. I said he'd be sorry. Either I'd kill myself or him. Like I said, I wanted to scare him. I thought if I put some rat poison in his food he'd just get sick and that woman would forget about him. I swear I didn't know rat poison could kill you.

The headphones are still on my ears and I'm typing away, but I can feel commotion in the newsroom. Emily puts a hand on my shoulder and with her other hand slips a note under a stack of papers on my desk.

I take the headphones off.

She seems frightened. "Keep this address. It's the case of that under-eighteen kid they plan to hang. Remember? I'm supposed to be at the victim's family's house tonight. Maybe we can get them to pardon the boy. But you'll have to go instead of me if . . ."

I'm staring at Emily in disbelief, not quite understanding all that she's saying. Somebody runs into the newsroom and shouts, "The Security Police are downstairs. They're coming up!"

The newsroom doors swing open. There's more than half a dozen of them, uniformed and plainclothes. Behind them staggers the editor in chief of the paper, looking stunned. The security men are polite. They call Emily's name and several others who work the politics desk.

Emily casually lets her cell phone drop into my lap. "There's a lot of names in there. Hide it." Then she starts to slowly walk toward the man who has called her name.

When they're all gone, there's a moment when the newsroom is in freeze-frame. Then everybody starts talking at once. The editor in chief tries to calm us down. "It's not like they haven't done this before," he keeps repeating. He's right. It's really more like mowing the lawn for them—just haul a few journalists in every few months to make sure they don't get cheeky. Though it's usually the politics desk people that get thrown in jail.

I examine the piece of paper Emily has left me. The address is near Vanak Circle. Eight p.m.

I let Ali know about it.

He doesn't look worried, but asks, "You really want to go there?"

"I think so."

"It's not safe. You do realize they arrested Emily for this very reason, her activism against the death penalty."

"I know it."

"All right then," he sighs. "Let's go home. I want you to get an interview out of Orzala. Afterward, I'll take you myself to the address Emily left you."

This is what I like about Ali, his talent for staying calm and carrying on. Our closest friend just got arrested in front of us and we're going home to get an interview out of Nasir's wife.

He drops me off on our street before driving over to the police station to see if the cops will reveal anything new. When Orzala lets me in, I notice that more than seeming shocked, she appears restless and ill. She holds her little girl in her arms. Her mother is there too. Except for the small New Year's spread on the mantelpiece and the little goldfish beside it, the house looks exactly like a few months ago when I'd come to interview her for my article. It's your typical single room belonging to a building's super, with the kitchen and fridge on one side and the rolled-up bedding on the other. The satellite TV is on. Next to it is an open closet, nearly empty save for a new set of child's clothes and an unworn red manteau on a coat hanger.

I comment on their New Year's clothes and wish them a good year.

It's the most inappropriate thing I could have said under the circumstances, of course, and I curse myself for it. In return, Orzala's eyes begin to water and she lets out a flood of tears and words: "Just this morning I had a fight with Nasir over the clothes. Yesterday he gave me money to buy something for myself and for Khorshid. Then he came home really late. He'd been out trying to sell all those fireworks for Chaharshanbe Suri. I told him he couldn't bring fireworks into the house. He said he just brought a few for Khorshid. He was lying. I had no idea he was hiding a whole pile of them in the storage room too. I showed him what I'd bought and immediately he started yelling at me. He said we were going back to Afghanistan soon. Did I think a woman could wear a red manteau over there? He ordered me to go return it."

This is the first I'm hearing about Nasir deciding to return to Afghanistan. Orzala seems spent and goes silent. Her mother hands her a glass of sugar water, then starts rubbing Orzala's back and explains how Nasir's family lives in a village not far from Kabul. Apparently, a month ago Nasir's father stepped on a mine and died. The family has no one now. So Nasir had to go back. He'd saved a good chunk of money these past few years working in Tehran and his mother has been waiting for him to return and start taking care of her and his younger brothers and sisters.

"I knew if my daughter went back to Afghanistan she'd be miserable. I tried my best to dissuade Nasir. But he wouldn't listen. He said he had to go and he had to take Orzala and the child with him. I asked him if he'd forgotten how dangerous it is over there. That civil war, when will it end? I told him he was tempting fate. But how could I forget that fate will get you no matter if it's in Iran or Afghanistan? Look at the hand it dealt us—Nasir's father gets blown up over there and his son blows up right here. We can do nothing with fate. Nothing, nothing, nothing."

Orzala stares with dead eyes at her mother, who walks to the stove to make some tea for us.

I ask, "You didn't really want to go back, did you?"

Orzala turns her gaze to me; it's a hardened face, filled with intent and resolve. "I'm not an Afghan. I'm Iranian. I grew up here. Here in Tehran. I'm a Tehran resident."

Orzala's mother nearly shouts from the stove, "It was this sort of nonsense you said to your husband that made him beat you! What do you mean we're not Afghans? We've always been Afghans. You're Afghan and so is your daughter!"

The old woman's words make me focus on her daughter's face and I pay more attention to the bruise under her left eye. I'd noticed it earlier but imagined it came from the constant crying.

A knock at the door. It's my husband, Ali. He gives a quick, awkward condolence to both women from the threshold without entering. Then he gestures for me to come out. He practically drags me to the car. "The traffic is something awful. If you want us to get to that address Emily left you today, we have to really hurry."

In the car he hands me the summary of the medical examiner's report about Nasir: *Death from explosion of fireworks. Nasir, a young Afghan man carrying approximately 3 kilograms of fireworks related to the Chaharshanbe Suri celebrations, was found dead due to the unexpected explosion of said fireworks.*

I turn to Ali. "Did you know Nasir was planning to go back to Afghanistan?"

Ali keeps his eyes on the traffic. "Hmm! Maybe that explains a thing or two."

"What do you mean?"

"Nothing. Look, can you get your laptop out and start putting together Nasir's story for the paper until we get to that address?"

"I'll do my best."

The sun is slowly setting. On every street corner you can hear the *pop-pop* sounds of fireworks going off. Here and there, behind the railings of house gates, we can also see the little bonfires families have set up for the celebrations. Excited and happy children skip and jump over the flames. My phone rings. It's Ali's mom. When I tell her we're on a job and probably won't get to her place until late, she offers her usual complaint before hanging up: "What kind of a job is this you two have that you never get a moment's peace?"

"Your mother was pretty mad."

"When is she not?"

"She's right, you know."

"About what?"

"Our jobs."

The farther north we drive, the louder and more expensive the fireworks sound. Then, as we get closer to Vanak Circle, block parties off the main streets take over. Teenagers jump over the fires and dance. Loud music blasts out from homes and car stereos. All around us police and *basij* units futilely chase after the kids. Every block has lookouts, and before the cops can arrive the kids run inside and lock the doors. It's a festive game of cat-and-mouse with the authorities. First there's a chase, then locked doors and an empty street; then a police or militia loudspeaker telling the neighborhood that, New Year's or not, they need to follow proper Islamic etiquette and quit dancing and jumping up and down in the street. I almost feel sorry for the cops. They're chasing the wind. As soon as they leave one street, the whole block erupts back outside and the dancing resumes. It's a beautiful thing.

And somehow, despite that circus outside, I still manage to type up the report about Nasir. "My laptop's battery is almost empty," I tell Ali.

"No way. You need to e-mail it to the paper for me. You have wireless?"

I nod and do what he asks. Then, as if on cue, my laptop dies as we get to our destination.

We're late though. Emily's human rights lawyer friend and some other middle-aged women are there. They look pretty down and appear to be walking back to their cars. Ali asks the lawyer what happened.

"It was useless." She notices my questioning expression and explains, "This here is the house of the victim and his family. The condemned is set to be executed next week. Emily found these people's address, got in touch with them, and set up an appointment. I guess they've talked long enough with her that they trust her. But only her. They wouldn't even open the door for me. For us, actually," she says, pointing to the rest of the women. "They say they'll only talk to Emily. I couldn't exactly tell them Emily's in jail right now. You know?"

She doesn't wait for a reply before getting in her car. Ali and I stand there for another minute and then he jokes, "What's the execution for this time? Another unhappy woman feeding poison to her cheating husband?"

His tone irritates me. "What difference does it make what the execution is for? It's wrong. But if you really care to know, it was over a street fight this time. Three years ago the kid was all of fifteen. He accidentally killed the other guy during the fight. Now that he's eighteen and of age, the victim's family wants him dead."

"Hmm, I really thought it was another husband-killing again."

"What's with you? It's not as if every murder is a husband-killing."

"Well, it's just that since yesterday I've heard about two of them."

"Two?"

In the lowest voice he can muster, Ali says, "Yes. The second case is the death of Nasir."

Now I'm screaming at him, "Nasir killed by Orzala? What the hell is wrong with you? Have you been affected by that bitch Aqdas *khanum* too! Do you think all Afghans are thieves and murderers?"

"Just kidding. Calm down." He isn't kidding, but I let him change the subject anyway. "This is the first New Year's we're actually physically together. Don't you want to get some *haft-seen* and take it home with us?"

I don't answer, showing my displeasure. We start driving again, this time toward the Tajrish *bazaar* where the riot of fireworks is more deafening than anywhere else. Ali jumps out the car and quickly returns with what we need for *haft-seen*, including a dish of wheatgrass and a pair of goldfish swimming in a small glass bowl.

"Don't be mad at me, love."

I still don't answer.

"I just have one more thing to take care of. We need some *arrack*."

Our connection for the booze lives near Tajrish. And Ali is only one of a handful of people who knows his address and can go right up to his door for the stuff. Otherwise you have to call for delivery. On the way there Ali tries to make me laugh. But I stay quiet. My head is spinning with thoughts of Shahla who was hung yesterday and that eighteen-year-old boy who'll probably be hung next week, and Nasir and Orzala. I can't wrap my mind around any of this and Ali's usual calm is just grating on me tonight. So much so that I only notice we've been parked in front of the connection's place when Ali returns with a twenty-liter container of booze which he hides in the trunk of the car to make it look like it's spare gasoline.

We drive on Moddares Freeway. It's mostly quiet on the open road and there are far fewer sounds of firecrackers. It's getting past eleven and we're both silent until we come upon a parked car with its blinkers on. Ali slows down. Loud music is blasting from inside the car. Suddenly the back door opens and we watch in shock as a foot kicks a young woman out. I notice three guys inside the car laughing. The driver gives us the finger, then offers another howl before stepping on the gas and disappearing down the road. For a few moments we linger there watching the girl dust off her clothes. Without a care in the world, she takes out her pocket mirror right there on the freeway to refresh her lipstick and fix herself up.

She finally turns to us and addresses Ali: "Hey, handsome, you already have a nice piece of ass sitting next to you. Get going from here and let me make a living tonight."

Ali drives.

We can barely look at each other the rest of the way. When we get home there are two police cars parked square in front of our building.

"My God," I croak, "they've probably come for me, Ali. It must have to do with Emily."

"Damn! And all that liquor in the trunk."

I try not to blow up at him again. "They might be hauling me to jail and you're worried about your stupid liquor?"

"My love, they're not here for you," he says coolly. "I know what they're here for. Just keep calm. Act natural."

Ali parks behind the cops and we wait and watch as one of them slowly approaches our car. He sticks his face into the open window where Ali is already displaying his journalist's ID.

"Good evening, officer. We live here and I work for the crime pages of the newspaper. What's happening?"

The policeman takes his eyes off Ali and zooms in on me. "Madam!"

Trying to keep an even voice I manage to bring out one word: "Yes?"

"That fishbowl. Be careful with it. It's about to spill."

I utter a barely audible thanks.

Ali speaks: "It's about that blast this morning, isn't it?"

"We just arrested someone."

The gate to Nasir's building suddenly swings open and out march Orzala and several cops. She is handcuffed and is being led out by a severe-looking woman. Her mother runs behind them carrying her granddaughter in her arms and screaming. Next comes Aqdas *khanum*. She sees us and hurries triumphantly toward the car and just about pushes the cop out of the way to tell us her news.

"I knew it. I knew it! It was that Afghan whore's doing. They got a confession out of her already. Her husband was walking down the street with all those firecrackers and somehow she managed to slip a live one at him. All these Afghans are bomb makers. I was sure of it. The poor man didn't have a chance."

I whisper to Ali, "You knew about this?"

"I heard something about it at the police station. They were suspicious of Orzala from the start."

Aqdas *khanum* and the cop move off. My phone rings. It's Emily. They've let her out. She tells me it was just a simple interrogation. The usual stuff about her having to cease and desist with all that "human rights nonsense."

The volume on the phone was loud enough that Ali heard it too. He grabs my hand and squeezes it.

"Thank you," I sigh.

"I guess this is a lesson to take home: don't mess with a woman's geography. Orzala will be going where Shahla went yesterday, and for exactly the same reason.

"Ali, please! Don't start."

He caresses my hand. "I'm sorry. I won't. Forgive me."

We hear several blasts of firecrackers all at once, and when we look up it's as if a rainbow has just appeared in the night sky. It is so lovely. So beautiful.

PART II

WHEN A WAR'S NOT OVER

THE SHELF LIFE OF REVENGE

BY SIMA SAEEDI

Karim-Khan, Villa

T he satellite TV news mentioned it only in passing—
several of the surviving *mujahedin*, across the border at
their longtime base camp in Iraq, had just had their heads
cut off.

Fariba sat staring for a few minutes in disbelief at a television
screen that had quickly gone to other programs, as if a few cut-off
heads was no more newsworthy than tomorrow's weather. Then,
leaping out of her trance, she hurriedly got up and turned on her
laptop. The Internet might tell her what the television hadn't, the
names of the dead at that camp. Names she might still recall, and
maybe even names she'd forgotten among the long list of possibly
dead comrades of years and years before.

Yes, she'd find out the truth. But here was the catch: Fariba
Tajadod, a woman nearing fifty, was no longer sure if the truth
even mattered anymore. And if it did, she was still not sure if this
truth was something owned by the dead or by those who had, for
better or worse, continued living.

Thirty-two years had passed. Thirty-two years of names. Yet
besides her own brother Ali, there was just one other name she'd
thought about often: Ahmad Fard. Ali was long dead. Though
there had never been a grave to go cry over. But what of Ahmad
Fard? Punching in his name in the search box revealed that Ahmad Fard was actually quite alive and well. He was not only alive,
he happened to be rather busy writing articles and giving lectures
these days. Ahmad Fard, alive! This name would not leave her be.

Ahmad Fard had not even had the decency to be among the victims at that accursed camp in Iraq where the last of the vanquished *mujahedin* foot soldiers had been allowed, first by the Iraqis and later by the Americans, to eke out a miserable living and count their days.

How old would this man be now? Fifty-seven? More or less Ali's age. Except that Ali's body parts had long ago been thrown in some unknown ditch set aside for enemies of the state, while Ahmad Fard—Ali's superior, his mentor, his comrade-in-arms and *brother*—was all over the Internet, still advising, still lending guidance, still telling people what to think. With a difference, though: today Ahmad Fard mostly talked about peace and "social cohesion," whatever that meant, instead of telling subordinates how they should be brave and always carry a cyanide capsule and a grenade to quickly kill themselves if they were ever in danger of being caught by the police or the militias.

But what had happened to Ahmad Fard's own cyanide capsule and grenade? Why was he still alive, and circulating freely in Tehran, when so many whom he'd preached to at one time were dead and gone?

Fariba wanted answers.

No, actually, she didn't want answers.

The uncertainty had begun again, like the years in jail, when she had been just another political prisoner who had too much time to overthink everything. She noticed that the same e-mail address was underneath all of Ahmad Fard's articles. Why had she never thought until today to do a simple search for him? She wrote the e-mail address down and began pacing around her living room. The pacing, too, took her back to prison, to solitary confinement, to nights when she prayed that in the morning they'd come with the blindfold for real this time and put her against the wall and finish her off so that this mad ticking of her brain would stop at last. Fariba Tajadod felt tainted. She felt dirty through and through. And she wanted to write Ahmad Fard right now and ask him if he ever felt an iota of this dirt in his soul. Did he ever pace the room like this? Did he ever feel guilty for giving so many people away to his interrogators? Did he also have to take sedatives around the clock to keep himself from going crazy?

Back in those days the revolution was still just a year old; their world had turned into something like a dangerous carnival. The king had abdicated and left the country. And good riddance! Everything seemed possible then and everyone had something to say about what the "possible" should be. Their own house had turned into a revolving door of young men and women full of revolutionary zeal. Fariba and Ali's father did his best to try to put some restraint on the youngsters' enthusiasm, but the talk was always of resorting to guerrilla warfare if the religious clerics and their supporters decided to push for an endgame and wipe all the other revolutionary groups out of the picture.

Fariba was only in high school back then—wide-eyed and excited and scared, walking the streets of the pulsating city where on every block adversaries—Communists, Marxist-Leninists, and fundamentalist Muslims—all vied for pieces of territory and listeners' ears. It was a time of committing to this or that ideology. You had to hurry, choose a side, and worry about understanding it all later. Or, as her brother Ali used to say, "The train is leaving the station soon and if we don't get moving on, the doors of this revolution will close on us for good." Fariba worshipped her brother. Her brother who was twenty-two and at the top of his class at the College of Engineering and who had finally decided to throw in his lot with the *mujahedin*. Ali said that only the *mujahedin* had the right combination of devoutness and commitment to social justice to stand up to the new bullies—the clerics and their street thugs.

She'd never forget that first time Ali brought Ahmad Fard to their house. The newcomer had big, penetrating eyes that would rest on the seventeen-year-old girl's face and make her knees weak. She was in love from that first day without even knowing it, in love with Ahmad Fard's seeming coolness under fire, his sense of command, his maturity, and the way he would not budge on things that mattered. He was the one who was going to guide her brother through this labyrinth of revolution. She felt it, as did many others. But on that day when the introductions had been made with the family and Ahmad was about to take Ali with him to a *mujahedin* meeting, her father had pointedly asked, "Don't you think these people you are throwing in your lot with are a bit violent?"

Her father had wanted a straight answer to a straight question. But Ahmad Fard's composure would not be shaken. Calmly he answered, "The experience of revolution is something new for all of us. Everything is possible."

She remembered how Ali would barely look at their father as the two young men left the house for the meeting. That had been the beginning. And the end.

A life of empty chores—that was what she'd been left with ever since coming out of prison. She'd been let out of jail exactly a quarter-century ago, twenty-five years of running errands to keep herself busy and not think about the dead. Ahmad Fard had told them, "We have to sacrifice ourselves so that the people of this country will have peace, so that there'll be justice, so that there won't be hunger anymore, not even sadness." From that first day that she'd met him at their house, until almost two years later when he showed up again suddenly and stayed hidden there for six months, an unbearable ache had taken hold of her.

Afterward in jail, the interrogators told her that Ahmad Fard had been finally executed. But when they released her a few years later, forcing her to have compulsory weekly meetings with a handler, it was hinted that Ahmad Fard might still be alive. She didn't believe it. Yet information was a one-way street. It had to go from you to them and not the other way around. So she'd never found out anything more. If Ahmad Fard was really alive, did he know what finally happened to her brother? There had been a girl in her cell block who always said she'd kill herself if she found out Ahmad Fard was dead. There had been a lot of girls who felt that way about him.

And they were all dead today. Ahmad Fard was not.

Seven in the morning and not a wink of sleep yet. All night she'd weighed Ahmad Fard's guilt and innocence. She was back to a summer day of a lifetime ago. After months of having no news of him, Ali was suddenly at the door. Fariba was so happy to see her brother that she'd hung onto him with both hands and would not let go. Their mother and father were in the kitchen preparing a feast together for their son's return. Ali had whispered to her, "Things are really bad, Fariba. There's nowhere to stay. We're getting caught right and left."

"What about Ahmad?"

"Forget him. No one knows where he is. Some say he pulled a grenade on himself before they got to him. Some say he left the country. Others say he's in jail."

"But if he was in jail, they'd have come for us too by now. No?"

"True. None of us must get caught alive. You mustn't forget. Whoever gets caught will eventually give ten more people away. It's like dominoes. Fariba, listen to me." He'd held her and looked hard into her eyes. "If you have a chance to leave this country, do it. Don't stay here. I doubt I'll be alive long. I took a big risk coming here today." Ali was breathless, talking fast, trying to get it all in before their parents came out of the kitchen. It was then that she realized this was probably goodbye. He'd continued, "You're not that involved, which is good. But you need to know what's going on out there. I see death in front of me every day. There's no longer any turning back for people like me. Do you remember Turkish Saeed? They identified him over at Laleh Park. I was supposed to meet him over there. So I took Jalil's daughter with me. I figured that way I'd look like a regular father out for a stroll with his child. I'd barely gotten to the park when there was a blast. Saeed saw them coming for him and pulled the pin before they could snatch him. I held the child close to me. She was screaming. Everyone was. I came out on the other side of the park and bought her some ice cream. If Saeed hadn't acted fast, they'd have caught me too. And with the kid with me, there was no option of blowing myself up. Are you getting the picture now?"

She had gotten the picture, yes. The last memory she had of that day was of their father yelling at Ali to stop his death wish, their mother weeping, and Ali with his head hung low putting an apple in his pocket and shutting the front door gently behind him. He had said to her, "You know, sister—one day somebody has to write about these days and how we all lived it. What I'm really afraid of is dying for nothing. I'm afraid that no one will ever know what we did and why we did it. Are we martyrs or traitors to this country? Was all this for nothing? Pray for me!"

She had prayed. For Ali and for all the people from those days. In fact, she was still living in that time. The anger of it crushed her sometimes. But so did the love.

Now she had to get ready for work after a night with no sleep. Her job was usually a breath of fresh air for her. For several years now she'd been working at a day care run by one of her friends from college. Fariba was good at the job and loved being around kids; it made her forget herself, made her forget everything. People told her she should open her own day care. But she always gave a thousand reasons why she couldn't. She told her friends that she'd looked into it and found out they wouldn't give a day care permit to a former political prisoner. But it wasn't true. It was more like she simply didn't want to own anything. Ever. She couldn't. Everything for her was at an end point. It had been like that for a long time. As if she didn't want to leave any trace of herself in this world. Nothing that could ever prove she had once lived. Which was why she never finished anything. Piles and piles of half-written stories. Projects that started well but were set aside. Small businesses that she'd open and then hand over to others who'd run with it.

That's right, for twenty-five years she hadn't fought for anything. Except her friendships. She worked hard at those. It was important to her to maintain them. In truth, the only thing she felt she owned in this world was her telephone book. Later on, when cell phones appeared and she started entering numbers into the gadget, she realized she was going to have upward of eight hundred names in there. She dreaded losing even one of these people. But what of the names who were already lost? Ali, Turkish Saeed, Sudabeh, Mohammad, Rasul, Homa . . . That would be a fairly long list too, though thankfully nowhere near as long as the people who were alive. Sometimes she wondered how the dead would judge her if they saw her now. Would they be disapproving because the living ones had gone "soft" and lost their revolutionary fervor? What, for instance, would they think of someone like her best friend Maryam?

She had met Maryam at a party a few years ago and they'd become fast friends because, unlike everyone else at the gathering, they'd both been intimates of the cell blocks and the solitary confinements and the interrogations. But Maryam always insisted, "I crave to simply lose my long-term memory and never get it back. What I want is to have fun, fun from now until the day I die." Back in the day, they had executed Maryam's sister while letting Maryam go on living. Had that been another form of torture? You let some of the people go so they would remember? And could Fariba really blame Maryam if all she wanted to do these days was drink until she was sick and dance until she had to be carried from the weekend parties at the end of the night?

So Maryam had become the sister Fariba never had. If only she could be more like Maryam! Carefree. Not so fixated on the past. Still, even Maryam had mentioned Ahmad Fard's name that one time: "Do you remember that guy? Of course you do. How could anyone forget *him*? My little sister was one of his charges in the organization. One time there were a whole bunch of weapons that needed to be transported. They just needed the stuff stashed for one night in a safe place. So they chose our place. Well, that same night the militia broke into our house out of the blue, ransacked it, found the weapons, and took me and my sister away. Somebody had to have told them about it."

Those overnight raids, she remembered, were a lot more nightmarish than daytime ones. When they broke into your house at night, it was as if you had been devoured by the darkness. No turning back. Fariba's own turn had come one midnight. They hadn't even bothered knocking; they just broke in. Three armed men. Took them two hours to search the place. They'd taken everything, every single photograph and piece of writing she possessed. Her mother and father standing there in shock and Fariba telling the men that she had her final language exam in the morning. The man told her to not worry; she'd be back in no time. "No time" had turned into five years.

She recalled every minute of that drive in the cream-colored Chevrolet from her home to Evin Prison. They had told her to put her head down on her knees so she wouldn't see where they were going. But it wasn't exactly difficult to guess. Then at some point one of the men had remarked, "Almost there, we're at the 'turn of repentance.'" Everybody knew what that meant; it meant the final road that ended at the dreaded Evin cells—it meant the place where loyalties went out the window and all secrets would eventually be pulled out of you.

Ahmad Fard. It all came down to him, she thought. Was it in Evin that he had started giving names away? Or had he started singing for them even earlier? So many young men and women had fallen under the sway of that tall, handsome leader. But how many of them had actually lived under the same roof with him for six months as Fariba had?

It had happened on an early autumn morning. She was walking down her street when a hand had grabbed her shoulder and directed her to the house, telling her to look only straight ahead. Her heart had dropped. Ahmad Fard, here! When they'd entered the house, her mother had almost collapsed from the shock of seeing him; while her father, in a voice filled with bitterness and rage, had pointed his finger at Ahmad.

"Where's Ali? I didn't raise a son so that he would turn into a killer."

"Ali is fine. He cannot be seen right now."

"So it is not all right for my son to come to his own house but it is all right for you to come here?"

"Mr. Tajadod, Ali is known in this neighborhood. If he shows up, they'll be at your door in no time. But me, they don't know. I just need a place to hide for a few days and then I'll be on my way. But if you are not comfortable with that . . ."

Of course he'd stayed. What else was there to do about it? Fariba's mother even insisted. In a way, Ahmad Fard was the last thread they had to Ali. It was better to have him here than not have him.

And so a few days had turned into a few weeks, and then into more than six months.

It was six months of strangeness and quiet love on Fariba's part. Ahmad Fard would of course never know her feelings for him. He would have called it bourgeois, antirevolutionary, or just plain silly. He spent his days exercising, praying, helping around the house, and telling Fariba that she needed to build her character and become strong.

"How does one build character?" she'd asked him.

"Start by reporting on your day. Try to find your weaknesses. Write everything down and show it to me."

"But there's nothing to report. I don't do much of anything."

"That's just it. If there's nothing to report, then something is wrong with your character. You need to become strong. Our revolution needs toughness, stamina."

During that winter, the most important *mujahedin* leader who was still at large or hadn't escaped the country was finally gunned down. The order from up above had always been clear-cut: kill yourself before they catch you. But when it came down to it, a lot

of the leaders had chosen jail rather than death. And by doing so
they'd gone on to net some of their unsuspecting subordinates for
their captors. She could see the frustration in Ahmad Fard's face
during those days. And the arguments between Ahmad and her
father were getting worse by the day. Her father, who wrestled constantly with the fury of a man who'd lost a child over nothing, had
asked Ahmad, "You people still think taking up guns is the answer?"

"The path we are on requires blood to be spilled."

"Whose blood? Yours or the twenty-year-olds you're sending
to the gallows?"

That night over dinner Ahmad finally announced that he'd be
leaving in a few days.

And so he did. Then, in the summer, word finally came that
Ali had been killed. A note was quietly slipped under their door
reporting Ali's "martyrdom." They wrote that he had bitten on
the cyanide capsule and blown himself up at the same time so as
to make sure he got the job done.

How would they know? Fariba had wondered even back then.
If someone blows himself up, how do you know he bit on the cyanide too? They had written in the note about "martyrdom for the
sake of freedom." It was the kind of language Ahmad Fard used to
perfection. Yet it did nothing for Fariba's mother who began her
downward spiral from that day on, and her father who went completely mute for the next decade until his death.

On the day Ahmad was leaving she had finally told him she
was no longer interested in working with the organization. She
had never taken up guns; she was only a sympathizer. Now she
didn't even want to be that. She'd had enough. She had to look
after her parents.

His answer had been predictable, typical Ahmad Fard, typical
mujahedin: "Fariba, having a family is only good when everyone
can have one. How is justice to be carried out if everybody thought
like you? Think again. Do you really believe you're more entitled
than a simple laborer?"

There was nothing to say to that. How did you argue against ready-made sentences? In the long run, she thought she had forgiven him, just as she'd forgiven her interrogator at Evin. Nowadays she thought of "Brother Amir"—the fellow who had put all those questions in front of her when they brought her in—as just another soldier, another clerk doing his job. All that time answering the questions of someone you never got to see. The blindfold they had you wear was actually the perfect prop for forgetting.

Her interrogation had begun with Ahmad Fard's name. She had read the question several times, not knowing whether she was supposed to write about an Ahmad who was dead or one who was still alive. All she wrote in response was, *He was my brother's friend.*

But both Fariba and her interrogator knew there was no longer a brother in the picture. Ali was dead. Which meant Ahmad had to be alive. The nature of the question made her almost sure of that. After an hour, when her interrogator came back and her blindfold was slipped back down, he asked her, "That's it? That's all you know about Ahmad Fard? That he was your brother's friend?"

"Yes."

"Then we start again," Brother Amir had snapped. "If you want to stay alive, start writing. Don't leave a word out about Ahmad Fard."

What was she to write? Ahmad had taught her to write the most ordinary stuff if she ever got caught, pretend she was just a teenage girl interested in school and getting married. If they made her name names, which they would, she should name those who had already died. She should do her best to waste the interrogator's time. That way she would be buying time for others who were still not caught. Some things were not too hard to write. But writing about the dead was.

When it was time, she began with her brother: *They told us Ali was dead. They told us there was no body to recover. They told us not to hold a funeral for him.*

It was a cat-and-mouse game between her and her interrogator, Brother Amir. But it was also the truest part of her confession. Writing about those who had been killed or blown themselves up or bitten on the cyanide didn't cost the dead anything; it only cost *her*. It was a list that could fill a couple of pages—Abbas, Nahid, Mehyar, Nasser, Reza, Ebrahim, Lida, Shahin, Roya, Simin . . .

At sixteen I joined the student wing of the mujahedin organiza-tion. My brother Ali introduced me. I don't consider myself a member of the mujahedin, but a sympathizer. I did not contrib-ute much, because my parents were very much against it.

I never carried a gun. I haven't had paramilitary train-ing. The only thing I learned was to make Molotov cocktails. I joined some of the demonstrations, but a lot of us didn't realize there would be armed conflict. They'd only told us to bring newspapers and matches, so that if teargas was thrown at us we'd be able to build fires and protect our eyes from burning. This was simple self-defense. It didn't harm anyone.

I have not had any contact with the organization since last year. With my brother's disappearance and the death of my friends, all my contacts were severed.

She had handed the paper to the guard outside her cell to give to Brother Amir. An hour later she had her blindfold pulled back down and the cell door was violently thrown open.

"You're writing homework for us? Is this high school? You're playing us? You didn't even write a word about this fellow Ahmad Fard. Until you write something real, you can stay here and rot. I keep giving you the benefit of the doubt because of your age, but it looks like you're bent on destroying yourself."

Ahmad Fard had also taught them to never come out of the role they'd created for themselves under interrogation. Killing time was important. But why should Fariba kill time? All of her time had already been killed.

The next morning Brother Amir held a piece of paper in front of her on top of which Ahmad Fard's name was written in large letters. There was no getting around it now. Ahmad Fard was the closest person in the world to her, and the person she knew least. It was a one-way intimacy. Ahmad Fard was important, both for her and for her interrogator.

So her strategy turned to assuming Ahmad Fard was dead. It was the safest way to approach this part of her confession. She realized that imagining Ahmad dead was not too difficult for her. How could someone like him be alive when so many lesser people in the organization had died? She remembered how easily Ahmad Fard had always spoken of necessary suicide. His eyes shone when he mentioned pulling a grenade's safety pin or biting on the cyanide. He became more beautiful than ever talking like that. More serious. More complete. She told herself if her brother Ali, who'd had the softest heart in the world, could do it, then it must be as easy as one-two-three for someone of Ahmad's caliber. Ahmad who was one of the theoreticians of martyrdom for the cause of revolution.

But she also had to be even more careful of what she wrote now. The cat-and-mouse game had entered a new stage. Ahmad had had an operational name, for instance. Everyone had taken one on after things became more serious. But should she dwell on that? She didn't know. It was tricky. Even trickier was the idea of Ahmad Fard having been to their house at all. That would mean her mother and father knew about him. Her confession then had to steer clear of their house at all costs:

I met Ahmad Fard for the first time at a headquarters meeting during the new year. I had gone there with Ali, my brother. Ahmad Fard talked to everyone, including me. Then I found out he was an engineer and had gone to the same university that my brother went to. I can't even say for sure if Ahmad Fard was his real name. I saw him at all the later meetings I attended as well. He was always very serious. I was never

sure which branch of the organization he was responsible for.
Honestly, I don't have a good idea of the organization's hierar-
chy. A little over a year ago I ran into him accidentally on the
street. He paid us a visit at the house and told my parents Ali
was doing all right.

Work was out of the question today. She had a headache and felt
like throwing up from lack of sleep. She left a text message at work
that she wasn't feeling well and couldn't come in. Being Thursday,
the beginning of the weekend, it was only half a day at the day care
center anyway; they could do without her.

She stared at that laptop screen. It was time. His e-mail address sat in front of her. She figured it wasn't necessary to write
anything out of the ordinary. She'd cut to the chase. She'd tell him
she wanted to see him for old time's sake. And what should she tell
her therapist about this new development in her life? Should she
even mention it? Probably not. Her therapist wasn't keen on the
idea of sudden decisions.

Greetings. I am Fariba Tajadod. Ali Tajadod's sister. I hope you
remember me. A recent piece of unfortunate news on television
made me do a search on the Internet and I managed to find
your contact information. I hope you don't mind. I would like
to see you, if possible. But in case you don't remember me, I
can write again and give you further information about myself.
Though I am fairly sure you will know who I am. Thank you.
p.s. Finding out just now that you are alive made me very
happy. Truly.

She sat staring at what she had written. Maybe she should
keep it as a draft and send it another day. No, now was the time to
do it. She clicked so hard on the mouse that it hurt her index finger. Then she jumped up and started pacing around. Deep breath!
Get out of the house, Fariba. She had to hit the streets before she

went stir-crazy. She should get in touch with her therapist. That's what she should do. She'd often told her therapist how she lived in two worlds, but she had never said a word about Ahmad Fard and why he contributed so much to that feeling. There were things you could simply never talk about. Even in therapy. And that man, Ahmad Fard, had become the dead bolt across her mouth a long time ago. She had thought she was reprieving his life by saying as little as she could about him at the interrogations, giving him a chance to make a break for it, or else die a noble death—like Ali and so many others.

A noble death was the key; that was what she'd imagined for him. Cyanide, grenade—whatever it took to do himself in and save others. She could not imagine anything less for a man of Ahmad Fard's stature. Which was why until last night he had been lying in some unmarked grave that no one, least of all Fariba, was ever supposed to discover. But now this convenient illusion, too, was finally over and suddenly all of the many dead, every last one of them, were up and about and marching in front of her with a vengeance, asking her the same question: *What about Ahmad Fard? Why is he not with us?*

She drove aimlessly. Or so she thought at first. But before long she was staring at the outside barriers of Evin Prison at the foot of the mountains in the far north of Tehran. The area had changed so much since those days. So much had been built in this part of town. And with every building frenzy so much had been buried and forgotten.

Ahmad Fard . . . he was a part of all this, his life having merged into the very fabric of lies and ridicule that was the end result of three months of interrogation. Brother Amir had only been toying with her all that time. They'd all been toying with her, as they already seemed to have mounds of confession from none other than Ahmad Fard himself, written no doubt in his impossibly neat handwriting. He'd told them everything. Even the operational name that he himself had given her, "Leyli." She was dumbfounded. In her mind, at first, she put it to his trying to protect her, to show the men questioning him that Fariba Tajadod was not someone they should worry about at all. She was not a threat, just a teenage girl who ate and slept and worried about her brother and didn't have the kind of discipline that a true guerrilla needed to have. What Ahmad Fard had not written about, of course, was her love for him, because that was the one thing she always kept to herself. So the day when Brother Amir finally laughed past her blindfold and disclosed how worthless she had really been to the "cause," she felt an utter emptiness: three months of cat-and-mouse for nothing. They'd already had all the answers. They already had Ahmad Fard. And if he had written about her—even if it was only meaningless stuff—what of the others who were more important than her? What else had he written? Whom had he given away and to what extent? Ahmad Fard hadn't died that noble death after all. No cyanide or grenade for him. Rather, they would probably just kill him here in Evin, she'd imagined.

Maybe there was still some nobility in that.

Unless he gave *everything* away. Unless he sang like a lark for them and didn't stop singing and betraying people until they commuted his death sentence to some jail time and a slap on the back of the hand.

Back at home Fariba made straight for the laptop. There was a reply.

A warm hello to you, dear Fariba. I too am so glad that you as well are alive. I am on a trip until late Friday. I can see you Saturday morning at my office. Say about 11 AM.

There was an address. Even a telephone number. He remembered her, obviously. What else did he remember? And what had he willfully forgotten?

She did more searches online until she came upon a video link of him at some industrial seminar in Istanbul. At first when she clicked the link she shut her eyes and just listened to him speak for a while. It was him, all right. That same voice of pure command and total control. What was he saying? It didn't matter. She opened her eyes and was astonished. Photos could be deceiving, but even on video he'd barely changed at all. Some gray hair on the side, making him look more distinguished. Otherwise it was the same Ahmad Fard. You couldn't mistake him for anyone else.

Two days left until Saturday.

She went to the mirror and stared at herself for a long time. A woman, alone, with more white hair than Ahmad Fard. Some age lines under her eyes, though not too bad. But her lips had long lost that freshness of youth. Smoking had seen to that. She also noticed her eyebrows were all over the place lately. Maybe she could pay a quick visit to that chatty makeup girl who worked near Vanak Circle. She was good with eyebrows, but she talked way too much.

She heard the ding of her cell phone by the laptop. It was Maryam with a text message: *You better not cancel on the party tonight. AGAIN!* She hadn't forgotten about the party, but had decided she wouldn't go. Now she changed her mind. Why not? She'd drink a little and get herself out of herself. Maybe she'd dance. She and Maryam would dance next to each other and her friend would give her that look of utter disbelief that appeared on her face once every six months when Fariba decided to dance for five minutes at one of these Thursday-night parties.

I'll see you there, don't worry, she wrote back to Maryam. Then she started digging around the bathroom for her eyebrow trimmer. It wasn't anywhere to be found, but she did come across a sharp little cutter-blade. The blade was not for trimming; it was for loneliness. Every solitary woman and man in Tehran probably had a cutter like this that they kept for those times when enough was enough. But cutting one's wrist was inefficient, unlike exploding oneself with a grenade or biting on a cyanide capsule. Even with the cyanide you could not be sure. She recalled Mahbubeh, a girl in her cell block who had bitten on the capsule, but they'd managed to catch her in time and bring her around. There was nothing worse than being saved after you chewed on the poison, because then they assumed you had to know some real secrets to have taken extreme measures like that. They saved you and then the real nightmare began.

That night the party had more than its usual share of the city's literati. For a minute she thought about turning back, going home, and having a quiet night to herself. She saw Maryam in the kitchen chatting with the host, a blue-eyed woman who acted in TV soaps, wrote poetry, considered herself a painter and a photographer, and lately was supposed to be working on a novel which, undoubtedly, would win a bunch of prizes. She even had a business card where she mentioned all the things she did. Except, Fariba thought matter-of-factly, she didn't do any one of those things well. But who cared? People came to these parties to get shit-faced drunk, dance, flirt, sleep with each other's wives and husbands afterward because they were supposed to be intellectuals, and then repeat it all next week and next month and all the months and years after. The same people. The same parties. And the same infidelities.

But tonight, Fariba at last decided, she'd go ahead with her original intent: she'd lose herself in that crowd. She went to the liquor table and poured herself some *arrack*. And when Maryam joined her she drank more and managed to actually hold her own with her friend for the next two hours.

"Well, you're a surprise tonight," Maryam said at some point after they'd been dancing for a half hour straight.

Fariba stopped dancing all of a sudden. She wasn't sure if she should say anything about what she'd discovered yesterday. She stood there immersed in the din of music and the dancing bodies around them, looking uncertainly at her friend.

"Well?" Maryam said. "Out with it."

She brought her lips close to Maryam's ear. "Ahmad Fard is alive."

"What did you say?"

"I've found him . . . I'm sorry, I think I upset you."

"No, no. Just, well, it's a shock. I mean . . . how come he's alive? And why and how did you find him?"

Fariba explained while Maryam kept shaking her head. They had slowly made their way to a corner where there was less music and people.

Maryam asked, "What kind of a man is he now?"

"The same, I think. Has his own engineering firm. Goes around giving speeches a lot. Writes articles. About all sorts of things. Basically he's still being Ahmad Fard. I can't believe we didn't run into him at one of these parties before this."

"Fuck him!"

"I wrote to him. Made an appointment to see him."

The shock came back to Maryam's face. "Why would you do that?"

"Unanswered questions."

Maryam scoffed. "Good luck with that. It's hard to fathom why they didn't kill someone of his importance. Then again, how many upper-echelon types like him do we know who bought their own lives at the expense of the rest of us? Am I right or am I right?"

"They weren't all like that."

"But more than a few of them were."

"Yes," Fariba muttered resignedly, "more than a few of them were."

Maryam threw her hands up. "Oh, the hell with it. Let's not ruin our night over this."

"Do we have any nights that are not already ruined?"

"Stop this gloom right now! Tonight I've seen you drink and dance. And it's a beautiful thing to see for a change."

"I don't know what came over me."

"Ahmad Fard, maybe?" Maryam smiled and pulled on Fariba's arm. "Forget that traitor. Let's go dance some more."

Fariba pulled back. "Wait!"

Maryam turned to face her again. "What?"

"Do you want to come with me to see him?"

"Are you kidding? I'd only shoot him."

"With what?"

"God! I'm kidding. All right. We'll go see him together. I wouldn't want you to go there alone, anyway."

"I'll text you his address. It's off Villa, a few blocks south of Saint Sarkis Church. Saturday morning. Eleven o'clock. Meet me nearby, let's say at Café Lord, a half hour before that. We'll walk from there."

Maryam nodded. "All right. Can we dance now?"

She spent most of Friday trying to recover from a hangover. She barely left her bed and had all day to imagine tomorrow morning when she'd come face-to-face with Ahmad Fard again. His office was just a few blocks away from the house she'd grown up in—the house that Ahmad Fard had stayed in for six months all those years ago.

How would she comport herself tomorrow at his office? She probably had to deal with one of those stuck-up secretaries first. The ones with the nose jobs and voices like a cat's meow. The girl would make her sit while she called *Dr.* Fard's line. She'd have to make sure not to make any nervous movements. Then what? When the secretary finally guided her to Ahmad's office, what would be the first thing he'd do? Would they shake hands? *Miss Tajadod, I am so pleased to see you.* Is that what he'd say? Or would he call her Fariba? Or even "Leyli," that needless operational name that he himself had given her. She had a lot of things to ask him. But maybe she'd start with how his life was. Are you happy? Do you sleep well at nights? Do you ever think about those black years? Do you think about all the friends and comrades we lost? Do you still believe that everyday life should be sacrificed for some greater cause, like a revolution? Or are you too just another hostage of day-to-day existence like the rest of us small people in this world?

Maybe she'd get tongue-tied and not utter a single word. It wasn't impossible that could happen. But even if she had to get drunk again to be able to speak her mind, she'd do it. Thankfully, Maryam would be with her. Or would she? Now she could no longer imagine Maryam being there tomorrow. Actually, she shouldn't have told Maryam anything. That was stupid of her. Because, well, there was a storm inside her that only Ahmad Fard could address, and for that she needed to be alone with him. She wanted to tell him about her nightmares of going back to prison. The sound of the last bullets delivered to this or that prisoner. The sound of the names of the women who were called one by one to present themselves for their own execution. She wanted to tell him how she'd tried but still could not bury the past. But also . . . this: how glad she was that she never killed in the name of revolution. That no one's blood was on her hands. But what of her brother? What of Ali? She had lived three decades with this one thought: what if before dying Ali had killed others? Would Ahmad Fard be able to tell her the truth about that? Or would he feed her another one of his old sound bites—*Fariba, war is war and freedom has a price.*

This Friday hangover was the worst she'd had in years. There was always a price to pay, wasn't there? *Ahmad Fard, I have had to pay the biggest price because of you. You changed the course of my life. And my brother's life. You are my ancient love who never knew what was in my heart. And today I'm a middle-aged woman with a trunkful of regrets and what-ifs. No, I don't want to recover that past. There's nothing left to recover. I just need some information. And a commander like you always had the information, right? What did you do with all that information? Serve it lock, stock, and barrel to your interrogators? Is that what you did? People like you always talked about dying for the cause. And yet here you are: alive! What does that say for the rest of us? That we were all your cannon fodder?*

She stayed up most of the night and the hangover stayed with her. She wished she had just one cyanide capsule left from those days. No doubt its expiration date would be long over, but still she wanted to take it to Ahmad Fard and see if he'd have the balls to at least put it in his mouth, even if he didn't sink his teeth into it. Of course he wouldn't. Instead he'd probably say something like, *Oh come, Fariba, get over it. All us Iranians experienced these things back then. You need to find the peace within yourself.*

People like that always had something to say about reaching peace within yourself. She'd give him peace all right. She'd finish him. Better yet, she'd finish herself.

She lit a cigarette and searched for the cutter she'd found earlier. Maybe there was a way to do it efficiently with a blade after all. Cut up and down rather than sideways. She found the blade on the ledge of the bathtub where she'd left it earlier. She kept the bathroom door open. After all these years since leaving prison she still got claustrophobic from closed doors and small spaces. Wasn't that funny? She wanted to kill herself and was still afraid of a closed door! She was afraid of death too. But she was also numb. In fact, suddenly the roller coaster ride of the past couple of days was over. She stood under the shower in her clothes and turned the water on for a few seconds. Then she made a cut on her wrist. Nothing deep. Just enough for some blood to come out. It felt ridiculous. It was as if a bee had stung her. She dropped the blade into the tub, grabbed the end of her shirt, pressed it over the cut, and left the bathroom.

On her bed she sat staring at the fast-approaching daylight. The sting from the cut made her aware of her body for the first time in days. She felt weak and dizzy. She pulled a sheet over herself, closed her eyes, and let go.

When she woke up she felt even worse than before. She noticed the trails of blood on the sheet and was disoriented for a minute. Now she dragged herself in front of the TV and searched for one of those classical music stations. Mozart's "Requiem in D Minor." Seemed appropriate enough this morning. Slowly her wits were coming together. The dampness in her clothes brought on a sudden chill and she felt a grogginess that kept her from being able to move around easily. The cell phone was on the kitchen counter. One missed call and a message from Maryam: "You're not answering. I'll just see you at 11 at his office. I can't make it to the café before that. So don't come earlier."

The phone showed it was already past eleven thirty. Music on the television stopped playing and a woman began speaking in Russian. All Fariba could understand was "Mozart." She called Maryam. Her phone was off.

Worry. It suddenly came in a wave and made her scurry for fresh clothes. In the car she thought how Maryam must be waiting for her at Ahmad Fard's office by now, or maybe she was outside the building wearing her usual bright red lipstick and smoking a cigarette. This image made her smile. She still couldn't smoke cigarettes out on the street like Maryam. It didn't feel ladylike. And Maryam always made fun of her about such things. How she ached to be more carefree like Maryam. Just have a good time and not give a damn about the world and its ways. To this day she had never asked how Maryam managed to go on living after they pulled her sister out of their cell and took her to be executed. How could Maryam dance and laugh and party like that when she'd had to witness a horror of that magnitude?

Fariba was glad she'd never asked Maryam about this.

The traffic barely budged this morning. But she didn't have far to go. They'd probably give her a ticket at some point for driving through midtown on a weekday morning without a special traffic permit. But who cared! She had to hurry. She called Maryam again. No answer. Another ten minutes, she figured, before she got there.

At the corner of Sepand, the street was completely closed off. A soldier directing traffic told her to turn the other way. Instead she got out of the car. There were police in front of the building where Ahmad Fard's office was supposed to be. The soldier started waving at her and telling her to get back into her car. Other vehicles began honking and several more soldiers came from behind and made them do U-turns. Fariba pushed the soldier's hand away and the young conscript appeared to simply give up on her. More police cars arrived from the other direction. When she tried to walk toward the building on Sepand Street, one of the policemen shouted to her to not come closer. She swallowed hard and froze.

Just then she saw him as they came out of the building, Ahmad Fard surrounded by half a dozen cops. He wasn't in handcuffs though. He just looked completely shaken up and scared. A good ten years older than how he'd appeared in that video. Fariba remained motionless, watching him, wondering where they were going. When she realized they were not getting into one of the police cars, she started to say in a voice that was barely above a whisper, "Mr. Fard, it's me. Fariba Tajadod. We had a meeting this morning."

Ahmad Fard neither heard her nor looked her way. He was talking a mile a minute to one of the policemen who kept nodding his head as they walked right by her. Another cop came unhurriedly out of a corner store smoking and speaking on his cell phone. He was a small man with a voice twice his size and he seemed pleased with himself. Fariba listened to him talk.

"Yeah, the woman stood right in front of the guy and shot herself in the head. Can you believe that? Sure I'm sure. I saw her dead body myself. Happened around ten. She was pretty too. In a beat-up sort of way. Poor thing. Had on that red lipstick you like to wear. And she had your name too, love. Maryam! . . . What? How should I know which Maryam? There's a lot of Maryams in this town. Half of them want to kill themselves and the other half want to kill somebody else." He paused and laughed. "Sure, I just hope you belong to neither of those halves."

THE CORPSE FIXER

BY MAJED NEISI

Shahrak-e-Gharb

Afghanistan

A lot of people wanted to steal his corpse. But Mullah Qader belonged to me. Because I was the only real corpse fixer who operated on the front lines between the Taliban and the *mujahideen*. Everyone knew I could get the goods like no one else. But no one is born into this world with the title *corpse thief* written on his forehead, you know? War does that. It takes away opportunities and it brings other opportunities. It was a job no one else really wanted, or could handle. So it fell upon me and my mule. Whenever one side wanted a corpse of one of their own brought back from the other side, I was the man to do it. And they both let me operate with impunity. Why? Because both sides needed me. Families wanted their dear ones properly buried. Comrades wanted comrades to have a suitable resting place on the right side of the battlefield. So Asef—that's me—and his mule were there to do the job: take dead Taliban fallen on the wrong side back to the Taliban, and take dead *mujahideen* back to the *mujahideen*.

I figured after delivering the body of the great commander, Mullah Qader, back to the Taliban and coming away with a decent payday, I could retire, go next door to Iran, get out of this hellhole of endless war. Like other Afghans I could get me a laborer's job there or, better yet, I'd become a super to a building or a groundskeeper at some rich folks' home and enjoy a peaceful life at last.

It all started on that fateful night when I was in the Taliban camp getting the order for a corpse that Mullah Qader himself wanted back. Suddenly they bring in this *mujahideen* boy who can't be more than sixteen. He looks like a peach. He looks better than a peach with those beautiful green eyes of his. The Taliban fighters can barely contain their excitement. They're going to have a night with him, and then some. But then, in the middle of our deal about the corpse, Mullah Qader's eyes fall on the boy too and the deal is forgotten. I saw the mullah zoom in on that kid like he wanted to tear into him right there and then. He jumped up, pushed his soldiers aside, took the boy's hand, and led him away. There were murmurs, but who could argue with the mullah? Only last week he had lashed one of his men within an inch of his life for raping a prisoner, yet tonight all he could think of was the green-eyed boy. I even tried calling him back to finish our deal. But no dice. The mullah and the boy disappeared into the only tent at that camp and I had no choice but to gather my things and head for the *mujahideen* line; I had a fresh corpse for them that was but a day old.

Later on, I heard the story the boy told of how he captured the mullah and brought him to the *mujahideen* lines. He only told half the story, of course. There was nothing about how he'd had to take it up the ass first from Mullah Qader and make sure the man fell asleep, satisfied, before he stole the commander's Colt and took him as his prisoner right out of that Taliban camp. And this is where I—poor old Asef and his mule—came in. The kid made the mullah drive them out in the wee hours of the morning before the morning call to prayer. They were heading toward the Panjshir Valley where the *mujahideen* were camped. But the kid knew it was only a matter of time before the Taliban realized their commander was gone and came looking for them. So he had the mullah drive his own Land Cruiser off a cliff and went the rest of the way on foot.

And they were lost.

Until they ran into me, poor Asef the corpse fixer.

The kid ran up to me, my mule, and my corpse, his gun pointed at us. I was thunderstruck. He should have still been back in the

Taliban camp and under the mullah; what was he doing in this no-man's-land between the two battle lines?

He said, "This is a fighting zone. Where are you headed with the mule and the woman?"

The "woman" was only the corpse, of course. With fresh corpses I always shaved them and put some makeup and a *burqa* on them to keep people from asking too many questions.

"She's a new bride. She's not feeling too well. I'm taking her to see a doctor."

"A doctor? In this wilderness!" He came closer to the mule and noticed the henna I'd daubed on the dead body's hands. The mullah stood to the side watching all this with a face that promised plenty of evil and blood. The kid gave a not-so-light slap to the mule's rear and the thing bucked, throwing my corpse to the ground. "A bride, did you say?"

I have to give it to him; even though he'd been buggered just a few hours ago the kid had some balls. He motioned with his gun to the mullah to come over. Then he put me and the mullah next to each other and made me talk.

I told the kid what I did for a living.

"I've heard of you."

"Well, here I am in flesh and blood." I didn't tell him I'd witnessed his being taken into the mullah's tent a little while back.

He asked, "Why the henna on the dead man's hands?"

"Makes them more womanly, in case I run into trouble and people have questions."

"All right. Forget the corpse. Take the *burqa* off him and put it on the mullah."

Was he kidding? Put a woman's *burqa* on the one and only Mullah Qader? When I hesitated, he flashed the weapon in my face. So I took the *burqa* off the dead man and without looking into the mullah's eyes put the thing on him. The kid seemed to know exactly what he was doing. He searched me for weapons and took my knife away. Then he rifled through the mule's packing and found a blade for shaving, some henna, and another set of women's clothes. I was wishing just then this latest corpse hadn't been so damn new so I wouldn't have had to dress it up like that. The best remains were the oldest ones, far past their stink. No one ever argued with those, not even if you made a mistake about the body sometimes.

The kid said, "How far are we from my side's front positions?"

"Half a day."

"You must help me deliver this whore's son to my people."

I took one look at the boy and another at Mullah Qader. What was I going to do? I'd always dealt only with the dead and it was a good enough job. It brought peace to the living to see their dead buried where they should be. But now I had to choose between the living—Mullah Qader and this boy. If I helped the mullah, the kid would die; if I helped the kid, Mullah Qader would die. If I helped no one, I was the one who'd probably be killed. Damn this war that someone would have to die for, either way you looked at it.

I barely mumbled, "Whatever you say."

The kid gave me a meaningful look and said, "Now, get to work. First cut off Mullah's beard and put henna on his hands and feet."

Hearing this, Mullah Qader sprang from his feet and, throwing the *burqa* off, roared like a lion. Anyone else would have soiled their pants hearing the invincible mullah's roar just then. But that kid, it was like he'd come to this world to do just one thing: put the mullah to shame. He shot a round next to the mullah's feet and we both saw he could shoot, and shoot well.

I can't describe what I was feeling then. Here, in the middle of nowhere, in Afghanistan, on a path that no one but myself was familiar with, I had to run into this boy and Mullah Qader. I was hoping someone, anyone, would show up and put all three of us and my mule out of our misery. I stood there frozen while the mullah took his clothes off. His massive belly hung over his balls like something obscene, and all I could think just then was how those balls had taken care of the boy's behind just a few hours ago.

The kid pushed me toward Mullah Qader. "It's time. You are in charge of fucking him."

I fell to the ground, crying and begging. "Do you know what you are saying? God Himself couldn't do that to Mullah Qader. How can you expect me, poor Asef, to be a part of something like this?"

But the boy was enjoying this. He was in his element. His eyes were bright with anticipation. He watched Mullah Qader, who was chalk-white now, and said, "Mullah, a bullet for a bullet, an ass for an ass. It's time to give up your ass."

I continued to beg. I took off my pants and showed him, "Look at this shriveled little thing of mine. I'm in shock. How do you expect me to fuck Mullah Qader with this?"

The kid nodded and went and got my shovel.

"No, I beg you. That shovel is just for digging up graves."

He pointed the gun at me and said, "He's going to bend over for you and you're going to push this handle as far in as it will go. If you don't, I'll shove it up your own ass."

Mullah Qader could barely stand on his feet. He had begun crying. I could not believe it. Was this the same Mullah Qader whose very name would make the enemy lose its resolve? Was this really you, Mullah? You pathetic fat turd crying like a bitch! You should have made a move just then, put up a struggle and fought for your life and died like a man. Instead you bent over and let the kid make me shove that handle inside you and tear your ass up. Yes, that kid was clever. He knew that after doing this to you, I would never consider helping you again, because the first person you'd take revenge on if you stayed alive would be me, poor Asef!

The mullah was half dead by the time we were done with him. The kid had me splash water on his face and then I had to shave him. I put the henna on his hands and feet and helped him into the *burqa* again. The mullah wasn't saying a word. He looked like a mute bride being sent to her husband's home. It's amazing how quickly you can reduce a man like that.

As we got close to the *mujahideen* lines, I handed the muzzle to the kid. "This is as far as I go with you. Please send my mule this way so I can go back and fetch my corpse before it's too late. And I beg you not to tell anyone I helped you with Mullah Qader or I'll lose my means of livelihood."

The boy laughed and said that I'd done my job well; he'd send the mule back to me in no time.

As they took off, Mullah Qader turned back to me. And from behind the *burqa* he said the words that would follow me for years: "I'll kill you."

Tehran

The Mrs. had told me, "Asef, you have two choices. By the time I get back from Paris, you either find my dog, or if he's dead I want his body back. Otherwise you leave my house."

So here I was, far from the Afghan battlefields. I was no longer pulling corpses from one side to the other. I had a comfortable job, one that was a lot better than the backbreaking construction work my Afghan brethren did for these ungrateful Iranians. But now the bitch's dog was lost and she'd handed me several hundred color copies of her Poopi's mug. I had to go around sticking Poopi on every wall and traffic pole in the Shahrak-e-Gharb District in the hopes that someone would recognize and bring him back so the Mrs. would award the lucky bastard with more money than I made in two years.

And that's exactly what I did.

All up and down Shahrak-e-Gharb, Poopi's face competed with photos of some of those dog-faced presidential candidates. I even paid off the local garbage collectors to let me know if they saw Poopi. I suppose my lot in life was to always be digging after the dead, whether dog or human. That fucking dog could be any-where. All these huge villas in this district. All these rich Tehranis. Half of them with dogs who eat dinners I can only dream of. I would hit the streets in early evenings and watch young men and women in their latest-model cars cruising Iranzamin Boulevard, flirting and exchanging phone numbers. I saw a lot of Poopi-like dogs in some of those cars and thought about stealing one and taking it to the Mrs. But the Mrs. knew her dog well. The thing slept next to her in bed at night and licked her pussy. Now, I can't say this for sure. But another of my compatriots, Baig Jaan, who worked three blocks up from me, swore that he'd seen his Mrs. getting licked by her dog. And I had to ask myself, why else would the Mrs. have Poopi in that bed? It didn't seem natural. Maybe all I had to do was find another small dog to lick the Mrs. and she'd forget Poopi altogether. I mean, here I was, with Rex and Juli, two monster-size guard dogs who also belonged to the Mrs. But the three of us had to live together in some shack at the end of the garden while Poopi got to have the Mrs. all to himself.

Wasn't right.

So the Mrs. called again and asked about Poopi. I told her I was still searching. She told me to go print more posters and stick them in every side street too. I figured this was a good sign. As long as she wasn't giving up on Poopi she wasn't giving up on me. Also, I didn't mind going out there searching for the dog. Come twilight I'd go to the construction sites in the area where fellow Afghans worked and slept at night. We'd drink tea, reminisce, and occasionally some pretty young Afghan boy would show up and we'd play music and have him dance and shake his ass for us.

On this fateful night Baig Jaan had told me he'd be at a half-finished site near his Mrs.' villa. He said there were a bunch of new Afghans working the area who'd be there too. I went to see who they were and maybe find something out about Poopi.

When I got there, the green tea was up and steaming. It was freezing out and they had wood burning in a metal trash can where men stood around warming their hands. Baig Jaan's foul mouth was running as usual, telling the newcomers about his Mrs. and how she liked the dog to eat her out. I'd told him more than once not to say these things to just anyone. One of these poor horny bastards, so far from home, would get it to his head to go pay Baig Jaan's Mrs. a visit. Worse still, the police would probably blame Baig Jaan as an accomplice afterward, because that's what they always do to us Afghans.

I joined the group around the fire and splayed my legs a little so my balls would warm up. Then I looked up to see who was who. That's when our eyes met. Those intense, full-of-hate eyes of Mullah Qader himself. The very mullah I'd supposedly dug from underground and delivered for a nice sum to the Taliban so they could have their legendary commander's body back. Except Mullah Qader hadn't died. Only a few select people amongst the *mujahideen*—and of course yours truly, Asef, who knows everything about the dead—knew about the mullah's escape and survival back then. Much later, I found that the mullah had caught up to the kid and finished him off. Now it was my turn.

My knees went weak. It was him all right. And he knew perfectly well who I was. How could he not? How can you stick the handle of a shovel up a man's ass, tear him up, make him bleed, shave him, put henna on his hands and feet, and finish his transformation with a woman's *burqa*, and not have him remember you? *I'll kill you.* Those had been his exact words all those years ago. And probably in his mind's eye he'd already killed me a thousand times.

I sat, trying to act normal. Baig Jaan handed me a cup of green tea and continued with his story of how the rich cunt liked having herself licked by her dog.

This was an impossible situation. Several times I looked up and those eyes on the other side of the fire would not stop staring at me. I finished my tea quickly and stood up.

Baig Jaan turned to me. "Where so fast?"

"I have to find the woman's dog. Dead or alive, I have to find it."

Baig Jaan sighed. "Go to Farahzadi then. Over there, there's a fellow called Jasem. They call him Jasem Lovedog. He's an Arab from the south. He's not a bad sort. He's more like us, really.

Around here any dog that goes missing ends up at Jasem's. I've even sold him a few dogs myself. Tell him Baig Jaan sent you."

I started to leave. Mullah Qader still hadn't taken his eyes off me. He'd grown old, but he hadn't lost that fearsome look and he was still huge. I felt faint and could barely hear Baig Jaan telling the new crew that my name was Asef and that they used to call me Asef the Corpse Lover back in Afghanistan.

Out on the street I kept turning back to see if the mullah was after me. On Iranzamin Boulevard, kids were busy in their cars doing what they always did this time of night. A little farther up, a teenage girl stood in the middle of the road wailing. She kept screaming at the young driver of a Hummer who sat there smoking hash with his friends and smiling at her. "You ran over my dog!" she screamed. "You murderer! I'll kill you!" The Hummer started up all of a sudden and growled off. A crowd joined the girl in the middle of the road. She wouldn't stop wailing. Before long police showed up, and like a fool I just stood there until they came right up to me.

"You an Afghan?"

"Yes, officer."

"Got your alien papers?"

"Yes, officer."

"Forget your damn papers. Go over there and throw the dead dog in the trash. Hurry up!"

The cops pushed the people away so I could collect the dead animal. The girl screamed for her dog but the cops held her off. In fact, the dog didn't look unlike Poopi. Maybe I could bury it in the yard and tell the Mrs. I'd found him but he was dead. Wasn't that what I'd done for the Taliban? Supposedly given their commander back to them? I cursed myself. When oh when are you going to stop stealing the dead, Asef? What if you bury this dog for the Mrs. and then the real Poopi suddenly shows up? This is why you can never return to Afghanistan. The Taliban will kill you for selling them a fake. I'd heard that after killing the boy, Mullah Qader simply disappeared. He was never a commander again. I guess the shame for him was too much. He took his revenge on the kid and now he was here for me. Tonight, oh Asef . . . tonight is your reckoning night.

I took the dog and carried it a ways before I dumped it. It had begun snowing again. I waited for a taxi to take me to Farahzadi and to Jasem Lovedog. Several cabbies slowed down, but as soon as they saw my face and suspected I was an Afghan they'd speed up again and leave me there in the snow. I guess they figured I'd cut their throats or something. They forget not a building would get finished in this city and not a restaurant could stay open if it weren't for us doing the dirty work. Lazy fucking Iranians! You'd think we'd stolen their mothers' inheritances.

The cold was in my bones now. I had no idea what to do. My options were nonexistent. On one side I had Mullah Qader who was out here to finish me; on the other I had the Mrs. who'd finish me if I didn't find her Poopi. I stood there feeling sorry for myself and getting covered in snow until a cab finally stopped. By the time I got off in Farahzadi the layer of snow had blanketed everything. Afghan workers stood in front of kebab houses directing customers this way and that. The scent and sweat of roasting meat was in the air. I felt him. I felt Mullah Qader's shadow behind me, though I knew that was ridiculous and he hadn't followed me up here. Now I recognized a fellow Afghan and asked him if he knew Jasem Lovedog's whereabouts.

Jasem lived in the back of one of the kebab houses. You could hear the barking of at least a dozen dogs in there. I rang the buzzer and a deep voice asked who it was. He didn't wait for me to answer but opened the door. Immediately three enormous dogs showed their teeth. Jasem himself looked to be in his midforties. He had disheveled hair and had a sleepy face.

"What do you want?"

"I'm looking for my Mrs.' dog."

"You're an Afghan?"

I nodded. He motioned me to come in. There was hardly any room in there. Dogs of every size and color climbed on top of each other and the smell of the place was not quite as bad as a three-day-old corpse in summertime, but close. Jasem sat me by the heater and handed me a cup of tea.

He asked, "How long have you been here? In Iran, I mean."

"I came just before the Americans attacked Afghanistan."

"What did you do over there?"

He had a friendly, familiar face. I felt at ease with him, despite all those dogs. I told him the truth: "I hauled dead bodies. I stole them. They had different names for me . . . Asef the Corpse Thief was one of them."

"You're like me, displaced by war."

"But there hasn't been a war in Iran for a long time."

"A war may end but the shrapnel stays, my brother. I'm an Arab from the south. I was twelve, maybe thirteen when the war started. We were living in Ahvaz then. When the Iraqis attacked, we had to come to Tehran. Refugees. Me, you—we're all a bunch of refugees living under these racist Iranians."

"At least this is still your own country."

He laughed. "In the beginning they used to call me Jasem the Arab around here. But after a while I changed my name to Jasem Lovedog. It stuck. They don't like us Arabs here. They like us even less than they like you. Even though I carry the passport of this damn country, they still despise me. So I figured, these rich motherfuckers out in Shahrak-e-Gharb, they love their dogs. If I become Jasem Lovedog they'll love me too. Tell me, your Mrs. loves her dog a lot?"

"She kicked me out of the house a few times saying I didn't respect her dog enough. Each time I stood behind her door and wagged my tail until she let me back in. She has two others, but they're big guard dogs. The three of us, me and the guard dogs, we live in a little shack away from the main house. A thin wall separates us."

"I told you, they love their dogs here. If you want to survive, keep wagging your tail for them. But if you want to really live, that's another thing; then you have to leave this country."

He got up and opened the door to another room and a whole bunch of Poopi lookalikes came running.

I noticed Poopi right away.

"How did you know it would be one of these?" I asked.

I know the type your Mrs. is and the type of dog she likes to keep her company. I steal them and sell them back. "

"But why steal them?"

"Why? Because I want to survive."

"My Mrs. will give you a good reward."

"Fuck her reward. You keep it. Keep it and tell her you gave it to me."

I bowed and shook his hand. "You're a good man." I took Poopi and squeezed him under my coat. He recognized me right away and didn't put up a fight or bark. Jasem was about to close the door behind me. I put a hand up: "I have one question."

"Ask."

"If you were in a war and could have killed someone but didn't . . . and now the war's over for you, but this guy has come to hunt you down—what are you supposed to do?"

"You have to finish a war on the battlefield. If you don't finish it, then that war's not over. You still have to fight."

I walked from Farahzadi to the Phase One area of Shahrak-e-Gharb with Poopi underneath my coat. I was shivering from cold and from fear. Mullah Qader had come to finish his war, and this white snow had changed the landscape completely.

I came through the back gate, quickly untied Juli and Rex, and let them run the yard. I'd never been more glad to share a hovel with these two giant dogs. If Mullah Qader was here, I would have known it by now. But he'd show up sooner or later. He hadn't traveled all the way to Tehran to build houses for Iranians or water their damn gardens. He'd come for me. He'd come because of his shame. I went over to the main house, fed Poopi, and let him loose. He jumped on the Mrs.' bed and immediately began licking her pillow.

It was past two in the morning now. There was no way I could fall asleep. It was like salt had been sprinkled in my eyes. I set my chair in the garden and built a fire. It was bitterly cold. As cold as some of those winter nights in the mountains of Afghanistan. Rex and Juli sat beside me, alert. They sensed something wasn't quite right. Like me, they were waiting. It got colder and the wind picked up, squealing through those trees like it was the end of the world. Because it really was the end of the world. But no more running away for me. This was the last stop. One of us had to finish it tonight. Deep down I knew it was me who was finished. So I waited and thought and thought: *Why didn't the mujahideen kill him right away back then? Were they waiting to exchange him for a prisoner as valuable as he was?*

But then when he escaped they spread the word that he'd been raped by the boy and been brought into their camp wearing a *burqa*. They'd even taken pictures of him like that. This meant the mullah's time as a Taliban commander was finished. He may have escaped, but he had lost face in the worst way a man can lose face in this world. They said they'd shot him trying to escape, which was a lie. But I used the opportunity to sell another body back to his own people and took off for Iran. Mullah Qader became the wild man of the mountains. He had nowhere to go. A week after I delivered the body, as is customary his family gave away the mullah's young wife to his brother. You poor fucked-up-the-ass bastard, Mullah Qader! You got buggered with a shovel, you lost your wife, you lost your command, you lost everything. And what did you gain in return? You had to satisfy yourself with killing that young boy.

And I was next.

There was a thump by the back gate, like a ball hitting the

ground. Rex and Juli ran barking toward the sound. In a minute the barking turned to moans and whimpers. Still the same Mullah Qader, a guy who could take on two man-killer dogs.

The pick I was holding in my hand felt like a ton of lead all of a sudden and I started shaking. After a while I couldn't hear Juli at all anymore. But Rex was still moaning somewhere back there in the dark. Then I noticed the dog dragging itself toward me and bleeding from several places. She'd be dead soon. I could see the two spots where the axe had gotten him. Apparently he had killed the kid with an axe too. Maybe the same axe! I bent down and ran my hand over Rex's half-alive body. Blood everywhere.

I stood up and held onto the pick for all I was worth. Its handle looked a lot like the one I'd had to shove up Mullah Qader's ass. I heard the sound of his footsteps. Before long we were facing each other. The dogs had torn his clothes, but he was still frightening and intimidating and holding his axe like it was an extension of his body.

Rex was panting desperately now. These were his last moments, I thought. I could barely breathe. I watched the Mullah watching me.

I said, "Mullah, that wasn't my war. It was yours. I was just a corpse fixer. That's all."

"War is war. It doesn't know a soldier from a corpse thief."

"So you've come to finish your war now?"

"A war has to be finished somewhere. That place happens to be here, and now."

My hand went limp on the pick. I took a peek at Rex. The unlucky animal was dying for nothing. Just like me who was about to die for nothing. Like a lot of people who die for nothing. The truth is that so many people come into this world to die over nothing. Like that kid who the mullah finally killed. Even the mullah himself—what had he been fighting for all those years? I bet he didn't even know.

I said, "Look, I was never at war with anyone."

"I don't care about that. I used to be a great commander. I'm not here to negotiate with you."

I saw his grip go hard on the axe. Rex shifted a bit next to my foot. The mullah took another step toward me and in that moment Rex, God bless him, gathered every ounce of life left in him and jumped the mullah.

The axe pounded clean and deep into Rex's head. My own grip went stiff on the pick. I saw Mullah Qader struggling to pull the axe out of Rex's head and without realizing quite what I was doing, I made my move. I hit him as hard as I could right on top of his skull. Blood went spewing every which way and the mullah, the great Mullah Qader, fell dead right next to Rex, my savior.

I stood over the dead man and dead dog until first light, freezing but unable to move. I don't know how those hours passed or what went through my head. I can't recall. At some point I heard Poopi's barking and finally shook myself out of that numbness and went over to the main house and gave the dog his breakfast. There was blood all over my clothes. I washed up a little and regarded myself in the mirror. Still the same. Still Asef the Corpse Thief. Nothing had changed about me all these years. I had to get moving. I had to get rid of the mullah's body. The first thing I had to do was buy a couple of big dogs from Jasem Lovedog. The Mrs. wouldn't know the difference. She barely knew what the big dogs had looked like.

I went back into the garden, picked up the mullah's axe, and started chopping him up. It was not easy work. He was frozen solid and I had to put up more fire to thaw him a bit. But I went at this with a ferocity I'd never known I possessed until Mullah Qader's biggest pieces were his ears.

Next I fetched the mosque-sized soup pot that the Mrs. sometimes used to feed the poor. The poor in this neighborhood of course only meant the Afghan laborers. I got a good fire going and started depositing the mullah in the pot one chunk at a time. I added some snow and before long Mullah Qader was cooking nicely in there. While that went on, I buried Rex and Juli.

The dogs I ended up buying from Jasem Lovedog had themselves a feast of Mullah Qader meat over the next several days. Even Poopi had a go at the mullah whenever I tied up the big dogs and brought him outside for his walk.

Now it was just me and the dogs. The Mrs. cut her trip short when I told her on the phone I'd found her Poopi. She was going to give me a raise, she said. So Poopi and I waited for her return. And I was sure Poopi was eager to get back to gifting the Mrs. her orgasms.

Everything had turned out fine, after all.

And poor old Asef is all right now.

LARIYAN'S DAY IN THE SUN

BY AIDA MORADI AHANI

Qeytarieh

I t begins like this. my gallery staff had left, so I bolted the place shut and stood on Shariati Avenue to light up a cigarette. Little did I know then that this long-suffering street would soon be in the world's headlines, and that I would have something to do with those headlines.

Another one of my stores, Piano Royal, was a little ways down the road. I headed in that direction. It was raining hard and I was thinking of the thirty-three-year-old bottle of red wine that I'd had in my mind to open for the past few weeks. Yes, it was time to give myself a present. I intended to jump in the old Dodge Challenger, head home, spread myself comfortably on the terrace, and let Avitall Gerstetter's lovely voice transport me to Jerusalem while I undid another cork that spoke of a life of waiting—thirty-three years of it, to be exact.

The last of the piano store employees was waiting for me. I brushed past him and the rows of pianos looking like raised graves standing at attention before us.

"You haven't been waiting long for me, have you?"

"No, boss."

"What about the order for that other upright piano?"

"Taken care of, boss."

"Don't be late tomorrow."

He said another "No, boss" and was gone. For a few minutes I leaned into my laptop's screen trying to figure out the latest import duties I had to dole out. Before long I heard an ugly banging on piano keys. I could tell it came from the grand that sat in the middle row of the store. I waited to hear if it would continue before I told whoever it was to come back the next day if they were interested in a piano.

A familiar voice: "Eshaq Lariyan. Past thirty-three years I've seen every kind of malady in you except deafness."

He was used to calling men by their first and last names. A habit he'd no doubt picked up thirty-three years ago when he was an interrogator at the Towhid Detention Center. I recalled those interrogation tables and the ever-present lamps overhead and this man staring into your face telling you he knew exactly who you were and what you did and now that the Islamic Revolution had won the day he was not going to let up on you. Yes, this was the man I knew then and I knew now.

Except everything had changed since that time. The Towhid Detention Center had become a museum. And I was no longer that junior antique smuggler who had sold his soul to this guy fresh out of Tehran University's School of Law. He with his thin beard back then and a headful of giddy thoughts about revolution. He had gone into the Sepah, a colonel now with more than thirty years of active duty behind him. Thirty years and a collection of shrapnel in his body as gifts from the Iran-Iraq War.

I stood up and watched him lean into the grand and regard me in his expensive, cream-colored winter coat that was far too warm for this weather.

"So, you went and bought the building next to the gas station too? Don't tell me you want to open a Jewish ghetto right here on Shariati Avenue, Eshaq Lariyan!"

"It's too soon for that," I said, walking across the room to the window.

Men are readable creatures. Let them say a few words to you and you know where they're heading. Not so with Colonel Said Isaar. Decades of experience with him had proved this time and again. I stood by the store window and watched him through the glass long enough to grow bored. Then my eyes fell on some dried mud on my shoes and I felt a terrible irritation take hold of me.

Until he finally spoke again: "It's possible I can promise this is the last time I have business with you."

"You are not a man to make empty promises. I'm all ears."

"But remember, I only said it's *possible* that I can promise."

"That's lovely. I suppose that could mean I might die this time around."

The rain outside wasn't letting up. It was the kind of weather that made you imagine anything was possible. You could imagine you were a poet. Or a killer. Or both. You could start trouble for yourself. Or else finish something for good.

Isaar came and stood next to me. "The place I want to talk to you about isn't far from here."

"Maybe it's my art gallery?"

"Actually, you only have to look outside to see the job I have for you, Eshaq Lariyan."

An ambulance from Iranmehr Hospital howled outside and then was gone. I felt a cold sweat envelop me; the only job I could see from this window was the wall of the sprawling British embassy summer grounds directly across the street.

I kept my eyes on those walls until Isaar continued. "I think you got it right. Except it's a few hundred meters to the south of where you're looking."

"You mean at the end of the British grounds?"

"I mean the cemetery for their war dead."

"It's been a long time since I dug graves for you."

He laughed. "But I'm sure your digging skills are still intact."

"Which one of your beloveds do you need to bury this time?"

He turned away from me and started back toward the pianos. We'd been so still that had some passerby looked up they might have taken us for a couple of mannequins in a display window. "Do you recall that time when all the public statues in Tehran started disappearing?"

"How could I forget?"

"What do you know about it?"

"Is this an interrogation?"

"If you like."

"All I know is it was three or so years back. They must have stolen a good dozen of them from the parks and traffic circles. I think when the bust of Ferdowsi disappeared, people finally began to make some noise. Actually, a lot of noise."

"And?" His voice was even and patient. He really did sound like his old interrogator self just then.

"The papers said that the municipality had a project and needed casts of the statues. Some bullshit like that. Soon the statues were all back in their places. Though I have my doubts they were the originals."

"And why would you think that?"

The redbricks of the British embassy walls stared back at me like a set of bloody teeth and I still hadn't a clue what the serial theft of Tehran's sculptures had to do with the British and their cemetery down the road.

I toyed with a cigarette without lighting it. "I heard some rumors back then."

"Go on."

"Some thought it was the work of religious fanatics. Type of guys who believe having figures like that in public places is against Islam. Others put the thefts to pros working with somebody high up in the government. But everybody, and I mean everybody, asked the same question at the time."

"Which was?"

"With all the closed-circuit cameras and all the cops on every street of this city, not to mention the boys from the Etelaa'at and their tentacles in every nook and cranny here, how could anyone just lift a statue in plain sight and not get caught? The question made one imagine the orders to steal the statues went way, way up."

Isaar said nothing for a minute. I kept my eye on the embassy walls and the little diplomatic police booth where a lone soldier sat staring out. Besides him, there were a couple of other soldiers striding up and down the other side of the street glued to their AK47s. It was at times like this when you imagined anything could happen in this city at any time.

Isaar broke the silence: "There was one other rumor."

We had arrived at the gist of the matter. I said, "Well, I'm honored that you've come to tell me about it."

He stepped quietly behind my work desk and sat down. "The rumor had it that one of the statues was taken on the direct orders of someone from the British embassy."

My blood ran cold. Had he, Colonel Said Isaar, come here tonight to order me to take a stolen statue back from inside the British embassy? I tried to keep a calm voice. "Your plan is bound to make a man nervous."

"But I haven't told you my plan yet."

"What I want to know is how the British managed something like this without Sepah and Etelaa'at finding out."

"Sepah and Etelaa'at both had a hand in it. Or, as it is officially put, corrupt elements therein. When people started asking questions and shit hit the fan, the guys involved were arrested and now we're just waiting to take the statue back and return it to its place."

"I thought it was already put in its place."

"A fake. As you correctly guessed."

"So why don't you just go in with your own people and take the thing back?"

"Because thirty-three years ago at the Towhid Detention Center we didn't place our bet on a Jewish horse for no reason. You are our man, Eshaq Lariyan."

I took out my handkerchief and wiped the sweat off my forehead. "You still haven't told me your plan."

"In the cemetery for their war dead, the English have a grave for a certain William Mason. I'm told the statue is there for the time being."

"Why there and not inside the embassy?"

"I'm simply given the information. I don't care about the why and why not. Nor do I care why someone at the embassy would be foolish enough to want a statue off the streets of Tehran. The secondary questions don't concern me."

He stood up, buttoned his coat, and moved with purposeful slowness toward the door, as if to allow me time to let things sink in.

I could see his Mercedes had arrived and was waiting for him outside.

"You have two months to plan this out, Eshaq Lariyan."

I nodded.

"You can get inside the cemetery without much problem. The day I have you down for is a day when the *basij* will take over the British embassy."

I could barely talk above a whisper. "You mean the *basij* are going to attack the British embassy so that I can steal back a statue?"

His thick eyebrows converged. "Steal it? No. They are not attacking the embassy for you. But . . . because they happen to be attacking the embassy on that particular day, you will have a chance to take back the statue for us. And like I said, you got two months to figure out a proper plan."

"Which statue is it then?"

"The waist-up piece by Mohammad Madadi. They say it's a masterpiece. Whatever that means!"

The door closed gently behind him. I watched Isaar get in the backseat of the Mercedes, which immediately took off down the wide, wet street like a shark nosing for blood. I knew, of course, about the piece he had been talking about. It was one of two statues that had been stolen from Iranshahr Park and afterward replaced with another fake. A hundred years back the British, who were in the habit of taking everything from everywhere, had appropriated a Qajar painting which had recently sold at a Christie's auction for some astronomical price. I did not think much of this so-called masterpiece of Mohammad Madadi and doubted that a hundred years from now it would fetch much of anything. But what did I know? All I knew was that whoever had had a hand in this job was probably a bit out of their mind, and now they'd pulled me into the vortex of their madness as well. I realized I had been grinding my teeth this whole time. Then I took a deep breath, loosened my jaws, and my right hand automatically felt for the Chiappa Rhino that was always by my side. I caressed that snub-nosed Italian revolver like you would a pet, or an insurance policy that one should never leave home without.

The cemetery was an oddity. It was at the very bottom end of the British grounds and only soldiers from their two world wars were buried there. Next to it was a police station which made things slightly complicated. But not enough for me to not be able to pay off someone in there to make sure at six p.m. sharp Jamshid Godarzi and I could cross over into the cemetery. I'd been working with Jamshid for a good ten years now. He was the sort of guy who switched jobs the way some men switch women. He tried anything once. And whenever I had a job for him, he would find a way to make it happen. He was dark skinned and thick and wasn't in the habit of brushing his teeth or taking showers. And he was my go-to guy for a day like this.

The *basij* had started amassing in front of the embassy by three p.m. I had the gallery closed all day. Now I closed up the piano store too and watched the last of the day's employees make a beeline for the metro station. A half hour later the chants and shouts of the *basij* were so loud that you could have taken a machine gun to a man right there and no one would have heard it. They were the usual shouts—the English were faithless, they were treacherous, down with the British imperialists, et cetera. In the past few months the Brits had sided firmly with the Americans against the Islamic Republic and its drive for nuclear power and voted for more economic sanctions. So, it seemed, it was time to let the rabble-rousing *basij* into the embassy to give the British a taste of how it felt to be besieged. Soon rocks and Molotov cocktails were flying at the embassy doors and walls. By the time the mob broke through the entrance of the place, I was ready. I'd let my beard grow the past two months and with the untucked black shirt that hid the revolver, plus my ugly drab pants, I could have easily passed for one of the apish-looking gentlemen now scaling the walls of the embassy.

I could never think about a job during the last few hours before it began. Today was no different. I sat there watching the developments across the street until a quarter to six. When I finally came out of the store, a woman with wild dog's eyes and wearing a full *chador* looked me up and down like she had found her long-lost brother, then she waved the anti-imperialist placard she was getting well paid to carry that day and shouted, "Down with Israel, down with the British!"

I raised my fist in a gesture of complete solidarity and shouted pretty much the same. And then I was running. The smoke from burning Union Jacks was so thick in front of Cinema Farhang that you had to cover your nose and eyes to get past it. I crossed Shariati Avenue and moved inside Dowlat, where a crowd of bystanders was busy taking videos with their cell phones. I'm sure they took plenty pictures of me too—a typical *basiji* thug running down the street, heading for the cemetery and the police station.

I saw Jamshid waiting for me. He sat quietly behind the wheel of a crane whose hook was already dancing over the wall of the cemetery. As I passed him, Jamshid jumped out of the driver's seat and began to follow me. He must have already set up all our other tools on the other side of those walls with the crane.

No sign of anyone in the courtyard of the police station.

Jamshid said, "They're all out there on the street with their stupid AKs and batons and walkie-talkies. But their orders are to just stand and watch while the *basij* do their thing."

A lone soldier, looking stoned out of his mind and not paying any attention to us, manned the station booth. I imagined that the guy we'd paid off must have seen to it this kid was well provided for on this historic day. We moved quickly. The area between the first and second floors smelled like something between old tea and a toilet.

Jamshid called from behind me: "You know, these damn British deserve everything they have coming to them. The cowardly bastards." He laughed. Then he began panting. We reached the third floor where our inside man had said we'd have a way into the cemetery. Still panting, Jamshid added, "One always knows a shit job from the number of stairs he has to climb for it."

I paused in front of the designated door on the third floor. As expected, the room was empty. Nice leather seats. Too nice for a dump like this place. We moved to the window. Just as our man had said, there was a giant air conditioner we could use as a jump-off point to get over the wall of the cemetery and then inside.

Jamshid gestured, *Shall we?* And then without waiting for me, he threw all of his 220 pounds out that window. I stood there for a second like a man who had to pull himself out of a mudbath of shit. Then I jumped after him like we were a couple of mad felines chasing each other.

I glanced north of us at the embassy garden. The trees were too tall here and I couldn't see what was happening on the other side. But the sounds of yelling and glass breaking were unmistakable. There was smoke too. Jamshid said something about how they must have a lot of toys to burn over there, and then the both of us took aim at the grass and threw ourselves into the cemetery.

The gravestones stood like a congregation facing a turquoise-blue dome and a cross. I hurried to William Mason's stone—dead in 1917, WWI, first grave in the third row. Jamshid trudged up with the dolly, rope, and the ladder he'd placed there earlier with the crane.

"Hurry," I called, "we only got as much time as it'll take for them to start and finish their praying."

And like clockwork, the sound of *azan* started just then from the main mosque of Gholhak directly across the street from us. I figured all the *basij* forces inside and outside the embassy would immediately put everything down for their late-afternoon prayer. We were in sync and everything was going as planned.

Jamshid went at it, digging with all he had. Before long we were looking at a safe that seemed to have crushed the casket underneath it. Poor William Mason! The bust sat wrapped in a white cloth inside the box and from my vantage point it resembled anything but the representation of a human being. But what did I know? Jamshid closed the box, knotted the rope around it, and began to work the thing out of the hole.

A voice from behind us called, "Take your time, stupid! Not so fast."

For a moment Jamshid and I stood nonplussed, looking at each other. Jamshid kept holding the rope.

"You with the rope, keep working. And you, don't turn around until your hands are up."

I did as he said. It was another *basiji*. He stood next to the cross holding a rifle which I'm sure he had "borrowed" from the diplomatic police who were supposed to be guarding the embassy. His facial hair started somewhere below his eyeballs and didn't end anywhere that I could see. But other than the magnificent beard, with our cheap pants and *chafiyes* all three of us were dressed pretty much alike for the occasion.

Jamshid gasped and kept pulling.

It felt like it took a year before Jamshid got that box onto the level surface. The *basiji* took a look at the crane dangling over the cemetery wall and ordered Jamshid to open the box. He came closer and gestured with the weapon for us to stand back. We retreated and watched him looking bewildered at the grave and what was inside the box.

Jamshid whispered, "I bet you he doesn't even know how to use the damn gun properly."

"Which is why you and me just might get killed today."

The fellow turned to us. "The two of you dress like *basij* and come here searching for treasures?"

"And now there's three of us," I replied.

"Is that so? Then let me call my boys in to come and finish our job."

He took his walkie-talkie out of his pocket. We could hear the prayers ending. This wasn't good, we'd fallen behind schedule.

"Shouldn't you be at your prayers now?" I forced myself to ask him.

Jamshid laughed.

The *basiji* looked nervous, unsure of what he was supposed to do next with us and his newfound treasure. He raised his voice, "Can't you see the gun in my hand?"

"Look, you can have a share of the spoils too."

He shut the box with his foot. "Then you'll take this thing exactly where I tell you to take it. Afterward, you go and get your boss."

"Listen, son, when I say you'll have your share, it means only one thing: we don't have a boss."

I had his full attention now. He looked excited, scared, and confused all at the same time. I had to act fast. Since he was thinking so hard, I asked if I could light up a smoke.

He nodded.

I pointed to Jamshid. "Can I take it out of his pocket?"

He came over and forced Jamshid's arms up with the tip of the rifle. It was getting dark now. As I removed the cigarette and lighter from Jamshid's pocket I winked, gesturing to one of the sprinkler heads among the yellowing grass.

Jamshid smiled. "Brother, light one up for me too, will you?"

The *basiji* eyed us with that same look of suspicion and excitement and went and stood over the grave. He too lit a cigarette while still pointing the muzzle of his gun at Jamshid.

"Don't play with my heart like that, brother *basiji*," Jamshid said, laughing.

Again we heard the sounds of breaking glass over at the embassy. I was thinking of Isaar and what he'd do to me if I screwed this one up. Everything hung in the balance, especially for the poor *basij* fuck who was gawking at us with a face that was turning more stupid by the second. He had a right to look like that and was probably thinking of the fortune that had suddenly fallen in his lap and would change his life forever. The seconds passed and the half-burned cigarette rested between my fingers like a ton of bricks. It hadn't rained since that night when Isaar paid me a visit at the piano store and the grass looked glorious just then in all its dryness. This was it; I only had to aim correctly for the last time in my life to finish this thirty-three-year contract with Isaar and be done. I flicked the lit butt at the first sprinkler head between ourselves and the safebox. Seeing this, Jamshid started laughing crazily.

The *basiji* shouted for Jamshid to shut up.

Jamshid flicked his cigarette too. It had been a gamble and I'd hardly expected it to work. But the fire began to catch in startlingly quick time, its smoke drifting inevitably toward that automatic sprinkler head.

I said, "Look, friend, if you don't do something about that smoke, you'll soon have to be explaining to your brothers why you've been keeping your walkie-talkie quiet all this time."

I wasn't sure if he got what I was talking about. Meanwhile, I also had the dreadful thought that maybe the sprinklers weren't even working. The guy's face lit up now. He didn't care about the smoke or maybe didn't even see it. He began to mumble, "We'll take the thing where I say we'll . . ."

The sudden splash of water from all the sprinklers coming alive transformed the cemetery in an instant. And an instant was all I needed to pull the Chiappa Rhino out of my pocket. I saw him fall to his knees, his head tilting at the sky for a moment before his chin hit the ground and the dancing water rained on his face. But the bullet hadn't been from my piece. I turned to Jamshid and saw him sticking his hidden Colt back in his pocket.

He said, "Boss, it's really time to hurry now." He pushed the safe onto the dolly and started.

I'll never forget the scene—that twilight and the sprinklers and the cemetery and the dolly and Jamshid slowly passing by the corpse of a *basiji* who lay at the edge of William Mason's grave in the Gholhak District.

From the embassy garden we could hear a *basij* commander telling his men to finish up and start vacating the smashed-up embassy. This meant there was no time left to fill in poor old William Mason's grave. There was no going through the police station either. But Dowlat Avenue was supposed to stay closed down. And I'd paid the inside man at the station to make sure no uniformed cop suddenly stopped us while we transported the safe from the crane into the Land Cruiser waiting down the street.

Once Jamshid had the safe hitched to the crane hook, he opened the ladder against the wall. The sprinklers had turned off by now and before climbing up I took one last look at the guy we'd dropped. It was as if William Mason had returned from the next world and pushed aside a whole lot of dirt to start living one more time, but as soon as he'd touched ground a German soldier had deported him back to where he belonged.

I told Jamshid I'd meet him later on. Now I sat alone in the Land Cruiser, with the safebox in the back, thinking of what I could possibly say to Isaar about some dead *basiji* at the cemetery. The truth was that neither the British nor the *basij* forces could raise an issue about the dead man next to that grave. The Brits wouldn't open their mouths because it wasn't in their interest; and the *basij* would stay hush because, well, how were they to even explain the presence of one of their own at that cemetery and not in the embassy garden in the first place? But I was still in the shit with Isaar.

And the whole way driving to his place in the Qeytarieh District I swore at myself for not having had the presence of mind to have a backup plan if something like this happened.

I put my window down and drove slowly, listening to the sound of the running rivulets of the city next to the sidewalks. I took in the trees and the silhouettes of housewives in their kitchens readying dinner. The image was one of a city at peace. So much so that you'd hardly believe just a little ways down the road the people of this very place had just raped the hallowed grounds of the embassy of another country.

I stopped in front of Isaar's gated mansion. How many times had I done this? How many times had I shown up here after a job to give him my report? Tonight I'd come to tell him I was done. I'd given them what I owed them and then some. It was time to let me go. That's right, I wanted to sell everything here and add it to what I'd stashed abroad. Then Hawaii, or Tahiti, or the Canary Islands. Anywhere there was sun and ocean and where they didn't overrun other people's embassies. I'd find a place like that and operate the biggest, best bar on the island. And so what if I could barely get it up nowadays, even on pills? I'd still keep a bevy of the sexiest women around. And once a year I'd run along to Jerusalem and cry my heart out and feel cleansed.

The automatic gate finally opened but the lights in the garden were off. I drove slowly up to the house where only the lights to the first floor were illuminated. It was odd not see Isaar already standing there waiting for me with his dogs and a bodyguard or two by his side. But then I saw the top of his head through the window, sitting in his usual chair in the living room. I entered the old, familiar place with its excess furniture without knocking, not minding that I was rubbing those muddy shoes, compliments of the sprinkler system of the British cemetery, into the expensive silk carpet.

"You know what, Isaar? Statues are like people: they too can get themselves into trouble."

"Not as much trouble as you're in."

The voice came from my nine o'clock. Now I smelled cigar smoke. And of course I'd never known Isaar to have a cigar. As I turned, the first thing I saw was the corpse of one of his longtime bodyguards by the stairway. Then I saw the owner of the voice, directly to my left. His head was erect but his shoulders slumped awkwardly a little forward. He also had a pair of blue eyes set deep in skin so white that it made me almost gag to look at him. I'd never liked the look of Englishmen and I guess I didn't like it now.

I felt the muzzle of an automatic in my back. "Move," the new voice behind me said. "I'd like to keep all my ammo intact today, if possible."

The Englishman was putting out his cigar in one of Isaar's antique dishes. "Take his gun and his car keys."

He had said all this in Persian. Almost without an accent. In that blue suit, almost the color of his eyes, and the reddish hair with tinges of white, he looked like the devil itself to me. His man now came around and stuck his piece under my chin. A familiar face. One of Isaar's men whom I'd seen alongside the dead one for years. A traitor. He took the car keys and the Rhino revolver out of my pockets. Then he put the muzzle to the back of my neck and pushed me toward the fireplace. It was only now that I had clarity. Isaar, dead! Just like that. His head hanging slightly to one side and not a word out of his mouth.

"Keep moving."

I did. The thing I had wished for thirty-three years ago in that interrogation room had finally come true. Isaar with his mouth open and blood spread over his fancy white shirt. But a man has to be careful what he wishes for, because I had never felt more alone and more vulnerable than that moment. I kept moving until my foot caught on something and I went tumbling against the fireplace. I grabbed onto a bronze statue of a woman with wings and pulled myself up. Then, turning to the corpse again, I saw that his dog, a boxer with her guts hanging out, lay just as dead as its owner under Isaar's splayed-out legs. It was the dead dog's paw that my foot had caught. Men and dog were fresh kills. I bent down and noticed the blood and piece of gut stuck to my muddy shoes, and doubling over myself I threw up on the bronze woman with the wings. Me! Eshaq Lariyan, who had seen his share of death for ten lifetimes and more! I was sick so long that the Englishman finally got bored with me.

"All right, Eshaq, enough acting for one day."

He didn't have to say my name like that for me to understand he knew everything there was to know about me. I tried wiping my mouth with my shirt sleeve, but Isaar's old bodyguard whacked me hard on my forearm with the automatic.

I sighed and took another look at Isaar. "You realize," I raised my head to face the Englishman again, "you're messing with a military branch of the Iranian government here."

"Wipe your dirty mouth."

I didn't. "They're going to get hard on you when they find out. Very hard."

He laughed. "They? They'll cut him up so bad you won't be able to tell the dog from its owner."

I froze. I was sure he was bluffing at this point. Nevertheless, I tried holding my ground since it was all I had left. "I suppose they're going to replace him with you?"

"With *me?*" His smile made me cringe. He came forward with those sloping shoulders of his. "They forced your dear Isaar to retire a few months ago. I suppose you didn't know. And why should you? *Corruption*, they called it."

The room smelled like lead and iron and staleness, and it was all I could do not to throw up on the Englishman and his sidekick right there. He didn't have to explain any further. I saw exactly what had happened. They'd made Isaar retire. But he knew about the statue from way before. And for whatever reason that I'll never understand, he wanted to swindle the Sepah he had so diligently and profitably worked for one last time. It couldn't have been just the money, though. Isaar had plenty of that already. Maybe it was out of spite for having to retire before he was ready. He wanted to swindle the special military arm of the Islamic Republic and the Englishman wanted to play games with the embassy of his own country. So they had found each other. More likely, they'd done these types of jobs plenty of times already. Isaar would take his cut for the statue and the Englishman would take the thing across the border—for whoever and whatever, probably some insane collector who got a kick out of possessing stolen statues from the public places of closed countries.

The Englishman said, "As long as Isaar had you believing you were still working for the Sepah, it was good enough for us."

I let him talk. First I had to take care of the guy with the gun. I was slowly collecting myself and thinking of a way out of this mess. I pretended to feel weaker than I was after all the vomiting. I barely whispered, "Well, Isaar took care of me, and you took care of Isaar. Nice job. Congratulations!"

The Englishman kept on talking, proud of himself and his treachery. I figured I could buy my freedom from the Sepah once and for all if I just did this right. I'd give them back the statue and tell them I'd been a part of Isaar's plan all along and was simply biding my time. That's what I'd do. It was a workable plan, if only I could manage to—

A slow but insistent beeping, like that of a clock or a bomb, suddenly began. Maybe for a fraction of a second all three of us froze in the moment listening to it. But then, without bothering to locate the source, I quickly crouched low and elbowed the bodyguard in the nuts as hard as I could. After the second quick blow he let go of the automatic and fell to the floor. I took back my Rhino and pointed it at the Englishman. For good measure I gave a vicious kick to the prone man's balls and saw the light go out of him.

All this maybe took a total of two seconds and yet the Englishman hadn't moved.

The beeping continued. Isaar's cell phone. Maybe a text message from someone. They hadn't bothered to take it off of him when they'd killed him. It was a telephone that had saved me.

I watched the Englishman, who returned my gaze with a look that was too cool to understand. Back then I still didn't realize how many centuries of practice in the art of being of an imperial race stood behind that unflappability of his. He could have tried to reach for the bodyguard's weapon, but he didn't. And now, with a gesture from me, he put his hands up and waited calmly.

I took the other gun off the floor too, and seeing the bodyguard start to moan and move a bit I gave him another smash with the heel of my bloody shoes right on the nose and kicked him over onto his stomach and took my car keys out of his side pocket.

"Make a move and it will be the second time in my life I sent an English bastard to the next world."

There hadn't been a first time, actually. And if I knew what was good for me, I had to leave that place today without another murder taking place. I couldn't let the Sepah have any reason to hold me back in Iran or give me up to the British as a fall guy.

The Englishman did not bat an eye. "I would like to make a suggestion."

I stepped over to Isaar and fished the phone out of his pocket. It had finally stopped beeping. "You are in no position to offer suggestions."

I saw that my number was the only one in the cell. Everything else had been deleted. They'd left the phone on Isaar on purpose and it had fucked them. Such symmetry! And what should those last persistent texts that had saved my life be? Several random messages from some local mosque about the upcoming Ashura ceremonies in the neighborhood.

I had to search the Englishman. I stepped over the entrails of the dead dog and did just that. He had nothing on him but more cigars and a lighter inside a leather bag. I wiped my mouth with the back of the bag and threw it to the ground. The man's cool was unnerving me. I felt I was only a step away from gifting him one of the bullets from my Rhino. But that would have been a deep mistake. First of all, this guy had done for me what I'd been aching to do for thirty-three years. Isaar was gone. Gone for good. And by killing this man, all I'd achieve would be to have the Sepah string me up as the mastermind behind everything that had gone wrong.

The bodyguard began moaning again. But I knew it would be a long time before the poor bastard could get his bearings. I stepped backward toward the door. "You can stay for as long as you like in this accursed place. My only command is that until that outside gate is shut behind me, you concentrate long and hard on your boy's balls. He's in need of serious attention."

And I was out of there. The garden was still dark. I hurried to the car and had my hand on the door when it was as if half the lights in the world suddenly came on. For a second I was blinded and in shock. In that second the sound of a bullet echoed in my ear a thousand times and I was on the ground before I knew what was happening. The next few seconds, or maybe minutes, I felt like some underwater diver who was stuck in an ocean of seaweed. I saw the Englishman step right past me without another look. I saw the glint of what looked like a Magnum. And I felt the fire in my spine.

Then there was the sound of a car door opening and closing. The start of an engine. And wheels missing my ears by inches. Everything was muffled and subdued and happening as if through a screen. Only as I felt myself passing out did I recall Isaar's phone which, miraculously, was still in my hand. I dialed emergency and mumbled, "Qeytarieh, Kajvari Street, number 36," before everything went black.

Maybe the Englishman thought even if I wasn't dead, I would be soon enough. Maybe he didn't want to risk the sound of a gun going off again in that house. Or maybe he'd thought that with Isaar's cell in my hand and my number in there, the Sepah higher-ups would simply put this to an endgame between two onetime partners. Whatever it was, he didn't kill me, and maybe he hadn't intended to all along. Which meant I'd jumped the gun.

I had a lot of time to think about all this over the next few months. Three surgeries in four months at Milad Hospital were just enough to turn a half-dead man into a live paraplegic. And a neutered one at that. I had been transformed into a half-thing, a bust, just like that statue that the Englishman took with him when he left.

When I finally came out of the hospital, they sent a messenger to tell me a few things. For instance, the night in question the ambulance had managed to get me quickly to the hospital. But afterward the folks in the Sepah would not let the police come anywhere near the case again. They closed the file on it and sent word that I could leave the country. In fact, they said I had no choice but to leave, and I had a month to do it. After thirty-three years they were retiring me too. And killing me had no benefit for them, while having a live Jew abroad who still owed them was far more desirable. They only mentioned in passing that everything I owned in Tehran would have to stay here and one month was long enough to do the paperwork and sign over what I had to the gentlemen of the Sepah. That was all right with me. I had expected a day like this would come. I'd prepared for it, and what I had abroad remained intact. I signed over my life in Tehran and they stayed true to their word and let me go. For them, the presence of one dead bodyguard next to Isaar and one semi-live one could explain everything. Symmetry again. Besides, who would want to build a case that had a Jew with a gun in it? It wouldn't do.

So yes, I was let go. And now in this not-so-quiet little island in the Caribbean I run what many customers swear is the perfect bar/restaurant, with plenty of delectable island girls to serve and smile at me, their boss. I sit here in my wheelchair and think now and then of Jerusalem, which I've never actually visited and probably never will, and I smile back at my pretty girls and recall all the things I can never do again before reminding myself that I'm still lucky to be here instead of a corpse in Tehran.

THE WHITEST SET OF TEETH IN TEHRAN

BY SALAR ABDOH

Karim-Khan, Kuche Aban

T he caretaker of the synagogue and his son carried the barrel to the garbage dump outside and emptied it. The thing seemed heavy and its contents looked like mud. Man and son glanced up for a moment in that dawn light, looking right at Lotfi's apartment window on the third floor, and Lotfi imagined their worried faces asked him to turn a blind eye on them.

He figured they were making wine for the synagogue. It wasn't illegal. Not for them. But they still dumped the leftover grape skin and mixed it with earth so no one could tell it was alcohol they'd made.

Lotfi had a headache. It came from a bad batch of bootleg vodka he'd bought from an Assyrian Christian. He wouldn't buy from that damn Christian again. *I'm an alcoholic in a supposedly dry country,* he thought. Yet if anything, Tehran was the wettest place on earth. People drank like fish here. All that homemade *arrack* and the overpriced booze that came across the border from Iraqi Kurdistan. Except you never knew what was legit liquor and what could kill you. The *khakham's* wine wouldn't kill him, that was for sure. And maybe he'd just go down there one of these days and ask to buy some of their wine from them. Of all the places in Tehran he could have gotten himself an apartment, he had to end up right across from a synagogue. Again! Just like all the years he'd lived just off Eastern Parkway in Brooklyn, New York.

He heard water running and came and stood by the bathroom.

The door was open. She'd lit a fat blue candle and was washing him off of her. He considered her skin. Milky. Breasts, full and firm. She had short hair and the way her neckline sloped to her shoulders made him want to join her in that shower. They'd met two months ago at some rich folks' weekend party a half hour drive away in Lavasan where mostly BMWs and Mercedes lined the driveway. He'd promised himself this was the very last time he was going to one of these gatherings. White pasta sauce dribbled from the mouths of potbellied merchants, and bleach-haired women who dressed like the Colombian soap opera whores they loved to watch on Iranian satellite television danced till the wee hours of the morning with their short chicken legs and gaudy, extra-high-heeled shoes. They were ugly, these rich people. They were ugly everywhere, not just here. Yet Lotfi had sat there wondering why he hadn't chosen another part of the planet to move to instead of Tehran. What with the score he'd made on his one and only book, and the tidy sum from his brother's life insurance policy back in America, for the first time in his adult life he had money in abundance. He was a millionaire suddenly. He could go anywhere he wanted to. If he had come to Tehran it was because he had unfinished business here. And maybe when he was done with this unfinished business he'd pack up and go again, go somewhere Mediterranean, a place with real liquor and with cops who were corrupt only half of the time.

The woman turned to fully face him and smiled. She had a bruise near her right earlobe that showed clearly even in dim candle-light. It wasn't too bad of a bruise. In fact it gave her boyish face a used look that aroused him. And now she beckoned him, but he only stood there watching.

"Do you want me to talk to him?" he asked quietly.

"Who?"

"Your husband. *Bache khoshgele*." It was his put-down for Ai-da's husband, *pretty boy*. Lotfi could never get himself to call the guy anything else.

"It's not a good time for talking about it," she said.

"Why not?"

"Because of the demonstrations."

Maybe she was right. It really was a peculiar time. The two months that they'd known each other had also been a time of street protests. At first Lotfi thought it was just a passing phase. But after a while there were pitched battles all across the city and wholesale arrests. Lotfi couldn't care less about the protesters. They were just the sons and daughters of the same fools who had marched on these streets thirty years earlier. They'd brought on a revolution back then and the revolution had stolen everything his father had worked for. Later on, some bitch in Los Angeles had stolen his only brother's life too. That was what Lotfi cared to focus on, the people who had done him wrong. He was a vengeful, hot-blooded Azeri Turk and he preferred to stay that way.

He asked, "If you don't want me to talk to him, then what do you want me to do?"

"Love me hard."

He nodded. In the year he'd come back to live here, he had met a lot of women who wanted him for his American passport and his money. They would approach him at parties like the one he'd met Aida at and push him to dance with them. Tehran was a city of fourteen million, but there were circles where you always saw the same faces. These faces already knew he'd written some third-rate book back in the States about a gang of computer hackers and an improbable bank heist that Hollywood had given him a bunch of money for. What they didn't know was how he'd come to write that book and why he was here. The night of the party, he had sat in a dark corner of the garden next to Aida and told her things. Maybe it was the good liquor that the host supplied in abundance, or the impression that this was the first time a Tehran woman had not tried to con him after two minutes; whatever it was, he decided he liked her. She wore neither gaudy high heels nor had her eyebrows plucked and lifted to get that sinister look of

surprise that women liked so much around here. She was pleas-
ant to look at and her rich, pretty-faced husband was on the other
side of the garden just then talking about politics and street
demonstrations.

Lotfi had told Aida his story because he was lonely. Told her
how the revolution had taken everything they had. Their house.
His dad's pharmaceutical factory in their hometown, Tabriz. He
even told her how it had all been instigated by one of his old man's
lackeys who'd suddenly turned religious, grown a beard, and testified at the Islamic court that Lotfi's father was a godless apostate
who should have all his properties taken from him. Thirty years
later that piece of shit, a fellow named Sarkeshik, owned the very
same pharmaceutical factory and was living merrily with his two
wives up there in a mansion in the northern part of the city while
his sons ran jewelry stores in Houston and Albuquerque.

"You are one bitter man," she had said to him.

Bitter? Bitter was right. His father had died bitter in jail. And
once Lotfi and his brother escaped the country, Lotfi promised
himself he would never speak a word of Persian again. He'd only
speak the Azeri Turkish of his own father as a protest to what
these people had done to his family. All those years of growing up
in Tehran and hearing jokes about his native Turks. His father had
once told him, *Everything these Persians have, they have because of
us Azeris. The bastards don't want to do a day's honest labor and they
can't stand to see us make money. So they make jokes about us. The
joke's on them and they don't even know it.*

Yet here he was, speaking Persian again. Being amongst Persians again. And desiring their women. "And you?" he had asked
Aida. "What's your story?"

She pointed in her husband's direction. "Like I said, I'm married to him." It was as if she were talking about a used car, not a
husband.

Lotfi glanced his way. Unlike most of the other men there,
Aida's husband was tall and fit looking. But the unmistakable lilt

of his voice gave him away as queer. He also had full, shiny black hair tied into a severe ponytail and his silky face was smooth and unnaturally unblemished.

Lotfi observed, "But he doesn't look like the marrying kind to me, does he?"

"I am what they call a Phillips screwdriver in this town," she said.

"A screwdriver?"

"He's the son of a *bazaar* merchant. His father knows half the people in the government. It wouldn't do for the son not to have a wife. I am a tool, an instrument. I'm a front. The family needed a wife and here I am."

"But why agree to it?"

She laughed. "Agree? You forget where you're living, Mr. Lotfi! One night the militia stormed into someone's house, a house very much like this one. I was there, he was there, and some other people were there. The rest of the guests were couples. Except me and him. They took us to jail and the next day the judge forced us to marry."

"So it was a setup? He paid the militia to storm the place?"

"Well, probably his father paid them off."

It didn't make a difference to ask why; with all the women in Tehran who would have gladly said yes to marrying into a wealthy *bazaari* family like that, they had forced Aida to become their bride. Things happened here and they had their own mad logic. Maybe it was just luck of the draw, or maybe Pretty Boy had simply insisted to Daddy that if they were forcing a Phillips screw-wife on him, it had to be this one and none other.

He was surprised that she revealed as much as she did, though. It wasn't usual to give a stranger at some party all this personal information. And in Tehran, city of rumors and backstabbers, at that! Maybe she was just fed up with it all and didn't care any-more. He knew something about that, about hitting rock bottom and no longer giving a damn. He had returned to Tehran thirsting for belated revenge. His intentions had been focused. As focused as when he'd decided to write that silly book to make money. Or when he'd fought those spineless insurance people to get his brother's life insurance pay. But then something had happened in the months he'd been in the city. His resolve had gone soft. He had taken the apartment in the heart of the capital so that, he reasoned, he could be with the common people rather than around these rich bastards he'd grown up with. He liked venturing out on foot or on the cheap motorcycle he'd bought so he could lose himself in that Middle Eastern chaos. He thought he was living in history. His place was in one of the old quarters below Jomhuri Avenue where, despite the shoddy building frenzy of the last couple of decades, mosques and synagogues and churches and even Zoroastrian schools still stood within a few short blocks of each other.

Yes, it was all quaint. Like living in some goddamn sepia-colored picture postcard from another time. But what about his resolve? It was only when the demonstrations had started that Lotfi began to find his purpose again. That, and the night when Aida told him about her "setup" marriage while he explained why he was in Tehran. It was like a pact. They knew each other's secrets even before they knew each other. It was crazy. It was furious love. It was dangerous and not overly romantic and it drew them to pound into each other like it was the end of the world—therefore the bruise by her earlobe this morning.

"Pass me the towel."

He did.

She drew up and kissed him deeply. "As long as you stay in Tehran, I don't care if I'm a prisoner of this awful city. I don't need to travel anywhere else. I don't need a passport. You're my passport."

The law was explicit about this stuff: she needed Pretty Boy's consent to get a passport to travel outside the country. But Pretty Boy wouldn't give it, worrying that if he permitted her to leave she'd never come back. And he couldn't have that. They had to keep up appearances.

Lotfi asked, "Doesn't he care you didn't come home last night?"

They'd been careful all these weeks. Meeting in secret and setting up times to see each other in advance rather than telephoning beforehand. But it was unnecessary precaution. The street demonstrations seemed to have put people outside of themselves. Times were different. In the past couple of weeks Pretty Boy had even become some kind of Internet hero amongst the protesters. He kept posting photos of the street marches on social media websites and commenting on how important it was for people to show up at the rallies in force. *The little fucker,* Lotfi thought, *has become a freedom fighter all of a sudden. The same ladyboy who won't let his wife have a passport and travel now wants liberty for the masses. Fuck your masses!*

Aida, seeming to read his thoughts, answered, "He's too busy these days to care where I'm at. Not that he ever cared much anyway."

"But not coming home at all last night . . . I mean, this is a first."

She wrapped a towel around herself and started for the bedroom. Halfway there she turned around and looked at him intensely. "His father called me the other day. He was angry. He said that that son of his is playing with fire going to all those street demonstrations and posting pictures about it online."

"Well, he is."

"He said not even he has the pull to get his son out of jail if something should happen to him at a protest."

"Worse things can happen to a guy at a demonstration than going to jail."

She loosened the towel and let it drop to her feet. In that half-light he could still see how firm her nipples had gotten. So here was that hard bruise he had given her earlier while making love and those hard nipples that she was offering him now. He exhaled deeply. He was thinking revenge again. When you started to go down that road, you could just keep on going. It became easier and easier to work up hatred and love in measures you hardly knew existed.

"Yes," she said, "a lot worse things can happen to a guy at a demonstration. I've seen it with my own eyes, baby."

The Afghan groundskeeper and his family lived in a separate dwelling at the end of the sprawling garden several hundred yards to the south of the mansion. There was happiness here, you could tell. They plied Lotfi with sweet sherbets and tea. Little Afghan boys played soccer on the grass and two young girls wearing bright-colored headscarves fussed about him with a string of little delicacies from their mother's kitchen. Afghans were that way, hospitable to a fault. It was a scene from his own childhood of having servants. Except that this whole arrangement with the household help belonged not to his father but to the man who had stolen everything from them thirty years earlier.

The Afghan looked visibly ecstatic at being able to host a guest of his *agha*. He didn't look a day over thirty-five and already had a brood of half a dozen. "You've known our *agha* for a long time?"

"Since I was a child. He worked with my father."

"Too bad *agha* is not in Tehran. He has a factory, you know. Medicines. All kinds of medicines. He has gone there to oversee something. But he will be back tomorrow. You should stay with us until he comes. Both *khanums*, his wives, stay abroad this time of year. It's just *agha* here now. He will be happy to see an old friend."

"Tell me . . . his *khanums*, I don't suppose they get along with each other."

The Afghan gave an uneasy laugh. "The *khanums* are like cheese and knife. They are like a strong wind and a mosquito."

"Ah! So they don't get along at all."

"*Agha* built two separate quarters for them, as far away as possible. God be praised, but women can be mischievous creatures. And I have spoken too much."

Lotfi consoled himself that having two wives had done its damage to old Sarkeshik. The women's hatred for each other made his domestic life miserable. It was small consolation, but better than

nothing. Women, alas, could always take your revenge for you—
and in this case, for all those falsely signed personal checks that
Sarkeshik had produced at the Islamic court saying that Lotfi's
father owed him millions.

He watched the Afghan, who actually looked like he might
have walked off a set from one of those epic Chinese war films.
The fellow appeared visibly wretched all of a sudden for having
given his *agha*'s secret away so soon.

"Your *agha* is good to you, is he?"

The Afghan's gaze went soft. "There is never-ending war in my
country. Without *agha*, I would be back home digging graves now."
After a while he added, "My own grave probably. I have been with
agha since I was seventeen. He has been very good to me."

Lotfi knew something about this kind of immigrant life. All the
shit jobs he and his brother had had to suffer in America until they
managed to pull themselves together. For Afghans in Iran, it was
the same. They did all the menial work and received the blame for
every crime imaginable. Still, there was something wrong with this
picture. Here was his old nemesis, Sarkeshik, having apparently
become a lifesaver to an Afghan immigrant and his family. The
man had become a goddamn angel. What did that mean? *And why
am I even here?* Lotfi didn't know. He'd had this vague idea of how
to go about taking his revenge. And today, after Aida had said
goodbye to him and gone home, he'd decided he'd finally do something about it. He'd ridden out to Velenjak and hovered by the tall
walls of the huge place, forgetting that a moneyed neighborhood
like this in north Tehran was full of private security. Before long
a pair of men were on him asking what he was doing there. He'd
had no choice but to ring the bell to Sarkeshik's house with the
men watching. And now he sat in the servants' quarters drinking
sherbet and tea.

He asked, "Has your *agha* always been this generous?"

"As long as I've known him. I started working for him when
I didn't even have a shirt on my back. Five years ago two of my

younger brothers came to Tehran looking for work too. Do you know what *agha* did? He fixed their papers to stay in Iran and paid for them to go to college. Both of them are in college now. Two Afghans in college, if you can believe it."

He hadn't come here to hear all this. It ruined his case. It dampened his hatred. He had nursed this hatred for thirty years. Watered and nourished it like a famished plant. He had had an idea of becoming a writer when he was younger. But he'd done the sensible thing and studied computer software and played it safe. As had his brother who'd been an engineer. It meant they'd both become levelheaded, middle-of-the-road immigrants in the new country. For Lotfi's brother what was past was past. Buried. They never talked about it. Never talked about Iran or their father or Sarkeshik. And when one day his brother had told him he was ready to get married and have a bunch of children, Lotfi had no choice but to give his blessing, even if he didn't have a good feeling about it. His brother had met some bovine-looking number in Los Angeles when he'd gone to have a teeth cleaning one day. Some Iranian gold digger who was tired of working in a dentist's office. She had his brother by the balls out there in California, and within six months they were married and talking kids. Four years later, still no kids and the woman wanted a divorce. Soon she was taking his brother to the cleaners. He lost the house, half his pension, and most of his savings. That was the New World for you! There was no balance anywhere in the world. Here in Iran all the rules favored men. Over there in America they favored women. All that bullshit talk of equality of the sexes. What equality? The woman had put his brother in the poorhouse. Another year passed and one day Lotfi got an official call to hurry to LA. His brother was dead. Massive stroke. But Lotfi knew better: it was heartbreak that had killed his brother. America had killed his brother. And Iran had killed him. And Sarkeshik had killed him. And, especially, that cow who was now living in the house his brother had sweated so long to get a mortgage for.

The Afghan was saying to him, "Do you want me to call *agha* and tell him you are here?"

"Not necessary." He began to get up.

The Afghan insisted he stay for dinner. Lotfi smiled to put the man at ease and reminded him that dinner was another eight hours away. Then he thanked the entire family, brought cash from his pocket, and left it next to his tea glass. The Afghan protested and Lotfi insisted.

"I will be back the day after tomorrow. Don't tell your *agha* I came by. I want to surprise him. I know it will make him happy."

The Afghan nodded good-naturedly. Anything to make his *agha* happy.

He rode in a daze to Vanak Circle where heavy police presence had brought a hush to the usually chaotic main thoroughfare. He didn't even know how he got here. All he knew was that a sickness had come over him as soon as he was out of Sarkeshik's place. It was the sickness of knowing that thirty years of entertaining revenge had suddenly become dust. After seeing the Afghan and his family he had no choice but to shed his hatred for Sarkeshik. He felt naked without this old hatred; he had to leave it behind and ride away.

The cops in Vanak eyed him but didn't order him to stop his motorbike. They must have gotten word that a street demonstration was heading this way. He rounded the circle and headed south on Gandhi Avenue. The city seemed at a standstill, waiting. It was usually on Fridays when the demonstrations would erupt. Some of them were planned weeks in advance. Those were the really big demonstrations. Others just sort of happened by themselves. Ad hoc gatherings in different neighborhoods. Often they might begin with university students chanting against the regime. Then others would join. And before long, helmeted men would arrive to beat people up and take busloads of students to Evin Prison. This looked to be a day like that, everything hanging in balance.

Lotfi wondered what Aida was doing now. She was . . . a good woman. Though he imagined he didn't even know what a good woman was anymore. After his brother's death, he'd made a conscious decision to relegate women to the extreme peripheries of his life. He would never forget the day he'd entered that sunless studio apartment in Van Nuys that his brother had been renting after the divorce. A hole-in-the-wall near Sherman Way in Los Angeles Valley that stank of unwashed dishes and garbage and death. The place was an utter wreck of Salvation Army furniture and hand-me-downs. The two brothers had survived America so it could come down to this? Then Lotfi's eyes had fallen on a shelf full of books. He had never taken his brother for much of a reader. But now he saw dozens of manuals about how to write crime novels. Books about poisons and guns and learning how to create a plausible private eye for your story. There were even notes in his brother's meticulous engineer's handwriting in a small red notebook about the things he had learned. His brother had tried to exit the rot of his new life by writing his way through it. Then the massive stroke. And soon a letter from the insurance company that Lotfi was his brother's beneficiary, but—

And wasn't there always a "but"?

He'd fought them. They had tried to get away with not giving him most of the insurance money. His brother, God bless him, had done one thing right these past few years and changed his beneficiary to be Lotfi. And then he'd upped and died and left Lotfi half a million dollars. The first thing Lotfi did was to quit his software job. The second was to hunker down back in his apartment in Brooklyn and go through those books his brother had left behind. Now that he had time and money, it was his one chance in life to try his hand at being a writer. The result was that ridiculous pseudo-tech novel about computer hackers and a heist. And yet, incredibly, in no time he had found an agent for it and then a publisher and a miraculous option from the movie that brought him another big chunk of change. Life was just that stupid and arbitrary. His brother had died in a miasma of bitterness and heart-break and Lotfi was, as the insurance claim said, the beneficiary of that.

He saw an open store on Gandhi Avenue and parked the bike to get a pack of cigarettes. Gandhi! Now that was a man who had never thought of revenge. Old man Gandhi and his shaved head and his glasses and his loincloth. For the second time that day Lotfi asked himself the question: *Why am I here?* But of course he knew exactly why he'd ended up riding down Gandhi Avenue. The Cow's family lived off of one of the smaller streets here. The Cow! His brother's ex-wife. She'd even tried to squeeze him out of the life insurance. But he'd beaten her fair and square. The paperwork was clear: Lotfi was the beneficiary, not the Cow. Nevertheless, beating her in court in America wasn't enough anymore. He knew she came to Tehran every other year to visit family. Lotfi had bided his time. It was amazing what money could do in this country. In any country, really. He kept a tab on her and when he got word that she was in Tehran again, all it took was a bribe in the right place to keep her from going back to the States. On the day she had gone to the airport to catch her flight out of Tehran, they'd taken her passport away and told her to go home until they contacted her. That was six months ago. Six months that she couldn't be in Los Angeles in the home she'd stolen from Lotfi's brother. Six months that she couldn't meet her mortgage. Six months that she couldn't go to the nail salon or eat her stupid Jenny Craig weight-loss diets. O sweet justice. Iranian justice. Fuck with me in the United States and I'll fuck with you in Iran. The Cow of course had no idea why they'd taken her passport away and how and when she would get it back. He took comfort in assuming she must be beside herself. That was good. But was it enough?

He knew himself well enough to realize he had ended up on Gandhi Avenue out of frustration over losing his taste for revenge against Sarkeshik. The Cow, though, was still his prey, his prisoner here. She wasn't going anywhere anytime soon. Lotfi had come to

Gandhi Avenue for something more definitive. He would hurt her, he decided. He'd just wait for her to come out of that house near the Channel 2 building off Gandhi, and he'd do what his brother should have done a long time ago. He was carrying a Czech-made police baton that could fit in the palm of the hand but would open out to a vicious-looking metal rod with the slightest flick of the wrist. It was an instrument of hurt. It could bash a window in. Or a head. Or a face. He had brought it along to rearrange Sarkeshik's face; instead he'd use it on the Cow today.

How he missed Aida! And how he hated missing anyone. The irony didn't go past him that he had done to his brother's ex-wife what Aida's husband was doing to her, not letting her out of the country. This was a country owned by men, after all. And for better or worse, Lotfi was comfortable with that.

"Can you spare a cigarette, brother?"

He had been sitting on the bike, daydreaming and smoking one of the cigarettes he'd just bought. They were two men and they had him surrounded. Not the toughest-looking men. But guys who obviously knew the business of intimidation. Lotfi kept his right hand close to his pants pocket where the flick-baton bulged a little bit. With his other hand, he threw the pack of cigarettes to one of them. "Keep all of it."

The other man said, "Aida *khanum* didn't come home last night."

"Come home to what? A eunuch?"

The one he hadn't thrown the cigarette to grabbed Lotfi's shirt. "Best be polite when talking about our boss."

Lotfi didn't flinch. If they were going to take him down this second, he had no chance. He was sitting on the bike and couldn't open the baton until he had some space.

"Who sent you? His father?"

"None of your business. Stay away from Aida *khanum*."

"Oh, so it is *baba-jaan* who is looking out for the son. I was sure it couldn't be the eunuch who sent you guys to follow me."

The man he'd thrown the pack to gave Lotfi a backhanded slap. He felt his face flush and it made him angry. The anger in turn made him feel alive. He could kill these guys. He could kill them right now. They weren't the carrying kind. They were small muscle for a motherfucker of a *bazaari* merchant. The same holier-than-thou *bazaari* fucks who had financed the stupid revolution thirty years ago.

He bit his words, "What happens to Aida now?"

"That's none of your business either, you whore's son! Just stay away from her."

"If she gets hurt—"

"If she gets hurt, what? You'll do something about it?" Both their faces were inches away from his own now. They looked like brothers. Bald, short, and broad-shouldered. They were probably failed wrestlers.

Lotfi put his hands up in a gesture of resignation. "Tell *baba-jaan* I've received his message. Loud and clear."

"Good." The man with the cigarettes stuffed the pack in his own shirt and then gave a short, painful squeeze to Lotfi's cheek. "It's nice you learn so fast."

It happened instantly. As soon as they turned to go, Lotfi reached into his pocket, flicked the baton open, and rained a succession of quick blows on them. They went down faster than he had expected and were immediately howling like sissies. They were belly-down and holding their hands over their heads to protect themselves. He could not believe how easy it was. They just lay there howling and pleading for him to stop even when he'd already stopped hitting them.

This show of weakness was in poor taste, Lotfi thought, and it made him even angrier with the men. He saw that inside the store people were staring at them but no one dared come out.

"Tell that fucking *baba bazaari* I'm going to stay away from his eunuch son's wife. But . . . if I hear anything has happened to her, and I mean *anything*, I will come after him hard." He reached into the back pocket of one of the men and pulled an identity card from his wallet. "Stay down!" he shouted when the other man tried to turn on his back.

He kick-started the bike. He felt exhilarated. This was the best thing that could have happened to him today. Suddenly Sarkeshik meant nothing. Nor the Cow. It dawned on him he had no idea what Sarkeshik looked like after so long, and he hadn't seen the Cow in over three years. They could look like anything. And it didn't matter anymore.

He squeezed hard on the gas so that the noise from the exhaust would screech right into the prone men's ears. Two semitough guys sprawled on the ground with just several whips of the baton. It was too easy to kill people. And even easier to put the fear of God in them.

Lotfi jammed the baton shut, returned it back to his pocket, put the bike in gear, and peeled off into a side street and away from Gandhi Avenue.

The next two weeks were a cloud of overdrinking. He had to call the Christian back and ask him to deliver more bad vodka in those plastic gas containers. Despite the momentary elation of that day on Gandhi Avenue, Lotfi had lost his center and knew it. What could you do when the settling of scores no longer haunted you day and night? It was like training for the biggest fight of your career and then being told the match was canceled and the opponent was gone. In the fog of alcohol, with his brother's former wife and Sarkeshik no longer of consequence to him, Lotfi sat behind his computer and followed the news of the street demonstrations instead.

And he drank and drank.

He kept the lights in his apartment dimmed and the shades drawn. The two men he had pummeled didn't come around. But he couldn't be too careful. He rarely ventured out and called the local grocer, a fellow Azeri Turk, to send his boy with periodic deliveries. Then one morning he received a call. The voice simply asked if Lotfi wished to "renew" his account. Which meant if he wanted to keep his brother's wife in the country another six months, he had to pay more money.

"No, you can close my account. I'm satisfied with the return."

The voice seemed disappointed and asked if Lotfi was absolutely sure.

"Yes, I'm sure. You can give the bird her wings back. Thank you for your services. My satisfaction is complete."

But he wasn't satisfied. Not the least bit. He missed Aida more and more. Which made him drink more. And what made it worse was that his Internet service suddenly went bad and there were long stretches of days when it was simply nonexistent. He felt like a ship adrift. Then, on another Friday morning, he was staring through half-shut shades at the synagogue when he heard a ping on the computer. Miraculously, despite his shoddy connection, there was an e-mail from Aida in his inbox.

Miss you.

What could he do? He didn't want to be rash and get her hurt. He began to follow her husband's postings online. By now Pretty Boy was virtually a rock star. He posted seemingly every hour, telling friends and followers that they needed to stay the course— *Freedom is around the corner . . . Long live the movement!*

Garbage. Garbage that made Lotfi want to puke his guts out with all that bad *raisin* vodka he'd been drinking. In one especially sickening post Pretty Boy had written that since green was the color of the protest movement, everybody should wear green not just on the streets but also inside their own homes. *We should wear green day and night. We should go to sleep green and wake up green. We should dream in green: Verde que te quiero verde.*

The son of a bitch was now quoting García Lorca in Spanish.

Lotfi told himself he had always hated that senseless, overrated poem of the Spaniard's anyway. "Another faggot freedom fighter!"

he cursed aloud like the ugly alcoholic he felt himself becoming.

Now he was tempted to post his own note online letting everyone know this was the same sick punk who was keeping his wife a prisoner in Tehran.

He realized he had turned into a caged animal. He almost wished those two men would show up again so he could finish all this. Die if he had to. Why was he feeling this way? All that money he had in American and Iranian bank accounts, and yet he was more miserable than ever. What was the use of money? He envied that *khakham* and his son across the street; he envied how every other day they went about their business of taking such loving care of their little patch of earth, watering the synagogue trees and sweeping and preparing the place for Saturdays. How he wished he could be like them.

Then, when the self-loathing reached boiling point, he had a revelation: Pretty Boy had to be working for the government. He was a rat, a snitch, a stool pigeon. All those so-called Internet friends of his, they were going to be rounded up sooner or later. Pretty Boy was collecting names and e-mail addresses for the government.

Once Lotfi thought he had put two and two together, he knew what he had to do. He had always known. *They* had always known—he and Aida. From that moment on, his recently lost resolve found a fresh center of focus.

He was forced to spend the next few days in the wasteland of onlinelessness, as the government censors were again clamping down on Internet access. He had not stepped out of the house in almost three weeks. His vodka was just about gone. He stunk. And he thought obsessively about Pretty Boy. He had to know what the guy was up to or he'd go crazy inside the four walls of his apartment. He sat and stared at that frozen computer screen until the connection returned in the wee hours of one of those mornings. It was like emerging from the bottom of the sea.

There had been fewer postings. Pretty Boy acknowledged that

the Internet situation was getting worse, but if any friends could read this note they should meet him—wearing green, of course—in front of Maskan Bank on Bahar Avenue at nine thirty sharp this coming Friday morning. From there they would join the crowds that were supposed to gather at 7-Tir Square a half hour later.

Lotfi breathed. He showered. He ate some rice and yogurt. He made a point not to drink any alcohol. Friday was only two days away.

A terrible chill took over his entire body. Lotfi was guessing they were in the garage of an unoccupied building.

A half hour. That was all the difference there was in being in the world and not being in it anymore. A half hour ago he had been gazing north toward Karim-Khan Avenue, the sea of people he had been a part of these past few hours now completely dispersed. It had felt good to be a part of the demonstration. This feeling had surprised him and he had had to will himself to stay focused on his quarry. Then on Kargar Street, where the fight with the police began in earnest, Lotfi discovered, at last, that he was no killer. He watched as scuffles broke out, rocks began flying, and people scattered like ants. Tens of thousands of people running every which way. It was beautiful. It was life itself in all its glory. It was combat. It was hunger and pain and reason for living. But what was he going to do about Pretty Boy? Nothing. He was going to do nothing. Lotfi had aged during this demonstration. He had become wise. What had he been thinking? That armed with his baton and a medium-sized kitchen knife he'd stick it to Pretty Boy and walk away?

In an alley off of Kargar Street, he'd watched as Pretty Boy tended to a teenage kid who had been hit with a brick. Pretty Boy wasn't running away like the others; even when plainclothes militiamen were a hundred yards away and advancing, he still didn't dash off. If Lotfi was going to stick it to him, this was the moment to do it. In that chaos of teargas and burning motorcycles no one would notice or care. All he had to do was go up and be as fearless and as quick as he'd been on the day he took on those two men on Gandhi Avenue. But he couldn't do it. He realized the last thing in the world Pretty Boy could be was an undercover snitch for the government. At that moment, Lotfi saw the blood and the expression of utter shock on the face of the kid that Aida's husband was trying to help get off the ground and he knew that he, Lotfi, was a sucker and a fool.

Lotfi ran toward Pretty Boy and the kid. Together they quickly lifted the boy and dragged him to the next alley where they laid him behind a parked car. The kid was moaning but he seemed like he'd be all right. It was just a deep gash on his face, more shock than anything.

"Thank you," Pretty Boy said. "I know you."

Several of the white-shirted plainclothes men ran right past them without stopping. The popping of gun rounds could be heard in the distance. A woman shrieked somewhere, and when the plainclothes men were gone someone called to them from a balcony that they should get off the street before they got arrested.

Neither paid the woman any mind. Lotfi said, "I am your wife's lover."

"Yes, you are." That same lilting voice that had rubbed Lotfi the wrong way. But a sober voice too. Sober, and meeting Lotfi with a gaze that was more curious than scared or surprised.

"Your father sent two thugs to beat me up."

"My father is a busybody. I apologize."

"So you knew about it?"

"I didn't. Until you took out my father's men. My father came to me then. They wanted to kill you. I talked them out of it."

"And why would you do that?"

Pretty Boy sighed. "Because, I suppose, I've been waiting for someone like you to come along."

Now it was Lotfi's turn to sigh. He couldn't figure this guy out. And this wasn't the time to play a game of twenty questions with each other. He said, "You stop to help a kid in the middle of all this. You risk getting beaten up and arrested. But you won't allow your wife out of the country. Why?"

He watched as Pretty Boy glanced down at the teenager who was quietly weeping to himself and not making any attempt to get up off the ground. Suddenly the area seemed hushed. As if they had all been part of a film set that had wrapped for the day. His adversary truly did look pretty. Not pretty; beautiful. Beautiful with his green bandanna and those dark eyes shining bright with courage on this Friday afternoon.

"The kind of family I come from, I can't have a wife disappear on me for good. And I know she would do that if she had a passport. But this much I can offer: if she stays in Tehran, she can do what she wants. *Anything* she wants!" He gave Lotfi a meaningful look and added, "Especially if I know she is seeing somebody I can trust."

"I'm that man. You can trust me."

"Yes, I know I can." Pretty Boy stuck his hand out.

Lotfi took the hand. "And what about your father?"

"It's time he saw some things differently about me. I love my wife, in my own roundabout way. I don't want her to go. But I don't want her to be miserable either."

There was an easy pause, intimate. And then Lotfi asked, "Do you not wonder how I happened to be here today?"

"It doesn't matter. What I want to do right now is take this boy home. He's hurting."

Lotfi nodded. It was as if all of his life had converged onto that moment. For the first time in years he felt himself becoming a better man. He had transcended something today. The street march, the talk with Aida's husband, the bloodied boy they'd helped together—it all seemed as if the universe was trying to tell him something: he was earning some serious karma points, for a change.

On his way back to fetch his motorcycle, Lotfi even decided

that he would go see his brother's wife soon and apologize for what he'd done to her.

Backtracking from Kargar Street to Hafez Avenue took unusually long; he had to keep to the smaller streets and avoid the militias. He was excited. He'd stay in Tehran. It wasn't so bad. He'd have Aida. At the same time, because she was married, he would never have to worry about her insisting that they wed. He'd have the best of both worlds. Maybe he'd write another book now. A real book this time. He'd sit himself down and read the Persian classics at his leisure and then write a historical novel or something. He'd give his life some meaning. He'd honor his brother's memory.

The speeding car hit him just as he was crossing the turnoff at the bottom of Aban Street. The collision got him on the side and sent him flying in the air and landing hard on the sidewalk. He closed his eyes, unable to move. He felt himself immediately being lifted and thrown into the back of a car. The next time he opened his eyes he was in that empty garage.

A half hour.

Why was his mind intent that only a half hour had passed? Maybe it had been hours and hours. Days even. He was lying flat on that concrete floor and a man was smoking a cigarette, gazing out through the iron bars of the gate to the outside. When Lotfi tried to cough, every bone in his body revolted against it. Pain shot through his right side and he gagged.

The man came and stood over him. "You should have renewed our deal."

He dragged Lotfi to a wall and made him sit upright. Surprisingly, this lessened the pain at first. Lotfi's breaths were shallow and fast. Surely he had broken ribs. Did this mean a punctured lung? Did he have internal bleeding? Would he die?

"If we're near where you hit me, then Aban Hospital is just up the road. Take me to the emergency room and I'll give you all the money you want."

The man laughed. Flicking his cigarette butt away, he replied, "Every offer has a time and a place. And you, my friend, have run out of time and places."

"Why are you doing this to me?" Lotfi's voice had a gurgle to it. He could feel every organ in his body working double-time to keep him breathing. He had a craving for chocolate all of a sudden. He had paid this nondescript man with the pencil mustache and ridiculous brown loafers a whole bunch of money a half year ago to pay somebody off to pay somebody else off to take away his brother's wife's passport and keep her a prisoner in Tehran. Lotfi felt a choking in his throat. It wasn't from pain, but sadness. What goes around comes around. Doesn't it? He thought of how Aida would never get to leave Tehran again. He wished he had bought a bottle of wine from the *khakham* so he and Aida could have drank it together.

The man was talking on his cell phone. "Yes, the last building. You can't miss it. It's a new building . . . Yes, you're almost here. After you pass Aban Hospital, you'll get to Warsaw Street. After Warsaw, it's two more short blocks south. Then take a right. I'll open the garage door."

So he'd been right. Aban Hospital was just up the road and they were but a stone's throw from where he'd been hit by the car. He groaned, "You went to her, didn't you?"

The man turned around. "What? Sure I went to her. I told her if she wanted her passport back, she could pay."

"And she wanted to know who did this to her?" He was actually crying now. He should have bought a bottle of wine from those synagogue people. He should have written a better book than that stupid Hollywood crap. He should have told his brother not to marry the Cow when there was still time to tell him what not to do.

"Of course she wanted to know who did this to her," the man answered. "And when she found out, she made me an offer I couldn't refuse."

"I'll pay you triple what she's paying if you get me to the hospital right now."

"Stop your crying, man. What's done is done. Like we say, *Eat a whole melon, and accept the shit that comes afterward.*"

"I'll pay you," Lotfi bawled. "Just get me out of here."

A car turned into the driveway and the man hurried to open the gate.

She must have had her Jenny Craig diets shipped to Tehran. She didn't look terrible, although she still had that awful chicken wattle. If anything, because of the dieting, the drooping skin beneath her chin looked more pronounced than ever.

"Leave him here." She didn't even bother addressing Lotfi. "They'll think he got beat up by the police today and crawled in here to die. It's the best day for it."

The man went to the car and came back with Lotfi's knife and the baton. "Look what I found on him."

She took the baton and played with it. "You think you can handle it?"

"What? You mean with that?" The man pointed to the baton.

"Yes, this," she said with impatience.

"I don't know. I mean—"

"Forget what you mean. I'll do it myself." Now she faced Lotfi, who had wiped the tears from his face and remained silent. "Don't you know days like today can be hazardous to your health, Mr. Lotfi?"

"You are an evil woman."

"All of you Lotfis are fools. Just a bunch of stupid Turks. You're even more stupid than your dead brother."

"I should have killed you when I had the chance," Lotfi murmured.

"What?" she barked.

Lotfi twisted his neck to address the man behind them. "I swear she'll eventually destroy you too."

"The lady has class. She's a dentist."

"She's just a dental hygienist, you fool. You're going to have the whitest teeth in all of Tehran. But that's all you're going to have."

He closed his eyes and heard the *click-click* of her high heels.

"Enough of your stupidity, *Tork e khar*, dumb Turk."

The baton connected over Lotfi's jaw and he felt the tooth-bridge on the right side of his mouth snap right off. He tasted warm blood dripping over his smashed face.

As he was letting go and keeling over, again he thought of the synagogue wine he never got to share with Aida. "The whitest set of teeth . . ." he whispered with half-open eyes.

"What?" she yelled.

Click-click. Now the Cow with the wattled chin changed her footing to get a good angle for the finish. And Lotfi, seeing the stick come down, thought for one last time of all these at once: red wine, white teeth, Aida.

This story was originally written in English.

PART III

PROPER BURIAL

THE RESTLESSNESS OF A SERIAL KILLER AT THE FINISH LINE

BY JAVAD AFHAMI

Shush

The apartment was on the third floor of a building at the outer edge of Shush. The heavyset officer's full name: Sergeant Major Haj Ali Mohammadi Ezzati-Rad. Ezzati was a seasoned veteran of the area's third precinct. Yet in those early hours of the cold, rainy day, just minutes before several SWAT teams from NAJA surrounded the building in question, Ezzati appeared dazed, his presence there a product of the sudden frenzy that had come over him as soon as he read the coded instructions from the NAJA central office.

He'd used the cover of darkness to get himself over to the place before the SWATs made their way to the Sirus crossroad. Ezzati hustled up the three floors of the adjacent building, panting and in pain each step of the way. On the rooftop he had to tiptoe on the thin ledge until he was past the emergency door of his target and outside the apartment.

The whole thing had taken him twenty minutes. For a man Ezzati's age, especially with those damaged lungs of his, it was something of a feat. And it had all started with that coded message from NAJA SWAT to every precinct in the district. Ezzati had been sitting on his small prayer rug in a corner of the communication room, his sleeves rolled up and a Koran in his hands, when a conscript handed him the decoded transmission. One look at the note and Ezzati was rushing to the commander's office.

Captain Salehi-Moqadam glanced at the note and nodded his head. "Well, well! So they finally traced our infamous Midnight

Bat, did they? And where should he be of all places—right around the block at the corner of Shush and Sirus!"

Salehi was a tough-looking, square-shouldered, middle-aged cop with a thin beard. Nothing seemed to ever faze him—not even the news that they had finally discovered the Midnight Bat's whereabouts.

He went on: "As soon as they uncovered that private little cemetery of his, I knew his days were numbered. It's just like all those other suspects that came before him. What were their names?"

Still standing respectfully by the door, Ezzati answered, "Sir, one was called the Cinderella of Karaj and the other the Scorpion of Eslam-Shahr."

Salehi stared back and forth between the *Wanted* flyers on his walls and a large map of Tehran. "But, you know, this last one could have ended better than this. It's too bad the Midnight Bat spoiled it for all of us. He shit on everything. He didn't have to." Now he turned his gaze back to his subordinate. "You and I understand each other perfectly, Sergeant Ezzati. I think you know what I mean. We were both in the war. We fought for our country. What I'm saying is, it's not a good thing when the capital of a true Muslim country, a Shia country, should be so riddled with scum. Every single block in this town is named after our war martyrs, men who fought right alongside us and died so our children could live in peace, and yet these same streets are jam-packed with school-age whores and every other kind of garbage you can name. You have an opinion on this, sergeant?"

Ezzati pulled himself a little straighter and answered, "Truth be told, I have no opinion, captain."

Salehi offered a bitter smile. "Or else maybe it would be easier to just change the names of all our streets again. At least our martyrs could finally rest in peace." Then, as if he had suddenly caught on to the gravity of the situation, he quickly added, "We don't have a lot of time, sergeant. Contact Captain Ahmadi and all the other patrols in the area and tell them to pull back on the double. The SWATs will be here in twenty minutes. I don't want a single patrol car to remain on Shush. Make sure no one leaves the station either. No one! The entire area has to be empty of our cars and uniforms. SWAT will handle it. They'll probably want to set a trap for him."

Ezzati waited. His night duty was over. He'd finished his morning prayer and had been ready to go home when the message arrived.

The captain continued, "By the way, tell the duty officer to be sharp. I want all the boys to get what they need from the weapons room. Tell everyone they must remain at their posts. As for you, I want you to stay in the radio room and keep an ear on everything. I have a feeling it's going to be a busy day. The SWATs might even ask for our backup. I hope to God he doesn't get away this time."

Ezzati clicked his heels and was ready to retreat from the room when the captain called out to him: "Look, Ezzati, what I'm asking from you—I mean you personally—is not an order. I know you're done for the day. But we're low on men today. Stay awhile. Help us out."

"Yes sir."

Ezzati went straight to the top floor of the precinct and told the duty officer what was happening.

Sergeant Ghanbari nodded thoughtfully. He was a big man. A few years younger than Ezzati and all muscle. Not the kind of cop you wanted to run into on the street. He said, "No wonder they call him a bat. He's been a hard catch so far. I'd love to be there when they finish him. I'll bet you he's not the kind to give in without a firefight. They won't catch him alive."

The two men walked together to the weapons room. Ghanbari was still talking: "They say the killer buries his victims with all the pomp of a proper Muslim burial. Can you believe that? He digs exactly according to the *sharia*. I mean, the guy's precise—two meters long, one meter wide, and ninety centimeters deep, and he faces the bodies toward Mecca. All the corpses they pulled out of the ground were properly shrouded too. The medical examiner says he even washes the bodies with camphor and cedar powder before putting them in a shroud. It's as if the guy had a whole mortuary to conduct his work. I bet you he even recites the prayer for the dead."

The weapons room officer had overheard the conversation and joined it. "I have to admit, I kind of like this guy. I don't like his method. No. But he strikes me as the kind of man who backs his words with real deeds, even if those deeds are the murder of a bunch of disgusting street whores. Are we, after all, Muslims or not? I swear to you, every time I have to go out there on a patrol and bust these bitches, I feel tainted to the core. But the Midnight Bat, he's a real man. A year and a half ago he began something and stuck with it. And that rumor they say about him lately fucking his victims, I don't believe it. No one believes it. It's just misinformation. Character assassination. What this guy did with the cheap cunts of this city, he must have had the heart of a lion to do. That man would never stoop to raping them."

Ghanbari asked for a Colt 45 and an AK-47 with extra magazines. The other man looked at him doubtfully. "What, you think he's going to attack the precinct?"

"A man can't go wrong with a full arsenal."

The weapons room officer, a thin older fellow who was always telling jokes, smiled. "While you're at it, why don't I call central and ask them to send us a fifty-caliber DShK too? After all, a man can't go wrong going heavy."

Ghanbari and the other man laughed. But Ezzati remained cold and quiet. He stuck the Colt he had just received in the pocket of his worn military overcoat and went off quickly.

The weapons room officer called after him, "Sergeant Ezzati, you *are* the man, brother. Your word is my command."

Ezzati called back, "I'll tell the sentry myself about the situation."

Now Ezzati was in the little kitchen of the police station trying to get some water into those useless lungs of his when he saw that Ghanbari had followed him. The duty officer stood there, the AK slung on his back, watching Ezzati who had suddenly fallen into a terrible coughing fit.

"How do you feel?"

"Good enough."

Ghanbari stepped toward his fellow sergeant. "I'll bet you'll be coughing up blood in a minute. Forget the captain's orders. Go home and rest. We'll take care of it."

"I'm going."

Ghanbari's gaze remained on his friend. "You're lying. You have no intention of going home, do you?"

Ezzati turned away.

"Tell me the truth. Where are you going?"

"Give me a break, will you!"

The duty officer blocked Ezzati's path. "You're a mess again, man. And it has something to do with that bitch, Zivar. Am I right?" He didn't wait for Ezzati to answer. "You still haven't learned your lesson, brother. That good-for-nothing woman is never coming back. And you're insane if you think you can still have her."

Ezzati tried to push Ghanbari away, but the guy easily wristlocked him and pushed him back against the wall.

"How long do you want to torture yourself with that cunt?" Ghanbari's voice rose in anger. "Zivar is gone. Get it? Just pretend she's dead. She wasn't yours to begin with. You should have thought about it a lot earlier. Back when you imagined bringing a girl twenty years younger into your house would do you good. Did you think it was a game? You think you can just replace one woman with another? Your wife, now that was a real woman. And Masumeh stayed faithful to you till the last day of her life. But this bitch you brought in to replace her—her head might have been in your house, but the rest of her body was with others. And you still don't get it."

Ezzati went into another coughing fit. He could barely breathe.

The duty officer let go of him and pulled back a bit. "Forgive me. I didn't want to make you upset; I just wanted to talk some sense into you." He refilled the glass of water and offered it to Ezzati.

He slowly drank the water, still unable to look into his friend's face. Then he mumbled, "You're imagining things. I'm all right."

Ghanbari slung the AK to his other shoulder. "Why can't you listen to some logic? You're a wounded war veteran. You don't even have to be here if you don't want to. You think it's some kind of sacrifice showing up at the job every day? For a guy like you it's suicide. And suicide is a sin. Aren't you a man of God? If I were in your place, I wouldn't stay in this godforsaken dump one minute more than I had to. Have you forgotten the Iraqis hit you with chemicals during the war? What do you think that cough is from? It'll be the death of you. Go home, Ezzati. I beg you to go home."

"The cough is nothing. I just can't find the foreign meds for it in the market. All they have is the domestic garbage. But I'll be all right."

Ghanbari brought his face close to Ezzati's one last time. "Go home and rest. Try, if you can, to forget that bitch."

Ezzati quietly brushed past his friend. On his way out of the police station he gave a casual nod to the sentry and headed away from the garage.

Now here he was, inside this apartment on the fringes of Shush. His knees were still shaking from the climb. Colt in hand, Ezzati finally managed to stand upright and stagger over to the middle of the living room where a corpse lay faceup on the floor. Young woman. Girl, really. No more than sixteen. Her disheveled black hair covered most of her face and the headscarf was knotted around her throat. Ezzati reached over and undid the knot of the scarf with his index finger. Her pale white skin was bruised underneath. The sergeant got up again and moved to the heater to warm his hands a little. His intermittent coughing left him spent. Now he took note of the time and began inspecting the place with a cop's eyes. The windows all had heavy curtains. There was a small desk in the corner of the living room. A woman's brown handbag sat on it. Next to the bag was a watch, two rings, and three gold bracelets. In the bedroom everything appeared tidy. No one had slept there lately. A woman's coat hung in the closet. Next to it, a man's suit and a pair of loose Kurdish pants. The only other objects were a couple of spray bottles of air freshener and several bedsheets folded neatly inside a drawer.

He had been there all of ten minutes when the sound of a key turning inside the door lock brought Ezzati out of himself. He made straight for the bathroom and left the door ajar so he could peer inside the living room. A woman entered the apartment. She had on a drenched and muddy black *chador*. She paused and gave the place a quick once-over. Now she let go of her umbrella and, as she made her way to the heater, the *chador* fell off her head and dropped to the floor. She was tall and looked distracted. In fact, it was as if she hardly saw the corpse lying right there in front of her. She took a cigarette from her bag and lit it. Her eyes fell on the brown handbag on the table next to the window. She went over and took the bracelets and rings but for some reason missed the watch.

Ezzati was keeping his cough in check and watching her every move. She headed for the bedroom. From his angle, Ezzati could see her hands reaching into the drawer and searching underneath the bedsheets. She came up with a wad of cash and stuffed it all in her pocket. She retreated from the bedroom and passed the corpse without so much as a look. She picked up her *chador* and umbrella and was about to reach for the door when Ezzati's bark made her freeze: "Stop!"

She gave a surprised cry and as she turned to face him the umbrella fell from her hands. She looked like she might scream. Ezzati took three quick steps to the door and grabbed her.

"Not a sound from you!"

"Mister, you scared me to death." She had a hand on her heart and was gazing at Ezzati in utter disbelief. "For a second I thought I was finished. I thought you were . . . the police?" Her wrinkles were full of dirt, and when she opened her mouth to speak the rot in her teeth was something awful. "Are you really police or . . . ?"

"Or what?" Ezzati asked, watching her curiously.

The woman seemed to shake off the initial shock. "Or nothing. I mean, the way you suddenly came behind me, I just got scared. That's all."

Ezzati glanced away from her for a second and tried to focus on what he had to do next. Immediately he heard the sound of the door opening and turned back to see the woman running into the dark of the hallway. He caught up to her by the stairway and grabbed hold of her headscarf. She tried screaming, but he already had his other hand on her mouth and was dragging her back into the apartment. He tossed her onto the floor next to the corpse.

"Key!"

The woman looked at him without understanding.

"Give me the key to the apartment. Now."

He took her key and locked the door with it. The woman had gotten up and dragged herself to the heater, the whole time not taking her terrified eyes off of him.

"Don't lie to me; what are you doing here?"

"Me? I'm Najmeh. Don't you know?" Her voice shook. She began to cry. "I swear to God I know nothing. For the love of your children, let me go. I'm innocent. I just do the work that—"

"Shut the fuck up. I'm not police."

The woman suddenly grew quiet and wiped her tears with the back of her hands.

Ezzati took the Colt from his pocket and stuck it in the back of his belt. "I'll ask you again—tell me exactly what you're doing here." He was speaking quietly now, but the woman continued shaking.

"I already said—my name is Najmeh. I clean houses. I work in people's homes."

He sprang at her, grabbed at the knot of the headscarf again, and hissed, "Bullshit me one more time and I'll destroy you. This is the last time I'll ask you: What are you doing here? What's your real job?"

The woman fell to pleading: "Mister, I'll tell you everything. I promise. Just don't hurt me. This thing," she pointed to the dead girl, "I had nothing to do with it. I never even saw her before today. I just come to wash the dead bodies he leaves behind. That's my job."

"How long have you been doing this?" Ezzati snapped.

"Can't say for sure. A year, maybe a bit longer."

"How did he find you?" Ezzati still held tight to the woman's headscarf.

"How should I know? He probably asked around. Everyone knows Najmeh the corpse washer. Everyone knows I'm always broke. When this guy called me, my child was already sick. She still is. I needed money for the hospital bills and the surgery. He told me over the phone there was good money in it."

"How does he get in touch with you?"

"He calls me. Tells me to get over here, and that there's a body to be washed and shrouded. The man is serious about the corpses being properly cared for. So I do exactly as he says. I go to the cloth market and buy some calico for the shroud. I wash the body in the bathroom, shroud it, and then I leave. That's it. I swear to you I know nothing about anything else. He never shows himself to me. I've never seen him in the flesh. He gives me specific times. He says I can't be a minute late or early."

Ezzati let go of the woman and took a few steps back until he was standing over the girl's corpse. "How many times have you done this?"

The woman paused. Ezzati watched her carefully. "I can't say for sure. Ten, twelve, maybe thirteen. I didn't keep count. Why should I? For the love of God, I'm a corpse washer. They say wash, I wash. If not here, then at the mortuary at Behesht e Zahra where I keep regular hours."

"How does he pay you?"

"Leaves the money in the drawer in the bedroom."

"How much?"

She hesitated. "Um, it's yours if—"

"How much?" Ezzati yelled.

"Hundred fifty."

"How much do they pay you at the cemetery for the same work?"

"Forty." The woman had begun shaking again. She stayed by the heater. "Can I smoke?"

Ezzati nodded. She fished a cigarette and stuck it between her rutted lips.

"Finish your smoke and get on with your work."

"Finish? Finish what?" she stammered.

"The job you got paid for."

She took quick drags of her cigarette and watched the corpse. There was no feeling in those eyes. Just another thing she had to wash. Ezzati went to the window and took a peek outside through the gap in the curtain. It didn't look like it would stop raining anytime soon.

"Hurry up!"

The woman took her last drag and went over to the body. She grabbed the girl under the arms and dragged her to the bathroom. She seemed to have a second wind now.

"Don't shut that door."

"But I have to strip her."

"Leave it ajar."

The woman nodded.

"How will you wash her? Only with water?"

The woman stared at him doubtfully.

"Answer my question. Don't you need to mix the water with anything else? Maybe with cedar powder and camphor?"

"It's not a must. It would be nice to have them. They give a body some fragrance. But it can be done without it. That's what the law says anyhow."

Ezzati stood there watching through the half-open door. "Talk. Every little thing you do in there, I want you to describe it to me."

"What's there to describe? I'll just strip the corpse and wash her. Like the rest of them."

Ezzati leaned against the wall behind him. "Have you known any of the bodies?"

"Personally, you mean? No. Why should I?"

"But you do know they were street women."

"Maybe I heard some things. Yes."

"Why do you think he asked you to wash and shroud the bodies according to the law?"

She was struggling to take the girl's clothes off and seemed annoyed. "How should I know? I guess he's a religious man. He believes in God and the Prophet. He prays. He's virtuous. Righteous. All that stuff. Whoever does something like this, he has to know right from wrong."

The girl's upper body was naked now, but the tight jeans seemed glued to her legs and wouldn't come off. It appeared that she was going to wash her outside the bathtub and let the water run off to the floor drain.

Ezzati turned away. "So you're saying the man who did this is virtuous?"

The woman was panting from the effort to strip the body. "These girls are not human. They're vermin. They need to be wiped off the face of the earth."

"How long since you stopped bothering to wash the corpses?"

Still panting, she began talking fast. "It was just this one time. I swear it. I was in a hurry. I told you I have a sickly child. There's no one to look after her. I have to get her to the hospital. She's been spitting blood since yesterday."

Ezzati let his glance linger on what was happening in there. The girl's white skin, her ankles and thighs, they would come into the sergeant's line of vision and then disappear as the woman worked on her.

"I have to rid her of the impurities before actually washing her," she explained.

"Which impurities?"

"You know, piss, shit, semen, blood, everything in every single hole." She was running the water now and had to talk loud over the noise. Steam came out of the bathroom. She spoke with revulsion in her voice. "This dirty bitch, she has everything you can name on her."

Ezzati barely moved. He kept his eyes on the blank wall and remained frozen.

"Now I wash her back. I have to run water over her three full times. Then I dry her and bring her out for shrouding. I'm going to take her into the bedroom."

Ezzati stayed in the living room. He could hear the woman's voice better now that the water was off.

"By the way, I had no chance to buy cloth at the market. If you permit it, I'll just use one of the sheets in the bedroom. As far as *sharia* law goes, it's allowed."

Ezzati said nothing. Slowly he lost track of time. He walked like some caged animal in that living room, stopping to lean on the heater and against the walls. When the woman finally appeared in front of him again, she had another cigarette in her mouth. "My job is finished," she said with emphasis. "I laid her in the bedroom nicely shrouded and facing *qeble*. She's ready for the prayer for the dead. If you are done with me, I'd like to go now."

Ezzati slowly lifted his eyes. "You said there were impurities on her?"

"I cleaned it all."

He asked the same question as if he hadn't heard what she just said. "There were impurities?"

The woman wiped her face with the edge of her *chador*. "With God as my witness, I cleaned everything. Why are you giving me a hard time? Let me go!"

Ezzati walked toward her. "You can't go anywhere. There's police all over the place."

"Please! What police? You? If there was other police, they would have broken the door down by now."

He pointed to the bathroom. "You have to stay in there until my job here is finished."

The woman was pleading with him again. He stood there for a second watching her, and then he pounced. He caught hold of her wrist and dragged her after him.

She was wailing now. "You are not a man. You promised to let me go if I did my job. I beseech you!"

He let go of her in a corner of the wet and still-steamy bathroom. "I have to tie you up. It won't be for long."

"I won't tell anyone anything," she cried. "I'll keep my mouth shut."

He bound her hands with a pair of cuffs. Then he took a bandanna from his pocket and expertly tied her mouth up too. "Don't you move from here."

Back in the living room Ezzati just about fell on the corner chair, exhausted. He leaned his head back and felt for the gun he was carrying. The weapon's presence bought him a measure of confidence. There were no more sounds from the woman. He stared at the water stains on the ceiling, his mind drawing blanks. Then, just as he was closing his eyes, there was a sound of steps in the corridor.

Ezzati willed himself off the chair and stood gazing at the door. There were no other apartments on this floor. Whoever it was, they seemed to be slowing down as they got closer to the door. Gun in hand, he tiptoed to the bedroom, but the vantage point from there wouldn't do. He was wheezing again and wanted to cough, but he managed to keep quiet and get himself to the bathroom just as the keys jangled at the door. He shushed the woman with a gesture of his index finger and turned to face outside.

A young man, thirtyish. His long hair soaked. He was skinny and wore a coat that reached below his knees. Ezzati kept his eyes on him from the gap in the bathroom door. The guy seemed to be taking the place in, though it was obvious it was hardly his first time here. He stood by the radiator and kept rubbing his hands to warm himself. He shook his hair out and Ezzati could hear the hiss of the water as it sizzled on the radiator. Over at the window the man took awhile carefully peeking outside. Then he walked over to the desk and his eyes fell on the watch.

"Gold!" he exclaimed. "This could be your lucky day today, *daash* Ebram."

Ezzati watched him as he made the rounds of the place, water still dripping from his hair and his poorly trimmed beard. Then he was standing still in that bedroom. Ezzati had to push the door open a little more to be able to see what he was up to. The man just stood there over the corpse, staring. Then he began talking to himself again: "The guy's like a bulldozer. Come rain or shine, he has to do his thing. It could be hailing stones from the skies and he still has to do his killing. The hell with him!"

He bent down and pulled the white shroud off the face of the dead girl. "O freshness! May Ebram here die for you a thousand deaths. You were a peach. Fuck the guy who did this to you. Fuck him and his mother. He gets his pleasure and leaves the bodies for me. The bastard."

Then, with one swift pull, he ripped the improvised shroud apart and let out a deep sigh. "I bet you were just a beginner, weren't you? May he that put an end to your sweet breath stop breathing himself."

From Ezzati's vantage it looked like the man had begun caressing the corpse's breasts. It was an appalling moment which Ezzati shared with the woman behind him. She had heard everything he'd heard and she turned away, embarrassed and uncomfortable. The man's moans were getting louder now. He sat on the girl's stomach and seemed to be undoing his pants.

"Forgive me, little angel. Just one single quickie and I'm done. Time is short and I have to get on with my work." His voice trembled with excitement and he kept repeating, "A quickie and I'm finished, I promise."

Ezzati's kick was vicious and it threw the man right off the corpse and against the wall. The sergeant stood there with his legs wide apart, gun in hand, dry coughing several times before he finally spoke. "Get up, you ungrateful piece of garbage. Do it now before I put a bullet in your head."

And then Ezzati was fighting to stay on his feet. A violent coughing attack took hold of him and wouldn't let go. The other man saw this and for a moment made a halfhearted attempt at closing the distance between them. But Ezzati held on, their eyes met, and then the man noticed he himself was bleeding from the nose. He must have smashed his face against the wall when Ezzati kicked him. The sight of blood appeared to purge him of any idea of a fight. He pulled his head back to stop the flow of blood and then dropped himself onto the floor. Ezzati's coughs soon subsided. He took a couple of steps toward the man and stuck the muzzle of the gun in his face. Ebram moaned. Ezzati's military boots crushed the guy's left ankle with such force that he didn't even try to protect them. He just grabbed his own face in his bony hands and let out another animal moan.

"You're afraid, are you? You're afraid, *daash* Ebram?"

The next kick was in the chest. Ezzati watched Ebram knot into himself from the pain. And he stood over him, coughing, spitting, yelling in truncated sentences. "You know, I owe you an apology. A year and a half ago. Thinking you had scruples. Killing your wife. Telling me you did it because . . . she betrayed you. Sorry for not arresting you back then. I let you escape. Thinking you deserved a second chance. Sorry. That's what I am. Sorry thinking you were a man."

Ebram lay prone on the floor. He was barely breathing and his face was covered in blood. Ezzati yanked his hair. Suddenly the other man opened his mouth and gulped air as if he'd been drowning. "Don't kill me. For the love of your children, don't! I'm innocent. It was the devil's work. I didn't mean to—"

Ezzati delivered a torrent of blows. "You know what I'm sorry for, you beast? I'm sorry I convinced myself you were partnering with me out of faith."

The blows landed every which way and brought only more resigned moaning from Ebram. They sounded like the groans of a man on his deathbed. Ezzati stopped for another attack of coughs; this time it made his body spasm. He fell to the floor. He was spitting blood and his gun lay next to him. The other man made a feeble move for the Colt, but Ezzati managed to pull himself together, grab the gun, and get up.

"On the blood of Imam Hossein, I implore you not to kill me. Forgiveness!"

"Forgiveness is not my style. Can't you see it? My job is revenge. I'm an instrument of punishment, you animal! I'm an instrument for doing God's work. A knife is made to cut, and I'm that knife." Ezzati took hold of the dead girl and dragged her one-handed until she was flush against the far wall. "Take a good look at her. When a sixteen-year-old girl can't be forgiven for going wrong, how does a vile creature like you imagine himself worthy of forgiveness? Huh?" He came back at Ebram and waved the gun at him. "Did you forget our deal? You were paid well to do a simple job. All you had to do was put them in the back of your cab, dig them a place, and give them a real burial. One meter wide, two meters long, and ninety centimeters deep—that's what a proper Muslim grave is supposed to look like. What happened? Your last four digs were not even thirty centimeters. Stray dogs found them and pulled them out by their legs. Now everything is blown. I don't know how they found out about this address, but they did. Now SWAT teams are out there. Any minute they'll break the door down."

"No. I swear. There's no one out there. I was careful. Nothing is blown. You're sick. That's what it is. You're obsessed. If there were police out there, they'd be in here by now."

Ezzati grabbed at the man's hair again. "They're everywhere, you fool. They know their job. They wait for an idiot like you to make a mistake. And idiots like you always make a mistake."

"Don't be so hard on me, sergeant. It was just a small slipup today. I got carried away."

"How did you give away our location? Were you taking speed again? Did you open your big mouth in your taxi and not stop talking? Your whole life's a mistake, *daash* Ebram. It's not just this girl here, you've been doing the same thing to all of them. I know, so don't lie to me." Ezzati turned, hurried to the bathroom, undid the woman's cuffs, and pulled her after him. He continued talking the whole time. "The fact is, we all messed up. All of us." He threw the woman who hadn't uttered a word all this time alongside Ebram and gave her a venomous stare. "And you too, you're wrong! The dead have to be washed exactly according to the laws. There's no choosing how you do it. First it has to be with the cedar, then with camphor, and finally with plain water. This was what you were getting paid for, to do exactly according to the *sharia*. But you too betrayed me. I'm willing to bet you haven't washed a single body properly for months and months. All you do is come here and take the money and their jewelry."

More coughing. Then he was on his knees once again. On his knees just like all those years ago when the Iraqi chemicals had first rained on his regiment during the war.

The woman started again about her sick child. Ebram wept.

Still on his knees, Ezzati pointed the gun at them. "Shut up. Both of you."

Ebram tried stupidly to protect his face from a bullet that wasn't coming. "Don't do it, man. Everyone makes mistakes. Even you. Are you a man or not?"

Ezzati slowly gained control of his breathing and stood up. "No, I'm not a man. If I was, I wouldn't be so alone right now."

The other guy suddenly raised his voice, taking Ezzati by surprise. "Stop that! We're all acting here. We're all trash. You're right about that. If you're going to kill us, go ahead. But don't for a second imagine Ebram here was a fool. I knew what was going on. Which part of it do you want me to tell you about? The part about the times I found condoms? You didn't even know how to use the damned things. That's right, you fucked them while they were alive and I fucked them when they were dead. There's no difference between us."

Ezzati cocked the gun. "Liar! You have no right to talk to me like that. I'll empty this thing in your evil face. I won't let you put the blame on me." Ebram didn't answer back. Ezzati booted him in the ankle. "What's the story with the condoms? Where are they? Talk!"

Writhing in pain, Ebram shouted back, "Why do you ask me? You already know where they are, they're in the drawer!"

Half crazed, Ezzati started throwing cans of air freshener from the top of the desk of drawers. It was as if the corpse no longer existed in that room. "I see nothing. What are you talking about?"

"I said inside the drawer, not on top of it."

Ezzati turned with wild eyes to the woman. "This is all lies. Tell him he's lying."

"Like they say," the woman groaned, "your ass has more shit in it than the two of us combined. Stop acting the part of the holy man. It's too late for that. I'm sure all that filth I found on her was your own and no one else's."

Ezzati's eyes were bloodshot. "You lie. Both of you are liars."

He waved the gun wildly at them. The woman screamed and tried to pull herself up onto the bed. "It was you. All you!" she yelled. Then she pointed to Ebram who was still lying on the floor. "This man must have always come to the apartment after me. So it had to be you."

Ebram echoed what she said. "She's right. They were always stained between the legs."

The woman gave Ebram an evil look. She seemed to finally understand the significance of all the talk about stains. "But wait, I washed them. I did wash them."

"You stopped washing them after the sixth or seventh one,

lying bitch. You're a couple of vultures living off dead bodies. The both of you."

The woman cried back from the bed, "Yes, it's true, I found the stains on them. It's what I do for a living. Been doing it for years. In the beginning you just killed them. But after a while . . . you lost track of who you are."

The gun shook in Ezzati's hand. Outside, the sound of pelting rain was wreaking havoc on the windows. Ezzati tried to speak, but coughed instead.

The woman continued as if possessed: "Dirty! Bloody. Full of come. Full of the disgusting monster that you are. You tore them up inside. You! You did it. Not this fool."

The sound of rain was momentarily lost in the noise of some car crashing to a halt. Ezzati scrambled over to the window and struggled to open it. The howling of the storm assaulted the bedroom like something alive. Ezzati saw that across the street wind had scattered the papers and magazines from the newspaper stand. He imagined the crime pages as they flew up in the air past him. He saw the faces of many girls, some laughing, some crying, girls with brown eyes and blue . . . all of them winging beyond him in a dance of victims until they became just one face staring back at him.

He shuddered. Now he saw that the newspaperman was carrying a machine gun and was hurrying across the street toward the building. The sergeant closed his eyes and watched his life pass before him. He imagined bullets whizzing by. He was back in the war and enemy tanks were approaching his platoon's position. He shouted to no one in particular, "Take cover! The Iraqis are coming in with chemicals! Everybody take cover now!"

This never-ending cough. Someone had a DShK aimed at them from a window of the building across the street. He was sure of that. The tanks were coming in two columns and behind them were soldiers wearing helmets and gas masks.

He shouted again: "Hurry! The enemy's on top of us!"

He stuck his gun out the window and fired until he'd emptied the magazine. Now the wheezing in his chest stopped and he wasn't coughing anymore. He opened his eyes and turned around. The woman lay flat on the bed pressing her hands to her ears. Ebram remained on the floor with a blank face, not moving. The monstrous sound that came next was the apartment door being smashed in. But Sergeant Ezzati paid it no mind. He turned his attention back to the street where he was sure the enemy was fast approaching. He glimpsed the abandoned newspaper kiosk. It was the last thing that Sergeant Major Haj Ali Mohammadi Ezzati-Rad would see on that cold, rainy day in the Shush District of Tehran.

MY OWN MARBLE JESUS

BY MAHSA MOHEBALI

Dibaji

I slow down and stop in front of the kid. He smiles, comes around to the passenger side, rests one hand on the roof of the car, lowers his face into the half-rolled-down window, and gives me the once-over. He has a thick wad of gel in his hair and a farmer's tanned face. You could tell he's not from Tehran. Probably made straight for Vanak Circle as soon as he got off the bus from some godforsaken village. I'd say this boy here needs another six, seven months and he'll shed that smug, stupid gaze and become truly worth the money.

"How much?" I ask him.

He grins. A car passes by and its light shines on his white teeth. "How many rounds?" he asks.

"I want you all night."

He grins some more and casts a glance at a newspaper stand some two hundred yards down the road. I can't see the faces of the two guys standing there and they most definitely can't see me. Later on maybe they'll be able to testify they saw their friend get inside a Porsche. That's about it.

He asks, "Just for you?"

"It's not a party. Just me."

He opens the door and slithers in. He has a firm body and a sexy little cut right under his chin. I press his window up, do a U-turn to avoid driving past the paper stand, and then step on the gas.

"You still didn't tell me how much."

"As much as it gives you pleasure, lady."

"What if it doesn't give me pleasure?"

Another one of those stupid grins. One of his gelled locks falls over his face. "Trust me, lady, you'll be pleasured."

The kid's tongue works fast for a beginner.

"Listen," I say, "across from the park they got uniforms inspecting cars. If they stop us, you're my husband's cousin. Understood?"

"Understood."

"What's your name?"

"Kamran."

He's lying. It suits him better to be called Yadollah. Or some other peasant name like that. A little ways up the road the patrol cars are pulled alongside both lanes checking on late-night party-goers. This may be the trickiest part of the whole evening; I don't want to have to roll my window down. Still, I push the hair sticking out of my headscarf back in and put on my best mother face. Without the makeup I don't exactly look like the type to have come out cruising for a hustler. As luck would have it, the patrol decides to shine his light from the sidewalk side where he's just been giving a hard time to some college-age girls. The kid rolls the window down and the light travels from his face to the back of the car where I've strapped in the baby seat on purpose. The baby seat does the trick; the light swings away and we're told to drive on.

The kid, whom I'll call Yadollah from now on, says, "Your husband left you or you're just a widow?"

I turn into Esfandiyar and push on the pedal. "Not in the mood for flirtation, boy. You'll do me two, three times good and that's all I require from you. Now roll that window back up."

He does what he's told, then slides his ass down on the seat and rests his knees on the dashboard. "Good, because I'm in no mood for another Miss Lonely Hearts either."

He acts like a professional, but his looks and his village accent give him away. He's a rank beginner. He probably has some family here and one of them called and said, "Yadollah, put down your hoe and shovel right this minute and come to Tehran. Here's where the money is." The two guys by that paper booth must have been his relatives. They stand there making sure he doesn't get in the wrong car. It's a dangerous job. Sometimes you'll get picked up by some girl and end up in a house where six hairy gorillas fall on top of you and dig you a nice new asshole.

I turn on Niyayesh and drive fast. A Camry and a BMW fall right behind me. They can't see through my tinted windows to know there's a woman behind the wheel, but it still hurts their manhoods to have the Porsche leave them in the dust like that. The Camry catches up in the tunnel, its driver a shitty little kid probably driving his papa's second or third spare car. I let him pass for the sake of his wounded pride, then right after the tunnel I squeeze past and leave him in the traffic again.

Yadollah is impressed. "You can drive."

I turn at the exit of East Hemmat and head up Pasdaran. Bumper-to-bumper traffic here.

Yadollah sits up. "Where are you taking me, love?"

"Nowhere bad. Don't worry."

"If we're going this way, why didn't you just take Sadr instead?"

"Lately they close Sadr up after nine p.m. If you really lived in Tehran you'd know this."

"I haven't been up this way for a while."

He's full of shit. There's not a soul in Tehran who doesn't know they've been building that overpass on Sadr for God knows how long. But it doesn't matter. We're stuck on Pasdaran for now and that's not the worst thing in the world. Weekend nights like this, it's serious cruising here and getting from one end of Pasdaran to the other can take an hour. That gives me plenty of time to make sure Mrs. Ebtehaj, our neighbor, is sleeping. The woman always sits behind the window sipping her tea, with one eye on her TV and the other on the street. She thinks she's invisible. The good thing is that the rest of the neighbors aren't nosy like her, because a single Mrs. Ebtehaj is enough for the entire neighborhood. She sits at her sentry duty till one a.m. every night, then she swallows three or four different pills and goes dead until seven a.m. Her schedule is one you can count on, and tonight I count on her.

A cutie tries unsuccessfully to peek into our car from inside her brand-new Santa Fe. Yadollah starts to bring his window down again. For a second I want to tell him to stop. But what the hell, let him! She can't see me. He shows his teeth to the girl, who immediately stretches out a hand and throws him a folded piece of paper. The boy takes it, smiles again, and puts the paper away in his pocket. But I can tell from his face he has no clue what's going on. All around us telephone numbers are being passed from one car to another. Boys to girls, girls to boys. I know he's dying to ask me who's receiving and who's giving money in this situation. It doesn't enter his mind that these kids are just out here for the hell of it. They take the telephone numbers, call each other and flirt a little bit, and then it's on to one address or another. They score a little coke and a couple shots of something and get to work. Next morning each to his own, and half the time they won't even remember each other's names. I could tell Yadollah all this. Clue him in. I could tell him that Pasdaran on a Thursday night is an automobile club. Or more like those old drive-in movie theaters. Except here you first check out the car to get a sense of the price tag on it, then you look to see if the merchandise inside is any good. Yes, I could tell poor Yadollah all this, but I don't; I can't be bothered.

"Look," I say, "these are all rich kids here. They're only out for a good time."

Another cutie stretches a hand out of her SUV and passes my boy a piece of paper. Yadollah takes that too and stuffs it in the same pocket.

"You don't mind, do you?" he asks.

"Do what you have to. But remember, these girls are not customers."

"I know."

He's full of it again. He doesn't know a thing. Eventually I pass a couple of Peugeots and make a sharp turn onto South Ekhti-yarieh, a street for people who don't want to take the risk of being seen by their wives and kids while exchanging telephone numbers. Once I pass the red light on Dowlat, I know I'm home free.

Next door, Mrs. Ebtehaj's lights are off. Good. And once Naser's Porsche is parked in front of the house where it can be seen, instead of in our garage, everything is set. A typical weekend night for Dr. Naser Zarafshan, my husband. Except that this weekend the usual gathering is at the house of one of his other friends and not here. Meanwhile, our two kids and I are supposed to be sleeping at my parents' house, because that is what Dr. Zarafshan has decreed. In fact, I called him just two hours earlier. He barked into the phone that he was heading straight from the airport to the weekend get-together at one of his friend's. Didn't say which friend, though, and it doesn't matter. What matters is that he is physically in Tehran now.

As soon as I open the door, the stink of one week's worth of after-party garbage almost floors me. The house is a riot of cigarette butts, unwashed dishes, and half-eaten food left to rot in every room, even the children's room. You see, the first thing you have to know about Dr. Naser Zarafshan is that this is a man who has an obsession with cleanliness. But his obsession works in strange ways. He will not trust anyone else to clean the house. And when there are servants, he has to closely supervise them and work them to death. Thus the state of the house tonight as Yadollah and I enter it—the sickly combined smell of a garbage truck and a public urinal in Mr. Clean's house because Naser had to fly abroad right after his party last weekend.

Yadollah throws himself on one of the couches and takes out a pack of Marlboros. "Want one?"

I shake my head. He pulls out his lighter, one of those kitsch numbers that plays a stupid tune when you light it. He pretends to be casual and not at all interested in the house. He doesn't even ask why the place is overflowing with garbage.

I remove my headscarf and manteau and throw them next to him on the couch. He can't take his eyes off the black satin nightie I've been wearing underneath. He travels down the length of my body, stopping at my thighs. Now he offers an odd look seeing me wearing men's boots, Naser's, before returning his gaze to my shoulders and onto the black gloves I'm wearing.

"Come here, baby."

He seems to have forgotten what he does for a living, speaking as if he's the one who picked *me* up. In a firm, even voice I say, "Take your clothes off and go lie on the bed in that room."

All my life I've wanted to say these words in exactly this tone of voice.

He puts out his cigarette in a bowlful of old pistachio shells. "So businesslike so soon? At least give us something to drink before we get to work."

I move behind the minibar and pour him a whiskey and hand it to him. I pour myself a gin and tonic.

He gulps the alcohol down. "You don't look like the type, you know."

He's right. Without makeup I look like your everyday Mother Mary. Makeup would have left traces behind. Lipstick on the bed-sheets, eyeliner flaking off on the pillow. Wouldn't do. I pour a second shot. "I said get in the bedroom."

He follows me, whiskey in hand. He takes his T-shirt off. Then shoes and socks. The shoes are dusty. He hasn't gotten around to cleaning them. Another dead giveaway he's not from Tehran. Now it's time to take off his pants. He plays with his belt and hesitates. You'd think it was his very first time.

"Hurry up!"

Once he pulls his pants down I finally understand his hesitation. He's got a massive hard-on under those shorts. He jumps under the covers thinking I didn't see it. Why is it men believe it's not cool to show their card so early? I suppose they just don't want you to know how eager they are when they've been playing it so cool.

"You don't want to take your shorts off?"

He's like a little bitch of a coquette. Slowly he pulls off the shorts and lays them on the pillow next to him. Without the shorts, his hard-on is like a tent under the covers. He reaches for it and tries taming it. No good. The thing sticks right back up. I hand him the rest of the bottle of whiskey and suck on my own bottle of gin. Then I sit on the ottoman across from the bed and cross my legs for him. He eye-fucks me big time and I let him.

"How long you been on the job?" I ask.

"For a while," he says, and guzzles the bottle like he's never drank whiskey before.

"You make good money?"

"Good enough."

Why shouldn't it be good enough? Back in his hometown the most he could hope for was probably a laborer's job or waiting tables, or—if he was lucky—a gig as a chauffeur. And on weekends he'd find some cheap cunt to service him and his friends. Now he's here. All he has to do is keep down a Viagra pill and some Tramadol and stand on a street corner. He should be thanking his lucky stars.

"Come sit on it," he says with a heavy look. The whiskey he's been downing like a champ is already getting to him.

"I'll come. Let me drink a little more."

"You've drank plenty, love. Come sit on it, won't you?"

I turn into a little girl for him. "Close your eyes. I don't like being watched when I'm coming."

"Baby, just sit on the General and I promise I'll keep my eyes shut."

I take several of Naser's neckties out of the drawer and go sit next to him on the bed. "Now close your eyes. Promise you won't cheat."

He stuffs his face in my cleavage.

I hand him one of the ties. "First your eyes."

He sighs. "Your skin is like cream, love." Reluctantly, he takes the tie from me and draws a tight knot to cover his eyes. Then he inches a hand between my thighs.

"You won't mind if I tie up your hands and legs too?"

He stops. The hand withdraws. He pushes the tie from one eye and gives me a frown. "You've been watching too many movies."

"Not really. I just want you to be all mine tonight. No one else's."

I want to laugh at my own words. They are so ridiculous. But Yadollah doesn't care. He pushes the tie back over the eye and slides down on the bed some more.

"Do what you will to me, love. Just fuck me soon. You want me your prisoner, I'm your man. You want me in chains, you got me. Just do me soon, I'm dying."

He has the hard-on of a true champion. I knew he was a novice at this. I take the rest of Naser's ties and bind the kid's hands and feet to the corners of the bed. Then I fetch the syringe and the massive dose of ketamine I've prepared for him.

"Love, what are you doing? Sit on it already, I'm begging you."

"Wait a bit. I want you good and horny."

"Horny? I'm dying here."

I pull the cover off of him. His dick stands at attention. Whoever circumcised this boy did a fine job of it. That's a luscious prick he has. I take another tie and slide it up and down his dick, massaging it. He's in seventh heaven, biting his lips and squirming with pleasure. I want him in his best moment; I want to freeze his absolutely finest expression when I do to him what I have to do. I keep the syringe in one hand and take the tie off his eyes. He looks like some Jesus close to bliss. He sucks in the air between his teeth and is about to call me "love" again when I push him over to his side, hold him down, and stick the needle right into his ass cheek. He wiggles and shakes to free himself but it's already too late. All I need is a few minutes. He doesn't yell or scream, but tries hard at first to reach the knots tied to his hands and feet. The strangeness of what has happened has muted him. It's as if instinctively he knows that to have a fighting chance he needs to preserve his energy. But it's no use. It's like watching a man slowly go underwater. For a minute he gives it everything he has, at one point shaking the bed so violently that I fear it might come apart. But the animal tranquilizer is working its inevitable magic. The muscles gradually give up on him. And the terror in his eyes becomes complete.

It's too bad. I wanted his eyes to look like he wanted to eat me. He is quite still now. Except his tower of power is still standing as erect as before. Maybe a few more seconds and that thing too will go limp.

I take the packet of cigarettes and his kitschy lighter and sit facing him drinking my gin right out of the bottle. My frozen man. My own marble Jesus.

"Forgive me, this is not personal."

I suspect he can hear everything. His gaze is still on me, fear and longing locked in those eyes in some eternal clash of desire and horror.

"Look, none of this is your fault. Maybe you're wondering why you're frozen like that. I could give you a lecture about it, but I'm long past my nursing school days and can't remember half the whys and hows. I just know what works. In any case, I owe you an explanation, don't I? It's only fair, right? Well, it's like this: What you are experiencing is part of a family reckoning. It's about a husband-and-wife fight. And you just happened to get trapped in the middle of it. I apologize."

I feel the coolness of the bottle of gin between my legs travel the length of my skin. His thingamajig is still standing at attention. I had no idea that even with the drug it could stay up like that. Maybe he downed a whole bunch of Viagra pills beforehand. Now my boy has an eternal hard-on. A marble Jesus with a hard-on that won't quit.

"Don't you just love what I've made of you?"

No answer, of course.

"I don't know when I cooked up this plan. It's not like you

wake up one day and decide to do it. These things take time. They need to percolate through your head a little bit. Then one night . . . I don't know, I couldn't fall asleep, and then it all came to me. Just like one of those murder mysteries. I worked out the whole plan in my head."

I press hard on the gin bottle between my wet legs.

"I have to give it to you, you've got one of the best rods I've ever seen. You could have been a fabulous gigolo once you stopped being a dumb peasant. You wouldn't have had to work the street anymore. All you'd need is one of these horny rich bitches to discover you. She'd give your number to all her friends and you'd be home free. Your phone would ring off the hook. You'd be the king. But boy do I want to watch Naser's face when he sees your dick. You know his own dick is more like spaghetti. When he sticks it in I feel like there's a little lizard paying a visit. It tickles, feels slippery, half dead. But I still have to make all the sounds, you know. He loves my sounds, otherwise he can't even stay hard. As for me, I'm happy to do it once a week. Once a week you open your legs, make a little aah-ooh noise, and the slippery little lizard goes his merry way.

I take another big swig of the gin. I'm feeling it.

"I like the fact you shaved off your pubes. Easier to keep things clean that way. But you have to tell your friends this isn't quite the fashion nowadays; the fashion is to let it grow. Like that faggot boyfriend of mine. I don't know why I'm thinking of him tonight. Maybe it's because of the shape of your dick. Reminds me of his a little bit. Except his was smaller. That faggot! I met him at the university before I became Naser's wife. Those were the days!"

I drink some more.

"What say you we go a round together? I mean, why waste that lovely specimen of manhood that refuses to go down for the count?"

I take out a condom and pull it over his hard-as-rock prick. I'm so wet that as soon as I sit on him the thing pumps right up to my navel. I ride him hard, still with Naser's boots on, and before I know it I've come three or four times. Four times. Let's be precise here. My body feels almost numb and I'm getting sleepy. But tonight's not a night for sleeping; there's a whole lot of work ahead.

I get off of him, grab a garbage bag, and throw away the condom and the syringe. Then I clean his skyscraper and all around the area. Naser won't be here until much later, but I have to finish the job as quickly as possible.

"I know you're a beginner, but you did well. You shouldn't put so much gel on that lovely hair of yours, though. I say let it grow. I'm a sucker for men with long hair. That faggot boyfriend I told you about, he had really long hair. He'd always wrap and hide it under a hat at the university so they wouldn't give him a hard time about it. But when we went to parties together, boy, everyone and their mother wanted to fuck him. Truth is, this whole business started with that piece-of-shit boyfriend. One day he comes to me and says so and so would like to take you out for a date. I look at my faggot boyfriend like the faggot he is and you know what he says? He says, *The guy's head of surgery on campus. He's just an old fart. He'll take you for a nice steak uptown and at most maybe you guys will rub legs under the table. What's the harm in that?* Can you imagine? I wasn't even the guy's student, but apparently he'd seen me through the glass when we were watching him perform an autopsy and he'd gone and asked the faggot about me. I've always wondered what that shit got out of the whole deal."

I take a last shot of my gin and throw that in the garbage bag too and light a cigarette.

"So that's how it all began, with a black Porsche waiting for me one afternoon by the girls' dorms. Naser was always a Porsche man. And seven, eight years ago it wasn't like today; you didn't see a Porsche every day in this town. I smelled the cool scent of expensive cologne when I got in his car. His fingernails were perfectly manicured and he wore a tasteful purple scarf. That night in the restaurant he didn't mince words—he asked if I'd marry him;

he needed a trophy bitch and a couple of kids. And I said yes. I'm thinking if that faggot boyfriend of mine had had any idea, he would have never pimped me to the doctor. And there you have it. That's the whole story. By the way, let's see what your real name is, kid. Let's take a look at your wallet."

His pants are on the floor. A worn black wallet in the back pocket. Inside it some torn-up money and those folded telephone numbers he just collected on Pasdaran. I put the pieces of paper with the numbers on them in my mouth and swallow them. It's an act of exaggeration and I don't mind doing it. His cheap cell phone shows three missed calls. I check the text messages too. Nothing incriminating me. And finally his national ID card: *Hamid Abasqorbani, 22 years old.*

"Boy, you're still just a little chick. But it's good this way. By the time you were thirty you could have had yourself a nice little nest egg for a wife and kids. You'd just have to be careful not to fuck it up and spend too much as you went along. Otherwise you'd have woken up one day and you'd be forty without a pot to piss in."

His balls look odd, one side up and the other down. I imagine his eyes are pleading with me. And so what if they are? I bring my lips close to his ear and whisper, "Naser has serious OCD, you know. He thinks his house has to be sterilized like a surgery room. He attacks the place with every kind of cleaning agent you can imagine. He puts his gloves on and goes to work. And when the kids shower, he stands there like a prison guard making sure they scrub themselves to death. Now, you might look at this stinking place and think I'm just feeding you a bunch of crazy lies. But I'm not. The doctor will come home ready to make the house spotless. But today he'll have a lot more work to do than usual."

I feel for his heartbeat. There's still a trace of something there. I don't want to start until I'm sure he is finished. So I light another cigarette and start blowing smoke rings in his face.

"You like how I make these rings? I learned that at the college dorm. Imagine a girl like me coming from the backwoods is suddenly thrown in this city and has to learn everything from the beginning, and all the while those fucking girls from Tehran with their nose jobs and painted hair are making your life hell. Yes, that's how it was at the start. But then you learn to wax that facial hair and do something about your eyebrows and throw away the damn *chador* at last. You feel like you've been tossed in the middle of some Disneyland and have to negotiate everything for the very first time. Slowly you come around. You fix your hair, tattoo your eyebrows, get the nose job, and learn to down *arrack* like the best of them. It's a lot easier, of course, if you manage to find the right boyfriend. A guy can show you the ropes a lot faster. Me? I had pocketed half the boys in our college by my second year here. I loved strutting around campus after my latest catch while those Tehran bitches gave me the evil eye for stealing their boyfriends. A girl from the village fucking with them like that. They deserved what they had coming to them. I know that you, of all people, can appreciate what I'm talking about."

His hard-on is no more. I get up and feel for his heartbeat a second time.

"Why doesn't your damn heart stop beating? I wanted to make it easy on you, but it's getting late. Hurry up already."

I fetch the gin bottle out of the garbage bag again and take a shot. One last cigarette too. My watch says two fifteen a.m.

"You and me, we have a little bit more time left. But not much. I'm worried about my children, see? The older one is already six years old and he's sharp. He said, *Maman, why do I need to drink cough syrup tonight? I'm not sick.* As for my parents, they're out cold. Ever since they moved to Tehran they have to take sleeping pills. They can't get used to the sound of traffic. Poor things! Alongside my brother, they all came as part of the package. Naser had already done his homework on me. He knew my brother hadn't gotten into college and my parents were just simple people living far from Tehran. He made an offer I couldn't refuse: he'd buy a nice big place for my parents right here in Tehran and he'd take care of my brother too. But you know, after sitting in that Porsche I'd have married him without the package. I'd have married him even if it was Godzilla behind the wheel. He said all he wanted in return was to be left alone on weekends. The weekend nights belonged to him and his friends. Poker night, he said. Poker night my ass. I started to get the picture after a while. Poker is just the excuse. Every weekend, whoever loses the most has to take care of business and pay for the delivery. *What's the delivery?* you ask. Mostly young boys, pretty as peaches. That's their taste. It sickened me. I brought in somebody to install a microphone. But it didn't work. Some of these guys won't go anywhere without their jammers. When I asked the electrician about it, he said, *What can I tell you? The ladies buy microphones from us and their men buy jammers.* But then I had him run a hidden camera that wasn't wireless. Did you know you can only jam wireless? The guy ran wires for me right through the ceiling lights and . . . well, I got some of the most disgusting videos you'll ever see in your life. I've hidden them right here. Naser will never find them. But the police, once they start turning this place upside down, that's a whole other story. Kiss poker night bye-bye."

I glance at my watch.

"Apologies to my marble Jesus, but I have to start now. Can't delay it any longer."

Naser keeps a bagful of surgical tools in the bedroom. Gloves. Knife. And we're off. "I'm truly sorry, young man. Who knows, had we met under different circumstances, some spark might have even come to life between us. Though I doubt it. What is it Christians say? Jesus was crucified for our sins? Well, here you are, aren't you?"

Blood gushes out from the first cut and immediately I feel faint. I take the gin and leave him for a minute. The living room stinks of leftover pizza and half-eaten bowls of yogurt and reeking cheese slices and rotted fruit. I think about all the times Naser would collect this garbage with a long set of pliers. The absurdity of seeing this obsessive-compulsive pedophile wearing surgical gloves and daintily picking up one piece of garbage after another with pliers and putting them in an industrial-size plastic bag. Then taking the bag out the back door, as if he's too ashamed of himself to carry it out the front. But tomorrow—I mean today—how's he going to clean this particular mess?

I force myself to chew on a piece of chocolate. I can't afford to act the part of a spoiled little bitch. I studied nursing for three years, for God's sake. All that blood and gore we had to see every day. So: back to Jesus. A pool of blood has collected around his torso and the sheet is soaked in red. I make for a deeper cut this time. Then I stick my hands through and open him up. The bowel spills out a bit. By now Jesus has lost color. I stick my hand in deeper to get a better grip, but I can't tell where the intestines begin and end. So I just start pulling and walk what I have in my hand across the living room before I cut it all up good. The stench of it. The half-digested lettuce and tomato swimming in a sea of near shit. My boy must have had a sandwich for lunch.

The third cut is a neat cross in the chest area. More blood. The end of the knife hits a rib and gets stuck there. It's handwork from here. I have to dig deep. Be methodical. Just like we were taught in school. Except half these things, I don't know which is which anymore. Liver, spleen, kidneys, gallbladder, out you come. I almost apologize to my Jesus again but then feel silly about it. It's all about quick work from now on. The heart fits nicely in front of the antique candelabra Naser claims his dear grandmama gave him. Dr. Naser Zarafshan of ancient royal blood. So he says. If he's so royal, why would he want to marry a girl from a working-class family? Past eight years I didn't see a single one of his relatives. He says they're all in the US, but I couldn't give two shits if they are on the moon or if they're royal or not. That's right, cut those veins. Spill everything across the house. I make sure the liver graces the face of that Marilyn Monroe. I mean, what kind of fool would have a Marilyn Monroe face woven for him on a carpet?

I rush back to Jesus: "Darling, I did tell you it's just a fight between me and that sick bastard. Yes? I'm sorry you had to get pulled into it. I truly am. But the day I saw him looking funny at his own children when they were taking their daily showers, I knew I'd had enough. And the luck of the draw fell on you. I'll be grateful to you till the end of time. And by the way, don't worry about my getting caught. Won't happen. I've thought of everything. When we're done here, I'll put my jogging suit on, I'll change out of Naser's boots, I'll throw away the Porsche's spare keys in the garbage bag, and I'll stick the bag in the backpack.

"Then out the back and away from here. From the Sadr overpass to the park in Ekhtiyarieh, it's only a half-hour jog. I'll run around the park like always and make sure the guard there sees me. I'll have to dump the pack beforehand, and don't you worry, there's plenty of places for that between here and the park. Some scavenger will have happy hunting; he'll throw away the garbage bag and be on his merry way with the pack in no time. This leaves the most delicate part of our morning. I'll go back to my parents' home and they'll think I've returned from my usual morning jog. The kids will still be sleeping. And I'll start calling Naser. He won't answer. Like I told you earlier, he went straight from the airport to one of his friend's homes for an all-nighter buggering little boys. I know, you're thinking this leaves a few loose ends. But I'm here to tell you otherwise. Say your pals at that paper stand identify you. All they saw was a black Porsche—and everybody knows Dr. Zarafshan doesn't lend his Porsche to anybody, especially his wife. What? How did I drive the car out today without being seen by the neighbors? Good question. I drove it out at five in the morning yesterday when everyone was still asleep. By seven I had left it at a busy garage on Jomhuri near the Friday *bazaar*. There's so much coming and going around there nobody has time to pay attention to you. So I left the car and took a cab back home. I know, I know: there are cameras all over the city. I can't help that. Some things you just have to leave to luck. Luck and careful planning. In any case, no camera is going to get past the Porsche's tinted windows, except when you and I were stuck in traffic in Pasdaran and you were collecting phone numbers from the ladies. And that's okay. It wouldn't have been right to keep you from collecting business, would it? Besides, I figure with all the evidence it'll be such an open-and-shut case that they won't ever get to thinking about cameras.

"Does all this satisfy your unquenchable curiosity? What? Still no? Listen, you really don't have to be worried about Naser's friends; I know these men. They'll have been too wasted by the time he joined them to wonder if he came in his own car or a cab. These guys are all doctors and their sick schedules are in sync. As for my parents, they'll just be waking up by the time I get home. Once the kids are up too, they'll jump into my lap and I'll make them cereal and toast and we'll all sit together in front of the TV watching weekend cartoons. What do you think? Are we in the clear now?"

I take off the gloves and my nightie and throw them in the pack too. Now I'm looking pretty outlandish, standing here naked except for the pair of black gloves I'd kept under the surgical gloves, plus Naser's three-sizes-too-big black boots. I drop down on the couch and suck on my gin bottle. Is this what ecstasy feels like?

All I can do is sit staring at my gutted Jesus for a few minutes more.

"You know what, my love? The best part of it, the absolute most gorgeous moment, is when Naser opens the door and sees all the blood and body parts on his floors. I can just picture it. His mouth hanging open, his knees giving out. By then I will have begun my strategic phone calls to nosy Mrs. Ebtehaj next door. I'll tell her that I can't find Naser and I'm worried. Mrs. Ebtehaj will hurry to our door. It'll be eleven o'clock by then and Naser will be home. Say what? You're asking me how I can be so sure Naser will get home by then? Because he's the famous Dr. Zarafshan. His entire existence is by the book. Even when he sticks a bottle up a little kid's ass, he does it with care. That's right, I have the video on that one too. So no matter what kind of filthy exploit he's been up to on Thursday night, he has to be home by eleven on Friday morning for the rest of the weekend. He needs his coffee, brewed by himself, and he needs to make sure the house is spick-and-span for the week to come. Now just imagine Mrs. Ebtehaj behind that door ringing our bell. Either Naser is so in shock that he automatically opens the door, or he's desperately trying to get rid of every trace of you. Either way, he's finished. Mrs. Ebtehaj is not one to give up. She'll call the fire station, she'll call the police, she'll have the whole neighborhood behind that door wondering what's happened to my husband. How sweet it's going to be! Naser's and his friends' fingerprints all over this place from last week's smut. One morning, when he was in a stupor from the night before, I made sure I got his prints all over the videos too. But today all Dr. Naser Zarafshan will be thinking about when the police bust open the door is that he needs to clean the house, clean his *maman joon's* candelabra and his blood-smeared Marilyn Monroe.

"Sweetness, you're getting on my nerves now with all your questions. Of course no one is going to believe his friends when and if they testify that he was with them all night. Who's going to believe a bunch of pedophiles whose nasty work is all over those videos, videos that Dr. Zarafshan took for his own sick pleasure? Naser's fellow sickos will be lucky if they're not dragged into court themselves. At most they'll say that they were too drunk to notice if Naser left in the middle of their party. Their lawyers and the hospital's lawyers will spend any amount of money to keep things under the radar. So who is to doubt Naser could have picked you, his own little private marble Jesus, on his way home? Or picked you up earlier and left you here, so he could come back and properly butcher you afterward. What's that, you say? Why would Dr. Zarafshan even do this? Oh, don't be so naive, my love; by now everyone will know the famous doctor is a psycho. Even his own colleagues will testify to that, if they testify to anything. They're all major stockholders in the same hospital. Their lawyers might even call me in and promise to turn over all of Naser's stocks to me, no questions asked, as long as I don't open my mouth. That way the hospital's name will never be mentioned in Naser's trial. They'll pay everybody off, including the judge. And all I have to do is look innocent and sad and weep and visit my husband regularly. I'll tell him I'm going to get him a top-notch lawyer. He'll swear it wasn't him who did it and I'll say he was probably so out of it that he doesn't remember anymore. He'll cry and I'll cry. I'll promise him I'll do anything to get them to only give him life without parole and not execute him. I'll get him the best toothbrush money can buy so he can clean every little nook and cranny of his cell. If they allow it, I'll bring him every kind of cleaning agent he asks for. I can just see him, on his hands and knees, scrubbing and scouring every inch of the prison to the end of his days. The great, very, very great Dr. Naser Zarafshan. Indeed, I have to do my best to commute his sentence to only life without parole. I have to spend some serious money on that and get him the best lawyer in Tehran. It's the least I can do for my dear old husband whose Porsche I'll be driving back and forth on my weekly visits to jail."

IN THE FLOPHOUSE

BY FARHAAD HEIDARI GOORAN

Gomrok

I could hear the woman's voice coming from the bottom of the deep pit right in the middle of that traffic circle. A sentry stood over the hole. Some soldier boy with the initials *M.R.* written on his uniform.

"Can't you just throw her a rope and let her climb out?"

He glared at me. "My job's to guard. Nothing else."

His accent said it all. A Kurd from Kermanshah. Hometown kid. I put my own accent in high gear and told him to be a good sport and listen to the advice of a guy from back home.

He glared at me again and barked, "Speak proper Persian and I'll listen to you."

"All right then. Don't you feel anything for her? Look at this hole. She could be hurt. She could be pregnant."

Soldier boy sneered, "Sure, must have been the cat made her pregnant."

I persisted, "But what's she done wrong? Why keep her in there?"

Now soldier boy stepped up and eyeballed me hard. "The Public Decency Patrol and the guys from the Office of Combat Against Corrupt and Immoral Behavior will be around soon. They'll know what to do with the likes of her. Besides, what's it to you? What do *you* do for a living? Huh?"

"I work in textiles and fabrics. I'm an engineer."

He gave me a once-over and zeroed in on my beat-up shoes. "The last thing you look like to me is an engineer."

I might have stood up to him a little more, but he was armed and I saw that he had his trigger finger ready. I didn't like how he was scowling at me either. Suddenly I felt fearful and pulled back from him. There were trees in the middle of the traffic circle. Black trees thick with soot. I leaned against one that had a single crow perched on its branch. The bird kept flapping its wings but didn't make a sound. That woman, though, the one in the pit—she was definitely making a sound. Bawling, I suppose.

I'd only arrived in town that morning at the Azadi terminal. Exhausted and thirsty, I'd gotten the *Help Wanted* ads right away and went to work. No time for stopping to eat or drink. I'd pop into one office after another and fill their job application forms. *Sure, we'll get back to you.* That was mostly what I heard from one faceless human resources manager after another.

By sunset I was half dead and my stomach was sour and hurting from too much lemonade, which was the only thing I'd had all day. It was as if I could see that accursed drink making its way through my intestines. But I still had to get myself to a Coffee Net run by an old college friend of mine. There was one company that had asked for an e-mail attachment of my résumé. They were interested in designs of civilian and military clothes and they also manufactured shrouds for corpses. Your typical semigovernmental company with a hand in everything. I'd found them in a narrow old labyrinth of a building decorated with too many colored lamps. I suppose the lamps were there for Eid e Ghadeer celebrations. And, of course, there was another bearded human resources guy there with a stuffy white shirt and dark glasses sitting behind the desk telling me what I expected to hear: "First you have to give a design sample. Management will take a look at it. Then we might give you a call for an interview."

Their ad had said something about designing a variety of dress gear for wholesalers, and it turned out they weren't exactly particular about what designs you gave them. It was an orgy of designs, really: design for waterproof fabrics, design for black *chadors*, design for towels, design for sofa fabrics, design for velvet and corduroy . . . the list went on and on.

Now then, I happened to have a few designs just for a day like this and I'd stuffed them all in a plastic carry-on. Up until this particular company, the only things I'd been offered were a couple of nowhere jobs by those human resources automatons—job number one, overseeing a city garbage recycling program; job number two, manager of a private funeral home. I wasn't interested. I hadn't gone to school all these years for things of that sort. And I didn't care if I had to walk around until I fell into a manhole like that poor woman.

Or else I could just return to the abandoned village of my father. But no, I was determined to make it right here in Tehran. I just had to keep walking this leviathan of a city until evening came, and then I'd find myself one of those decrepit old guest-houses near the Zakaria Razi Circle and rest for a bit.

Well, old Zakaria was right there, all right. As a statue. The great Persian Zakaria Razi, of the inventor-of-alcohol fame. Mr. Alcohol! And in his honor, they'd laid out empty bottles of booze around the statue itself. Ninety-nine percent pure medicinal and industrial alcohol in yellow and white bottles. To the south of the circle were a string of bicycle shops, and if you followed on down that road you'd eventually get to the main rail terminal. To the north were several secondhand shoe sellers on South Karegar Avenue. These guys had every kind of footwear you could think of, from half-rotted boots of dead soldiers to beaten-up safety boots for factory work. I managed to get me a pair of old boots with a nice recent shine on them. The secondhand dealer told me, "They may have been to war and back, those boots. But I tell you, they're made for walking in Tehran."

I didn't disagree.

Now clad in my "new" boots, I caught a motorcycle cab off Razi Circle to Komeyl Bridge where my old schoolmate's Coffee Net was supposed to be. The motorcab guy was dozing on his bike even as we rode. Poor junkie was a bundle of sniffles and nose drip and was jonesing hard. When I wrapped my hand around his puny waist it was like holding on to a skeleton. But he still got us there in one piece and soon I was standing in front of the Coffee Net.

At first my old friend pretended he didn't believe it was me. "I would have thought you'd be six feet under by now."

The man had always been a bit of a downer, to put it mildly. And I didn't bother asking him what kind of a greeting this was after so long. I just needed one of those computer screens. He didn't even bother asking me what I was doing there and how I'd managed to get his address.

Now he started nagging about times not being so good. "We don't have enough customers," he announced. "Sooner or later the bank's going to take this place over and throw yours truly in jail." He poured us some piss-weak tea from a flask. "So tell me, are you one of these Facebook fanatics now too, or are you still playing around with that damn diary notebook of yours?"

"I still have my diary. But I also got this blog going where I write down everything that comes to my head."

"Like what?"

"Like writing about my old Kurdish village. Remember, I took you there one time? Remember when I showed you one of our Yarsan graveyards, you asked why they had the same words written on all the gravestones?"

"What words were those?"

"*The dead always return.*"

"Quit that talk!" he said with sudden worry on his face. "Or one of these days they'll put a bullet in your head too, and in the heads of all your Kurds—and your Yarsan followers. Do you think I'm kidding? Just the other night they found the body of a girl near our house. Rape. But they left some dumb letter on her to make it seem like she killed herself. You think anyone is going to bother with the truth? You think anyone cares if she killed herself or someone killed her? Allah *a'lam*, only God knows, my friend. Only God!"

I'll admit, he was actually one of those friends you'll miss once in a while. But we lived hundreds of miles apart and didn't much see eye to eye on anything. Besides, his chronic pessimism really got under my skin after a bit. He just never stopped braying about how hopeless everything was.

Now he said, "So, did you ever take care of your military service? Did the powers that be manage to finally pull you under their holy flag?"

"No, I still haven't done my service."

"You want my advice: go serve your time and come back before the next war starts."

"But look at me, I've already reached my midlife crisis. How can I go become a soldier at this point?"

"Then you have to keep dreaming about a passport, or even a simple driver's license, until the day you die. You know they won't give you either until you put in your time." He peered at my ancient but shiny boots and added, "Looks like you'll be searching for a job till you drop dead too."

As soon as I sat down behind one of those shabby computers at the Coffee Net, words started to pour. *Hole in the ground . . . woman . . . Soldier M.R.* I was annoyed at myself for not having had the balls to stick my head in the hole to at least see what the woman's face looked like. I was dedicated to this blog and wanted it to be as true to life as possible. I wanted to describe that woman, but instead had to content myself with a description of her groans. Then I described soldier boy. *His dark skin, his hawkish nose. Soldier M.R.* You could see he'd written the letters himself with a black magic marker on the pocket of his green uniform.

I spent a good two pages describing the Public Decency squads roaming the streets. I was scared of them. Scared shitless, to be honest. What if I could be a real writer and describe these kinds of feelings? What if I didn't have to limit myself to just a notebook of diaries?

I wrote in the blog:

The woman squashed a fourth cockroach and threw it out the window. The smog blanketed the city from here all the way to the Elburz Mountains. "What a city!" she muttered to herself. "The south side scorches the earth, the north side snuffs out the sky."

Now she went and stood in front of the mirror and got her lipstick out. Next she put on some rouge and fixed her ponytail. Then, before she knew it, she'd put on a pair of high heels, a bright wrinkled headscarf, and a low-cut manteau and was heading outside. The door to the flophouse smelled of urine. She walked past Razi's statue and went and stood on the other side of the traffic circle. Lights flickered every which way and the monstrous sound of the garbage truck deafened her ears. She watched the men collecting the garbage. "Poor guys!"

A rundown white Paykan stopped at her feet. The guy stuck his head out the window and spoke through the cigarette in his mouth. "Where to at this time of night, missy?"

"Nowhere."

The cigarette fell from the man's mouth. "If you want a better-model car to pick you up, best move uptown," the man sneered. "I'll take you uptown myself and drop you off in a profitable corner if you like."

"Mind your own business. I've come to get some fresh air, all right?" She had to laugh at her words—getting some fresh air next to all that garbage!

The car rolled out and she could hear the man's voice saying something about her ankles looking like marble.

The sanitation department men showed her where the park was and a street cat seemed to want to lead her in that general direction too. It turned out to be a small park with some old spruce trees and a few sorry-looking pines. There were several metal benches around a small empty pool. The cat sprang into the pool and meowed.

She spoke to it, "Are you a boy or a girl?"

The cat continued to meow. She went and sat on one of the benches. Somewhere nearby a voice was saying, "You'll get so high in a minute you'll be crawling on the ground." After a while the same voice added, "The Public Decency patrols be damned!"

The cat had come closer to her and was waving its tail.

She spoke to it again, "I asked are you a boy or a girl?"

A different voice answered, "The cat's a eunuch, miss." He was a tall cop with a baton in hand. "What are you doing here this time of night?"

"Sitting down."

"Your identity card?"

"I left it at the desk in the guesthouse."

"Go back home. Now!"

"Home? You mean the guesthouse?"

"Whatever shithole you belong to, return there now. Don't linger."

"But I came outside to get some air."

She was bleeding a lot today and could see the cop's eyes following the trail of her blood trickling from her crotch down to her ankles and onto her high heels.

She stood up and shuffled back in the same direction she'd come. The cat followed her each step of the way. "What? Looks like you're as lonely as I am. How about you remain my guest tonight?" She picked up the hairy animal and planted a kiss on its nose before climbing up the stairs of the flophouse.

After finishing with the blog, I sent out my résumé and left the Coffee Net without bothering to say goodbye. The street off of Komeyl Boulevard was mostly military. One side of it was housing for army personnel and the other was a sprawling barracks protected with a double row of barbed wire. On the walls, as far as the eye could see, they'd painted pictures of war martyrs. Martyrs and their words of wisdom before they went happily to their deaths.

I kept on walking till I was back at Razi Circle. No sign of that soldier who had been guarding the hole. No sign of the woman and her moans and groans either.

It was time. I ended up at an old flophouse nearby. You could tell the building went back a ways. It was not one of these cardboard-box affairs they built these days. Its brick facade and latticed windows definitely set it apart from all its surroundings. I got to chatting with the desk clerk, thinking he might give me a discount on the room. I told him about my job hunt and some of the ridiculous ads they'd put in the paper that day. I told him a story about Qazvin Gate, one of the original twelve city gates of old Tehran, and how in the last century they used to have a guy sitting at it all the time, writing up the funeral processions that passed through so they would be reported to the royal court.

"Qazvin Gate was right around here," he concurred. "Now it's lost, like everything else. Probably hidden inside the belly of the central train station or somewhere like that."

He looked fifty but was younger. Good-natured and fat. Kind of guy you like right away. He was also baby-ass bald and kept scratching his head with all ten fingers. I think he could tell I was feeling low, because right away he added, "Don't you worry about a thing here, friend. Our guesthouse is a safe place for everybody. They come here from all over the country. Soldiers. Officers. Laborers. Office workers. College students. And another thing, all our rooms have a study desk. Yes. I'll take care of you. Count on it."

Out the window of the lobby my eyes fell on a pair of ravens. I asked, "Is there a chance a man could get a real drink around here?"

"Don't even think about booze in these parts. If they catch you, it's seventy lashes of the whip. Then they'll just throw you in the slammer with the drug addicts and alcoholics." He pointed with his index finger. "Their detention center is right around the corner behind the railway station."

* * *

It was stifling hot that night and the cockroaches wouldn't leave me alone. From the room to my left I could hear the sound of someone working a sewing machine. Several times I thought to peep through the keyhole to see who it was. Though I already knew it was just another poor Afghan with a tall order of funeral shrouds he had to finish. The desk clerk, being helpful, had volunteered, "There's an Afghani in one of the rooms next to yours. The guy sews night and day. If he makes too much noise with that sewing machine of his, let me know and I'll shut his electricity off."

The lights to the room on the other side of me were already off. But I could hear heavy breathing in there. After a while I couldn't take it anymore and went and looked through the keyhole. It was dark. Still, I could just barely make out a pair of bodies enmeshed in each other rolling around on the bed. Maybe I was dreaming this. No, I wasn't. I'd simply fallen into the chasm of my own thoughts and there was no way out of it. I was picturing myself walking the streets of this endless city, newspaper in hand, looking for work that wasn't there. I was a textiles designer and a man who was still dodging his military service after all these years. If only I'd finished those twenty-seven months of compulsory army duty and gotten them out of the way when I was younger! But it was wartime back then. And if they saw so much as a hint of fuzz over your lips, you were sent in for a quick boot camp and then off to the front lines.

Even so, I really should have turned myself in the day they showed up at our farm. Didn't matter how afraid I was. Hadn't I seen enough corpses already? Every day they'd haul in more dead soldiers and bury them in our village. I thought of that soldier at the pit in Razi Circle; him too—they would have delivered his corpse during that decade of never-ending war.

Now this black hole of what-ifs was driving me up the wall. This was just the first night here. How many more nights could I last like this? What was I supposed to do during daytime? How many more job ads should I answer? What if I returned empty-handed back to our village and faced the wandering ghosts of the dead in those deserted fields? My father used to always say, "Don't go wandering, son. Nest the bird of your dreams in your own house. Even if it's a house you don't yet possess." That was his refrain: "Seize the day. Don't let time slip away."

But the only thing I had left was time, time to let everything slide by. Maybe I could go get a job in that other sweatshop I'd visited today. The one with the four Afghans in it. Three men, one woman. All of them in a trance with the work of spool and thread and needle, and those sewing machine pedals with the interminable din they made. Those Afghans too were working around the clock making corpse shrouds. For some reason seeing all that white cloth on special order for the dead had made me dizzy and I'd gagged. Which then inspired the sweatshop boss to try to revive me with a nasty concoction of lemonade.

The guy had had an awful stutter. "You are an engineer. A d-designer. You know s-something about t-textiles and the rules of b-burial, I hope, yes?"

"No."

"Look! M-Muslims need to be buried with v-various cloths. A *l-long* and a shirt. The *long* has to cover from b-belly button to the knee of the corpse. And it's b-better from ch-chest to the feet that you—"

I cut in, "But my proposed design does not go with—"

He didn't want to hear what I had to say and kept stuttering away, "Sh-shirt must cover whole body. Long enough to m-make a kn-knot down there . . ."

I was getting ready to gag again listening to him go on like that. And may God bless the ancestors of one of the Afghan tailors who caught a finger in a sewing machine just then and began screaming. The boss turned to the Afghan and I got out of there with quickness—far away from that moldy basement filled to the brim with reels upon reels of yarn and fabric for the dead.

My bed! It stunk of industrial alcohol and there were drops of dried blood all over the sheets. *The bird of your dreams*, my father had said. If he could see me now. I started to imagine I was leaving the city from the old Qazvin Gate when my friend the Coffee Net owner suddenly showed up in my head: "Come with me."

"Where to?"

"Office of the main cemetery at Behesht e Zahra."

I pictured him walking ahead of me a few steps, emptying some kind of liquor into his gullet like there was no tomorrow. "On a night like this, it wouldn't do *not* to get shit-faced drunk. We need to forget the world, my friend." He had turned and was staring at the pair of old soldier's boots I'd just bought—the very boots that had gone to war but ended up in the Gomrok District today. We were standing now in front of an enormous building somewhere south of the city. "Listen, this is the place where they keep the fanciest machines for finding missing corpses. You know, the same ones they used during the war to find dead soldiers. Go look in their files; maybe you'll find your own name there."

I imagined us entering the building and going up the escalators. There was a room full of ledgers and metal filing cabinets. The wind blew hard out the window.

"That's right, friend, all of our names are here. Me, you, everyone."

Enough daydreaming!

I rolled off that stinking bed and splashed some cold water to my face in the bathroom. Surprisingly, there was actually an imported bar of soap on the sink. Made-to-order for a quick jerk-off. I threw the soap out the window. Then my eyes fell on a picture someone had taped to the bathroom mirror. It was Marion Crane in the movie *Psycho*. No doubt this was the doing of some penniless film school graduate who had come to the city looking for work and ended up here like me.

The guy had wanted to be remembered.

Out of boredom I killed a few more cockroaches with my sandal. There were train whistles from the near distance. My stomach hurt from all that gas trapped in my belly. Back in the bathroom the bidet had a screw loose and as soon as I turned it on, water hit the ceiling. It wouldn't turn off, so I left it as best I could and returned to the room.

I peered through that keyhole again.

Soldier M.R. from down the road. There was a reddish light in there now and I could see him plainly on that bed. He was holding onto a woman's body beneath him. The woman's eyes were open.

I don't know how I fell asleep, but I did. And I was immediately back in my diary again. I was back to that woman. I seemed to have decided to name her "Sheen," as in the letter Sh.

Then I woke back up and glued myself to the keyhole once more. I was trembling. First there was Soldier M.R. Then there were others. Or at least I imagined there were others and they were pouring alcohol on the woman's nude body. I was sure I saw everyone. Even the unmistakable hands of the desk clerk who at one point had begun to tie a corpse shroud on the belly button of the dead body. I thought I even saw the sweatshop manager: him of the stutter and the white shrouds. His words were still in my head—*For a M-Muslim, you have to co-cover everything. Kn-knees. B-Breasts.* Then there was my friend the Coffee Net owner—*Listen, brother, in this insane city, who knows what's real and what's not. Who's dead and who's not. Where's that thin line between life and death? You know, they've taken her corpse to the medical examiner's office. They've confirmed it was rape. They're still looking for the killer . . .*

I slept.

In the morning I woke up to police sirens and ambulance alarms. I ran to the window. Several uniforms were leading Soldier M.R. and the desk clerk out of the building and throwing them in the back of a police car. Next they brought the woman's corpse on a gurney and placed it in the ambulance. I was running a fever and my face was drenched in sweat. In a few minutes the uniforms would be searching the rest of the building and they'd start asking questions. They would knock on my door. They'd want fingerprints and signatures from everyone. Maybe they'd call me in as a witness. Whatever was going to happen, I must get rid of this notebook. That was the first thing I had to do, throw away the diary. I had to dump it somewhere far, far away. Somewhere behind the old Qazvin Gate where no one would think twice to look for it for a thousand and one wretched eons.

A STONING BEFORE BREAKFAST

BY AZARDOKHT BAHRAMI

Salehabad

Afterward, people would argue with me that it had been more than twenty years since they stoned anyone to death in Tehran. Sure, it still happened in the provinces now and then; they still stoned adulterers in places far from the capital, far from this cultured and sophisticated metropolis that we live in. You would read about a man or woman wrapped in a tall sack and placed in a hole dug in the ground. Then they'd cover their heads and invite the neighborhood to gather and stone them—smash them from a designated distance until they were good and dead. Yes, I know all about the laws of stoning. I have studied the subject. But I'm here to ask you two things: One, does it really matter if this particular stoning took place twenty years ago or last week? And does it really make a difference if it took place in the middle of Tehran or a hundred miles away?

It doesn't.

They stoned my Elika.

And they did it right here.

And this is how it happened:

A young man is shouting in the crowd: "Kill that piece of dirt!" But folks just stare at each other and then glance away. In the last half hour a good forty or so people have gathered to form a semicircle around her.

One of the women asks out loud why they haven't covered her face. She insists that this is the law. It's as if she's some kind of Minister of Stoning. Again she asks why they brought her here wearing a white shroud. Shouldn't she be placed in the usual sack-cloth? Shouldn't her hands be inside the hole as well? Again, no one answers her questions. And after a while the woman retreats and walks away from there, mumbling under her breath and disappointed in this flawed carrying-out of a stoning so early in the morning.

I see Elika's lips moving. She's talking to herself. Quietly. She must be exhausted. Maybe she's still hoping, as I am, that Liza will arrive. Liza will. But it won't change a thing.

Now another stoning expert, a second woman, wonders why Elika's hair is still wet. It shows through the white headdress they've put on her.

An old woman in a black *chador* whispers next to me, "You know, before putting them in the hole they are supposed to wash them. I'm sure that's the law. They must wash them with cedar powder and camphor." Then she gestures to the woman who's been wondering about Elika's wet hair and adds in a mocking voice, "Well, they haven't brought a hair dryer to blow-dry her hair, have they?"

A young man picks up a couple pieces of rock and throws one of them at Elika. It doesn't hit her. Immediately one of the two officers runs up to the man and says something in his ear. Then he points to *haj agha* and the young man nods and takes a step back and drops the other piece of stone and waits.

Elika scans the crowd. I'm sure she's looking for Liza. Liza had visited her a few months ago back in jail and sworn she'd find the girl. If she did, we don't know about it. Because we haven't seen Liza since then.

Now a sharp voice from behind me asks what we are waiting for. "Let's finish her already."

Another woman joins in, "May you fry in hell for making sinners out of our men."

An old woman adds, "May you fry twice in hell."

A couple of people laugh at this. But most say nothing.

Her back must be in pain. Or maybe it's itching like mad. She'd always be scratching herself whenever we left the house to-gether. She'd laugh and joke that it was all these Islamic clothes that she was allergic to. I wish I could go up to that hole and somehow scratch her back for her and take a look at her wounds. We would always take turns scratching each other while making howling noises like dogs. We'd usually do that on the big sofa. The same big sofa all four of us used for our customers. Kati didn't like the job all that much. She'd say she wished the men would hurry up, fuck, and leave. But Elika said that wasn't fair. Some of the men were truly attentive to us. We had to appreciate them. She'd insist that there were customers and then there were *customers*. In the mornings we'd meet at the infamous sofa and laugh at the stu-pid things the men had done the previous evening. The nervous types. The ones afraid of their wives. The ones who couldn't keep it erect. The list was as long as the neighborhood.

The court had judged that she should also be lashed a hun-dred times. I wish I knew when they did that. Does she still have the gashes on her back? I wish somebody would just pick up a couple of huge rocks and quickly finish her off.

Sixty or seventy people are here now, all of them with one eye on *haj agha* and that man from the prosecutor's office. But *haj agha* is in no hurry. Maybe he's waiting for more people to show up. Maybe he wants the entire fourteen million people of Tehran to come here at the northernmost point of Khorsandi Street in the Western Salehabad District. When he first showed up in the morning he gave us a long speech. Something about the law and religion and keeping the foundations of the family strong. And so this devout crowd has gathered near the intersection of Tond-guyan and Azadegan freeways to make the foundations of their families strong. Families who mostly make their living off the drug business and whose daughters disappear from their homes before they're fourteen and, if they're very lucky, end up selling them-selves to high-rolling Arab sheikhs down south in the Persian Gulf.

I wonder who those little kids are. They are too young to know what they're here for. Maybe they've just come along for the show with their fathers. There are also several young men whom I've never seen before in these parts. It's as if they've come for a party. They wear expensive jeans and spotless shoes. *Haj agha's* special ass-kissers. They've picked up the largest stones they could find and are ready to go. I guess they weren't here when *haj agha* gave another lecture about the lawful size of the stones. They're not supposed to be bigger than a walnut. It's these guys I count on. I'm hoping they'll start and finish the job as fast as possible. Smaller stones will just prolong the torment.

Well, it looks like *haj agha* has finally given his go-ahead. He gestures to the man from the prosecutor's office who in turn tells the uniforms to get out of the way. Next, he sends out a loud *salevat* and the crowd repeats after him. It's time. Suddenly there's fresh, pulsating energy in the crowd. Three stones simultaneously fly at Elika. None hit her though. Everybody turns to see who threw them. In court they'd said that the witnesses who testified against her should go first, then the rest of the crowd could follow.

The fourth stone finally hits Elika square in the forehead. There's blood now between her eyebrows. Elika barely bats an eye. Her gaze remains on the women and men facing her.

I know what she's thinking: she's hoping that Liza won't show up, after all. The stoning has begun and it's too late now to try to save her. You see, the video that doomed Elika had nothing to do with the woman in that hole. That wasn't Elika in the video. The couple in the porn scene had both worn masks. So it is only they who can prove the woman was not Elika. But how would they know what their little film has accomplished? And even if they knew, why should they come forward? So that they can take Elika's place? I don't think so! Liza promised she'd move mountains to find that couple and bring them in to testify. But we already knew that was just wishful thinking.

And by now I'm sure all Elika wants is for this to be over.

It's also what I want.

The crowd's aim is getting better. A small rock hits her left ear. Another smacks her shoulder. The law says if the condemned can pull herself out of the hole she'll be set free. It's exactly the same thing when they hang a man and the rope doesn't hold: they have to let him go. I'm sure she could pull herself out if she tried hard enough. She'd blossom then like a fresh plant growing out of the earth. Like her very own name, in fact. I'll never forget the time we were all sitting in the park smoking when she finally told us what her name really meant. *Elika, the Mother of the Earth.*

Elika, rooting out of the ground.

Most of the men's hands are shaking. They can't meet each other's eyes. A lot of them did not want to be here, I'm sure. But they had to show their faces for the sake of *haj agha.* They had to prove to each other they're pious men. They can barely look Elika's way though. Which is why most of their stones don't meet the target.

Yet the stones get bigger. One of them eventually hits Elika's hand with such force that you can hear the wrist bone cracking. It's the same wrist that always held her expensive gold bracelet. She'd given it to me that day when *haj agha's* men came for her. "Take it. I don't want it to fall in their hands." Then she'd called Kati and handed over her ring too, the ring Ali *agha* had given her. She knew how much Kati loved that ring, and of course Kati loved that ring because she loved Ali *agha,* our neighborhood carpenter. But the man was all work and no play. We'd made a bet on him. Kati insisted there was not a man on earth who would stay faithful for long. Except maybe the prophet Adam, and that was only because in his particular sad case there wasn't a second option. And so Kati had tried every trick in the book, but Ali *agha* wouldn't take the bait. Until finally Elika invited him one day to the house to take a look at our "broken" dining table.

There's a little kid who can barely stay in his skin from excitement. His stone lands on Elika's forehead, again. More blood.

Elika's hands don't move to protect her face. That woman was right: those hands should not even be outside of the hole. Why are they? This is a stoning performed incompetently. Nothing's been done right. They seem unable to kill her with a measure of efficiency and compassion.

I look everywhere to see if Ali *agha* has shown up. He hasn't. After that first time with Elika, he came around several more times. And every time with a different excuse—he'd forgotten his measuring tape, he had to sand the table leg a little bit more, he had to make sure the whole thing was steady. And he left more money afterward. Liza quipped that he'd probably consulted with the other men in the neighborhood and found out we only gave discounts the first time around. Kati didn't like any jokes about Ali *agha* though. One time she'd taken the money he'd left for Elika and tenderly rubbed it on her own eyes before giving it back to her: "You've worked hard for it, love. Enjoy."

Elika's eyes are tired. No one's hit them yet. Bull's-eye. The smaller kids are mostly hanging around Taher. They point to their fathers' hopeless pitches and laugh. Taher really grew this past year. It was his stone hitting our door that warned us they were coming for Elika. Now this other stone he throws today only scrapes Elika's ear. One stone for another; we're even now. I remember the first time Elika noticed Taher outside our house. It was a mourning day for some imam. Black flags all over the neighborhood. Elika was standing out there waiting for a bike messenger to arrive as Taher passed by. I was inside watching them through the window and failing at studying for my end-of-term college exams. Elika said something, and I saw Taher's eyes zero in on her painted toenails. The good thing about sixteen-to-seventeen-year-old boys was they finished fast and took off running. We loved their innocence. We'd do them for free and charge their fathers twice as much. I remember thinking back then how Elika could really teach Taher a few things. Things *agha* Nosrat, Taher's dad, could never teach him. *Agha* Nosrat himself came to us at least once a month. And his wife, who knew us only as college students from the provinces, brought us *aash* sometimes. Elika loved her cooking and would run her tongue all over the bowl till the last bit of food was gone. Kati always laughed at that: "If she only knew what else that belongs to her you've sucked on, she'd strangle you with those huge hands of hers."

Now Taher lays a hand on his father and says something to him. Reluctantly, *agha* Nosrat bends down to pick up a stone. He examines it carefully, probably trying to make sure there are no sharp edges to it. He looks weary and frustrated. He puts little into throwing the rock and it lands far from Elika. Taher lowers his head and begins walking away. *Agha* Nosrat goes up to *haj agha* and bids him goodbye before following his son. Father and son look like a couple with bad hangovers. They can hardly walk straight as they disappear from sight.

I notice a newcomer to the scene and immediately know it's Liza. She's wearing an expensive-looking *chador* and trying not to be noticed. But how could I not know it's her? I can even tell that under the *chador* her body is shaking and she's weeping. No, she was not able to find the witnesses; she could not save Elika. Whatever made her think she could? I turn my attention back to Elika. There seems to be a pause in the stone-throwing. The scarf over her head is sticky with blood and she looks like she might pass out. But then she too notices Liza and suddenly straightens her neck and opens her eyes wide, as if to show Liza she should not be afraid.

Could it be that the austere *haj agha* is having second thoughts? Now he's decided to remind everyone that the law says the condemned can save herself and be pardoned if she can climb out. But why would Elika want a pardon? So she can go back to that same husband, Sayan, who disappeared on her eight years ago and only sent his friends back now to testify against her as an adulterer? The second time they'd met, Elika told us, he'd taken her to the rooftop of his place and pretended he needed a hand to help fix their air conditioner. One thing led to another and by the time Sayan's mother and sister caught them up there, it was too late to put their clothes back on. Sayan's mother had smiled a big smile and said something ridiculous about how boys would always be boys and this was quite all right in her book. The way Elika described it, *maman joon* seemed so proud of her son just then she looked like she might make a grab for his thing and give it a big kiss for good measure.

One of the men in the back of the crowd addresses *haj agha*. He's asking a question, but *haj agha* hasn't heard him. So he repeats the question. Something about the number of stones that the law allows the crowd to use. *Haj agha* picks up the microphone and gives another one of his little lectures—he tells us there's no definite agreement about the number of stones. Some say they should be limited, others say people should use as many as needed to finish off the condemned. Saying this, *haj agha* finally picks up a piece of rock himself. He's cool and patient and seems to be saying a quiet prayer before he hurls the rock. It hits Elika on her ear. The energy level of the crowd immediately goes up a couple of notches. Others gather up more rocks and start throwing with renewed vigor.

The women don't throw anything. But the kids have made a sport out of it by now. They're taking bets amongst themselves and goading each other. And there's that one little kid who never misses. One of his tosses breaks Elika's nose. The kid does a little dance with that hit. It's like he's discovering himself for the very first time.

Elika, or what's left of her, takes her eyes off Liza and throws me a desperate glance. What is it she wants to tell me? That she's afraid even at this late stage someone might arrive to stop all this before it's over? That had been the curse of her marriage too—an untimely arrival. Back then Sayan had already disappeared from her life for nine months, then suddenly one day he reappears and insists they finally get married. I figure every woman has to try to turn a new page at least once in her life. And that one time for Elika was Sayan's marriage offer. Within half a year he had gone through all her savings, and after six months he disappeared from her life altogether. Only to reappear eight years later with a porn film and false witnesses.

That kid won't quit throwing one stone after another. He has a nearly perfect score. I can barely see Elika's face now. It looks like some strange fruit swelling out of the earth and surrounded by buzzing flies that can't get enough of the blood caking the dirt around it. The neighborhood crowd pulls back. Even those guys who are not from around here have stopped and are amusing themselves by taking pictures with their cell phones.

She always did want to be surrounded by people who couldn't stop taking pictures of her. She said a day would come when she'd be a supermodel and she'd take care of us, her best friends, her sisters. She ate little, always mindful of her figure. And sometimes in the house she did a catwalk for us, pretending to throw flowers to her fans and signing autographs. She never got tired of this and we never got tired of laughing with her when she strutted up and down the hall waving at all the invisible admirers.

The *click-clicks* of an orchestra of cell phones taking her picture continues. Elika has finally gotten her wish.

That same kid hasn't stopped, and catches a piece of rock smack on Elika's mouth. Her head is thrown back from the impact. This boy's a natural. They should bring him to every stoning within driving distance.

Her face is grisly now. And when she turns a bit to try to smile at me, I notice that there's a wide gap in her bloody mouth. Her front teeth are all broken. I glance Liza's way but she's no longer there. I don't blame her for leaving. I intend to stay, though, right to the end of it. As for Kati, she had said there was no way she could be a witness to this.

Haj agha has also sent word that there is no point in me and Kati and Liza staying in Salehabad after this.

But look at that kid throw! Such courage. He's run out of stones and now he does something that quiets the crowd: he starts walking toward Elika. *Haj agha* raises a hand telling the crowd not to throw anything. A voice calls to the boy and asks him where he thinks he's going. But the kid continues on, as if in a trance. Around Elika there is a heap of stones of all shapes and sizes, many of them wet with her blood. Her head looks like a puppet's now; it's slack and wobbly, her face an obscene veil of blood through which she still seems to see. Because now something like a grin comes over her and her crushed fingers move slightly and point at the biggest stone near her face. The boy picks it up to examine it but immediately throws it away. The thing is all bloody. He retreats a bit and then comes closer again; he sits on his haunches and stares at Elika. It is as if a toy of his had suddenly done something odd. Elika's grin is gone. She waits, only half conscious. The boy selects the stones he wants, taking only dry ones. He carries a bellyful of them in his upturned shirt and goes back to where he'd been standing. He lays the stones at his feet, then glancing up at Elika he chooses the biggest one he can find, spits on it, and gets ready to throw. Elika raises her head as best as she can. She's ready. They both are.

The kid's arm goes back. But at that moment a man slaps the stone out of his hand with such force that the thing rolls away to where *haj agha* is standing. The man delivers another hard slap at the boy's neck and, pinching his ears, drags him away from there. The crowd watches them leave, first with awe and then disappointment. It's as if with the boy's leaving their last hope is gone and now they have no idea what to do next. Everyone looks at one another in confusion. No one knows what to do. So no one does anything.

The wind has picked up and there is an odd smell in the air. No more stones are being thrown. Life has gone out of this crowd. Maybe they're all just waiting for the job to be done so they can complete the prayer for the dead behind *haj agha* and get away.

Maybe they're just tired and hungry. Most of them had shown up here right after the morning prayer. They haven't even had breakfast. The merchants must be itching to get to the local teahouse for their usual morning fare of bread, eggs, and tea before opening shop and beginning the day fresh. But nobody seems to want to be the one who throws the last rock.

What's left of Elika is turned my way. I cannot see her eyes anymore but I know what she's asking. She's lost hope that the people of Salehabad will finish this. Why won't someone in this crowd do something—one of these upstanding citizens who is determined to keep the foundations of his family and religion strong? Why doesn't someone try to prove to *haj agha* how manly and devout he is? Why doesn't someone, anyone, accept the last pitch?

I bend down and pick up the biggest piece of rock I can find. It's huge, way bigger than what the law allows. I have a sure aim. And I never miss when it really, really matters most.

PART IV

THE EXECUTIONER'S SONG

BRIDGE OF SIMON

BY YOURIK KARIM-MASIHI

Narmak

The people of Narmak and Zarkesh were wary of the canal that passed through their neighborhoods. Especially after that year when rains caused the waterline to come up a good two meters. That was the year Rafik's brother fell in and they eventually located his body dozens of miles away south of Tehran. Rafik's older brother had been a handsome young man. Handsome and smart. Which was all the more strange that he should have acted so rashly at the treacherous canal. He'd seen his girlfriend coming his way from the other end of the Bridge of Simon and tried to show off for her by hanging from the outside railings. Needless to say, he never got to her.

From then on Rafik's father refused to set eyes on the canal and that accursed bridge. He'd plead with his younger son to do the same. But Rafik wouldn't hear of it. This was absurd. The Bridge of Simon was the fastest, easiest way for him to get to the Narmak quarter where his cousin Edvin and their best friend Kamran lived.

Still, there was something about that canal, like a border of some sort. On one end of it were the people of Narmak, with a sizable population of Armenian Christians like Rafik's cousin Edvin. Narmak was also a much better-looking neighborhood than Zarkesh. But Zarkesh could boast that to be from there meant your word was your honor; a guy from Zarkesh never betrayed a partner. For the three friends, though, all this was just a lot of empty words. They were inseparable. And now that summer was coming to an end and there was nothing much to do but wait for another school year, they were more inseparable than ever.

One of those late-summer mornings Rafik started out as usual to meet his friends. The previous day, Edvin's father had gone on and on about all the improvements they'd done on Intersection 62 in Narmak and how you couldn't compare it with anything else in the quarter. So the three boys finally decided to see what all the fuss was about.

But rain was coming down hard that morning. For a minute Rafik hesitated. Then he just pulled his rain hoodie on tight and headed toward the Bridge of Simon. He hadn't gone far when to the left of the canal the flashing lights of several police cars caught his attention. They were all parked in front of a house with its front door open. Uniforms came and went. Something had happened there. It was wet and windy and nobody paid Rafik any mind as he made his way toward the place. Soon he was hanging about one of the windows to the house when a policeman stuck his head out and started shouting.

"Officer Ahmadi! Get over here on the double. This one's a mess. I need you."

The cop disappeared inside. Rafik stepped closer to the window. At first he could only see people standing and talking. Then, when a couple of them shifted around, he saw something on the floor that he couldn't quite make out right away. He rubbed his face to get the rain out of his eyes.

That thing inside was a body.

The lone body of a woman folded over a single stair, or more like a raised platform dividing two of the rooms. Her disheveled black hair covered most of the step, but you could still see the bloodstain next to her head. Rafik took a step back, his mouth agape. He felt a chill in his body. That same moment he saw the policeman who had been calling for Officer Ahmadi storming back to the window.

"What are you doing here, boy? You belong to this house? If

you don't belong here, get going. *Yallah*, get going right now!"

Rafik ran. But not to Edvin and Kamran. He ran all the way home.

The next day he tried again. His mind was only on one thing: 12 + 1. He didn't know at what point yesterday he had noticed the house number to the dead woman's place. It was like someone was playing a joke on the neighborhood. Thirteen! Why that unlucky number? So unlucky that the municipality let you use 12 + 1 on your door instead. Curiosity impelled him back to the place. The door was closed today. But when he peered through that window he could still clearly see the bloodstain. No one had bothered to clean it up.

"Don't let the oil get on you, boy!"

Rafik glanced around to see the door-to-door oil vendor pushing his decrepit little cart past the house. From across the street people were watching them curiously.

Rafik started running again.

Of course, neither Edvin nor Kamran believed him when he told them the story. They imagined he'd just gotten lazy yesterday and didn't want to get wet in the rain. But Rafik insisted.

"So, let's go see it then."

"I don't ever want to see that thing again."

"A dried pool of blood can't hurt you."

"But if you'd seen the dead body . . ."

So they ended up with their original plan to visit Intersection 62. And it turned out to be true what Edvin's father had said: the thoroughfare looked really good, like someone had taken high-quality paint to the facades of all the buildings and planted fresh trees along the boulevard. That day Rafik listened to his friends go on about how nice that intersection had become. But his mind was not with it and he said almost nothing until they pressed him.

"Yes, it's pretty here. I haven't seen anything so pretty in a long time."

* * *

From then on Rafik made it a point to avoid the 12 + 1 house as much as he could. Some time passed and the next occasion he found himself on that street, he saw that the place was already being worked on. There were laborers there instead of police this time around. And when he went and peeked through the window he saw that they'd laid new tiles on the floor and painted the walls. Soon somebody else would be living there and they'd have no idea of the house's past.

More than a year went by. A lot of Christians were moving abroad, especially to America. And one day Edvin told Rafik and Kamran that his family's papers were ready and they would be moving too.

Then Edvin was gone. Just like that. And with him leaving, neither Rafik nor Kamran had the heart to bring anyone else to replace him. But their own friendship grew tighter. And as the years passed, so did their fixation on a neighborhood girl called Hengameh. The curious thing about Hengameh was that she too lived in a 12 + 1 house, though on a different block. Rafik tried to put that little fact about Hengameh out of his mind. But there was another thing: in the fifteen years since Edvin's leaving, not once did he or Kamran work up the courage to say two words to the girl. Then at some point Hengameh's brother was sent abroad too and her parents followed. This left only Hengameh, who had recently gotten married. She took the bottom floor of the 12 + 1 house and had tenants living on the top floor.

Before long, Hengameh got tired of her famously lazy husband and sent him packing from that house. She had studied management in college, but her heart was in photography and soon she started taking it seriously enough to be able to make some money from it. She came and went, seeming to pay little attention to anyone or to the vicious rumor mill of the neighborhood about a beautiful divorcée. She was her own woman now. Which made Rafik and Kamran more crazy about her than they'd been when they were all teenagers. They imagined her firm yet deliciously ample body, with that long, flowing black hair they recalled from before she was old enough to have to wear a headscarf. When they were not working, the two of them would sit hours at a time at the same old traffic circle she passed through every day. She'd become their habit. A habit they could never get close to. With that perennial shoulder bag and camera dangling from her side, she seemed to them like a character from the classic foreign movies they were both addicted to.

Kamran had his own ideas about which characters Hengameh reminded him of:

"She laughs like Anouk Aimée in *La Dolce Vita*."

"She walks like Elizabeth Taylor in *Cat on a Hot Tin Roof*."

"She moves her head like Rita Hayworth in *Gilda*."

"Her glances are like Brigitte Bardot's in *And God Created Woman*."

"Her seduction is like Marilyn Monroe's in *Some Like It Hot*."

"The way she traps men is like Vivien Leigh in *Gone with the Wind*."

Of course, Rafik saw Hengameh in a completely different, much softer light. And he'd say things like:

"No, she's more like Greta Garbo in *Ninotchka* when she laughs."

"Grace Kelly in *Mogambo* when she sits."

"Audrey Hepburn in *Roman Holiday* the way she holds her bag."

"Kim Novak in *Vertigo* when she puts on her gloves."

"Anna Karina in *Vivre Sa Vie* when she watches a movie."

"Judy Garland's innocence in *The Wizard of Oz*."

One thing was for sure—a lot of people in the neighborhood were jealous of Hengameh. She was independent and that rubbed folks the wrong way. But for Rafik and Kamran she had become a stand-in for all the things they didn't have and all the places they hadn't gone. Sometimes the ache of desiring her seemed to break them and they could not figure why neither of them made a move.

It was as if getting rid of her husband had made Hengameh even more inaccessible than before.

Kamran would say, "Man, this girl is so doable. If I just sleep with her one night, I'll never grow old."

Rafik would squirm when he heard his friend talk like that about Hengameh. "That's stupid!"

"Why stupid?"

"If you sleep with her one night, you'll have to serve her forever."

"You think it's not worth it then?"

"I don't know. She's too much of an angel."

"Then if she ever gives you the green light, just send her my way. Please! Tell her there's a poor bastard called Kamran who's been dying for her for over a decade."

"She's a work of art. You can't talk about a work of art that way."

"So what am I supposed to do with Mona Lisa over there? Just stand by and look at her? That's all we've been doing since we were kids."

But what Kamran in fact did was to finally get married. His family forced a distant cousin on him. Nevertheless, even the marriage of one of them could not cure either man's itch. Every day, after Kamran was done driving his food distribution truck around town and Rafik was finished at his picture-framing workshop, the two men would go right back to the same bench and wait for Hengameh to pass by. It was a sickness that finally caused Kamran's mother to speak up.

This turned out to be a wake-up call. Their hunger had turned them into the butt of the neighborhood's jokes. Things happened fast after that: An uncle of Kamran's wife offered to give the newlyweds a discount for an apartment well away from Hengameh's block. Kamran had no choice but to accept. And barely a year later he had a daughter and told Rafik he was working double shifts to support his family. Rafik also tried to lose himself in work at the picture-frame shop. Gone were the languid afternoons on the bench where they killed time waiting for Hengameh to pass— Hengameh who often would smile but never, ever said a word.

It was another life. It was another time.

Then it happened. One day Rafik was walking down the same old streets minding his own business when he ran smack into Hengameh. They were standing inches apart. Face-to-face. This wasn't like all those times in the past when he and Kamran would stand to the side and watch her glide by. Rafik felt like he'd stuck his fingers in a wall socket. He couldn't move.

Hengameh broke the ice: "Rafik, say something. Are you mute?"

"Um, yes. I'm here."

She smiled. "How come you're always running from me?"

He could barely talk. "I don't run."

"You know what I mean. All these years . . ."

Rafik's mouth was dry. He stood there gaping.

"All right then. Tomorrow night come visit me. Nine o'clock sharp. I know you know where to find me." She smiled.

She left him there in the middle of the street disbelieving his own ears. Hengameh inviting him to her place? How would he break this news to Kamran? Should he even tell him about it? Kamran was married now; this would just mess with his head. But then . . . wasn't this the same as not sharing a meal with your best friend? Though Hengameh was not something two people could share, was she? In his frustration, confusion, and excitement, Rafik had to keep reminding himself that Kamran was married. *And I'm not.*

From the moment he ran into Hengameh until nine p.m. the next evening, it was as if a lifetime passed. Rafik had no idea what to do with himself. By seven p.m. he had showered, shaved, donned his fresh clothes, and dabbed a good amount of cologne. He was ready, with two more impossible hours to spare.

It was the end of spring and it got dark late these days. As he was coming out of the house, Rafik's mother gave him a once-over. He knew she could tell he was going out to meet a woman, but if she knew who she'd raise hell about it! He had to calm down. He didn't want to walk too much and start sweating. Maybe he'd smell bad and Hengameh would be turned off. No, he'd just go sit on the benches at Baharestan Park until ten minutes before nine and try to clear his head a bit.

The walk took him by a place he hadn't passed in a long time, the 12 + 1 house of old. The place that woman had been murdered in all those years ago. But had she really been murdered? The papers had written several pieces about it back then, but a culprit was never announced. Maybe she had just slipped and fallen. Rafik couldn't remember anymore if they had even identified a suspect.

He found himself just standing there and staring into that same window he'd peeped through back then. Before long a woman approached the window and gave him a quizzical look. She didn't say anything, she just stood there watching him watching the house. He could see they had carpeted the entire floor. Only the edge of that single stair was still visible from beneath the carpet. Now the woman finally palmed his hand on the window as if to push him away. This jolted Rafik out of his trance.

He murmured under his breath, "I beg your pardon," and turned away.

Eight p.m.

He'd thought he'd only stood there for a minute. It had nearly been a whole hour.

He sat in the park, not thinking about Hengameh now but about the house and the woman who had stared back at him. He felt completely disoriented.

"*Agha*, buy a fortune from me, won't you?"

It was one of those dirty little kids you usually saw at traffic lights selling fortunes of Persian poetry. Without thinking, Rafik took some money out of his pocket and handed it to the kid. Then he did something inexplicable to himself: while the kid held out the paper fortunes, Rafik deliberately counted through the envelopes and took the thirteenth one from his hands.

"Won't you read it, *agha*? It's good to read it right away."

"No, son. I'll read it later. I promise."

He knew he wouldn't read it later either. He didn't want to. He didn't want to connect Hengameh and that lady in the 12 + 1 house and this paper fortune together. He suddenly wished he hadn't bought the thing.

At exactly eight fifty p.m. he finally got up. To reach Hengameh's house from the park he had to pass by the Bridge of Simon again. He lingered there and watched the rough spring current rush underneath him. He thought of his dead brother. If only Razmik hadn't acted so recklessly years ago. Rafik stood there gazing until he felt light-headed and unsteady on his feet. A hand pulled him back from the edge.

"What are you doing? You almost fell over the rails."

It was a woman talking to him. She was looking at him like he was crazy. He apologized several times and thanked her. She looked at him doubtfully again and then was gone.

What if all this was a game? Why would the prettiest woman in all of Narmak and Zarkesh want to see *him*? And in her own house? Rafik began to doubt himself. He wished he hadn't let go of that paper fortune in the rushing water. Would the fortune be able to tell him if this invitation from Hengameh was real? He doubted that.

Most of the streetlamps in Hengameh's street were off. He stood in front of the door to her building and saw that it was already ajar. He passed into the hallway and was about to knock on her unit when she opened the door.

"How punctual of you," she said quietly, and let him in.

The lighting was dim and Rafik couldn't quite see where he was stepping. On the walls he could make out framed photographs. Probably Hengameh's own work. The sound of her high heels followed him. He was excited by that sound. She caught up to him and they faced each other. Now things came into focus. That sleeveless black dress she wore. The red lipstick and polished red nails. The delicate necklace and the little red earrings against her fresh white skin. She smiled and he felt his knees wanting to give. He was giddy and wished to hold onto this feeling forever. She grabbed his hand and pulled him toward the love seat in the living room.

"Watch out for that step. I keep the lights low on purpose. I like it better this way."

"Me too."

She had a lovely scent. He wanted to take it all in.

She said, "So if I didn't come up to you that day, you would have never made a move on me?"

"I'd kill to have you notice me."

"Then why didn't you come forward?"

It wasn't much of an excuse but Rafik pointed to his right eye. "I have a little problem here." There was a small spot on his eye and all his life he had been self-conscious of it. Just like Kamran who still worried about the little mark from the cleft lip of his childhood. "I just didn't believe you'd be interested in someone like me," he added.

Hengameh sighed. "When someone has something unique, they should be proud of it."

"Proud?"

"Yes. Your *little problem* makes a woman want you more."

She stood up and caressed Rafik's shoulder. "How about coffee? I know you Armenians love a cup of coffee. No?"

"I don't drink coffee at night. But tonight—it's a special night."

"Special? You mean you only want to see me this one night?"

She didn't wait for his answer and headed toward the kitchen. Rafik followed her with his eyes.

"Name?"

"Rafik Mahmudi."

"What kind of name is *Rafik?*"

"Armenian."

"Then how come you have a Muslim last name?"

"My ancestors were from the Salmas area of Azerbaijan. A lot of the Armenians there had my last name."

"Listen, Mr. Armenian, I want to help you. But it looks like you want to play with me."

"I'm not playing with anyone, officer."

"Do you admit you murdered Hengameh Farahbakhsh?"

Rafik stared blankly at the detective. If he felt anything, it was numbness—if even that.

"She was still wearing clothes. I don't suppose you got very far with her."

"We were about to have coffee."

"And?"

"I already told you."

"Tell it to me again."

Rafik took a deep breath. "Hengameh went to the kitchen to make coffee. She came back out saying she'd put it on low heat. Then . . . then the doorbell rang. She seemed scared. Said she hoped it wasn't the tenants from upstairs. She checked through the keyhole, then ran back to me and made me hide behind the sofa. I asked her who it was. *Uninvited guest*, she said. She told me to close my eyes and ears and not make a move. You can imagine how I felt. It was horrible. After a while I could hear arguing, but couldn't make out what they were saying. I felt like I had to do something. I felt cheap. Stupid. All I could do was pull myself up a little. I could see the light from the kitchen and two shadows in there moving. Hengameh came out first. She was carrying a tray. I wanted to believe she was bringing me my coffee. The man, he had something in his hand too. Like a small statue or something. I'm not sure. Then he . . . he just bashed her over the head with it. I saw it with my own eyes. Slammed it down on her head. Hard.

The tray flew out of her hand and made a horrible noise when it hit the floor. Horrible! Really loud. I heard doors opening on the second floor and neighbors running downstairs calling her name. I made myself small behind that sofa. I have no idea how that man left the building. I swear it. I couldn't move from there until the police broke down the door."

"Well, well, Mr. Rafik. Rafik the Armenian! I told you I wanted to help you. But this fairy tale you're feeding me—maybe you've been watching too many movies."

"I told you all I know."

"The windows to that building all have metal guards. And you yourself said as soon as the tray fell, there were people from upstairs banging on the door. You don't ask yourself how this ghost you're talking about managed to get out of the house? If you were me, would you believe yourself?"

"No."

"Good. Now we're getting somewhere."

"I only know I'm innocent."

"Maybe you were drunk and didn't know what you were doing."

"I'm not a drinker."

"Really? An Armenian who doesn't drink? That's a first."

"We were supposed to drink coffee and talk. I was in love with her."

"The woman is laid out on those stairs. Her head smashed in. Blood everywhere. Just like that scene you saw when you were a kid. Remember? That house at 12 + 1?"

"How do you know these things?"

"How do I know? Are you sure you're not still drunk? You told me all this just a half hour ago. First you told me about one 12 + 1 house, then about another 12 + 1 house, the victim's."

"Officer, I've loved Hengameh since I was fourteen."

"Sure you did. Maybe you just got a little overexcited. Admit it!"

"I didn't kill anyone. And I wasn't drunk. I loved her. And you want to make a murderer out of me."

"Don't tell me someone else was there! Don't give me lies. Do you understand, Armenian? You're insulting my intelligence, Armenian."

The Criminal Investigation Department building was crowded. Kamran made Rafik's father stand back while he spoke with the chief investigator on Rafik's case.

"Detective, I'm sure there's been mistake about Rafik Mahmudi."

"So you're an expert in murder cases?"

"I mean, there's no way my best friend would do something like this."

The investigator offered a thin smile. "Sure, we all know of your friend's innocence."

This was how it had gone the past few days, ever since Rafik's father had called Kamran and asked if Rafik was with him after not coming home the previous night. They'd waited and waited. And when there was still no word from Rafik, they'd driven together to the local police station. Still nothing. It was on their way back from the police that there was finally a call. Rafik was in custody at the Criminal Investigation Department. But there was no way they'd be allowed to see him now. Even a visit to the Armenian rep at the parliament hadn't helped. Now in the hallways of the CID, Kamran looked so spent that Rafik's father understood there was little chance left for his son.

"It's bad, isn't it?" the old man said. "What did that cop say to you?"

Kamran's voice cracked and he couldn't meet the old man's eyes. "We'll fight it, Uncle Garnik. We'll do whatever it takes for Rafik."

"I'll put down the deed to my house as collateral until his court date."

"It's a lot more serious than that, Uncle Garnik. They won't release him on bail. You already know that."

The old man moaned, "His mother won't survive this one."

"I know it," Kamran said, glancing away.

It turned out as they'd predicted: not long after Rafik's guilty verdict was read, his mother passed on. They'd done all they could to save Rafik's life. Even the chief investigator for the case had had a talk with the victim's brother when he came back from Europe for the court date. As her closest relative, Hengameh's brother insisted in court on *qesas*, an eye for an eye. And when the detective asked him how a guy who lived in a part of the world that didn't believe in capital punishment could come here and insist on it, the brother had said that the pictures of the crime scene left him no choice. That and the fact that Rafik would not even admit to what he'd done.

And so Rafik's execution was set for a year later.

It was a year during which Kamran did just about everything short of breaking Rafik out of jail. Now there were just two days left till the execution date. Kamran sat on the sofa with a blank face watching the twirls of steam rising from his teacup. He began to weep quietly. His wife noticed it and came and sat beside him.

"There's nothing you didn't do for him."

"They're going to kill him the day after tomorrow." He sniffled like a child. "I talked to everyone I know. I got enough money together to buy his life back. But Hengameh's brother won't budge. He says it's not blood money he wants. He wants justice. I thought since we all grew up together in the same neighborhood, maybe he'd show a little mercy for old time's sake. I don't know which bastard showed him the crime scene pictures. If only . . . I don't know. I've failed my best friend."

Kamran balled himself in a corner of the bedroom and continued to cry silently till dawn. In the morning he smiled at his anxious wife, kissed his daughter, and with an expression that betrayed a newfound sense of mission he headed out the door.

It took some time being passed around at the prosecutor's office before he finally found the right man to talk to.

"My name is Kamran Abrishami. I've come to confess to the murder of Hengameh Farahbakhsh."

The assistant attorney for the execution of verdicts stared back at Kamran, nonplussed. At last he said, "Well, well, Mr. Abrishami! So you are saying Rafik Mahmudi is innocent?"

"He is."

"Tell me, how long have you two known each other?"

"Forever."

"Right. So you must be truly like brothers if you're willing to make this sacrifice for him."

"It is not a sacrifice. I'm telling the truth. I'm willing to make a statement and sign it right now."

"Listen, man. I assume you have a family. Right? But that guy, he's single. And an Armenian on top of it. Why do you want to destroy yourself for a creature like that?"

"Because he's not the murderer. I am. This is my last chance to make it right. Tomorrow they're going to put the rope on an innocent man."

"I understand your friend is from Zarkesh. I've heard things about that neighborhood. They say folks from there stay true to their people."

Kamran stared at the ground. "But I'm not from there. I'm from next door, the Narmak quarter."

"Same difference."

"Not at all."

The attorney seemed to lose patience now. "All right, let's do this: instead of wasting each other's time with empty words like *honor* and *sacrifice*, how about we get down to what really matters? I'll ask you a simple question. If you answer correctly, we'll continue. If not, I want you to go home and let us get on with our work."

"I'm ready."

"Here are the facts: One, the victim's windows all had metal guards. Two, the neighbors were behind her door almost immediately after she was killed. Three, besides your friend, the police found no one else in that house."

"I know all this, yes."

"Then can you tell me how you managed to get out of there without being seen?"

Kamran was staring at the young attorney, who in turn was staring back at him with a got-you look. Another few seconds passed before Kamran finally answered: "In the storage room next to the backyard there is a closet with wall-to-wall carpeting. But if you pull the carpet back, you'll see a hidden trapdoor that connects to the boiler room."

Less than a half hour later word came back that Kamran Abrishami's account was true. The first thing the attorney did was to revoke Rafik Mahmudi's order of execution. Next, a new file had to be opened for Kamran.

"Why did you kill Hengameh Farahbakhsh?"

"I wanted to see her. But she said she didn't want to see me anymore. I couldn't resist. I went to her place that night. She didn't have to open the door. But I knew she would if I made noise. She was always afraid of the neighbors being in her business."

"And?"

"And . . . I saw it all. I saw the coffee brewing in the kitchen. The two cups. She must have had a guest or she was waiting for someone. She was mocking me. Said I made her sick. We hadn't even been seeing each other that long. I asked for one last kiss. One last kiss and I'd be out of her life forever. She mentioned the old cut on my lip. How it made her want to throw up. This from a woman who had always said how much she loved my scar. I lost it then. Hengameh was wearing that black dress and looking lovelier than ever. But now me and my lip made her sick. She told me to get out. And she started walking with the tray toward the living room. I still didn't know if anyone was there. And the last person

I would have thought of finding there was Rafik. I wasn't thinking straight anymore. I picked up the statuette of a samurai I'd given her myself. I hit her as hard as I could. And that tray, it flew, and what a noise it made. Only then did I realize what I'd done. I heard footsteps running downstairs. People calling her name, knocking on her door. I was afraid. The first time I was ever at her place, she'd showed me the escape hatch to the boiler room. She'd even caressed my ugly lip when she said it: *Just in case I ever need you to get out of here quickly*. I took the samurai I'd hit her with and ran out of there. I don't know where the statue is now; I threw it off the Bridge of Simon that same evening."

Kamran's confession was done. There was a lot of commotion and coming and going for the next hour until the attorney came and faced him.

"Well, Mr. Abrishami, this changes things a bit, doesn't it? We are releasing your friend, your so-called brother whom you held out on for a whole year and almost sent to his death."

Looking utterly worn-out, Kamran asked if he could see Rafik for just one minute.

"Out of the question. It's against the rules."

"But I already made my confession," he pleaded. "I'll see him in your presence if you like. Please . . . accept this last request of an already-dead man. I don't want to leave this world without him hearing it from my own mouth. We are brothers and were both in love with the same woman."

Rafik was brought in. As soon as his eyes fell on Kamran, he went over and hugged him. Then quietly, so no one else in the room could hear, he whispered to his friend, "I knew today was the day you'd come for me."

NOT EVERY BULLET IS MEANT FOR A KING

BY HOSSEIN ABKENAR

Shapur

Scene 1

The one holding the gun shouted, "All you motherfuckers lie on the floor right now!"

The bank's customers began screaming and drawing close together before they all threw themselves to the floor. There was a chubby young soldier working security holding a cup of hot tea in one hand and an old G3 rifle on his shoulder. As soon as he tried to move, the lead robber smacked him in the face with the butt of his handgun. The soldier went down with his tea, the strap of the G3 still in his hand. He received a kick to the ribs and quickly let go of the weapon.

There were two of them. They both had black stockings drawn over their faces so that their eyes were hidden. One of them was slim and had long hair bunched up underneath the stocking. Robber #1, who was doing the shouting and the gun-waving, cursed some more, picked up the soldier's gun, and gave it to Robber #2. Meanwhile the soldier, bleeding from the nose, slowly dragged himself to where the others were sprawled. Robber #2 appeared to have a bad leg and didn't know how to hold the rifle properly. Nevertheless, he or she managed to smash the bank's video camera with the rifle stock; the thing made a cracking sound and hung limp off of its hinges. In addition to the woman farther back at the safe-deposit desk, three other employees were still frozen behind the teller windows. Robber #1 now motioned them to join the others, which they did.

Since the bank manager was on vacation, his deputy sat in his chair to the side of the teller windows. The guy's knees were shaking violently and he was desperately trying to find the alarm button beneath the table. He pressed on something with his foot but nothing happened. Now, with the eyes of Robber #1 on him, he slowly stood up like a kid who had been found out and tiptoed over to where the other captives were. Sitting next to him there had also been a bearded man, maybe around sixty, who had a set of red prayer beads in his hand. The man kept squeezing the side of his coat as he got up to follow the vice-manager. The two of them now stood together over another guy who sat on the floor as if he was about to eat his lunch there. This other man, looking bewildered and lost, had a newly shaven head that he kept scratching hard at with the edge of his mortgage booklet.

The safe-deposit woman was the only staff still left on the other side of the glass divider. Mechanically, she began pushing stacks of money that had been sitting on her table into the drawer. It was as if she were in a trance. The vice-manager noticed her doing this and his eyebrows went up in surprise; it was a good thing the bank robbers were not looking her way just then.

Scene 2

Zahra said, "Push the damn button!" Then she struck at the elevator button herself. You could still hear music from inside the apartment. Two young guys came out of there and ran toward the elevator. When its door closed, they about-faced and went for the stairway.

Inside the elevator, the other girl, Samira, could barely keep her eyes open. She pressed herself against Zahra. "You danced like a queen tonight." She brought her face closer to kiss Zahra on the lips but Zahra pushed her away.

"How much did you drink? Your mouth smells like a toilet. Damn you, Samira!"

Samira continued laughing and trying to kiss Zahra with her

eyes closed. When the elevator door opened, Zahra pulled her out of there while yanking her *chador* out of her bag. The sound of the guys' footsteps was getting closer. She let go of Samira and threw the *chador* on.

One of the guys protested, "Zahra, you just got here. It's not even nine thirty."

"It's late for me. I gotta go, Ali *jaan*."

Arash whispered, "Did Milad say something to make you mad?"

Zahra glanced away. "Thanks for everything. Say goodbye to Rasul too. The cab's waiting outside."

"Do you want me to tell the driver to leave?" Arash volunteered. "One of us can drive you home later."

Samira giggled and hung onto Zahra's arm. "Come on! We were just starting to have fun. Let's stay."

Zahra's voice was full of irritation: "It's my mother. I've had a dozen missed calls from her already."

"Oooh, Mrs. Mayor's office!" Samira chuckled again.

"Shut up, Samira."

"Do you need some gum at least?" Ali asked.

"But Zahra didn't drink anything," Samira said, giggling.

The phone in Zahra's bag began to vibrate. "Goodbye, guys."

Scene 3

The flimsy shopping bag's handle tore out of Puri's hand and several of the oranges went rolling down the street. Before she could get to them, a passing motorcycle crushed one of them and raced on.

Puri sighed, then laughed in resignation when she saw Milad had caught up to her and was already salvaging the oranges that hadn't been damaged.

"Let me take the bags for you," he said.

"It's like you descended from the sky, Milad *jaan*." She gave him the bags but held onto the two big round flatbreads. "Thank you."

They walked past the local barbershop. Milad slowed down and got the guy's attention and pointed to his own head. *I'll be back*, he pantomimed.

The barber nodded and went about his work.

Puri said, "Why do you want to cut it? You look great with a ponytail."

"I'm tired of it, to be honest."

They walked several more blocks in easy silence until Puri stopped in front of an alms box and dropped a small bill in there. "I can take it from here."

"No, let me help you. I don't live too far."

"Don't you and your brother live back the other way?"

"We did. But I moved down here recently, to Vazir Daftar Street. It's that big old building over there. I'm renting just a small studio."

"What about your brother?"

"Well, he's got his family."

"Hmm. Does he want to cut his hair too? You guys look so similar."

"Actually, he does. Or maybe he has by now. Says it itches too much." He laughed. "Maybe I'll keep mine so we won't look so much alike." His attention now went to the other side of the street where several black-clad men stood in front of a mosque. You could hear the sounds of a *noha*, lamentation, coming from inside the place.

Puri nudged him with the bread. "Take a piece. It's fresh."

Milad tore off some bread and put it in his mouth. They started walking again. In front of her building, she paused for a second and gave a kick to one of the front wheels of her car.

"That tire needs some serious air in it," Milad remarked.

"I know," she said.

"It's dangerous like that—is it yours?"

"More of a gas-guzzler than a car, to be honest. It used to belong to Shahin's father. I don't think you ever met my kid, Shahin."

Milad shook his head.

Puri was about to ring the buzzer but then remembered that Goljaan, her Afghan helper, must be gone by now. It took her awhile to find her keys.

They climbed side by side up a dark and dank stairway.

"Come in for a minute," she offered.

He glanced down at his muddy boots. "I won't bother you."

"You're not a bother, come in."

As he went to set the shopping bags inside the door their hands brushed one other ever so slightly. Their eyes met.

"Only if you'd like to come in," she added.

There was noise from inside and they both peered in. A boy of about ten or eleven, drool hanging from his mouth, was staring at them with glazed eyes. Puri suddenly became nervous.

"I'm sorry, I . . . I know you're waiting for a loan from the bank. But my boss there still hasn't gotten around to any of the recent loan requests. He's on vacation."

Milad was back to gazing at his own boots. "Right. Sure thing."

"That last loan you took, how many more payments do you have on it?"

"Two."

"Pay those off first. I think it's better that way. Then I can speak to the bank manager."

"Of course. Whatever you say." He slowly retreated from the door and turned at the stairway.

Scene 4

"You think you're smart, don't you? I knew it. I fucking knew it. You've been acting strange for a while. Always nagging me about something. Making me look bad. I spit on myself. Yeah, on myself, for having a wife who sends me a court order after six years of being at her beck and call every moment of every day. Shut up! Shut your trap up and stop crying. What did you tell them? That your husband is an addict? That I'm crazy? That I beat you up?

That I don't give you enough pocket money? What did you say, bitch? Talk to me! So fucking what if I take a couple of tokes at the end of the day? I do it so I can keep working. Do you know how the pain in my back feels? Like pins and needles. I work so I can put food on the table. It takes a man, a real man, to sit sixteen hours a day behind the wheel of those buses. You think anyone can do it? You think these motherfuckers sitting in those real estate offices moving millions around and getting fatter every day—you think those pieces of shit could do what I do even for one day? Look at me. Look at this bank book I carry around and not a penny to my name. I tell you what I'll do: I'll shave my head. That's what I've decided. My scalp is itchy from my nerves, and this stupid bank book is only good for one thing: it's a head-scratcher. Excuse me, what? Stop that mumbling. You think your own husband can't ask where you go off to when I'm working? Always leaving your one-year-old baby with the neighbors and going off God knows where. You think I don't know? And I'm not supposed to ask? I spit on this fucking life I got! Not worth a shit. Work two shifts a day and what do I have to show for it? Nothing. Zilch. Zero. Just drive that fucking route up and down this nasty motherfucker of a city with no time off, no weekend, not an hour to call my own. And suddenly I'm the bad guy? The court wants *me* to explain myself? Fuck you all. And fuck those passengers who always give me shit. One guy says he doesn't have exact change. Another wants to get off before the next station. Another refuses to pay. Another curses me out and says I passed her stop and wishes hellfire on me and mine for seven generations. This is my lot in this miserable country. I spit on every Iranian that ever walked the earth. You want a divorce, do you? You want your freedom? Be my guest. Go! Go and see what's waiting for you out there. Plenty of streetwalkers where you're headed. And guess what? They're even glad to take a nobody like me for a ride. I know, because I see it every night on my way to the terminal. Sixteen-year-olds, forty-year-olds, doesn't matter. They got no place to stay. They won't get off the bus. I tell them, *Sister, it's time to get off. Go home.* But they got no home. They got nowhere. You crying now? Today you cry, tomorrow you'll have the cops on me. I know your kind. Just because I'm not rich, just because I don't own my own home, I don't have the latest-model car, I don't have a country house, I don't have . . . don't have a pot to piss in. What do you want me to do? Go rob a bank? Will you shut that baby up, for God's sake! Or are you above taking care of your own child now too? When you first came to Tehran you were a simple girl. None of this lipstick this, lipstick that. I should have known better, but I waited. Told myself you'd come around. It was just a new stage with all the makeup, I told myself. You'd settle down, I told myself. But it got worse. First you nagged my poor little brother so much that he ran off. The kid's just a college student. But do you care? Of course not. You don't care that he has to pay three hundred a month for a hole-in-the-wall two streets down from here. And you're still not satisfied, are you? Stop that crying. I swear I'll hit you. Ouch! What happened? I didn't mean it. Let me see. You happy now? Now you'll have more evidence for the judge, won't you? You can tell them your husband hit you in the face with his key ring. Who'll believe I didn't mean it? No one. But you know what? I don't give a damn anymore either way. You go your way, I'll go mine. What's a pauper like yours truly sup-posed to worry about—that they'll take my bread? I got news for you: they already took my bread; they took it from me a long, long time ago."

Scene 5

The man was in the middle of his evening prayer when his cell phone rang. He kept an eye on the screen even as he continued. As the sound became louder, his wife came and stood over him. He kept praying but signaled with his hand for her to not worry about it and get on with her own work. She complied.

After that he only went through the motions of the prayer and finished up as fast as he could.

He checked the phone while his wife asked from the kitchen if she should start serving dinner.

"I'm going to Kamali's house tonight," he answered.

She walked back out into the living room. "But . . . I put on a whole lot of rice for us. Why didn't you mention it earlier?"

The man didn't bother answering. He seemed annoyed about something and asked, "Where's that daughter of yours? Is she upstairs in her room? Tell her if she steals my car keys and goes out like that again I'll break both her legs. I'm not joking."

The woman nervously played with the button on her skirt. "*Haji*, please! She's a big girl. She didn't mean anything by it. She's sorry."

The man's voice grew louder. "She didn't mean anything by it? Where was she Friday night? Why did she come home so late?"

"She was at her friend's house. They were studying together."

"Studying, was she? Mark my words, if I catch her one more time . . ."

His phone began to beep again. He paused for a second before answering in an even tone, "*Salam alaykum, haj agha.*" He laughed. "No, certainly, yes. I'll be there. I just have to stop on the way at the office and get some documents. You honor us, *haj agha.* We'd be happy if you came here and we could host you for a change." As he spoke into the phone, he slowly folded his prayer rug and put it away in front of the hall mirror. "Certainly. But tomorrow the mayor's office is closed. Yes, because of Commander Jafari's fortieth day of mourning. I know, it's hard to believe. Forty days since his passing already. May he rest in peace. Yes, yes, absolutely."

Call over, he went to the coatrack next to the entrance and put on his overcoat.

His wife stood at the threshold of the kitchen watching his every move. She said, "I have the help coming in the morning to clean the house. Can I give him that other black coat you don't want anymore?"

"Give him the sneakers too. The ones Yasir sent from London. I don't wear those things."

She nodded.

He kept his eyes on her for a few seconds. "What's this thing you're wearing? Have you seen yourself in the mirror lately? You look like a maid."

The woman immediately became anxious and withdrew a little into the kitchen. "I . . . I don't know. It's just that I've put on a bit of weight. This skirt is just a lot more comfortable."

"I brought a whole suitcase full of new clothes for you from Turkey. They're all too tight already?"

A text message distracted him and she stood watching his back while he fiddled awkwardly with his phone. He put on his shoes and without turning to her again or saying goodbye, he muttered a *Bismillah* and exited the house.

The woman did not move for another minute. Then she went to the kitchen cabinet and took out a bottle of prescription medicine. Valium. Her hands were shaking. She filled a glass of water and took two pills out.

"Is his majesty finally gone?"

The woman jumped. "Zahra! You scared me. I guess you already heard how angry your father was with you."

"Don't worry about that man."

"One doesn't talk about one's father like that." She examined her daughter. "Why are you dressed up?"

Zahra was holding up a small mirror and putting on some gloss. "He thinks he has the right to tell you anything he wants. And you never say anything back. What are you scared of?"

"I asked why you're dressed for outside."

"Because that's what I'm doing—going out."

"Zahra, please! Don't you have an exam? You should learn a little bit from your brother Yasir."

Zahra sneered, "Yasir? That guy could barely get his high school diploma here. Now all of a sudden we hear he's getting a

PhD in London. Who did my father pay off this time? And how much?"

"Your father spent thirty-one months at war in the front lines." She stormed past the girl into the living room and started searching frantically for the TV remote. Zahra followed her. "Thirty-one months," she repeated. "Don't you ever forget that!"

"Well, your *haj agha* is certainly getting mileage out of those thirty-one months now. And all he has to do in return is sport a stupid prayer bead and let his beard grow a little. Everyone knows he's turned the city's Twelfth District into a thieves' den."

"Bite your tongue, girl!"

"Why do you let him push you around like that?"

"He's my husband. He's the man of the house."

"Don't play dumb. You know he's been having an affair with a married woman. Don't pretend you don't know."

"Zahra!"

"You were crying on the phone when you were talking to Aziz about it."

"I was talking to Aziz about someone else."

"Sure you were. You haven't slept together in over a year."

"That is none of your business."

"It *is* my business. You have to stop being such a weakling in front of him. I know what it is: you're afraid he'll divorce you and you'll have to go back to the provinces. Who'd want to give up all this luxury, right? The money and the fancy car and the country house and the fashionable address in the most expensive part of Tehran. You're afraid you'll be average again. So you take those stupid pills and keep putting on weight. Instead of taking all those meds, you should take a shot of whiskey every night. Works a lot better."

"Stop this talk, Zahra. Sacrilege! I don't know what kind of people you've been hanging around with. Your father is right: when a girl doesn't marry young, this is the result." TV remote in hand, she sighed and sat down on the sofa and began surfing the channels.

Zahra scoffed, "And tell him to stop bringing me suitors. If he still insists, tell him to at least let them know beforehand I lost my virginity a long time ago."

Her mother put a hand over her face. "God forgive us for her profanities."

"Don't worry. Our times are different than yours. Nowadays you won't find any girl my age in Tehran who hasn't known love and then some. Virginity is for fools." She went toward the door.

Her mother jumped from the sofa. "I swear I'll call him right now if you go out."

"So call. You think I'm scared? When you call him, tell him his daughter went to buy cigarettes. I'll be right back."

Scene 6

He tapped the motorcycle cabbie's shoulder and said, "This is a one-way lane for buses. What are you doing?" He was holding on for dear life and was glad that the guy had at least lent him his helmet.

The rider half turned to him in the wind. "No worries, I know the cop handling the lane today. He won't bother us."

A bus came straight at them. The rider angled his bike sharply onto the sidewalk where several cursing pedestrians had to jump out of the way.

On Manuchehri Street he gratefully got off the bike and breathed a sigh of relief. The area was filled with currency exchange shops and antique and black-market dealers. He handed the biker his fare and headed into the crowd of people.

"You selling dollars?" someone shouted.

"No."

"You buying them?"

No again. A little farther into the street there were less people. Several secondhand traders had laid out their goods on the sidewalk—watches, prayer beads, rings, old coins.

He stopped in front of one of them. The guy was selling

nineteenth-century teapots, ancient-looking locks and bolts, an old Zenith camera, a pair of brass trays, and a boxful of LPs from the 1970s.

Someone passed by whispering that he had "king-killers," *shah-kosh,* for sale.

What if the guy was undercover? He had to be careful before he asked around. He walked a bit farther on and squatted by another street dealer. Picking up a steel knuckle buster, he asked how much it was.

The seller didn't even bother looking at him.

He tried again, "How much is that knife?"

"Eighty," the man said, still not turning to him.

He took the knife and tried opening it but couldn't. The man grabbed the knife from him and flicked it open. "Switchblade."

He laughed nervously. "All right, how much for the knuckle buster?"

The man gave him a dead expression. "Don't beat around the bush. Tell me what it is you're after."

"A gun."

The guy kept a steady eye on him, measuring him. Now he slowly turned and gestured at a heavyset man with a thick mustache who slowly ambled over to them.

"He's looking for a king-killer."

The big guy ran a hand over his mustache and stared hard at the potential customer. "Come!"

He fell behind the big man.

On a smaller street they stopped in front of a ruin of a house and the man spoke: "You want American Colt or a Russian automatic?" He had a Kurdish accent.

"A king-killer. That's what I came for, a *shah-kosh.*"

"Can be arranged. It's secondhand, though. Forty-five caliber."

He wasn't sure what to do. He kept his hands in his pockets, feeling naked there.

The man said, "I have a secondhand Beretta too."

"The king-killer. How much?"

"Three-fifty. Fifty rounds thrown in."

"It works fine?"

"Fit for a king." The man rubbed his fingers together to indicate it was time to show him the money. There was no choice. He had to trust the guy. He brought a bundle of bills from his jacket pocket and counted before handing it to the Kurd. The guy counted again and then touched the bills to his forehead in a gesture of appreciation. "Wait right here."

After a while he began to feel stupid. Why had he trusted the guy like that? He lit a cigarette and smoked nervously, not sure what to do. The air felt dirty. He threw the half-finished cigarette away and slammed a fist against the wall in frustration.

Another five minutes and the man finally showed up.

First thing he did was give him the ammunition. Then the king-killer itself, wrapped in an old red rag.

He felt the thing in his hand, the rag still covering it. It was heavier than he'd expected.

Scene 7

"*May your hearts be of gold and your eyes sparkle and your mouths show laughter and may today's autumn afternoon be filled with joy for you and your . . .*"

"Turn that stupid bitch off, please," Puri said.

Goljaan, her Afghan helper, smiled and turned the radio off. "Shall I iron these ones also, *khanum jaan?*

"No. Go on home. I'll do the rest myself. I left your money next to the radiator. Don't forget to take it."

"May God always protect you. Thank you. A friend is headed for Kabul tonight; I can give them this money to take for my family."

"Good."

The boy was standing there, his eyes vacant as always and the ever-present drool hanging from his mouth. Puri pulled the sweater over his head. The kid stood motionless while she struggled with the sleeves. Impatiently, she said, "Shahin *jaan*, help me out here a bit. I can't wear your clothes for you."

The boy stood still and more drool came out of his mouth.

Goljaan picked up her envelope of cash. "What is this, *khanum?*" She pointed to a blue dress on the sofa.

Before Puri could answer, her phone rang. She answered it. "I'll call you back, *Maman jaan*. No, I can't come to your place. I know schools are closed, but the banks aren't. Yes, I do have to go to work. All right. No." She threw the mobile on the sofa and turned to Goljaan. "The dress is for you. Almost new. I only wore it one time at a wedding."

"You are an angel, *khanum jaan*." Goljaan went to the door to put on her shoes.

Puri was distracted. She began ironing a scarf, half talking to herself and half to Goljaan who was almost out the door. "Two of the employees have gone on vacation and they force me to do all their work. People tell me how lucky I am to work in a bank. Mrs. In-Charge-of-Safe-Deposit-Box. As if the money in there belongs to me. As if I won a prize or something. What do they know! Between last week and this week the price of milk tripled and I have an eleven-year-old child who hasn't spoken two words his entire life. Sure, I'm really lucky to work in a bank." She peered over at the boy who stood there gawking at her. "And guess what else? Now everything in the world is suddenly carcinogenic. Those new Chinese lamps: cancer. The plastic spatula I just bought and threw away: cancer."

The phone rang again. She stood the iron up and checked the number calling her. Taking a deep breath, she answered, "*Salam*. I'm home. I've just washed him. I'll give him the phone." She called the boy over. "Shahin, your father wants to talk to you."

The boy's mouth hung open from joy. He hurried to his mother who lifted the phone to his ear. Some nondescript sounds came out of his mouth and he listened. She sat him down on the sofa, caressed his head, and took the device away after a few moments and began talking into it. "It's me. Well, it's nice of you to remember him. No, I'm not being sarcastic. I'm almost out of his medicines. No pharmacy has them in the city. They say it's the American sanctions. Nothing's coming into the country. I asked one of the bank's customers. He has a son studying in London. Deputy mayor. Twelfth District. Travels a lot. I gave him the names of the medicines. He said he'd bring a couple of packages. What? No, I didn't flirt with him, for God's sake. Besides, you can tell from his face the guy has something to do with Etelaa'at. I don't even like him. But what can I do?"

She listened for a while longer, becoming increasingly agitated. The boy remained on the sofa swinging himself left and right. Finally she shouted into the phone, "What's it to you if I'm seeing anyone or not? Do I ever ask *you* these questions?" She hung up and turned the phone off completely and threw it next to the boy. The boy stared at her with wide eyes and she kissed him on the forehead before going over to the window and lighting a cigarette.

Scene 8

Arash sat in a corner of Milad's room, unseen, while Milad stood in the doorway listening to his doddering landlord ramble on in chopped sentences.

"Young man, I told you from day one . . . families live here . . . That friend you have, he doesn't look right . . . and girls, too many girls coming and going . . . I mean, I'm not traditional . . . but the other tenants . . . if you ask me, they're all thieves . . . but still my tenants . . . You should be careful of that Internet . . . I like the satellite TV myself . . . those Turkish soaps are nice . . . not all of them though . . . And you're telling me you don't have the rent and it's five days past the beginning of the month . . . and with my two daughters in college . . . Do you know how much college costs nowadays? . . . And then I have to climb up these stairs with my bad knees and bad back and bad everything . . . not right for an old man like me . . . And here, here is a lightbulb for your hallway . . . Screw it . . . screw it in yourself."

Milad nodded respectfully. "You are absolutely right. Give me one second." He set the lightbulb on his study desk, took some money from the drawer, and handed it over.

The old man counted with shaking hands. "But this is only half of it."

"Sure, I'll have the rest soon."

Slowly but firmly he closed the door in the old man's face and came back inside, looking both relieved and exhausted.

Arash was rolling a hashish joint on a small tray full of loose tobacco. "That old man should have his mouth sewn up. What a windbag! The bastard already owns six buildings in the neighborhood and he still has to come up here and knock on your door. You should tell him to go to hell."

"Don't be stupid," Milad snapped. "I'm lucky the guy rented me this place at all." He sat in front of his computer.

"There he goes again, Mr. Facebook. *Oh look, friends, my thousands and thousands of bullshit Internet friends—here's my pic drinking strong black coffee, here's me in my green outfit from last year, here's my cat and isn't she a jewel? And isn't meditating and thinking Zen thoughts so damn cool, guys? Let's everybody meditate together and jerk off.* God! People got nothing better to do in this town."

"Shut up, Arash! This computer's got a bug. Half my files are fucked. I'm frustrated as hell."

"You say it like the damn machine has the flu. What, you want to French kiss the computer screen? Fuck that thing and its files. Where do all these files and the papers you turn in for your engineering courses get us, college boy? Nowhere. We're still poor as shit." Arash lit the joint, took a couple of hits, and offered it to Milad. "Inhale, brother, it'll lighten you up."

Milad put the joint in his mouth and took a long, hard drag, gazing vacantly at the ceiling. He blew the smoke out toward Arash. "So what happened with your plan to leave this shithole country?"

"My old man says not to count on him for help. Motherfucker! He says he doesn't have the dough. And even if he did, he wouldn't give it to me. The asshole!"

"That kind of money is no joke."

"The man I talked to said he didn't need all the money at once. I can pay him off in three installments. The last one when the visa comes through."

"If you have to pay, you have to pay. Three installments or ten installment makes no difference when you don't have the bread."

"I know. My ass is fucked."

"Besides," Milad took another hit, "what if the guy takes your money and runs?"

"Nah. He's trustworthy. He does this kind of thing for a living. It's his livelihood. He'll lose customers if he fucks me. I asked around about him. Did my research. You remember that guy who was in love with himself?"

"I know a lot of assholes like that. Who?"

"You know, the guy who was in the gym like fifteen hours a day. Had muscles the size of Hercules's dick. Used to roll up his sleeves in the dead of winter and strut around like a pumped-up whore. My contact got him as far as Malaysia. Now he's waiting to get to Australia." Arash took the joint out of Milad's hand. "But forget that for a minute. Let's talk about this: I got a fail-safe plan. Something deep, something serious." He took a toke. "We'll be millionaires if we do it right. A one-shot deal."

Milad turned away. "Not another one of your get-rich-quick schemes."

"I swear, if you say no, I'll have to ask that dumbfuck Rasul the Limp, Samira's one-legged dick."

"You're high. Relax and shut up."

"This is real. And even if Rasul says no, I'll ask the bitch herself, Samira. That girl's willing to do anything. Remember the time she came to the stadium with us?"

Milad's phone started buzzing.

Arash persisted, "I swear, you're less than a cunt if you say no to my plan. It's foolproof." The phone continued vibrating on the sofa. Arash finally picked it up and checked the number. "You're going to answer your phone or not? It's your woman, Zahra."

"Don't answer it."

"You're wasting your time with that piece of ass. Better off jerking off."

"Shut up." Milad was clicking fast on the computer keyboard and didn't even bother to turn around when Arash slid the phone across the floor to him.

"She goes around acting like Ms. Innocent. I hear her big-shot father has picked the Twelfth District clean these past four years. Everyone and their mother in the Twelfth is on the take. I wish the bastard would at least give me a job there."

Without turning around, Milad stretched his hand out and took the joint from Arash.

"Let me guess," Arash went on, "you probably do her from the back, right? But why her? I mean, this town's filled with bitches—tall ones, short ones, ones with asses the size of a donut, others like a watermelon. We got the pick of the litter, and they're all looking for husbands. The stupid cunts."

The phone buzzed again.

Milad finally picked it up off the floor, silenced it, and shoved it in his pocket.

"Come on!" Arash whined. "Let me tell you my plan. We can go out and eat something and talk."

"I can make you an omelet right here."

"You're gonna turn into a fucking poached egg yourself if you keep eating so much of that shit. That's all you ever eat. Come, let's go out and get some fucking dog burger at least."

"All right, let me just change this lamp and we can go."

A minute later Arash heard a thud in the hallway and then Milad's voice groaning about his twisted ankle.

"Great," he muttered to himself, "now we got Rasul the Limp #2, and there goes my foolproof plan."

Scene 9

It was dark out and wet. The man drove into the main street. An Allah gold chain hanging off the rearview mirror quivered back and forth every time the car made a turn.

"I'm sorry if it scared you. I always carry one with me."

"It's all right," the woman answered quietly. "I'd never seen one up close."

"Don't be afraid. What's important is that the wrong kind of man doesn't carry one of these. It's just for protection." Saying this, he reached instinctively for the side of his coat and felt the weapon's hardness. Then he ran the same hand over the woman's thigh. She froze.

"Once the work on my country house up in Lavasan is finished, it'll be a lot better for us. It's a bit far, but safer."

The woman said nothing.

There was a long line in front of the New Moon ice-cream shop. He drove past it.

Now the woman said, "I can get off here."

"Too many people. I'll go around. You didn't tell me what happened to your forehead."

"It's nothing."

"How old's your child?"

"Almost one."

"May God preserve him. You are still going ahead with your divorce with that bus driver?" Instead of waiting for her to answer, he reached for a small leather Koran sitting on the dashboard. Inside it was a folded-up piece of paper. He handed it to the woman. "This will help you. It's a little note to the family court judge in the district you need to go to. Give it to him, and tell him I send my regards. He'll know what to do."

"You are very kind to me."

"But don't call my cell phone anymore. Just send me an empty text message. I'll know it's you. I'll call you back."

"I will."

He pulled out an envelope from his inner coat pocket. "Take this too."

The woman felt the money in the envelope and put the whole thing in her bag. "Thank you very much."

He rubbed her thigh one more time and she froze again.

"Can you get out here?"

"Yes. Thank you."

"I don't want to see you with a mark on your face again. Doesn't look good."

She nodded and hurriedly stepped out of the car. "Thank you, *haj agha*. Thank you."

Scene 10

From the back of the bus a woman shouted, "Driver, open the back door!"

There was hardly room to breathe in that bus. Everyone hung on to some sliver of metal railing and tried not to squeeze too hard against the next person. Even on the bus's steps people were sardined shoulder to shoulder and could barely move. The last guy in through the middle door had his briefcase half stuck outside and was desperately pulling on it with both hands.

The light turned green and the bus started to move again. The woman shouted, "I said I'm getting off! Stop the bus!"

A chorus rose, "Bus driver, stop! She needs to get off!"

The driver paid them no mind and kept driving. Somebody in the front noted that there was no bus stop here.

It was a gray morning. Early. The bus moved fast through the express lane. A man pushed his way with difficulty to the front. "Driver, please open the door when you can. I got on the wrong bus."

The driver didn't acknowledge him. Someone nearby said, "There's no more stops until Vanak Circle."

Someone else observed, "The poor guy got on by mistake. Why can't he just stop for him?"

From the opposite direction a motorbike came zooming illegally toward them. The driver didn't slow down at all. At the last moment the biker was forced to turn sharply onto the sidewalk and almost slammed against several pedestrians, who scattered like bowling pins.

The bus moved on.

At Vanak Circle the doors to the bus finally opened. Several men got on from the front and ran their metro cards through the machine. One guy had to buy his ticket first and stretched a bill toward the driver.

"Here you go."

The driver just sat there staring directly ahead of him. He saw no one and answered no one.

Now a large woman came barreling up front. "I hope you rot in hell!" she yelled. "Now I have to go all this way back because you wouldn't stop!" She threw her coins on the floor of the bus and stormed out.

The driver checked his watch. Almost ten o'clock. He pressed a button next to the steering wheel and slowly got up.

One of the passengers said, "Where's this guy going?"

"He's leaving. Hey, where are you going? This isn't the end of the line."

The passengers stuck their faces to the foggy windows of the bus and watched the driver as he walked toward the family court building in Vanak and eventually disappeared in the crowd.

Scene 11

As she rode him she pressed her palms into his chest, moving her head back and forth to caress his face with her long hair. He lifted his head and bit on her nipples one at a time and then sank back down and grabbed the back of her ass cheeks and pressed her deeper. She moaned. In one quick movement he turned her so that she hit the mattress on her back while he stayed inside her pumping harder.

She moaned again and so did he and they managed to come together.

He rolled off and lay on his back. She put her head on his sweaty chest.

His phone buzzed. He jumped up but didn't check it. As he was taking a piss the phone buzzed again. He went and stood by the window and listened to his messages.

It was Zahra: "Milad, I know Samira is there. It's not my business . . ." Her voice cracked as she spoke but she went on with the message. "If I made a mistake and slept with others, I was thinking what difference does it make? What's important is the heart. You know? Milad, listen to me—I'm failing all my college classes because of you. I can't concentrate. I swear to God, if you don't talk to me I'll kill myself."

He deleted the message and turned to see Samira stepping out of the bathroom. She sat naked in front of the computer and lit a cigarette.

"It was Zahra," she said. "Right? Poor thing. You should treat her better." She clicked on something and piano sounds came from the computer.

"Turn off that music."

She did so, then picked up an enormous textbook and asked, "What does this title mean? *Fluid Mechanics*. Is it a novel?"

Milad didn't answer.

"So what happened to your leg? Now you're walking like that dumb fiancé of mine, Rasul the Limp. He says he wants to wait until we have more money before we get married. *More money from where?* I asked him. He's so dumb." She laughed. "Have you seen how long he's grown his hair? He's looking more and more like you these days. Maybe he wants to be you. Everybody does. By the way, I saw Arash the other day. He's got some crazy idea in his head."

Milad was staring out the window. He spoke her name: "Samira."

She didn't hear him and continued to talk. "He said he'd told you all about it. I mean, I'm sitting there listening to him, thinking this guy is out of his mind. You should have seen Rasul's face. I thought he'd have a heart attack just listening to the plan. But then I thought—why not? I mean, his plan isn't all bad. So I say to Arash, *Do you want me to come instead of Rasul? I can even play like I got a limp like my fiancé. It'll throw off the police afterward. They'll be looking for a limping thief.*"

"Shut up, Samira," he said quietly.

"Milad, come to think of it, now that you're limping too, why don't all three of us—me, you, and Rasul—all go together with Arash?" She laughed louder this time. "Think about it: Arash and the limping bank robbers."

"Be quiet."

"Has a ring to it, no? I mean—"

"Samira!"

"Huh? What, love?"

He threw Samira's bra and panties at her. "Get lost!"

Scene 12

The hallway was pitch-black. Zahra peeked inside her mother's room. Her bed was next to the window. A shaft of light illuminated her glass of water and her bottle of pills on the nightstand. Her mother was fast asleep. Now she tiptoed to her father's room. The door was shut. She drew a deep breath, held it, and turned the doorknob. She stood there for a second. No sound except his heavy breathing. She brushed a hand against the clothes hanging near the door. Pants pocket. The car keys rattled when she reached for them. She fisted them with a sweaty hand and tiptoed back out without shutting the door all the way.

Downstairs, she put on her orange scarf and *manteau*. She took another deep breath and stepped out of the house.

Scene 13

It was past two in the morning. Except for a few neon signs here and there, everything appeared closed. Puri didn't remember which pharmacy was open this time of night. She passed several sanitation workers in their orange overalls. A man stood holding a backpack and as she passed him he tried to flag her down. She pressed on the gas and moved on.

Her phone rang. She didn't answer. In the distance she spotted a cigarette man. He sat next to a beat-up metal container and had himself a fire going with empty cigarette cartons. She pulled the window down a couple of inches.

"You got Marlboro Lights?"

The man nodded and she pushed some money out the window. He gave her the cigarette pack.

"Is there a twenty-four-hour pharmacy around here?"

He stared at her. "What are you looking for?" When she said nothing, he asked, "Meth? Crack? Pills—"

She didn't wait for him to finish. Several lights down she slowed the car and took out a smoke. Her hands were shaking. This time of night, most of the lights stayed yellow and just blinked nonstop. Her phone rang again. This time she answered.

"What do you want from me? I told you I'm not home." She listened for a minute and then snapped back, "The boy is running a fever! I've come looking for a pharmacy. No, you let *me* talk! If you're so worried about him, be my guest, come and take him. Take him and see if you can look after him for one day." She listened again, and now answered with a dull, tired voice, "We've been divorced four years and you still won't leave me alone. To hell with you. What makes you think you can call me at two in the morning anyway?" She sped up and shouted into the phone, "That's right! Actually, I'm planning to fuck some college kid twenty years my junior. He lives in my neighborhood. You happy now?"

She threw the phone on the passenger seat and drove faster and faster. The low pressure in the front left tire made the car hard to control. Still, she passed through several more yellow lights without slowing down. And though her cigarette wasn't finished she was already reaching for another one.

She did see it coming. The white Toyota approaching from the cross street at normal speed at first. Puri thought she'd pass it before they both got to the intersection. But then the Toyota seemed to be trying to do what Puri was doing, speeding up, and in an instant she was ramming right into that white car, lifting the thing and sending it spinning in the same direction it had come from. Puri's face banged against the side window upon impact but she didn't lose control of the wheel. She applied the brakes and simultaneously heard the sound of metal on asphalt and shattering glass as the other car careened and slid, upside down, before finally coming to a stop on the opposite side of the intersection.

When she finally turned, she saw what looked like an orange headscarf next to the car among all that shattered glass. It was not unlike the color of the overalls of those sanitation workers she'd driven past earlier. She felt like vomiting. The cigarette had fallen to the floor by her feet and was still burning. She lit the other one that was between her fingers and took a long drag. She didn't even glance back at the upended Toyota again. There were no cars anywhere. No one had seen this. Her engine was still idling. She put the car into gear and slowly inched away.

Final Scene

Bank Robber #1 kept pacing back and forth, nervously waving his gun in the air. He screamed, "Hurry up, all of you! You see what I'm holding in my hand? They don't call it a *shah-kosh* for nothing. And if it can kill a king, it can definitely kill you pieces of shit. Now out with everything you got in your pockets."

He turned to the woman in charge of the safe-deposit. "I want all the money you keep on this table, bitch." He slammed his hand on her table and returned to the customers. "Hurry!"

People were nervously emptying pockets and opening hand-bags and overturning briefcases.

Robber #1's attention went to the bald man who was still scratching his head with his mortgage booklet. He lingered for a second on the man before deciding to address the vice-manager instead. "Take this." He threw a black bag at him. "I want everything that's on the floor in that bag. Cash, phones, rings, everything."

Robber #2 was standing watch by the exit, one eye on the bank and the other on the street. There was a moment when everything seemed to come to a standstill, and then Robber #1 ran back to the safe-deposit woman.

"Didn't I tell you to put all the money on this table?"

The woman was watching him with a bewildered expression. There was a bruise on the side of her face the size of a ping-pong ball. This fact seemed to make Robber #1 more angry. He yanked her hair and pulled her out of her seat. The woman started scream-ing so loudly that Robber #2 had to run over and wrench Robber #1 off of her.

The two bank robbers whispered something amongst them-selves while the woman, crying, shuffled to where the others were still busy getting rid of their valuables.

Just then a cell phone went off. The sound of a *noha* lamenta-tion was coming out of it. The phone belonged to the man with the red prayer beads who had been standing with the vice-manager.

Robber #1 stormed up to him. "You old fart, didn't I tell you to cough up everything?" He smacked the man in the forehead with the gun. The phone fell out of the guy's hand, but the infer-nal dirge coming out of it continued.

"Shut it up!" Robber #1 screamed. "What kind of stupid ring-tone is that? Kill it." He pointed his king-killer to the ceiling and pulled the trigger. There was an awkward click but nothing hap-pened. The barrel had jammed. "Shit!" He tried again. Nothing.

The man he'd just hit, his face bleeding, seemed to come alive all of a sudden. He fingered the side of his coat, took a glance at the broken camera, pulled out his own gun, and released the safety. Robber #2, who was still standing by the safe-deposit table, now came running, rifle in hand, and immediately received a bullet to the throat.

"My daughter . . . hospital . . ." The prayer-bead man who'd just shot his gun off murmured these words to himself. No one heard him, of course. It was pandemonium in there. For a second the man even seemed to want to bend down and reach for the phone that had momentarily stopped ringing. People were screaming. A woman had passed out.

"Mercy!" Robber #1, standing there shaking, now croaked.

The phone started back up. The same song of lamentation. Robber #1's legs went limp and he fell to his knees next to Robber #2's body.

"Mercy," he repeated, this time barely managing a whisper.

The man fingered his red prayer bead and his face went dark. He put the gun to the masked man's forehead. "Mercy? Mercy, you say? Don't you know a king-killer that actually works knows nothing about that word?"

THE GROOM'S RETURN

BY MAHAK TAHERI

Behesht e Zahra Cemetery

H e told the man at the car wash he wanted the Peugeot made spotless for the wedding.

The man remarked, "Looks like you've been on the road a bit." Behdad nodded as the guy went around knocking some dried-up mud from the back wheels. "I'll wash it so good you'll think it just came out of the factory."

Behdad nodded again.

The man wanted to start with the inside of the car. Together they pulled out the oversized carton filled with old newspapers and clippings from the backseat. Then Behdad stood to the side and lit a cigarette. A crow perched nearby and stared right at him. There was loathing in the bird's expression, as if it had been witness to and could recall every wrong with this city. He thought: *That bird is the opposite of Tehran. Tehran's memory is empty. It doesn't exist.* After five years of being on the road, Behdad was sure of this. He found it incredible that a murderer could so easily come back to the scene of his crime and no one would remember him. The car wash guy said something he didn't hear. When his smoke was finished he began skimming through the old newspapers in the box looking for nothing in particular, just skimming them: *On Wednesday, the district inspector reported the body of a woman found in her own residence off of Si-e-Tir Street.*

The guy was working on the top of the car now, soaping and scrubbing as hard as he could. He called out to Behdad again, telling him he could wait inside if he wanted to. Behdad said no and went back to the newspaper clippings with her pictures in them. Elahe had resembled a movie star at those initial proceedings in court. She was beautiful and hardly needed makeup. Most of the later pictures were good too. But in those later ones she seemed more like a movie star in mourning. Behdad didn't like them so much. You could see some hair sticking out of her headscarf, showing the white at the root of her black hair. In the very beginning, when he'd first noticed her coming to the bank, she'd been blond. But the blond disappeared after a while in jail. Behdad knew that was part of her new act too. The white and black hair. The bereaved look. Elahe had been a first-rate role player. She loved to act. Loved refrains and catchwords. The whole time after the verdict, while waiting to be executed, she kept telling reporters how much she'd loved him. "You must see *him* through my mind," she'd insisted to them. Even back then he'd thought how Elahe's mind could turn the stink of a toilet into the scent of a rose.

> *A woman who took money from the bank account of the victim's husband on the day of the murder has been arrested. Judge Jafarzadeh of the criminal court stated that the murderer also confessed she had an illicit affair with the victim's spouse for the past four and a half years. The victim's spouse had been renting an apartment for her in a northern section of the city.*

After five years the car's natural blue was finally coming out from under all that dirt and grime. The guy kept calling out all the little extras he was doing to the car, hustling for a good tip. And Behdad kept nodding yes to everything. It had been the same with Elahe. She labored for the love they had for each other by asking him yes/no questions. *Do you love me? Yes. Do I look pretty today? Yes. You'll never leave me, right? No.* She named the apartment he'd rented for her "Our Tehran Afternoons." She called him her man. But always made sure to remind him she wasn't trying to take the place of his wife. "No, I'm not like that. I don't want to be a burden to you. I won't ever let her find out. Just tell me when you don't want me anymore and I'll go away. No questions asked."

She'd talked like that in jail too. There was no wall separating her words of love to him and the words she said to the newspapers: *My only crime is love. This is the story of our love, me and him. Love is not an illusion. It's real. My captivity for his freedom. I am good with that. None of this is fantasy.*

"Now you can really see the car," the man announced with satisfaction. His job was done. Delidad finally turned to him. And then both their gazes followed the crow who had begun to stir on the roof of the car wash. "Only a bird that size can survive in the pollution of this city," the guy said. "The sparrows couldn't last here. They're gone. Everything's gone."

Behdad, too, had left this city. But it wasn't voluntary. The order had come from above. They'd sent one of their messengers and made it clear: *Disappear and don't ever come back if you know what's good for you.* But who were *they*? He still didn't know. All he knew was that Tehran was theirs. The country was theirs. Regular folks called these kinds of people the "shadow government." You didn't see them. You just received orders. Once you were in their orbit, there was no getting out.

Behdad knew he was trapped from the first time they'd asked him to falsify bank documents. Later, when they were done with him, they worked on his wife. *Your husband is seeing a woman called Elahe. He spends his afternoons with her. When he comes home, it's her perfume he's carrying on him.* His wife never told him how she knew all this stuff. There were countless fights. She'd had no idea that these fights were what the shadow men were aiming for; they were setting her up for the day she'd be killed.

And he never figured out where these men were. Everywhere and nowhere. They only sent their henchmen. They sent guys on motorcycles who brought you directives, commands, threats, warnings. Until your entire life became a cycle of permanent anxiety. Until you were scared to pull down the window in case a motorcycle thug passed by.

Behdad peered to the north of the city, toward the mountains that you could barely see through the smog. Five years ago he had left this place via the Karaj Highway only to return on the same road. He had stayed in hundreds of no-name places that didn't even earn a spot on most maps. The longest he'd stayed anywhere was in a village not far from Bandar Abbas, off the Persian Gulf. His real home was this car and the teahouses along the road. If there was one thing he'd learned from his travels, it was this: you can't build a home on the white lines of the freeway. And now he was here, because . . . well, because the dead had finally summoned him.

In the hallway of the criminal court a reporter had asked him, "What verdict do you think they'll give Elahe?"

He didn't even have the energy to hate the reporter, and all the dozens of others who had hounded him during those days. He'd answered, "Verdict? The verdict they give will be for me too. We're both on trial."

"No," the reporter had said, as if Behdad was daft. "I'm asking so you can give a passionate answer for our readers. Don't be so cold about it, sir."

"You have your answer. Let your pen invent the passion."

The crow circled and landed on top of the car. The car wash man shooed it off. "Good as new," he said to Behdad. "Only I couldn't get some of those scratches off. For that I'd have to give it a thorough polish. It would take some time."

Behdad took a wad of money from his pocket and peeled off several large bills. The man examined the money with surprise. It was way more than the price of a car wash. "You can give the rest to the other guys," Behdad said.

There were no other guys, of course. The man smiled. "I'll get pastries and take them to the wife and kids. Make them happy. You are too generous."

He wanted to tell the man that dirty money never brought good luck. And this money—this very money that he had just taken out of his pocket—had passed through *their* hands, people who turned everything they touched to scum. But what did this car wash man know about all that? What you don't know can't hurt you. Seven years! That was how long he'd worked at the bank before they approached him. *Approach* was too weak a word for it; more like they'd made him an offer he could hardly refuse. They'd made it seem easy, and in fact it really was easy to create false letters of credit for imports. The imports were nonexistent. This way they managed to receive government-subsidized exchange rates and then flush the precious dollars out of the country but bring nothing back in return. It was the perfect setup. They'd bought him for peanuts because saying no was not in the equation. Then, when the little extras started coming in, he'd grown too comfortable with the good life, especially with the apartment called Our Tehran Afternoons.

He placed more bills in the man's hand. "Do something for me, then: get your family some really nice pastries. The very best."

"May God always provide for you. May your wedding bring you and yours fortune."

The murderer tried to deny her involvement in the crime. But in no time she confessed, stating that it was out of love that she committed the heinous act. Having taken the key from the victim's husband's pocket, she entered the house without being noticed and killed her victim with multiple knife wounds.

The newspapers devoted full-page articles to her. The story sold. It especially sold if they included pictures of her. There was always a waiting list of reporters to interview her. And she always obliged. She was in her element that way, playing the role of the brokenhearted lover to the very end and appearing carefully fragile and sorrow-stricken in the photographs. He recalled how she had always loved taking pictures, often insisting they go to one studio or another where they could get romantic shots with dreamy backgrounds. Funny how his own wife had been the exact opposite of that. A woman of no frills. Never spent money that she didn't have. Even when she noticed that their living situation had improved far beyond what a simple bank employee pushing thirty could afford, she still refused to spend. Maybe she suspected from the start that the money was dirty and didn't want to touch it.

The car wash man took the box of newspapers and placed it in the passenger seat up front. "You like reading newspapers obviously."

"Old newspapers."

"Good for cleaning windows."

Behdad said nothing. At the bottom of the box were copies of all the false documents he had ever put through at the bank. Everything was there. And this morning he'd sent scanned copies to every newspaper that had ever run articles about Elahe. In case the papers were too afraid to publish them, he'd taken the precaution of posting them online and forwarded the link around widely. Would they bite? He didn't know. But he had done his job. At last.

As soon as he sat back in the car, Elahe's voice was everywhere. She swam alongside the traffic and lingered behind the honk of cars stuck on Hafez Bridge. She was a symphony that never left him, confessing to all who would listen: *Yes, I did love him. And yes, I did kill. But who did I kill? I killed our own child. The one-month-old baby that was in my belly. That's who I killed. All of you whose job it is to collect evidence, why won't you try to find out the truth? I didn't kill his wife; I killed US.*

A motorcyclist stopped near him at the red light. *Must be one of their messengers*, he thought. Behdad didn't turn to look, but rolled his window down to see what the man had to say or deliver to him. A bullet maybe? Even before they'd killed his wife and thrown Elahe behind bars, it was always these bike riders who brought him the messages. *Do this, do that . . . get lost and never show your face in this city again.*

It had been that easy for them. As easy as creating fictitious bank documents. In the end they had themselves a fictitious murderer too, and were done with him.

The motorcycle rode away without a message or a command.

The offender's attorney insists that the method of procuring the confession was not legal and that the actual clues found at the crime scene do not correspond to Elahe's original admission of guilt under duress. Particularly, the attorney adds, the powerful thrusts of the knife to the victim's body cannot have come from a woman of Elahe's size and strength.

Elahe's grave was still warm. He was sure of it. People lied when they said the earth around the dead goes cold. Five years had passed and he still could not put her out of his mind. She was alive for him. And as he turned on Jomhuri Avenue, where a thousand TV screens in the windows of the electronics shops blinked at him, he imagined they'd all simultaneously show the same thing: Elahe's court appearance. All those LCD screens, large and small, had to be in on his secret. But, of course, they were mostly showing cartoons of fish swimming in the ocean and cats and mice chasing each other. He thought of how the true pulse of a city was always just underneath such wallpaper images. All you had to do was change from the cartoon channel to the city channel and then you'd know the truth. You'd really know. *Who am I to take someone else's life? Life comes from God and only He can take it back.* Elahe had wept and wept when she said those words to the judge.

But not once had she ever cried when they were home together in *Our Tehran Afternoons.*

He parked in front of a flower shop and told the wise-looking old man that he wanted wedding flowers fastened to the car. Lots of them.

"Anything in particular?"

"A few of everything."

The old guy smiled. "I could do that and charge you a lot of money. You're the customer and the customer is always right. But it's a wedding we're talking about. The flowers attached to the car need to have harmony. There's an art to it. We shouldn't overdo it."

"You decide then. As long as it's colorful. I want plenty of color."

It was the one thing his wife and Elahe had had in common: they both loved flowers. They both said they could understand the language of plants. He wondered if he had ever really understood either one of these women. His wife was gone and he'd barely thought of her these five years. As for Elahe, he could never get past those memories of her in court, talking: *They write that I like to watch violent movies. Somebody tell me, is* Gone with the Wind *violent? Is* Doctor Zhivago *violent?*

She had created a stir with such words and the judge would sometimes glare at her as if he wanted to hang her right then and there. Her attorney had protested to the court that from the very first day they'd taken to calling her "the murderer" rather than "the accused." It was branding someone who had not yet been proven guilty. It was this same lawyer who had insisted on yet a third appeals court. But by then the Elahe who showed up at the stand was hardly the Elahe of Our Tehran Afternoons. Her skin had turned ashen and she played the part of a lover who had been completely defeated. *I've said it before and I'll say it again, it wasn't me. I've proved my love already. I could not see him suffering like that.*

He had visited her in jail and said, "If you admit to the murder, these guys will leave me alone. I promise after that I'll get you out of jail myself. It'll be easy. I was her husband; I have the right to ask the court to let you go. It's the law."

It wasn't that simple, though. They'd offered him a choice: take the blame yourself or have Elahe take it. But they were bluffing, as usual. They didn't want him to take the blame. If he did, then there would be an investigation into his job and they might discover the false import documents. No, they wanted Elahe to take the fall, a straightforward case of a scorned and vindictive lover. He'd had plenty of time since then to think these things through. He'd been duped. When she was being readied for the gallows, they'd told him it was no use: they'd kill both of them if he asked the court for clemency. The papers had a field day during that period: *Jealous Woman Kills Her Lover's Spouse . . . Murderer Recants Her Confession . . . Elahe Says She'd Do Anything for Him . . .* Five years of living with these newspaper clippings. That's why he was back. Because nothing mattered anymore.

The flower man was telling him something. ". . . Take a look at this album, son. Maybe you'll like a few of the designs."

"It doesn't matter."

"But it does. Let me tell you, I've been in this business over thirty years. Rest assured, years down the road your lucky bride will be reminding you what beautiful flowers you had on the car. These old hands bring luck to young people."

Behdad winced. "I'm not so young anymore. But all right, whatever you say. Whichever design you think is best is fine with me."

He scanned the street as the flower man got to work. There were two motorcyclists on the other side of the road next to a juice stand. They both wore black leather jackets without helmets.

The newspapers had asked: *Elahe, is there anything else you want to tell us?* And she'd replied: *Only this: I'll keep buying flowers, just so the flower man won't know that my lover has left me for good.*

The car slowly became a feast of colors, just as the man had promised. He went about it patiently, fastening flowers and ribbons and leaves in two neat circles across the hood and trunk. Behdad came and stood outside watching the man work. Passersby made comments and offered congratulations. But the two men in leather jackets across the street barely turned his way.

"How do you like it?" The old man ran a hand through his

white hair and smiled at Behdad. He seemed pleased with his work.

"You are an artist." He took out another wad of bills from his pocket and counted. When the flower man protested that he was giving him too much, he put another bundle of cash in the man's hands. "Pray for me."

"May this happy occasion bring you a hundred years of happiness."

Behdad drove.

The execution had taken place on a late-autumn day inside the prison. He was there; they'd ordered him to go. He had to be there as the spouse of the victim insisting on *qesas*. Elahe's mother was there too and one of their relatives was holding her up with difficulty. Behdad could hardly look at them. "My daughter made a terrible mistake being with a married man," she cried, "but I know my daughter; she's not a killer." His memory stopped there. He could not recall the stool being pulled from under Elahe. He could not remember if she'd said anything. Elahe was up in the air and he was still down on earth, his eyes glued to the ground. Immediately afterward, his life had been voided—fired from his job for carrying on an illicit affair, thus bringing shame to the bank and his colleagues.

A big stamp of annulment on his life. The road his only option.

Until today.

He drove on, farther and farther south until he was on the freeway that led to the Behesht e Zahra Cemetery. They hadn't buried his wife at this place, but instead took her to her parents' graveyard in the town she'd grown up in. The police report had said they'd found the victim naked in bed. They lied; his wife never slept naked.

A white car moved past him and one of the passengers shouted out congratulations to the groom. Behdad rolled his window down and honked back. He wanted the sound of his wedding to echo through the entire city that he'd just left behind. In the meantime, as he'd expected, the two bikers were there in his side mirrors. They stayed on him like a pair of wings, one on each side, keeping pace exactly a car-length behind. He pressed on the gas and saw them speeding up too. The white ribbons hanging off the flower arrangements fluttered in the air. He was a groom who had arrived five years too late. But today he was in a hurry. The biker to his right gradually inched closer until he was almost flush against the rear door. Speeding up again, Behdad reached over, swung the front passenger seat open, and shoved the box out of the car. As he did, he lost control of the wheel and the vehicle made a sharp turn in the direction of the box and the biker. The sound of metal on asphalt. The car was making for the guardrails. He quickly grabbed the wheel and swung it the other way, then reached over and closed the flapping door without slowing down. The other bike had stayed on him, though it hung back a bit now. In the rearview mirror he saw that the crashed bike had slammed into the rails but the rider wasn't anywhere near it.

Newspapers and clippings scattering and dancing in the air on the freeway of the dead.

He pressed harder. At the Behesht e Zahra exit he slammed on the brakes and threw the car in reverse. The second motorcycle was fast coming on him now, followed in the distance by a semitruck. The whole thing took barely a couple of seconds. The bike smashed hard into the car's rear. Behdad watched the man fly up like a cartoon character and come crashing down next to his spinning bike. The driver of the semi had in the meantime pulled over in shock and the infernal sound of his horn would not let up.

As Behdad began to drive again, the smashed-up trunk kicked open and up, causing some of the loosened flowers to slide off. He could see nothing now in the rearview mirror. The smell of burning garbage was overpowering out here. He rolled up the window and headed for the cemetery entrance.

He should look his best for her today. He collected himself

in the parking lot. The tiny gravestone he had ordered sat in the trunk unharmed. He took it out and held it under his arm like a briefcase. He had to find row 253. The city of the dead had grown these past five years. Back then her plot had been the last in its row. But now the graves hugged the walls of this section from one end to the other. He walked fast, almost running, catching pieces of poetry on the other graves as he passed them. For her, though, he'd ordered a simple stone with just her name on it, *Elahe Sattari*.

He started running, like someone trying to catch up to a bus that was about to leave him behind. Her plot was easy to find: it was the only one in that area that didn't have a gravestone yet. He'd fix that right now. He placed the marker over her and took out the small music box he'd bought for her when they first met and started winding it up. He'd never done this part before. It was always Elahe who liked to wind the thing up. At dusk every night she'd sit on the balcony, draw a shawl over her bare shoulders, and let the thing play just once. It was a part of her act. The romantic in her.

The music began to play. *Ding-ding-ding* . . . He had no idea what the tune was. But its sound brought back the scent of Elahe's incense and the general smell of her apartment. Our Tehran Afternoons. He held his face closer to her. He could hear her breathing now. She was here, yes. He lay over her and listened and ran a finger over the name *Elahe Sattari*. He had instructed the mason to make her first name bigger than her last. So cold here! The dead don't give off any heat? But Elahe was breathing for him and he lay perfectly still and recalled just how much she hated the cold. He wound the music box a second time. Footsteps came toward him. Patient footsteps, footsteps with all the time in the world in this deserted section of the vast cemetery.

Behdad glanced up to see the first biker he'd crashed into standing there watching him. There was blood on the man. Blood and patience. Not anger, but determination. The guy brought his hand up, pointing something at him. Behdad rested his head back down and embraced his lover's name. A fierce noise rang out across the cemetery, and several bored-looking black crows took off from where they'd been perching nearby.

THE GRAVEDIGGER'S KADDISH
BY GINA B. NAHAI
Tehrangeles

The first to die were the carp, which became cloudy-eyed and disoriented, circling the lake in slow, awkward patterns and developing ulcers on their gills and in their kidneys till they washed, wasted, ashore. Then the seagulls started to go blind and slam into things, or they fell, midflight, into the water or grass, or stopped eating till they died of anorexia. By June, little kids who stuck their hands out of the paddleboats to feel the water went home with burned skin, and the old Russian and Iranian men who sat in the shade and played backgammon all day complained of headaches and nausea, and the few fishermen who were dumb enough to cook and eat the bluegill and tilapia they had caught and frozen before the blight had to be rushed to hospital.

The daily joggers suspected environmental calamity. They called and e-mailed the parks department, their councilman's office, city hall. They started a "Save the Lake" social media campaign, sent videos of sloshed birds and moldering fish to websites that covered the goings-on in the Valley and Los Angeles proper. If this were a little fishpond in Beverly Hills, they said, every resource in the city would have been drawn upon by now; if it were a swimming pool in Santa Monica, seven different environmental groups would have filed suit in state and federal courts. But this was Van Nuys—60 percent Latino and the rest are black or Armenian or Asian or Iranian, they got bigger worries than a lake being polluted in the park. They were lucky they had a park at all.

The good news was that some years ago, property owners around the park had strong-armed the city council into renaming part of the area "Lake Balboa"—which, truth to tell, sounded considerably more upscale than plain old Van Nuys—and that quite a few buyers fell for the posturing and paid a premium for the name, even poured good money in by renovating an old house or tearing it down to build a new one, which meant they had a bigger stake in not letting their investment turn into a cancer cluster. Among these residents were a husband-and-husband couple, Donny and Luca Goldberg-Ferraro, who had spent the previous nine months remodeling and redecorating their house. The younger spouse, Luca, was a fairly successful film producer with an even temper who, like anyone even remotely connected to the business in LA, believed he should not be subject to the same limitations as other mortals. For a while, he followed the news about the lake with dispassionate curiosity, trusting, as he told Donny, that "the city will take care of it." Then he noticed the scent of garbage that sometimes blew in the wind, and confessed to being "slightly irritated." A few weeks later, when a stray seagull crashed headfirst into their window and left traces of blood and feathers and brain tissue on the glass, he declared in the most docile tone, "I've run out of patience with that lake."

Donny was a writer with a good two decades on his husband and absolutely no interest in the park or the lake or, really, anything that had happened in the world since the O.J. Simpson trial in 1994. He had published two dozen novels and was still writing well into his seventies, but he couldn't remember the last time he had left the house except to go to a doctor's appointment or a fancy dinner with Luca. He had bought the house with money he made from selling his first book in 1962. Inside, he hung giant black-and-whites of old movie stars, Garbo and Dietrich and Bette Davis, on all the walls. He had silk flowers in the foyer and synthetic grass for a lawn, and he kept the curtains closed and installed only peach and yellow lightbulbs in the chandelier and the floor lamps.

His favorite part of the house was a glass coffee table he called "the cemetery" because it was covered with Lalique and Daum crystal figurines, "à la Tennessee Williams." The table was situated close to the window where the seagull had met its abrupt end, which was the only piece of the whole matter that interested Donny— "Can you imagine if the window were open?"

That was on Sunday morning, July 21, 2013. On Monday, three more birds met an untimely end outside Donny's crystal cemetery, prompting Luca to wonder aloud if he should "have my intern look into the matter of the lake."

Donny let a full minute pass, then announced, "My dear, fuck the lake."

But the next morning the front lawn was littered with avian remains, and Luca realized he was going to have to help cure the infestation or learn to live with the scents and sights of bird viscera.

On Wednesday the intern, a Harvard Business School graduate who was "working his way up"—that is, for free—with Luca, reported that the lake, in true LA fashion, was "staged." Rather than a natural occurence, it was a twenty-seven-acre, ten-foot-deep hole that had been filled, in 1992, with 72 million gallons of reclaimed sewage water from a nearby treatment plant. The park where it was situated had started out as Balboa Park but had more recently been renamed Anthony C. Beilenson Park—after a former congressman from the twenty-fourth district.

To Luca, the natural next step was to call the congressman at home.

Thursday morning a truck pulled up in front of the lake, and two men in official-looking uniforms started to collect samples. They came back the next day in hazmat gear to gather more samples and install orange glow-in-the-dark *Health Hazard! Do Not Touch!* signs. On Saturday, the district's representative on the city council made a personal appearance at the park. He wore a brand-new pair of Ray-Bans, a too-starched safari suit, and sunscreen with too much fragrance. Fashion statement notwithstanding, he looked genuinely absorbed in the report whispered to him by the city's "pollution complaint investigators" and "water-quality control agents." He had barely driven away in his black-on-black Subaru with the two college-age assistants forever tapping on their smartphones when the website of *LA Daily News* erupted with the headline, *Gold Discovered in Lake Balboa.*

The ensuing flash mob pummeled the grounds of the park and made scraps of the rental bikes, boats, and kayaks. Within the hour, the Japanese cherry blossom trees were stripped naked and the jogging path was pockmarked with ditches, and so many people converged on the lake and waded into the water with their shovels and pans and buckets, the fire department had to call in riot cops to break up the fights. The 101 and 134 freeways were backed up for miles in both directions, and surface streets turned into parking lots and police and news helicopters fought for airspace above the area. Their noise, combined with the sound of cars honking and pedestrians' voices, awakened Donny from his Ambien-induced, Xanax-aided, total-darkness-in-the-room-plus-black-eye-mask sleep that he likened, fondly, to being dead. Downstairs in the living room, he found Luca at the window, binoculars in hand, listening to his intern dish the details of the story on speakerphone.

The soil and water samples taken from the lake indicated not the existence of pure gold, but an inordinately high concentration of a number of chemical compounds found in gold. According to Wikipedia the compounds were known as "gold salts." At a reasonable concentration, if refined and mixed with other elements, they are sometimes used in treating illnesses and in certain medications. At higher doses, they can cause gold poisoning.

For the first time in recent memory, Donny became interested in the news. He went up to the window and took the binoculars from Luca, then called their "butler," Mehdi, from the kitchen to bring coffee.

"He's late," Luca reported. "He's called my cell four times already."

A middle-age Iranian man with washed-out good looks and a pathological drive to please, Mehdi had "been with" (that's how they put it, because it sounded more elegant than "worked for") Donny and Luca for nearly three years. He had started as a temporary chauffeur for Donny in 2010, to drive him to his physical therapy appointments after a knee replacement, and slowly moved to full-time status as housekeeper and cook and personal shopper and that amorphous hireling that is de rigueur for every ardent wannabe or unemployed has-been in LA, "personal assistant." He was so polite and deferential, so utterly self-effacing and low-maintenance, he could be a nuisance if not kept in check. Obsessively punctual, he synchronized his watch with the clock in Donny and Luca's dining room and made a point of being neither late nor early by so much as a minute. On the rare occasions when some calamity held him back by any fraction of an hour, he went into a state not unlike an anxiety attack that could only be tamped down with a cocktail of high-potency benzodiazepines.

He called twice more that morning to say he was still stuck in traffic, and he sounded so shaken up and harried, Luca suggested they "call it a day and let you go home and rest." Only that wasn't an option because the gridlock stretched in both directions, so Mehdi hacked it as long as he could, then simply turned off the engine, left the key in the ignition, and walked the rest of the way to work.

He showed up with his shirt drenched in sweat and hands visibly shaking, so overwhelmed with apprehension that he stuttered like a pro. The minute he started to apologize for his lateness, Donny raised a hand and signaled for him to shut up.

"My dear man, your abjectness is irritating."

Donny was still at the window with the binoculars, and he had stationed Luca on the computer and left the TV on CNN so they wouldn't miss a second of anything.

It took them both a minute or so to understand, from his silence and obvious confusion, that Mehdi did not know about the lake. Astonished, Donny lowered the binoculars and turned to him.

"Come here," he said, and Mehdi started toward him with jittery legs. His face was glistening with a new sheet of perspiration and his palms left tracks when he wiped them on his pants. He was rounding the corner of the Lalique cemetery when Donny added, "Haven't you heard? They found gold in Lake Balboa."

He said this with uncharacteristic enthusiasm, as if the gold had been discovered on their own property, and he expected Mehdi to at least feign excitement, as he did, just to be polite, whenever Donny or Luca shared with him some good news of their own. Instead, Mehdi let out a soft, truncated yelp, sank to his knees, and let the binoculars fall out of his hand.

⟐

His father had said they were going to buy shoes. Instead, they took a taxi to Vanak in North Tehran. There was snow everywhere, but his father insisted that the driver let them out a few streets away from their destination, so that their shoes and socks, even the bottom of their pants, were wet and frozen over by the time they reached the house. They waited for the buzzer, then hiked through the giant metal gates and up a long driveway. Mehdi shivered with cold, but his father had been perspiring since before they left home, and now he had to stop every few minutes and wipe his face with the side of his lapel. On either side of them, tall, naked trees, their branches powdered with snow, rose like ghosts over icy flowerbeds.

The front door was unlocked, so Mehdi's father, Alireza, had only to push down on the brass handle to let them in. But he had started to shake, and his hand was slippery from the sweat, so he gave up after two attempts and turned to Mehdi for help. Inside, the house was dark and cold and utterly quiet, as if no one had lived in it for decades, but Alireza seemed to know where he was going. Down the long hallway and past a black marble staircase, he led Mehdi into a round dining room with a circular table and twelve chairs. "Stay here," he said. "Don't wander out and don't come looking for me." But Mehdi followed him anyway, because he was afraid of being alone in this strange house and afraid too that Alireza would not come back for him. He had gotten as far as the bottom of the staircase when Alireza turned around and saw him.

"Go back and close the door," he snapped, "or I'll quash you," but by then it was already too late.

Golnessa Hayim—barefoot, flat-chested, and dark as a Gypsy—stood against the second-floor railing in a purple satin dress with one blooming rose painted on the front, and a single slit carved into the hem right up to the tip of her white lace garters and the mouth of her red, naked vagina. Her hair was a storm of black curls and her eyes were bottle green and transparent as glass, and when she smiled at Mehdi, he saw her one gold tooth and realized, to his utter delight and acute horror, that this was the shameless, ruinous, Jew-whore woman his mother had often raged against in the last few months.

Spellbound, Mehdi had the urge to follow his father up the steps and into Golnessa's arms and chest and soft, hollow places, though he was only eight years old and still thought his penis was for urinating. His eyes would not relent; they were locked into Golnessa's green gaze so that he had to walk backward to get away while Alireza, who had forgotten his son already, climbed two steps at a time and fell into Golnessa with a loud, aching moan that coursed through the house and made Mehdi's legs go limp.

He waited, alone, in the dining room. He was too nervous to sit, too agitated to walk without feeling as if his knees would buckle. Every few minutes, he thought he heard a sound—footsteps approaching, his name being called—only to realize it was just an echo in his ears. When he couldn't stand the tension anymore he ventured back into the hallway.

The rest of the house felt like no one had lived in it for decades, but Mehdi thought he could sense heat transpiring through the door frame of one of the rooms upstairs. Then he heard the song.

"*Dar in haal-eh mass-tee safaa kardaam.*"

Golnessa's voice spilled down the steps like warm water.

"*Tow-raa eyy khodaa man seh-daa kardaam.*"

It was an ode to God, a plea by a devout subject lost in euphoria and beckoning Him closer—though there was no mistaking, right at that moment, whom Golnessa beckoned.

That she sang so ably and with such abandon, people said about Golnessa, was no doubt thanks to her ancestors, who were traveling Jewish musicians from Shiraz—city of fine wine and loose morals whose women were considered de facto prostitutes. Besmirched from birth, Golnessa's mother was dark and similarly flat-chested and plain as a stick figure drawn with coal on a sidewalk. Her only choice in marriage was a gravedigger's son from that poorest of Jewish ghettos, the *mahalleh* in Yazd. Golnessa was her fourth child and first daughter, and she turned out to be the last as well because the pregnancy upset some essential symmetry in the mother, thinned out her blood or siphoned the milk of her muscles so that, even after her body had expelled the infant and rid itself of the extra fluids, her legs felt heavy and slack and reluctant, they fought her when she tried to walk and shifted if she stood, no matter how much vinegar and salt and mustard seeds and sage and turmeric she wrapped them in and how much garlic and coriander she added to her food or even how many freshly cut foreskins she swallowed at circumcision parties. She went from walking with a slight gait to dragging one leg around to walking with a pair of wooden sticks to, when Golnessa was about six years old, dragging herself on the ground.

On the bright side, Golnessa had come with her own, albeit unsubstantial, dowry—her lower left incisor, fully grown and permanent at birth, was pure gold.

She had been such a marvel as a baby—a loud, undersized creature with a fountain of curly black hair already longer than her own infant body, shiny dark skin and glass-green eyes and that one tooth gleaming in her mouth every time she let out a cry—that people lined up in the courtyard of the gravedigger's house just to catch a glimpse of her, even reached into her mouth and tried to wiggle the tooth or pull it out, held a magnet up to it to see if it was real gold, and went away convinced, yet again, that God was full of surprises.

The parents were going to leave the tooth in her mouth as a savings account of sorts—something of value she would take to her husband's house—but as she grew older and her mother's health declined, they decided to cash in early. One night when Golnessa was six years old, her father strapped her to a chair, poured a full glass of *arrack* down her throat, and launched a full-on attack with a pair of steel pliers. He pulled at the tooth till his hands blistered, grabbed the arms of the tool with a towel wrapped around them and pulled again. The harder he pulled, the less her jaw gave. He oiled Golnessa's gums and tried again, blew some opium smoke into her nostrils to put her to sleep, and cut the gums of her lower jaw along the length of the tooth to where he imagined the root should be. He even tried reasoning with the mouth—this is just a baby tooth; a bigger, stronger one will grow in its place if only you relinquish this one.

All the while Golnessa sat motionless on the chair, her eyes wide open and her senses immune to the wine and opium, and stared at her father without uttering a sound.

The next day, the father brought home one of the wooden, three-wheel carts they used to haul corpses at the cemetery, set his wife in it, and attached a harness to the handles. Then, as if in punishment for denying him the tooth, he put Golnessa in the harness and told her she would stay there until she either let go of the tooth or got married and left the house.

* * *

Her first husband, when she was barely fourteen, was a sixty-seven-year-old Zoroastrian *bache baaz*—molester of young boys—which was a polite name for men who did not like to be considered homosexual but saw nothing unmanly about spending quality time with youngsters. He had married Golnessa because he was getting on in years and wanted a young woman to take care of him. Given his well-known disinterest in the female sex, he wasn't expected to consummate the marriage. The night of the wedding he went into the "conjugal chambers" for formality's sake, took off his socks and shoes and asked the bride to rub his feet while he slept. He yelled for the relatives who had gathered outside the room to go home already, there would be no deflowering of the virgin that night, no presentation of a chiffon-and-lace handkerchief bloodied with the evidence. But oh, how wrong he was!

She must have *chiz-khored* the old man—secretly fed him a potion that put him, unsuspecting, under her spell—because not only did he emerge an hour after he had called it a night, looking radiant and self-satisfied and so very, very virile, to present the handkerchief as well as the bride's gown all smeared with proof of her deflowering, he never again showed the slightest interest in a boy. Instead, he applied himself body and soul to mining the depths of carnal gratification with Golnessa, maintained a strict diet of a dozen raw eggs for breakfast, twenty-four pitted dates stuffed with walnut for lunch, and ripe figs and goat head or devil's eyelashes with dinner. Whatever poison she was sneaking into his food or drink improved not only his constitution but also his luck, because from the day she stepped into his house till she left, six years later, one early morning in the midst of a rainstorm, the old *bache baaz* went from being utterly impecunious to more than moderately wealthy.

That's how she bought her freedom from the old man, how she would convince others to grant her a speedy divorce: she promised they could keep the luck she had brought them.

* * *

Her second husband was a forty-some-year-old Muslim carpet seller from Shemiran with a wife and half a dozen kids.

The third one was a thirty-year-old Jew from Tehran; he had been married two years and had no children—just a wife—to abandon for Golnessa.

The thing about her was, she had no fear. The worst fate that could befall a woman—being considered a harlot—had already happened to her at birth because of her family's inherited profession. The next few worst things—being poor, having a mother who could not care for her, being so dark and unattractive that she would be written off as a likely candidate for marriage to anyone at all—had also happened to her before she opened those green eyes of hers onto this world. The eyes, in fact, fooled some people into believing that she might be that rarest and most mythical of creatures—a good-luck woman—because they were, indeed, striking in their clarity and vividness, but then there was the Moor's skin and Mongol's body, the Berber hair and those African lips, and there was the fact that she had made a cripple out of a perfectly healthy mother, and that she was born to a man who washed corpses for a living, and soon enough it didn't matter how radiant the eyes were, you knew the girl was bad news.

Any other woman of her caliber would swallow the proverbial scorpion and resign herself to being less worthy than a bald canvas rug on the doorstep of a poor man's caravansary. Golnessa, instead, became the scorpion.

She had no fear, no shame, no (it seemed) need or desire for that most valuable of commodities in Iranian society—a good name. The only quality she seemed to favor in a man was youth, and the only compensation she offered for getting him to betray his family and become a social pariah was that certain euphoria she sang about, and the undeniable good fortune, albeit only financial, that traveled with her from house to house.

Not that the money—sudden, easy, and abundant as Golnessa's luck made it—couldn't have induced the euphoria, but greed alone, no matter how dire, would hardly account for the depth of devotion she inspired in her men, or the lengths to which they were eager to go for her. Her fourth husband, Davood Hayim, "stole" her from an employer who had treated Davood with greater generosity and more genuine kindness than his own father.

Davood's father, Moshe Hayim, was a Jew who converted to Islam so he could take advantage of the law that assigned sole rights of inheritance to any *jadid al-Islam*—new Muslim—no matter how distant the family connection might have been or how many male heirs were standing in line. Given the benefits, and the ease with which conversion was possible—all one had to do was to be sure he wanted to be a Muslim, and a Shia at that, and say the words, *La ilaha il Allah, Muhammadun rasulu-llah, wa aliyyun waliyyu-llah*— I testify that there is no god but Allah, Muhammad is the messenger of God, and Ali is the vice-regent of Allah. You could do this with or without witnesses, then wash yourself, and you were done—Moshe Hayim became a *jadid al-Islam* in a matter of minutes, changed his name to Muhammad Hakeem, added a *seyyed wa aliyyun waliyyu-llah*—descendant of the Prophet—as a bonus, and even took a Muslim wife. He kept the new wife in a separate house from the first one, visited them on alternate nights, and let each raise the children in her own religion.

Moshe Hayim, a.k.a. Muhammad Hakeem, had many daughters, but only two sons: Davood from the Jewish wife, and Alireza from the Muslim.

Touched with Golnessa's good luck, Davood became increasingly wealthy. He relished both the money and the social status that came with it, and was eager to keep it, but the richer and more popular he became, the easier it was for him to defy Golnessa, leave her side, forget that she was to be worshipped. That's why she *chiz-khored* Alireza.

For weeks after the visit to Vanak, Mehdi prayed that Alireza would take him back to the house. He dreamed of Golnessa even when awake, heard her voice, the words to her song, even in his sleep. At home, he went around sniffing like a bloodhound for that cold, bitter scent his father carried home on his skin and clothes some nights. It was the smell of Golnessa's house—her room or sheets or maybe just her breath—and it stuck to Alireza like a scar and caused his wife to erupt in anger and accuse him of being less honorable than a *dayoos*—a man whose wife whores around. For Mehdi, though, the scent was all that stood between him and absolute despondency. A few times in the ensuing months he ran away from school and boarded a bus to Vanak, trying in vain to find the house. He even asked Alireza if they could "go see the lady with the gold tooth again," but the only response he evoked was a firm slap and a bloody lower lip. He had nearly given up on ever seeing Golnessa again when Alireza had one fight too many with his wife, spat on the ground to mark the momentousness of the occasion, and declared he was leaving to marry his brother's wife.

To his mother and siblings, this was a calamity they would not overcome; to Mehdi, it was proof that God did exist, and that He did, in fact, hear young boys' prayers.

⁂

Donny and Luca had put an ad on Craigslist and interviewed two dozen applicants before Mehdi called. Donny had a hard time trusting anyone; he was raised poor and didn't take anything for granted. He liked Mehdi's shyness, the way he waited to be invited before he stepped into a room or sat down. He liked that Mehdi was handsome without being brazen, that he didn't ask what the salary was or how many hours he would work. He said he lived alone and had no family or romantic connections. When he told them he didn't have a smartphone they assumed he couldn't afford one, but he explained, ever so reverently, that that wasn't it, he also didn't have a TV or a radio, even in his car. He hadn't read a newspaper since New Year's Day 2000, and then only to find out if the world had ended as promised. He ate one meal a day, didn't smoke or drink, but he was an expert cook and knew his spirits as well as any barkeep.

His reclusiveness and purposeful disinterest in the world had Donny and Luca convinced he was gay and unable to accept it— "almost literally in the closet." They told him he would have to get a cell phone if he was going to work for them, even if it was only to communicate with them, and that he would be driving their car while on duty. They didn't mind his being a foreigner; they thought Iranians were delightful people. Indeed, the guy who cut their hair was an Assyrian from Iran; he opened his salon on Sundays just to do Donny's hair.

Mehdi was such a good employee, they raised his hourly wage without him asking, but their many attempts at having a conversation about his personal life or his past failed completely. They knew he was born in Iran and had come to the United States in 1992; that he had lived on the West Side for a while before moving to the Valley; that he had no religion, no next of kin, no friends, and that he didn't want any.

Sometimes, when he was especially tired or anxious, he would hum a tune under his breath with Persian words. "It's supposed to be a love song," he had told Donny once when he asked, "but in fact it's a gravedigger's kaddish."

⁂

Alireza didn't have money to give to his wife and children when he left them, and he didn't expect to make any once his perfidy had become public. Until he became *chiz-khored* by Golnessa, he was a storekeeper for a wealthy antiques salesman who did most of his business with foreign tourists. Afterward, he couldn't have paid an employer to let him keep anything, much less items of great monetary value. Nor could he convince the most gullible of merchants to enter into a partnership with a man who couldn't be trusted with his own brother's wife. His duplicity toward Davood rekindled within the community the memory of Moshe Hayim's conversion and his thieving of old widows' and young children's inheritances. Then Davood went and tried to kill himself by drinking a fair amount (but obviously not enough) of pure distilled alcohol, which made him completely blind and bore a few good-sized holes in his stomach and intestines but didn't finish the job, and any scraps of forgiveness or trust that might have been thrown at Alireza were as good as gone.

But while he and Golnessa might have managed to live on sex and song alone, his wife and children still needed bread and rice and maybe even shoes. To that end, Mehdi's mother took him out of school when he was nine and sent him into the streets to sell lottery tickets and chewing gum and cigarettes twelve hours a day; she took in people's dirty sheets and comforters, washed them in enormous pewter tubs till her hands were raw from the boiling water and abrasive soap; she begged her own family for handouts and went to the police every few weeks to demand that they arrest Alireza and bring him home to feed his children. A year later, when they were still hungry, she sent Mehdi to Golnessa's house to ask her and Alireza for help.

Once a month, from the time he was ten years old with a hollow stomach and a head that had to be shaved regularly to ward off lice, little Mehdi Hakeem drank from the same fountain of rapture that had poisoned his father, and lived to want more. Golnessa didn't lay a finger on him; that might have quelled some of the fury that had ignited within him the night in Vanak and became more crushing as he grew older. But whereas Alireza was spiteful and dismissive and cruel to Mehdi, whereas his own mother counted him as one of the great burdens of her life, a piece of the flotsam that remained of her wrecked marriage, Golnessa accorded him all her conqueror's magnanimity.

Who says kindness isn't more deadly than love?

Having nearly despaired of ever finding work again, Alireza had knocked on one last door—a Jewish-turned-Baha'i vendor of women's cosmetics and panty hose and undergarments—who took pity on him enough to risk eleven tubes of hand lotion.

"Sell these to whomever you can," he told Alireza, "and you can keep 10 percent of what you bring back."

The lotion was heavy and white and aromatic. It came in a toothpaste-type tube and had English letters on one side, Hebrew on the other. It was made in Israel, by a company named Ahava, with minerals extracted from the Dead Sea and avocado and hazelnuts. The Jew-turned-Baha'i had bought the lotion in Tel Aviv and tried to test its market potential by creating an attractive display in his shop and pushing it on every customer who came in, but he had managed to sell only one tube in six months. Alireza sold the rest in half a day.

He sold other items for the Jew-turned-Baha'i and took a larger percentage. Then he started to send for the lotion directly to Israel, rented a stall on Shah-Reza Avenue, and went into business for himself. A year later, he owned a real store. The year after that, he was distributing wholesale to other stores in Tehran. He was still devoted to Golnessa, but he couldn't spend his days at home anymore and didn't like it when she used her charms to keep him back. He adored Golnessa, but he also loved being rich and important, sitting in an office behind a desk, and giving orders instead of carrying them out. Like the other men before him, he started to believe the lies she had fed him—that he was special, better, more deserving, more worthy than the rest.

On the days of his visits, Mehdi would stand watch outside Golnessa's door until Alireza left. Then he would ring the bell and wait, like a wet dog on a cold night at its owner's doorstep, for Golnessa to let him in. Sometimes she took him into the drawing room, sometimes to her bedroom.

"Come, *Shazdeh Koochooloo*—Little Prince," she said as she dug into her purse or picked through a bowl of coins she kept on the table. "Let's see what we can find for you."

She called him Little Prince until he was 6'3" and seventeen years old, but as he grew older, she let him stay at the house longer, offered him tea at first, then *arrack* and opium.

"Sit down, Little Prince, and tell me what goes on outside these walls. My husband doesn't like to tell stories."

She never referred to Alireza by name, and it wouldn't have mattered if she did. Mehdi wouldn't have wanted Golnessa any less, or thought "the husband" any less worthy of her, because—Mehdi was convinced of this—no other man could love her as much as he did. That he hadn't already thrown himself at her feet, begged her to go away with him, and promised to carve out his own heart and liver and bring them to her on a platter if she refused him, was only because he was waiting to save enough money to buy himself a real suit and a pair of leather shoes, and to buy her a diamond ring, however small. He had gone from selling lottery tickets to working in a grocery store to (in the mid-1970s when Tehran was teeming with foreign tourists) renting space in the main bazaar and pushing handmade espadrilles and lamb's wool overcoats with a forced ethnic look. He worked himself to near exhaustion and lived on one meal a day, and still the money he brought home was barely enough to pay the rent and keep his mother and siblings eating. Then he turned seventeen and Golnessa let him into her bedroom one too many times.

❧

Out of Mehdi's earshot, Donny and Luca debated what they should do with him next. In the long run, they agreed, he would have to "find another position." He had always been neurotic, but in the past, his other qualities had compensated for this one flaw; clearly, his condition had worsened of late.

While Donny stayed put in the kitchen ("The man's ill; there's no telling if he may become violent."), Luca ventured out with a glass of Gatorade to gather some basic intelligence.

Mehdi tried but couldn't sit up straight or formulate whole sentences when responding. "Yes, I'm okay." "No thank you, I don't need an ambulance." "Yes, it's probably just my blood sugar." "No, I'm afraid I don't have health insurance." "Yes, I'll get a checkup at the first opportunity."

Back in the kitchen, the Goldberg-Ferraros decided against taking Mehdi to Harbor-UCLA or LA County or any of those hospitals that accepted patients who didn't have insurance. Even if they managed to get through the traffic, Luca would have to drive for an hour in any direction, then sit with Mehdi in an overcrowded emergency waiting room with legions of people each carrying some other germ. And they couldn't keep him at their house all day because he would be too much of a liability, if his condition worsened or (who knows?) he became violent. Not that he was able to drive anyway, but by now his car had either been stolen or confiscated where he left it. So Luca put on his own "I'm a producer, it's my job to iron out the wrinkles, no problem is too big or daunting for me" air, and went back to offer Mehdi a ride home.

You would think they were going to lead him to the abattoir.

He protested and thanked Luca and protested some more, mustered some ungodly strength and stood up and even walked to the door, insisting he would take the bus or hitch a ride, he wouldn't dream of inconveniencing his employers, especially on a weekend. He relented only when Donny "invited" him to settle down: "I don't want a lawsuit later because you weren't well and I let you loose."

They decided they would wait till the LAPD evacuated the park and cleared the traffic. To make himself less of a nuisance, Mehdi retired to the laundry room where he sat in a corner on the floor like a three-day-old puppy with a head cold, accepted every offer of food and water, but left it all untouched. In between bouts of apologizing to Luca and Donny every time they popped in to check on him, he pulled his legs to his chest, rested his forehead on his knees, and sobbed quietly.

* * *

For ten bitter, desperate months after their first union, Mehdi made a weekly, then daily, pilgrimage to Golnessa's house in hopes of seeing her again. A decade's worth of hunger and wanting, of jealousy and suspicion and rage and impotence, had ended, suddenly and oh-so-exquisitely, when she had opened her legs that blessed Thursday afternoon, minutes before sundown, and allowed Mehdi into the shadowy lowlands and savage enclaves of her cold, black flesh. She made love to him only once, then turned away and ordered him to leave. The next time he came calling, she didn't open the door to him.

That was in 1977. Alireza was hardly at home, too preoccupied with running his ever-thriving enterprise to so much as see Mehdi as he stood, forlorn and frantic, on the sidewalk opposite the house. He watched "the husband" leave early and return late in that metallic-blue, late-model BMW, in the expensive handmade suits and dark, reflective sunglasses, and he—Mehdi—couldn't help but resolve that "it"—the husband—was to blame for Golnessa's sudden estrangement. Alireza was older, cleaner, a thousand times more confident and imposing than Mehdi; no doubt he was also a better companion. He didn't stutter and quake when in Golnessa's presence, didn't lose himself so entirely in her arms. He wasn't a nobody, some little shopkeeper pawning worthless peasant duds in a dusty back alley; he was a businessman with throngs of employees who depended on his good graces and colleagues who wanted to shake his hand.

The longer she held Mehdi at bay, the more determined he became to remove the thing that stood between them. Then the revolution came.

The mullahs ordained that it was every believer's righteous duty to inform on actual or potential *taaghootis*—those belonging to the old regime—Zionists, or antirevolutionaries. Revolutionary tribunals were held in improvised courts, no defense attorney for the accused, and a fifteen-minute window in which to read the charges and issue a verdict. After that, the prisoner was taken up on the roof and executed by firing squad.

Throughout the '70s, Alireza had followed the example of many other wealthy Iranians who believed in the mighty dollar much more than the Iranian rial, and who therefore transferred large sums of money into American banks. Between 1977 and the latter days of '78, when the "disturbances" in the central bazaar in Tehran grew and spread to other parts of the capital and the country, he sold whatever he could of his assets and either sent the money out or used it to buy precious stones that he and Golnessa could easily hide. In 1978, he flew to New York and stashed most of the jewels in a safe-deposit box in an American branch of Credit Suisse. When he came back, he had Golnessa memorize the numbers of all the accounts, then burned every piece of paper associated with them. "In case we have to escape quickly," he had said.

How difficult would it be, in that atmosphere rife with death and destruction, to convince a tribunal that Alireza, whose father was, after all, a Jew (who says he didn't become *jadid al-Islam* only in name? Alireza who had become rich by selling products made in Palestine, thereby enriching not only himself but also the Zionist government; how difficult would it be to convince a mullah that Alireza was a Zionist spy deserving of at least an extended stay in Evin Prison?

Mehdi only pointed the finger. He said everything but the part about Golnessa knowing where their money was hidden and how to access it. Alireza was arrested at home on July 4, 1980. Months later, notice was sent to Golnessa that she was to collect his body at the central morgue where she would be charged the cost of all sixty-eight bullets used to kill him.

He was twenty years old; Golnessa was fifty. He was Muslim; she was Jewish by birth. He had sold out his father, left his aged mother and helpless siblings to beg or starve or sell their bodies, he didn't care what, as long as he didn't have to see them again. Any other time in recent history, these transgressions would unquestionably have led to prison time for Golnessa and forced exile for

Mehdi. But in 1980, greater crimes were being committed every day in every corner of the country, and few cared about or even noticed that an old woman had *chiz-khored* yet another young man. Mehdi was released to Golnessa's tidal wave of fervent worship and reckless lovemaking that left him dog tired and used up and still aching for more. A dozen times a day, Golnessa crooned the ode to God that Mehdi had heard her sing that first night to Alireza.

> *Na-haa-dam sar-eh sajdeh bar khaak-at,*
> *Tow-raa eyy khodaa man seh-daa kardaam.*

She bowed to the Lord and prayed at His feet and called out to Him, faithful penitent that she was, called out because He was "the Reason and the Source, the Key and the Cause."

He was so content in their little nest together, so awed and humbled by and grateful for the hand dealt him by fate, that it took nearly a year for him to realize that Golnessa walked with a pronounced gait. When he asked, she told him, in more than a rebuke, that nothing she did or felt or was would ever be his business. Somewhere in a past he no longer recognized as his own, Mehdi had heard stories about the mother with atrophied limbs, Golnessa harnessed to a cart, pulling the sick woman like a corpse. But he had not then, and could not now, consider the possibility that Golnessa was anything but perfect, or match the girl in the harness to the paragon of beauty before him.

⊱⊰

At eight o'clock Saturday night, Luca half-carried Mehdi into the convertible blue Lexus that came with the producer title at the studio.

"Where to?" Luca tried to sound cheerful, though he dreaded being locked in a confined space with Mehdi at that moment. He smelled of sweat and tears and fabric softener from the Goldberg-Ferraro laundry room. Though he had calmed down somewhat from the morning, he looked like he could easily fall into a new round of hysterics, which would be problematic out on the freeway, Luca thought, so he decided to take surface streets only. He made a big show of focusing his attention on the navigation screen in the car.

Mehdi uttered a name—Pacoima—but no address. Luca had a vague idea that Pacoima was a city, or neighborhood, somewhere in the Valley. He thought he had heard it mentioned in the context of the Latino gangs—twenty and counting—that roamed its streets. He spelled out the name on the navigation touch screen and waited for Mehdi to give a street address.

"It's far for you," Mehdi said instead. "And it's not very safe this time of night." It was 8:15. "Your car might draw attention."

In the three years he had worked for Donny and Luca, Mehdi had never given them reason to doubt his honesty. Now, sensing his reluctance to reveal where he lived, Luca wondered if he and Donny had been too trusting.

"Just say it!" he snapped at Mehdi. Luca never lost his temper; that's how he had managed to survive in the movie business without getting cancer or having a heart attack or stroke. But he knew when to act impatient or angry. That was the other secret to his success.

Glenoaks Boulevard was twenty-two miles long and stretched from Sylmar through Glendale. Around Van Nuys Boulevard, it ran parallel (and much too close) to the Golden State Freeway. The 11000 block where Mehdi lived was nearly all one- or two-story apartment buildings. A few were overpopulated with immigrant families; most were postforeclosure, in disrepair, and vacant. None was in as bad shape as Mehdi's house.

The lot, Luca guessed, was at most two thousand square feet, separated from the freeway by a low-rising cement barrier. The front door literally sat on the edge of the sidewalk; the windows were protected by metal bars.

"Just a minute," he forced half a smile at Mehdi, "I'm going to walk you in."

He saw Mehdi panic, which was incriminating to him and frightening to Luca. It was bad enough to be in a car with a man who had come unhinged for no comprehensible reason, but to walk willingly into what may well be a deadfall was another story altogether. Luca wrote a text to Donny. He gave the street address, touched *send*, then wrote a new one: *I'm going in. If you don't hear from me again in 15 minutes, call the police.*

※

Mehdi never knew when he stopped being Golnessa's lover and became her caretaker. He imagined it happened slowly, during the 1980s when it was just the two of them alone in Darband, in that house with the windows that opened onto the river. The house was all that the Islamic Republic had allowed Golnessa to keep of Alireza's estate—that, and the jewels she hid on her body when the Pasdars came to evict her from the main residence on Pahlavi Avenue, and the account numbers she had memorized. Mehdi didn't have to ask what the total was in either tomans or dollars; he was certain there was enough, and that, thanks to Golnessa's luck, there would be more every year. He had abandoned his own little business without giving it a second thought, decided they would sell the jewels one by one when the need arose, and committed himself to the work of adoring Golnessa in an appropriate manner and to a sufficient extent. He wasn't about to repeat Alireza's mistake—to leave a woman with her appetite and ardor alone, give her reason to feel underappreciated, allow other men time and space to get close to her.

There would be no other man in Golnessa's bed after Mehdi; he was certain of this. He wore the harness willingly and without regret.

Her right leg was barely functional when they moved together to Darband, so it was easy to overlook the weakness that had begun to spread in the rest of her limbs. By the mid-'80s, she was having trouble crossing the length of a room without holding on to the furniture and using the strength of her upper body to propel her legs forward. They had been married by a mullah as soon as Alireza's death certificate came through, but she had yet to let Mehdi spend a full night in her bedroom. Nor did he ever see her without her face painted and her nails and hair done, or in a plain dress, or engaged in a domestic activity. In the morning he waited, sometimes till eleven, to take a breakfast tray to her room. She was already bathed and dressed with a servant's help, but she ate in a chair next to the bed and spent most of the daylight hours at home and with the curtains closed. At dusk she changed into a formal gown and met Mehdi in the dining room. Then her arms began to fail.

The cook had made broiled mutton with saffron rice and sour currants for dinner, but Golnessa's plate remained nearly untouched, and her hands were folded on her lap. She sat up straight at the head of the table, Mehdi to her left, making small talk about the pirated and dubbed DVD of *The Godfather, Part III* they had watched the previous night.

She must have sensed that Mehdi was about to ask why she couldn't raise a spoon to her mouth, because she raised the pitch in her voice and fixed him with her green eyes and kept talking till the moment passed. Then she called for the maid to come gather their plates and bring tea. Just when the girl hovered over Golnessa with the tray, Mehdi said, "We're going to see a doctor this week."

A full three years would go by between the night he declared they were going to see a doctor "this week" and the day she finally arrived in a physician's office. She had lost use of her legs entirely and had to be pushed around in a wheelchair; her arms hung by her side like foreign objects; she could only move one hand. She had a hairdresser come to her three times a week, trained the maid to do her makeup, paid a seamstress to buy fabric and make dresses Golnessa picked out of smuggled European fashion magazines.

To get her to leave the house in Darband and submit to a medical examination by a team of doctors, Mehdi had to fight Golnessa for the first time since he had met her. Until then, he had had no idea just how scared he was of her disapproval, or how completely he relied on her to make every decision for both of them.

She was sixty years old; he was thirty. He had been possessed by her for twenty-two years and would continue to be—he knew this—until his last breath.

The doctors in Tehran had seen other patients with muscular atrophy of the kind affecting Golnessa, but they didn't have a name for the condition and didn't believe a cure was possible. Maybe it was MS or ALS, they said; maybe it wasn't. Maybe it would progress to other parts of the body; maybe it wouldn't. Maybe the United States would know more; maybe they wouldn't.

⸙

"Immaculate ruins" is how Luca would later describe Mehdi's place to Donny.

There was no telling how old the house was because it was made so cheaply, it could have started to disintegrate after a year. The backyard, which Luca saw first because the front door was jammed, was as dusty and desiccated as the high-noon desert in a Western movie set. The streetlamps were blown and there was no lighting on the outside of the house, so Luca had to rely entirely on Mehdi to keep him from tripping or, he was increasingly worried, falling into a gaping fault line. Donny always said those fault lines, so ubiquitous on the landscape, were nature's way of reminding Angelenos what imbeciles they were—to live on a part of the planet they knew was going to open up and swallow them all.

They went through a solid metal door with three separate locks that Mehdi had to open with different keys, then a wooden door fortified with metal strips and two locks, then a swinging aluminum panel with hinges that made a ghastly screeching sound as if to warn of trespassers. Mehdi stepped into the house first and tightened the bulb in a floor lamp, mumbled something about saving electricity, then switched on a second lamp.

The room was small with no windows, but it was the cleanest, most perfectly weird, ready-for-my-close-up-now, Mr. DeMille, set Luca had ever been on. The two chairs, one coffee table, end table, and bookcase were all covered with starched, gleaming-white, expensive-looking sheets. A three-foot-high stack of Persian-language magazines sat neatly against the wall. A small silver tray with a pair of clean tea glasses and a two-cup porcelain teapot was placed over the sheet, exactly at the center of the coffee table. The sheet, like all the other ones in the room, bore no mark of a human hand or body.

"Do you iron these every day?" Luca asked incredulously, but he already knew the answer.

❧

After the disastrous visit with the medical dream team Mehdi had gathered in Tehran, Golnessa reimposed the rule of silence about her physical condition. But she also let go of her efforts to hide it from Mehdi. When they made love, she let him lead; if he fell asleep to her singing, she didn't wake him up to go to his own room. He took over the job of feeding her, then of washing and dressing her. He did it all because he still loved her as much as ever, and because he sensed his blood run cold at the thought of her being absent from his life. Maybe, too, because she demanded it.

She didn't have to utter the words for him to know what she wanted; he'd spent too many years striving to please her. He had never put this to the test, but he was certain that the price of displeasing Golnessa would be complete and permanent banishment; it's what had happened to Alireza and, no doubt, the men before him. She must have planned to leave the old man from the start, but with the others she had taken a lover to replace a less-than-entirely-attentive husband.

And she had gone from each man to a younger one because, Mehdi now imagined, she realized what lay in wait for her. She had seen her mother become completely disabled and was preparing for the day when she too had to be lifted from the bed into a chair.

News was traveling faster from Europe and America, thanks in part to the dozen satellite radio and television stations that broadcast to Iran. In 1997 and '98, two Jewish brothers in Los Angeles, physicians both and who suffered a condition similar to Golnessa's, claimed they had identified the illness and were working hard to find a cure. They were interviewed on a few programs, and each time, they urged other patients to get in touch with them. One day, Mehdi called the radio station in LA and spoke on the air to the doctors. "We will find a cure," the more outspoken one assured Mehdi and other listeners.

More than the hope he offered, it was the doctor's confidence, the poise and self-assuredness with which he predicted success, that transformed Mehdi. He realized this was a largely American trait—the "can-do" attitude that was either the cause or a result of the country's strength and prosperity. Iranians had always admired this. Most even envied Americans for it. But few, if any, believed they could own it. The world turned on a different axis in the East than in the West; the horizon was closer, more modest, not nearly as lustrous.

Yet here was this Iranian doctor, already disabled and certain to become more so, and he sounded every bit as "can-do" as Ronald Reagan telling Gorbachev what to do with his wall. If the talk on Persian-language media was to be believed, a great many Iranian exiles had achieved abroad what would have been impossible in Iran. No doubt the circumstances—a better economy, infrastructure, opportunities—could account for this. Then again, maybe confidence bred success.

Without telling Golnessa, Mehdi hired an English tutor to come to the house every afternoon during the hour of her siesta and teach him basic phrases he imagined he would need to communicate. He had heard that a person could live a full and completely connected life in LA without speaking a word of English, and that some of the best doctors in the city were Iranian-born and spoke Persian. Half the taxi drivers were Iranian too, as were shop owners, teachers, therapists, fortune tellers, scientists, and generally successful people. Even so, Mehdi thought it might be a good idea to know a few words and sentences in the language of the majority of Angelenos. He couldn't find anyone to teach him Spanish, so he settled for the second most popular native tongue.

The English tutor, an Iranian who had been a student in Oregon when the revolution broke out, had an ex-girlfriend he was still in touch with. But for the fact that he wanted to return to Iran and take part in establishing *velaayaat e faghih*—Islamic government—the two would probably have married. Instead, she moved to LA, became a real estate agent, and used the few words and expressions he had taught her in Persian to draw business from the scores of refugees looking first for rental apartments, then for homes and condos to buy.

Kat Cohen, née Catherine Payne, was a Methodist-turned-Buddhist-turned-Scientologist who had converted to Judaism to marry a South African Jew. She had sold upward of three hundred houses on the West Side to Iranians, and she would be glad to help Mehdi out, rent a place for him and his wife for three months, but she felt obligated by her conscience and professional ethics to disclose what a mistake this would be on his part. To see doctors at UCLA or Cedar Sinai medical centers, you had to stay on the West Side. A semihabitable two-bedroom in Beverly Hills or Brentwood (Santa Monica was too far and too foggy; Holmby Hills was too expensive; Bel Air was fine if you wanted to get lost on your way home every single night because the streets were so entangled and the signs were useless) would cost a minimum of $12,000 a month. With a little bit of money down and a slightly longer commitment, a person could buy a house in LA for that kind of monthly payment. Then he could rent the house and keep the income, or use it as a summer home, or, who knows, be tempted to stay in LA and stop breathing the polluted air of Tehran. Kat Cohen suggested "something in a modest $6 million range." Since Mehdi had no credit history in the US, she told him he would have to pay all cash.

He didn't need to ask Golnessa for the money. She had seen this trip to Los Angeles coming for months. She knew he left the house for hours at a time, made secret phone calls, studied English. One night, as they lay in bed next to each other, she asked if he realized what leaving meant.

"You should know, too, that my luck doesn't travel."

&

Before Luca could stop him, Mehdi had pulled all the sheets off the furniture and, like a marine color guard, folded each one thirteen times into an "In God We Trust" triangle. He put the sheets in a box on the top shelf of the bookcase, motioned with his hand for Luca to "it's not worthy of you but, please, make yourself at home," and rushed into the small kitchen off the yard side of the room. Luca thought he heard the clicking of a burner on a gas stove. His phone vibrated for the umpteenth time since he had sent the last text to Donny, so he pulled it out and found a dozen voice and text messages, all demanding that he *Get out NOW* and warning that *I'm going to CALL THE POLICE if I don't hear from you in SIXTY SECONDS.*

It's all good, he texted back. *This guy is CRAZY.*

He heard a cabinet door close, so he leaned over to peer inside the kitchen.

"Are you making tea?"

Luca realized the question sounded more like an indictment—as in, *Are you nuts enough to make tea at a time like this?*—and felt terrible. Then he saw the embarrassed expression on Mehdi's face, and was ashamed.

Yes, even at a time like this, Mehdi had not forgotten his manners, the graciousness of the Iranian host who wouldn't dream of having a person, even a stranger, in his house without offering food and sweets and fruit or, at the very least, tea.

Mehdi was fussing with the tea leaves and pouring water from the kettle. He tore the wrapping off a box of See's Candies that Luca thought looked suspiciously like the one he and Donny had handed out to all the help at Christmastime, put a small sugar bowl filled with clear rock candy on the tray, and picked it up.

"Please, Luca, have a seat; it's not worthy of you, but make yourself at home."

It wasn't particularly hot for July, even for the Valley where temperatures were easily twenty degrees higher than on the West Side, but Luca realized he had been sweating. He went to the sink to pour cold water on his hands and let his body cool. He lifted the lever to the right, the left, straight back.

"Is this tap broken?" he called behind him at Mehdi.

There was a pause. Then Mehdi was next to him and trembling again. Without asking Luca, he grabbed a glass from a cabinet and started to pour water from a store-bought plastic container, but his hands were too unsteady. Luca noted that the sink was spotless, as if it had not been used in a while, and that there was no dish rack next to it. Instinctively, he put one knee on the ground and looked under the sink.

He wished he hadn't stopped Donny from calling the cops.

❧

The house on Sunset and Alpine, Kat Cohen informed Mehdi, was listed at well below market price for $8 million cash because the original owners were a Russian mob boss, his black Swedish wife, and their three children. The husband had been shot to death while taking a bath in the master bedroom, and while that was clearly a business decision, the wife had put the house on the market and moved with the children into a high-security condo on the Wilshire

Corridor. But it seemed Americans had a thing about buying a house in which someone had died. By law, the owner had to disclose the death to the new buyers, which was pretty silly if you thought about it—where but in one's house is a person supposed to die? Why would death be news to a stranger? Still, Mehdi was grateful for Americans' fear of ghosts and other unsavory remains of living people, so he took Kat Cohen's advice and "grabbed the dial."

He took her advice again when she told him that in Beverly Hills, if he drove a car worth less than $50,000, he would be mistaken for the help. People would cut him off on the road and valets at high-end restaurants would refuse to park his car—and don't even bother hoping you'll get invited to any parties once you're spotted getting into and out of a Camry.

He didn't have to worry about money or even ask Golnessa for permission to spend any of it: they were in the US with visas granted to patients seeking medical treatment. To obtain the visas, Mehdi had had to present letters from doctors in Iran and in Los Angeles, as well as proof that he and Golnessa would be able to pay their medical bills. Maybe she was desperate to get better; maybe she feared that, if she didn't go with him, Mehdi would leave alone for America. Either way, she gave him every account number and, once in LA, had the money transferred from New York and made Mehdi signatory.

He bought a Mercedes S-Class for $80,000. On a referral from Kat, he hired a decorator she was happy to recommend, and a husband-and-wife Filipino couple she was also happy to recommend. For $1,000 a week, the husband did the heavy lifting and food shopping and the wife cooked and cared for Golnessa. Only then did Mehdi wade into the quicksand of the medical system without health insurance.

The doctors at Cedars examined Golnessa and announced she had advanced hereditary inclusion body myopathy (HIBM)—a rare genetic muscle-wasting disorder with no cure and, so far, no treatment. Thanks to the two physician brothers and families of other patients, a cure was being aggressively pursued, and it would probably be found, as one can-do brother had promised, in his lifetime. But he was in his early forties; Golnessa was seventy-one.

She had submitted to the examination, the blood tests and MRIs and every invasive procedure, with an eerie calm that worried even Mehdi. She didn't understand English and wasn't interested in speaking in Persian with the Iranian doctors or the interpreters provided by the center. Her hands were completely disabled now but her organs remained unaffected and her voice was strong. Until Mehdi corrected it, the doctors were under the impression that she was his mother. Afterward, they assumed he was a kept man. They thought she should be approached to make a donation to the search for a cure, if not for herself then perhaps for her children or grandchildren who may be affected and not even know it yet. Who else but a very rich widow with throngs of progeny far away in the home country just waiting for her to die would snare a young, good-looking man nearly half her age? So they called the medical center's "development" staff who called their regular Iranian donors. Did others in the community know Golnessa Hakeem? the development people wanted to know. Was it safe to assume she should be "cultivated," possibly for estate planning? Could the regular donors be counted on to act as intermediaries? Suddenly, the phone in the Hakeem house started to ring.

Mehdi didn't know any of the callers but they seemed to know him and Golnessa. They knew his siblings too, and were happy to bring him up to date. And though they clearly remembered Alireza and Davood, and knew how Mehdi had ended up with Golnessa, they didn't seem to hold it against him.

Things had changed a great deal among Iranians in the West since the revolution. Memories were shorter; people had a higher tolerance for bad behavior. A person or a family's social status did not depend as much on their pedigree and good name as it had in Iran. Here, it was mostly about how much money you were thought to have. Compared to what went on every day in LA, the history that had made Golnessa a social pariah most of her life didn't seem as outrageous. Compared to the crimes committed during and after the revolution, Mehdi's virtual patricide was not an unforgivable sin.

There were parties on the West Side five nights or more a week, and before long Mehdi was invited to all of them. The Jews, who knew Golnessa was Jewish, assumed Mehdi was too. The Muslims, who had heard of Alireza, assumed he was one of them. For a while when they called, they invited "you and *khanum*"—the Mrs.—but he always went alone and they stopped mentioning the wife. He was still a good-looking man. The shyness that, had he been poor, would have explained "why he's such a loser," was deemed genteel and classy because he was rich. The fact that he showed up to parties without his wife, which would have meant he was "a disloyal, cruel, and dastardly ass" if he was poor, was a sign of his moral courage for subjecting himself to loneliness while he cared for an invalid spouse. He could have left her in Iran, or committed her to a government-funded home in LA. He could have taken another wife and had children while there was still time, enjoyed his money. They didn't just say this to each other about Mehdi; they told him too.

He had no idea how to interpret this sudden shift in his social standing. He was having enough trouble keeping track of the callers' names and their explanations of how he was related to them. The first time someone invited him to their house he nearly gagged in terror. When they insisted, he said what sprang to mind: "I'm not sophisticated and I wouldn't know what to wear." But the invitations kept coming and the Iranians on the boards of charities and the development people from the medical centers and various city organizations in Beverly Hills kept insisting that he was fine "as is. No need to wear anything special and you'll be among friends, we're all down-to-earth here."

That last claim wasn't true. When he did, at last, venture out for an hour, one night after he had sat with Golnessa while the Filipina woman fed her in bed, Mehdi was spellbound by the elegance and excess he saw at the gathering. The house was palatial and tastefully furnished, the women lean and elegant and mostly blond. There was enough food and music and flowers and alcohol to keep a shipload of sailors happy for a year on a deserted island. It was all so intimidating, Mehdi lingered against a wall for ten minutes, then rushed to get his car before the valet had had a chance to park it.

But he had been initiated, and after that it only became easier.

He didn't like to leave Golnessa alone with the help, because she didn't speak English and hardly let them touch her. Almost entirely immobilized, she had to be moved in bed or on the chair every three hours to prevent sores. This wasn't difficult, since she weighed barely eighty pounds and kept losing more weight. Mehdi cooked all her favorite meals and taught the Filipina as well, but it was no use, she ate like a small child and never seemed to enjoy it. She had the ability to speak but not, he sensed, the will. He knew that she was angry at him for bringing her to LA, that she felt betrayed by him, but unlike in the past when he wouldn't dare question her feelings, he told himself it made no difference to Golnessa what country they lived in—a bed was a bed anywhere, and the view from her window, while not as striking as the views in Darband, was rather idyllic. And he hadn't abandoned her here; he hardly left the house during the day and went out to parties only at night when she should have been sleeping. He still sat with her for hours at a time, just holding her hand and caressing her hair, running his finger along the length of her eyebrows and to her temples, down the bridge of her nose, onto her mouth, the way she used to like. Because she wouldn't sing to him, he sang to her:

Sabbab gar besoozad, Mossabeb tow has-ti,
Sabbab kaar eh in jahan tow-ee . . .

Slowly, he began to take meetings during the day. Then there were lunches and dinners hosted by solicitous volunteers, Shabbat dinners, birthdays, and graduations, and, counting American, Iranian, Muslim, and Jewish holidays, something to celebrate every other week. It was strange, Mehdi thought, how he was getting acquainted with his own people for the first time in his late forties. Those others he had known in Iran—the working-class families, the villagers who had migrated to the capital in search of jobs, the street urchins who, like him, worked twelve-hour days peddling chewing gum and cigarettes and, in the hours-long traffic jams of Tehran, washing car windows for whatever the driver threw at them—they had become strange and foreign to him during the two decades of self-imposed confinement in Darband. He had money then, but no way to use it beyond the necessities. The Iranians he was meeting in LA were friendly and hospitable and generous to a fault. They rarely brought up his relationship with Golnessa, and when they did, it was to say they realized he was a victim—a young boy *chiz-khored* by a "charming" stepmother.

By 2004, two and a half years into their stay in the US, the stepmother was severely malnourished and had to be fed intravenously from time to time. She had multiple recurring infections that required hospital stays or twenty-four-hour care at home by a nurse. The sicker she became, the more she seemed to blame Mehdi. He filled the void by getting "more involved" with the community, but "involvement" was not cheap, and Mehdi, who had not needed to watch his spending for decades, didn't know when to stop.

In 2005, when he had spent or donated most of their liquid assets, Kat Cohen helped him mortgage his house. In 2006, he took a second mortgage. In 2008, he sold the house and, after he had paid the bank, was left with a little under $1 million. This time, Kat Cohen found a rental condominium in the Wilshire Manning high-rise near Westwood. Golnessa was eighty years old, shrunken and stiff and unyielding as a wood carving. She stared at Mehdi with such fierce resentment, he could barely stand to be in the same room with her. He sold his expensive car and bought a Toyota, stopped writing checks and buying designer clothes and going out for meals, but he couldn't care for Golnessa alone.

He kept paying for the nurses and the live-in help after they moved out of the Manning in 2009 and into a smaller rental behind the row of Persian restaurants on Westwood Boulevard. He paid when they moved again in 2010 to an apartment on Valley Vista in Sherman Oaks. In 2011, when all he could afford was a one-bedroom on Glenoaks, he became her sole caretaker.

Luca had thought he was going to check the main valve under the sink, or that was the pretext anyway, because he could see Mehdi was hiding something (maybe a lot of things), and the kitchen was as good a place to start searching as any. There was a heap of pipes and joints and screws and washers, every piece gutted and taken apart then thrown into a pile. Whether metal or plastic, the outside of each part looked normal, but the inside—Luca reached for the flashlight in the front corner of the cabinet, turned it on, and stared in disbelief—was the color of gold.

Behind him, he could smell the angst rising like fumes from Mehdi. Without looking at him, Luca went into the main room and through it to the only bedroom in the house. There was a king-size bed with a frayed duvet cover and a set of pillows that had once been expensive, a rocking chair on one side and a closed wheelchair on the other. Luca moved into the bathroom and tried the faucet in the sink, then the shower.

"Did you turn the water off?" he asked.

Mehdi nodded.

"Where do you wash?"

Mehdi cleared his throat. "There's a twenty-four-hour fitness—"

"You shower at the gym?" Luca nearly screamed. "What? Is it the money?"

Mehdi didn't look like he was going to answer.

"What's that in the pipes under the sink?"

This time, Mehdi wasn't reticent. He walked over to the toilet and lifted the lid, then motioned gently for Luca to come closer. There was no water in the bowl, but the porcelain was painted gold.

"Look," Mehdi said, pointing with his chin to the floor of the shower. Here, the grout between the tiles was golden.

"Is it . . . ?" Luca could hardly gather the words.

Mehdi nodded.

"From the water?"

Mehdi nodded again.

"Like . . . in the . . . lake?"

⤬

He didn't know how to use a computer and didn't know enough English to search the Internet, but he had to find work because he and Golnessa needed money. A young boy who worked at the Persian grocery store in a strip mall on Glenoaks helped him out by looking on Craigslist. Mehdi hadn't told the boy or the store's owner that he was married, and he didn't tell Donny and Luca either. He didn't have neighbors because the few houses on his street were abandoned and boarded up, and he didn't have friends. All those people who had toasted and befriended him in Beverly Hills, who had called three times a week just to see if he was free for lunch, reached across the table and put a hand on his arm, gave it a firm squeeze, and said, "You're a good man, Mehdi, it's a real honor," when he wrote a check—he hadn't heard from any of them since he sold the house on Alpine.

One day, he realized that no one who knew him in the Valley was aware that he had a wife.

The job with the Goldberg-Ferraros was just a few hours a week at first, when all he had to do was drive Donny to his physical therapist in Encino and back. Mehdi would feed and change Golnessa before he left, and rushed home as soon as he was done with work. But then Donny raised his hourly pay and gave him more work, and Luca had him run errands for the studio, so that

Golnessa was sometimes alone all day. She now had bedsores and infections that no amount of antibiotics would clear, but since there was no money for doctors, all he could do was take her to the emergency room at Tarzana hospital every few days.

She had no death wish; Mehdi was sure of this. She refused to eat because she wanted to punish him, and that's why she was determined not to die either.

She did this—not die—until the morning of March 20, 2012. At 5:41, that day, Mehdi got out of bed, washed his face, brushed his teeth, then went back into the bedroom and put a pillow on Golnessa's face. He waited, but her chest rose and fell at the same pace as before. He pressed the pillow down and held it, but her breath was as steady as a metronome. He bore down, put one knee on the spot where the pillow rose and fell ever so slightly. His knuckles had turned white and his back ached, but she still kept breathing.

He left the pillow on her face and pulled the bedsheets off the mattress, folded them onto her like a shroud, and wrapped her with electrical tape. He had steel bars left over from the time they first moved into the house and had to fortify the windows. He taped two of them to Golnessa.

He had driven past the lake every day for months. He arrived at the park a little before seven. There were a few joggers on the track, a couple of older women walking their dog. He lifted Golnessa out of the trunk and carried her in his arms, like a mannequin encased in paper, to the lake, dropped her in the water, and watched her sink to the bottom. Then he walked back to his car, and waited for the police.

The running track circled the lake. One by one, the joggers finished their exercise, stretched, and drove away. The dog walkers went home. None of them even looked in Mehdi's direction.

He hadn't thought about this—what he would do after he had killed Golnessa. He assumed it would be planned for him. The arrest and interrogation, jail and prison and whatever came after.

It didn't occur to him that he would go unnoticed, that he could drop a body into the lake in daylight and not be seen.

Maybe the cops were late, held up by some major event—Obama flying in to LA to raise money and creating a traffic jam. He turned on the radio to 670 AM, the Persian-language channel. A woman with a clear, fluid voice was singing: "*Dar in haal-eh mass-tee safaa kardaam . . .*"

It was an old recording of the Iranian classical singer Elaheh, with poor sound quality, and it spooked him so much he got out of the car and walked back a few steps. It was eight thirty, almost time to go to Donny and Luca's, and there was still no sign of the police.

That night, he decided it may be some time before they caught up with him, so he started to put his affairs in order. He cleaned the house, covered the furniture with sheets, cleared the pantry and refrigerator. He washed the windows, the shower, the toilet. He cleaned and waited, cleaned and waited. The neighborhood had become more blighted every year after the recession, so he sealed the front door shut and installed the metal barrier in the back. Then he installed locks. Installed more locks.

He noticed the water running yellow, and tried to pretend it was rust from old pipes. His hair felt sticky after he took a shower, his skin itched, and he felt nauseated every time he poured a drink of water from the sink. One Sunday he decided to check the main valve.

"It's my wife, you see," he confessed to Luca in all seriousness. "She had a gold tooth that couldn't be extracted."

It was the tooth that had polluted the water and settled into the pipes while Golnessa was living in the house. And it was the tooth that polluted the water in Lake Balboa after she was buried in it.

"We had a pact, you see," he told Luca, "that I would not abandon her. She harnessed me with love at first, then with fear, and now, you see, she harnesses me with this gold."

This story was originally written in English.

PERSIAN GLOSSARY

Aash: A dish similar to soup. There are several varieties of *aash* in Iran.

Agha: Means Mr. or sir. The word is often used as a courtesy before a man's name to show respect.

Arrack: An alcoholic drink almost always made from raisins. In other countries such as Turkey and throughout the Arab world, it is made from anise and tastes entirely different.

Ashura: Ashura is commemorated by Shia Muslims as a day of mourning for the martyrdom of Imam Hossein, the grandson of the Prophet Muhammed.

Azan: The Islamic call to prayer, recited at prescribed times of the day from a mosque.

Azeri: Refers to the Turkic ethnic group of either the Republic of Azerbaijan or Iranian Azerbaijan.

Baba: Father.

Baha'i: The Baha'i faith, a syncretic religion founded in nineteenth-century Iran (where to this day it suffers persecution), is now spread worldwide with several million followers and a governing body in Haifa, Israel. Its three core principles are the belief in the unity of God, religion, and humanity.

Basij: A paramilitary volunteer militia established after the Islamic Revolution. The *basij* receive their orders from and are subordinate to the Sepah (Revolutionary Guards).

Bazaar: As a sprawling marketplace, the *bazaar* is similar to a *souq* in the Arab world.

Behesht e Zahra: The largest cemetery in Iran, located in the southern part of metropolitan Tehran.

Bismillah: Means, "In the name of God." Often said aloud when beginning something.

Burqa: An outer garment covering the entire body and face that is worn by women in some Islamic countries, most notably in Afghanistan.

Chador: : An outer garment or open cloak worn by more traditional Iranian women.

Chafiye: A traditional Middle Eastern headdress worn by men, and often nowadays worn as a scarf.

Chaharshanbe Suri: A celebration, which literally means the "Wednesday feast." It is held on the last Wednesday of the Persian calendar year in March. It is a Zoroastrian fire festival dating back to pre-Islamic Iran, and people often light bonfires in the street.

Daash: An abridged, more colloquial form of the word *dadash*, which can mean brother or friend.

Diyye: In Islamic law it is the financial compensation paid to the heirs of a victim.

Eid: Usually refers to Eid e Nowruz, the New Year, which in Iran begins with the first day of spring and is celebrated over a period of thirteen days.

Eid e Ghadeer: A festive day observed by Shia Muslims to commemorate the appointment of Imam Ali by the Prophet Muhammad as his immediate successor. Ali was the cousin and son-in-law of the Prophet.

Enshallah: A hopeful expression that means "God willing" or "God's will."

Etelaa'at: The primary intelligence agency of Iran. Its full name: Vezarat-e Etelaa'at Jomhuri-ye Eslami-ye Iran.

Ferdowsi: A highly revered Persian poet (940–1020 CE). He is the author of the Shahnameh, the national epic of Iran and the Persian-speaking world.

Haft-seen: *Haft-seen* (or the seven Ss) is a traditional table setting for the celebration of spring and the Persian New Year. The *haft-seen* spread includes seven items all starting with the letter S (*seen*) in the Persian alphabet.

Haj agha: A *haji* is a Muslim who has successfully completed the pilgrimage (*haj*) to Mecca and is therefore given this honorific title. The expression *haj agha* combines the title of *haji* with that of *agha* to convey respect to the person—often a cleric, or someone in a position of authority, or more commonly simply a man who is older. (Men are often called *haj agha* out of respect without having ever actually made the pilgrimage.)

Qajar: The Qajar dynasty ruled Iran from 1785 to 1925.

Imam: An Islamic leadership position, most commonly referring to the prayer leader of a mosque. However, in Shia Islam the title carries far more weight, and often specifically refers to the twelve spiritual and political successors of the Prophet who descended from his family.

Imam Hossein: The grandson of the Prophet Muhammad, and the son of Imam Ali, Hossein is one of the most important figures of Shia Islam. The annual commemoration of his martyrdom is a significant event.

Imam Reza: The eighth imam of Shia Islam; his shrine is in the city of Mashhad in northeastern Iran.

Jaan: A term of endearment used ubiquitously in Persian. Literally, it means life, but it is usually said along with someone's name to indicate intimacy and friendship with that person, and it can be variously interpreted as dear, beloved, brother, or friend.

Joon: A variation of *jaan* that suggests even more intimacy with the other person.

Khakham: Rabbi.

Khanum : Depending on the context, it can mean either Mrs. or lady, and often serves as a title of respect alongside an adult woman's first or last name.

Long: A sheet of cloth worn by men.

Lur: An Iranian ethnic group living mainly in southwestern Iran.

Maman: Mother.

Manteau: Derived from French, it is an outer garment or cloak worn by less traditional Iranian women.

Mujahideen: Loosely aligned resistance groups to the Soviet invasion of Afghanistan. After the Soviet withdrawal they fought amongst themselves and later, under the charismatic leadership of Ahmad Shah Massoud, who was the commander of the Northern Alliance, they fought the fundamentalist Taliban fighters backed by Pakistan.

Mujahedin: Refers to the People's Mujahedin of Iran. An Islamic/Marxist movement that at first fought against the Iranian monarchy and later against the Islamic Republic of Iran. During the Iran-Iraq War of the 1980s, the group was given refuge by Saddam Hussein and mounted attacks on Iran from within Iraqi territory. While some of its leadership has continued to reside in exile in Paris, the group's core members were confined for many years to a camp in Iraq and were disarmed after the American invasion of Iraq.

NAJA: The uniformed police force of Iran.

Nim e Shaban: The day Shia Muslims celebrate the birth of the twelfth and last imam, who is also known as the *mehdi* or messiah.

Noha: Shia lamentation and mourning.

Paykan: A mass-produced car in Iran since the 1960s that is based on the design of the British-made Hillman Hunter.

Qalyan: Better known in the West as a hookah, it is a water pipe for smoking flavored tobacco.

Qesas: An Islamic term meaning "equal retaliation," which follows the principle of "an eye for an eye." In the case of murder, it means the right of the relatives of a murder victim to demand execution of the murderer.

Qeble: The direction toward the Kaaba in Mecca, Saudi Arabia, that a Muslim should face when praying.

Salam alaykum: One of the most common forms of greeting in the

Muslim world. Literally means, "Peace be upon you," but is understood as a greeting. *Salam* is the shortened version which is used more commonly in Iran.

Salevat: The practice of formal worship in Islam. In Shia Islam, and particularly Iran, to utter a *salevat* is to salute the Prophet and his kin in one simple, often repeated sentence.

Sepah : Full name: Sepah e Pasdaran. Known in the West as the Revolutionary Guards, it is an important and powerful branch of Iran's military founded after the Islamic Revolution.

Sharia: The moral code and religious law of Islam.

Shah-kosh: Refers to handguns sold on the streets in Iran, but often more associated with smaller miniautomatics. The term *shah-kosh,* or "king-killer," is derived from *shah,* meaning "king," and *kosh,* which is the verb "to kill."

Shia: The second largest sect of Islam after Sunni Islam. The majority of the population of Iran is Shia, although there is a significant Sunni population as well.

Taliban: A Sunni Islamic fundamentalist movement that at times has fought as an insurgency group in Afghanistan and at other times has ruled major swaths of the country with the iron fist of religious law. The Taliban were displaced from their position of power after the American invasion of Afghanistan but have continued to fight.

Yallah: An expression meaning, "Hurry up!"

Yarsan: *Yarsan,* or *ahl-e-haqq* (People of the Truth), is a syncretic religion common among the Kurds of western Iran and Iraq, though there are smaller groups of Persian, Lur, Azeri, and Arab adherents among them.

ABOUT THE CONTRIBUTORS

Fereshteh Shoulani

SALAR ABDOH divides his time between Tehran and New York City, where he is codirector of the MFA program in creative writing at the City College of New York. He is the author of *The Poet Game*, *Opium*, and, most recently, *Tehran at Twilight*, which is also published by Akashic Books.

Faranak Sharifian

HOSSEIN ABKENAR was born in 1966 in Tehran. A veteran of the Iran-Iraq War, he has published two collections of short stories and the war novel *A Scorpion on the Steps of Andimeshk Railroad Station*, which won several of Iran's top literary prizes and has been translated into French, German, and Kurdish. His screenplay for the film *No One Knows about Persian Cats* won the Special Jury Prize at the Cannes Film Festival.

Ebrahim Shefaati

JAVAD AFHAMI, born in 1965, volunteered for the Iran-Iraq War at age fifteen. Years later, he wrote the award-winning book *Cold Sooran* based on his experiences. His other works include the highly acclaimed short story collections *The Tale of the Samand Taxicab* and *The Livid Umbrella*. His novels *Rendezvous in the Forest of Acorns* and *The Year of the Wolf* are forthcoming.

Meysam Hassanloo

AIDA MORADI AHANI was born in 1983 in Tehran. After graduating from college, she began writing articles and essays on literature and cinema. One of her short stories from her first collection, *Pins on a Cat's Tail*, has been adapted to film, and her widely acclaimed novel about the Iranian financial mafia, *Golfing on Gunpowder*, was published in 2013.

Alireza Dehghan

AZARDOKHT BAHRAMI was born in 1967. She is a writer of short stories, novels, plays, film scripts, and humor. Her book *Wednesday Evenings* won several of the top literary prizes in Iran. She has published four books, with two more novels and two short story collections forthcoming.

LILY FARHADPOUR is a writer and journalist. Her books include the story collection *The Window with a Blue Glass Opening to the Back Alley* and the novels *Striped Saturday and Leaden Seconds* and *Metro Line 4*. She has also been senior editor at a number of Iran's most important journals and newspapers.

Aco Salemi

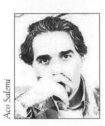

FARHAAD HEIDARI GOORAN, an Iranian of Kurdish descent, was born in 1972. He is a prominent writer and editor at several newspapers and journals in Tehran and also the author of three novels, *The Colors and Legends of Reincarnation*, *The Decadene Reader*, and *Shortness of Breath*, which won the influential Mehregan literary prize in Iran in 2008.

Amir Alami

DANIAL HAGHIGHI was born in 1988. With a degree in architecture and city planning, he considers himself something of a left-leaning underground researcher in Tehran whose first book, *Declaring a Vegetable State*, was—like countless others in Iran—banned from publication by the censorship department of the Ministry of Culture; it has since been published in London.

Karim Karim-Masihi

YOURIK KARIM-MASIHI is an Armenian-Iranian Christian born in 1963. He is an award-winning graphic artist and writer. His books include three collections of short stories: *Ground Floor*; *Dream, Memory, Happiness and Others*; and *The Long Highway*. He has also published a collection of four one-act plays and has written a two-volume collection of essays, *Night Becomes Dawn*, now in its third printing, about photography and cinema.

VALI KHALILI was born in 1984 in south Tehran, and has worked as a journalist since the age of eighteen for some of Iran's most important newspapers, including *Shargh* and *Etemaad*. Currently he is a crime reporter whose coverage ranges from rape and murder to public executions and earthquakes. He has also worked with the BBC in Turkey and Portugal, and is the recipient of two awards of excellence for his reportage.

Greg Bal

MAHSA MOHEBALI was born in 1972. Her publications include *The Voices, The Grey Spell, Lovemaking in Footnotes*, and *Don't You Worry*. She has won numerous awards for her fiction, including multiple prizes from the Golshiri Foundation. In 2013 she was awarded a residency at the international program of the Iowa Writers' Workshop.

GINA B. NAHAI is a best-selling author, columnist, and full-time lecturer at USC's Master of Professional Writing Program. Her novels have been translated into eighteen languages, and have been selected as "Best Books of the Year" by the *Los Angeles Times* and the *Chicago Tribune*. She has also been a finalist for the Orange Prize, the International IMPAC Dublin Literary Award, and the Harold U. Ribalow Prize. Her latest novel, *The Luminous Heart of Jonah S.*, is published by Akashic Books.

Salar Abdoh

MAJED NEISI is an Arab Iranian who was born in southern Iran during a bombardment in the Iran-Iraq War. Since then he has dedicated himself to examining the pathology of war in battlegrounds across Iraq, Lebanon, and Afghanistan. His dozen documentary films, including reports on combat and the international drug trade, examine ordinary people caught up in extraordinary circumstances, and have been screened in festivals in France, the US, Sweden, Holland, and South Africa.

Hanna Marjanian

SIMA SAEEDI was born in 1969 in Birjand, Iran. Imprisoned during the first years of the Islamic Revolution, she restarted high school in 1985. During President Khatami's reform period she worked as a journalist and also served as the chief editor of the online magazine *Tehran Avenue*. Her love for Tehran is inexhaustible and currently she runs a café in the nearby countryside.

Hosein Roozaneh

MAHAK TAHERI was born in Ahvaz, Iran, in 1973. For the last fifteen years she has worked in the field of architecture while publishing short stories in various journals and magazines in Iran. Her novel *Name & Surname* is forthcoming.